Patricia Highsmith

Ripley Under Ground

Penguin Books

Penguin Books Ltd, Harmondsworth, Middlesex, England
Penguin Books, 625 Madison Avenue, New York, New York 10022, U.S.A.
Penguin Books Australia Ltd, Ringwood, Victoria, Australia
Penguin Books Canada Ltd, 2801 John Street, Markham, Ontario, Canada L3R 1B4
Penguin Books (N.Z.) Ltd, 182–190 Wairau Road, Auckland 10, New Zealand

First published in the U.S.A. 1970
Published in Great Britain by Heinemann 1971
Published in Penguin Books 1973
Reprinted 1976, 1978, 1980, 1982

Made and printed in Great Britain by
Hazell Watson & Viney Ltd, Aylesbury, Bucks
Set in Linotype Granjon

Penguin Books
Ripley Under Ground

Patricia Highsmith was born in Fort Worth, Texas, in 1921. Her parents moved to New York when she was six, and she attended the Julia Richmond High School, then later Barnard College. In her senior years she edited the school magazine, and at the age of sixteen decided to become a writer. Miss Highsmith comments that she is 'interested in the effect of guilt on my heroes'. Her first novel, *Strangers on a Train*, was filmed by Alfred Hitchcock, and her third, *The Talented Mr Ripley*, was awarded the Edgar Allan Poe Scroll by the Mystery Writers of America. She enjoys gardening, carpentering, painting and sculpture; some of her works have been exhibited. She now lives in France.

Patricia Highsmith's books include *Deep Water*, *The Cry of the Owl*, *The Glass Cell*, *A Suspension of Mercy*, *This Sweet Sickness*, *Ripley's Game*, and *Eleven*, a collection of short stories (all published in Penguins). Her latest publications are *The Animal Lover's Book of Beastly Murder*, *Edith's Diary*, *Little Tales of Misogyny*, *The Boy Who Followed Ripley* and *The Black House*.

To my Polish neighbours,
Agnès and Georges Barylski,
my friends of France, 77.

I think I would more readily die for what I do not believe in than for what I hold to be true. . . Sometimes I think that the artistic life is a long and lovely suicide, and I am not sorry that it is so.

Oscar Wilde in his Personal Letters

I

Tom was in the garden when the telephone rang. He let Mme Annette, his housekeeper, answer it, and went on scraping at the soppy moss that clung to the sides of the stone steps. It was a wet October.

'M. *Tome* !' came Mme Annette's soprano voice. 'It's London !'

'Coming,' Tom called. He tossed down the trowel and went up the steps.

The downstairs telephone was in the living-room. Tom did not sit down on the yellow satin sofa, because he was in levis.

'Hello, Tom. Jeff Constant. Did you . . .' *Burp.*

'Can you talk louder? It's a bad connection.'

'Is this better? I can hear you fine.'

People in London always could. 'A little.'

'Did you get my letter?'

'No,' Tom said.

'Oh. We're in trouble. I wanted to warn you. There's a . . .'

Crackling, a buzz, a dull click, and they were cut off.

'Damn,' Tom said mildly. Warn him? Was something wrong at the gallery? With Derwatt Ltd? Warn *him*? Tom was hardly involved. He had dreamed up the idea of Derwatt Ltd, true, and he derived a little income from it, but – Tom glanced at the telephone, expecting it to ring again at any moment. Or should he ring Jeff? No, he didn't know if Jeff was at his studio or at the gallery. Jeff Constant was a photographer.

Tom walked towards the french windows that gave onto the back garden. He'd scrape a bit more at the moss, he thought. Tom gardened casually, and he liked spending an hour at it every day, mowing with the push-powered lawnmower, raking and burning twigs, weeding. It was exercise, and he could also daydream. He had hardly resumed with the trowel, when the telephone rang.

Mme Annette was coming into the living-room, carrying a duster. She was short and sturdy, about sixty, and rather jolly. She knew not a word of English and seemed incapable of learning any, even 'Good morning', which suited Tom perfectly.

'I'll get it, madame,' said Tom, and took the telephone.

'*Hello*,' Jeff's voice said. 'Look, Tom, I'm wondering if you could come over. To London, I . . .'

'You what?' It was again a poor connection, but not as bad.

'I said – I've explained it in a letter. I can't explain here. But it's important, Tom.'

'Has somebody made a mistake? – Bernard?'

'In a way. There's a man coming from New York, probably tomorrow.'

'Who?'

'I explained it in my letter. You know Derwatt's show opens on Tuesday. I'll hold him off till then. Ed and I just won't be available.' Jeff sounded quite anxious. 'Are you free, Tom?'

'Well – yes.' But Tom didn't want to go to London.

'Try to keep it from Heloise. That you're coming to London.'

'Heloise is in Greece.'

'Oh, that's good.' The first hint of relief in Jeff's voice.

Jeff's letter came that afternoon at five, express and registered.

104 Charles Place
N.W.8.

Dear Tom,

The new Derwatt show opens on Tuesday, the 15th, his first in two years. Bernard has nineteen new canvases and other pictures will be lent. Now for the bad news.

There is an American named Thomas Murchison, not a dealer but a collector – retired with plenty of lolly. He bought a Derwatt from us three years ago. He compared it with an earlier Derwatt he has just seen in the States, and now he says his is phoney. It is, of course, as it is one of Bernard's. He wrote to the Buckmaster Gallery (to me) saying he thinks the painting he has is not genuine, because the technique and colours belong to a period of five or six years ago in Derwatt's work. I have the distinct feeling Murchison intends to make a stink here. And what to do about it? You're always good on ideas, Tom.

Can you come over and talk to us? All expenses paid by the Buckmaster Gallery? We need an injection of confidence more than anything. I don't think Bernard has messed up any of the new canvases. But Bernard is in a flap, and we don't want him around even at the opening, especially at the opening.

Please come at once if you can!

Best,

Jeff.

P.S. Murchison's letter was courteous, but supposing he's the kind who who will insist on looking up Derwatt in Mexico to verify, etc?

The last was a point, Tom thought, because Derwatt didn't exist. The story (invented by Tom) which the Buckmaster Gallery and Derwatt's loyal little band of friends put out, was that Derwatt had gone to a tiny village in Mexico to live, and he saw no one, had no telephone, and forbade the gallery to give his address to anyone. Well, if Murchison went to Mexico, he would have an exhausting search, enough to keep any man busy for a lifetime.

What Tom could see happening was Murchison — who would probably bring his Derwatt painting over — talking to other art dealers and then the press. It could arouse suspicion, and Derwatt might go up in smoke. Would the gang drag him into it? (Tom always thought of the gallery batch, Derwatt's old friends, as 'the gang', though he hated the term every time it came into his head.) And Bernard might mention Tom Ripley, Tom thought, not out of malice but out of his own insane — almost Christlike — honesty.

Tom had kept his name and his reputation clean, amazingly clean, considering all he did. It would be most embarrassing if it were in the French papers that Thomas Ripley of Villeperce-sur-Seine, husband of Heloise Plisson, daughter of Jacques Plisson, millionaire owner of Pharmaceutiques Plisson, had dreamed up the money-making fraud of Derwatt Ltd, and had for years been deriving a percentage from it, even if it was only ten per cent. It would look exceedingly shabby. Even Heloise, whose morals Tom considered next to non-existent, might react to this, and certainly her father would put the pressure on her (by stopping her allowance) to get a divorce.

Derwatt Ltd was now big, and a collapse would have ramifications. Down would go the lucrative art supply line of materials labelled 'Derwatt', from which the gang, and Tom, got royalties also. Then there was the Derwatt School of Art in Perugia, mainly for nice old ladies and American girls on holiday, but still a source of income, too. The art school got its money not so much from teaching art and selling 'Derwatt' supplies as from acting as a rental agent, finding houses and furnished apartments, of the most expensive order, for well-heeled tourist-students, and taking a cut from it all. The school was run by a pair of English queens, who were not in on the Derwatt hoax.

Tom couldn't make up his mind whether to go to London or not. What could he say to them? And Tom didn't understand the problem: couldn't a painter conceivably return to an earlier technique, for one painting?

'Would m'sieur prefer lamb chops or cold ham this evening?' Mme Annette asked Tom.

'Lamb chops, I think. Thank you. And how is your tooth?' That morning, Mme Annette had been to the village dentist, in whom she had the greatest confidence, for a tooth that had kept her awake all night.

'No pain now. He is so nice, Dr Grenier! He said it was an abscess but he opened the tooth and he said the nerve would fall out.'

Tom nodded, but wondered how a nerve could fall out; gravity, presumably. They'd had to dig hard for one of his nerves once, and in an upper tooth, too.

'You had good news from London?'

'No, well – just a ring from a friend.'

'Any news from Mme Heloise?'

'Not today.'

'Ah, imagine sunlight! Greece!' Mme Annette was wiping the already shining surface of a large oak chest beside the fireplace. 'Look! Villeperce has no sun. The winter has arrived.'

'Yes.' Mme Annette said the same thing every day lately.

Tom didn't expect to see Heloise until close to Christmas. On the other hand, she could turn up unexpectedly – having had a slight but reparable tiff with her friends, or simply having changed her mind about staying on a boat so long. Heloise was impulsive.

Tom put on a Beatles record to lift his spirits, then walked about the large living-room, hands in his pockets. He loved the house. It was a two-storey squarish grey stone house with four turrets over four round rooms in the upstairs corners, making the house look like a little castle. The garden was vast, and even by American standards the place had cost a fortune. Heloise's father had given the house to them three years ago as a wedding present. In the days before he married, Tom had needed some extra money, the Greenleaf money not being enough for him to enjoy the kind of life he had come to prefer, and Tom had been interested in his cut of the Derwatt affair. Now he regretted that. He had accepted ten per cent, when ten per cent had been very little. Even he had not realized that Derwatt would flourish the way it had.

Tom spent that evening as he did most of his evenings, quietly and alone, but his thoughts were troubled. He played the stereo softly while he ate, and he read Servan-Schreiber in French. There were two words Tom didn't know. He would look them up tonight in his Harrap's beside his bed. He was good at holding words in his memory to look up.

After dinner he put on a raincoat, though it wasn't raining, and walked to a little bar-café a quarter of a mile distant. Here he took coffee some evenings, standing at the bar. Invariably the proprietor Georges inquired about Mme Heloise, and expressed regret that Tom had to spend so much time alone. Tonight Tom said cheeerfully:

'Oh, I am not sure she will stay on that yacht another two months. She will get bored.'

'*Quel luxe,*' murmured Georges dreamily. He was a paunchy man with a round face.

Tom mistrusted his mild and unfailing good-humour. His wife Marie, a big energetic brunette who wore bright red lipstick, was frankly tough, but she had a wild happy way of laughing that redeemed her. This was a workman's bar, and Tom did not object to that fact, but it was not his favourite bar. It just happened to be the closest. At least Georges and Marie had never referred to Dickie Greenleaf. A few people in Paris, acquaintances of his or Heloise's, had, and so had the owner of the Hotel St Pierre, Villeperce's only hostelry. The owner had asked, 'You are perhaps the M. Ripley who was a friend of the American Granelafe?' Tom had acknowledged that he was. But that had been three years ago, and such a question – if it never went any further – did not make Tom nervous, but he preferred to avoid the subject. The newspapers had said that he had received quite a sum of money, some said a regular income, which was true, from Dickie's will. At least no newspaper had ever implied that Tom had written the will himself, which he had. The French always remembered financial details.

After his coffee, Tom walked home, saying 'Bonsoir' to a villager or two on the road, slipping now and then in the sodden leaves that cluttered the edge of the road. There was no sidewalk to mention. He had brought a flashlight, because the streetlights were too infrequent. He caught glimpses of cosy families in kitchens, watching television, sitting around oilcloth-covered tables. Chained dogs barked in a few courtyards. Then he opened the iron gates – ten feet high – of his own house, and his shoes crunched on gravel. Mme Annette's light was on in her side room, Tom saw from the glow. She had her own television set. Often Tom painted at night, for his amusement only. He knew he was a bad painter, worse than Dickie. But tonight he was not in the mood. Instead, he wrote to a friend in Hamburg, Reeves Minot, an American, asking when did he expect to need him? Reeves was to plant a microfilm – or something – on a certain Italian Count Bertolozzi. The Count would then visit Tom for a day or so in Villeperce, and Tom would remove the object from the place in the suitcase or wherever, which Reeves would tell him, and post it to a man Tom didn't know at all in Paris. Tom frequently performed these fence-like services, sometimes for jewellery thefts. It was easier if Tom removed the objects from his guests, than if someone tried to do the same thing in a Paris hotel room, when the carrier was not in. Tom knew Count Bertolozzi slightly from a recent trip to Milan, when

Reeves, who lived in Hamburg, had been in Milan also. Tom had discussed paintings with the Count. It was usually easy for Tom to persuade people with a bit of leisure to stay with him a day or so in Villeperce and look at his paintings – he had, besides Derwatts, a Soutine, of whose work Tom was especially fond, a Van Gogh, two Magrittes, and drawings by Cocteau and Picasso, and many drawings of less famous painters which he thought equally good or better. Villeperce was near Paris, and it was nice for his guests to enjoy a bit of country before going up. In fact, Tom often fetched them from Orly in his car, Villeperce being some forty miles south of Orly. Only once had Tom failed, when an American guest had become immediately ill in Tom's house from something he must have eaten before arriving, and Tom had not been able to get to his suitcase because the guest was constantly in bed and awake in his room. That object – another microfilm of some sort – had been recovered with difficulty by a Reeves man in Paris. Tom could not understand the value of some of these things, but neither could he always when he read spy novels, and Reeves was only a fence himself and took a percentage. Tom always drove to another town to post these things, and he always sent them with a false return name and address.

That night, Tom could not fall asleep, so he got out of bed, put on his purple woollen dressing-gown – new and thick, full of military frogs and tassels, a birthday present from Heloise – and went down to the kitchen. He had thought of taking up a bottle of Super Valstar beer, but decided to make some tea. He almost never drank tea, so in a way it was appropriate, as he felt it was a strange night. He tiptoed around the kitchen, so as not to awake Mme Annette. The tea Tom made was dark red. He had put too much in the pot. He carried a tray into the living-room, poured a cup, and walked about, noiseless in felt house-shoes. Why not impersonate Derwatt, he thought. My God, yes! That was the solution, the perfect solution, and the only solution.

Derwatt was about his age, close enough – Tom was thirty-one and Derwatt would be about thirty-five. Blue-grey eyes, Tom remembered Cynthia (Bernard's girl friend) or maybe Bernard saying in one of their gushing descriptions of Derwatt the

Untarnishable. Derwatt had had a short beard, which was a tremendous help, would be, for Tom.

Jeff Constant would surely be pleased with the idea. A press interview. Tom must brush up on the questions he might have to answer, and the stories he would have to tell. Was Derwatt as tall as he? Well, who among the press would know? Derwatt's hair had been darker, Tom thought. But that could be fixed. Tom drank more tea. He continued walking about the room. His should be a surprise appearance, a surprise presumably even to Jeff and Ed – and Bernard, of course. Or so they would tell the press.

Tom tried to imagine confronting Mr Thomas Murchison. Be calm, self-assured, that was the essence. If Derwatt said a picture was his own, that he had painted it, who was Murchison to say him nay?

On a crest of enthusiasm, Tom went to his telephone. Often the operators were asleep at this hour – 2 A.M. and a bit after – and took ten minutes to answer. Tom sat patiently on the edge of the yellow sofa. He was thinking that Jeff or somebody would have to get some very good make-up in readiness. Tom wished he could count on a girl, Cynthia for instance, to supervise it, but Cynthia and Bernard had broken up two or three years ago. Cynthia knew the score about Derwatt and Bernard's forgeries, and would have none of it, not a penny of the profits, Tom remembered.

'Allo, j'écoute,' said the female operator in an annoyed tone, as if Tom had got her out of bed to do him a favour. Tom gave the number of Jeff's studio, which he had in an address book by the telephone. Tom was rather lucky, and the call came through in five minutes. He pulled his third cup of filthy tea nearer the telephone.

'Hello, Jeff. Tom. How are things?'

'Not any better. Ed's here. We were just thinking of ringing you. Are you coming over?'

'Yes, and I have a better idea. How about my playing – our missing friend – for a few hours, anyway?'

Jeff took an instant to comprehend. 'Oh, Tom, great! Can you be here for Tuesday?'

'Yes, sure.'

'Can you make it Monday. The day after tomorrow?'

'I don't think I can. But Tuesday, yes. Now listen, Jeff, the make-up – it's got to be good.'

'Don't worry! Just a sec!' He left off to speak with Ed, then returned. 'Ed says he has a source – of supply.'

'Don't announce it to the public,' Tom continued in his calm voice, because Jeff sounded as if he were leaping off his feet with joy. 'And another thing, if it doesn't work, if I fail – we must say it's a joke a friend of yours dreamed up – me. That it has nothing to do with – you know.' Tom meant with validating Murchison's forgery, but Jeff grasped this at once.

'Ed wants to say a word.'

'Hello, Tom,' Ed's deeper voice said. 'We're delighted you're coming over. It's a marvellous idea. And you know – Bernard's got some of his clothes and things.'

'I'll leave that to you.' Tom felt suddenly alarmed. 'The clothes are the least. It's the face. Get cracking, will you?'

'Right you are. Bless you.'

They hung up. Then Tom slumped back on the sofa and relaxed, almost horizontal. No, he wouldn't go to London too soon. Go on stage at the last moment, with dash and momentum. Too much briefing and rehearsal could be a bad thing.

Tom got up with the cold cup of tea. It would be amusing and funny if he could bring it off, he thought, as he stared at the Derwatt over his fireplace. This was a pinkish picture of a man in a chair, a man with several outlines, so it seemed one was looking at the picture through someone else's distorting eyeglasses. Some people said Derwatts hurt their eyes. But from a distance of three or four yards, they didn't. This was not a genuine Derwatt, but an early Bernard Tufts forgery. Across the room hung a genuine Derwatt, 'The Red Chairs'. Two little girls sat side by side, looking terrified, as if it were their first day in school, or as if they were listening to something frightening in church. 'The Red Chairs' was eight or nine years old. Behind the little girls, wherever they were sitting, the whole place was on fire. Yellow and red flames leapt about, hazed by touches of white, so that the fire didn't immediately catch the attention of the beholder. But when it did, the emotional effect was shattering. Tom loved both pictures. By now he had almost forgotten to remember, when he looked at them, that one was a forgery and the other genuine.

Tom recalled the early amorphous days of what was now Derwatt Ltd. Tom had met Jeffrey Constant and Bernard Tufts in London just after Derwatt had drowned – presumably intentionally – in Greece. Tom had just returned from Greece himself; it was not long after Dickie Greenleaf's death. Derwatt's body had never been found, but some fishermen of the village said they had seen him go swimming one morning, and had not seen him return. Derwatt's friends – and Tom had met Cynthia Gradnor on the same visit – had been profoundly disturbed, affected in a way that Tom had never seen after a death, not even in a family. Jeff, Ed, Cynthia, Bernard had been dazed. They had spoken dreamily, passionately, of Derwatt not only as an artist but as a friend, and as a human being. He had lived simply, in Islington, eating badly at times, but he had always been generous to others. Children in his neighbourhood had adored him, and had sat for him without expecting any payment, but Derwatt had always reached in his pockets for what were perhaps his last pennies to give them. Then just before he had gone to Greece, Derwatt had had a disappointment. He had painted a mural on a government assignment for a post office in a town in the north of England. It had been approved in sketch form, but rejected when finished: somebody was nude in it, or too nude, and Derwatt had refused to change it. ('And he was right, of course!' Derwatt's loyal friends had assured Tom.) But this had deprived Derwatt of a thousand pounds that he had counted on. It seemed to have been a last straw in a series of disappointments – the depth of which Derwatt's friends had not realized, and for this they reproached themselves. There had been a woman in the picture too, Tom recalled vaguley, the cause of another disappointment to Derwatt, but it seemed that the woman was not so important to him as his work disappointments. All Derwatt's friends were professionals also, mostly freelance, and were quite busy, and in the last days when Derwatt had called on them – not for money but for company on several evenings – they had said they hadn't time to see him. Unbeknownst to his friends, Derwatt had sold what furniture he had in his studio and got himself to Greece where he had written a long and depressed letter to Bernard. (Tom had never seen the letter.) Then had come the news of his disappearance or death.

The first thing Derwatt's friends, including Cynthia, had done was gather all his paintings and drawings and try to sell them. They had wanted to keep his name alive, had wanted the world to know and appreciate what he had done. Derwatt had had no relatives, and as Tom recalled, he had been a foundling without even known parents. The legend of his tragic death had helped instead of hindered; usually galleries were uninterested in paintings by a young and unknown artist who was already dead – but Edmund Banbury, a freelance journalist, had used his entrées and his talent for articles on Derwatt in newspapers, colour supplements and art magazines, and Jeffrey Constant had made photographs of Derwatt's paintings to illustrate them. Within a few months of Derwatt's death they found a gallery, the Buckmaster Gallery and moreover in Bond Street, which was willing to handle his work, and soon Derwatt's canvases were selling for six and eight hundred pounds.

Then had come the inevitable. The paintings were all sold, or nearly, and this was when Tom had been living in London (he had lived for two years in a flat in S.W.1, near Eaton Square) and had run into Jeff and Ed and Bernard one night in the Salisbury pub. They had again been sad, because Derwatt's paintings were coming to an end, and it had been Tom who had said, 'You're doing so well, it's a shame to end like this. Can't Bernard knock off a few paintings in Derwatt's style?' Tom had meant it as a joke, or a half-joke. He hardly knew the trio, only knew that Bernard was a painter. But Jeff, a practical type like Ed Banbury (and not a bit like Bernard), had turned to Bernard and said, 'I've thought of that, too. What do you think, Bernard?' Tom had forgot Bernard's exact reply, but he remembered that Bernard had lowered his head as if in shame or plain terror at the idea of falsifying his idol, Derwatt. Months later, Tom had encountered Ed Banbury in a street in London, and Ed had said cheerfully that Bernard had brought off two excellent 'Derwatts' and they had sold one at the Buckmaster as genuine.

Then still later, just after Tom had married Heloise, and was no longer living in London, Tom, Heloise, and Jeff were at the same party, a large cocktail party of the kind where you never meet or even see the host, and Jeff had beckoned Tom into a corner.

Jeff had said, 'Can we meet somewhere later? This is my address,' handing Tom a card. 'Can you come round about eleven tonight?'

So Tom had gone to Jeff's alone, which had been simple, because Heloise – who at that time did not speak much English – had had enough after the cocktail party, and wanted to go back to their hotel. Heloise loved London – English sweaters and Carnaby Street, and the shops that sold Union Jack wastebaskets and signs that said things like 'Piss off', things that Tom often had to translate for her, but she said her head ached after trying to speak English for an hour.

'Our problem is,' Jeff had said that night, 'we can't go on pretending we've found another Derwatt somewhere. Bernard is doing fine but – Do you think we could dare dig up a big trove of Derwatts somewhere, like Ireland where he painted for a bit, and sell them and then call it quits? Bernard isn't keen about going on. He feels he's betraying Derwatt – in a way.'

Tom had reflected a moment, then said, 'What's the matter with Derwatt being still alive somewhere? A recluse somewhere, sending his paintings to London? That is, if Bernard can keep going.'

'Um-m. Well – yes. Greece, maybe. What a super idea, Tom! It can go on for ever!'

'How about Mexico? I think it's safer than Greece. Let's say Derwatt's living in some little village. He won't tell anyone the name of the village – except maybe you and Ed and Cynthia –'

'Not Cynthia, She's – Well, Bernard doesn't see much of her any more. Consequently neither do we. Just as well she doesn't know too much about this.'

Jeff had rung up Ed that night to tell him the idea, Tom recalled.

'It's just an idea,' Tom had said. 'I don't know if it'll work.'

But it had worked. Derwatt's paintings had begun coming from Mexico, it was said, and the dramatic story of Derwatt's 'resurrection' had been exploited to advantage by Ed Banbury and Jeff Constant in more magazine articles, with photographs of Derwatt and his (Bernard's) latest paintings, though not of Derwatt himself *in* Mexico, because Derwatt permitted no interviewers or photographers. The paintings were sent from Vera Cruz and not even Jeff or Ed knew the name of his village. Derwatt was perhaps mentally sick to be such a recluse. His paintings were sick and depressed, according to some critics. But were now among the highest priced paintings of any living artist in England or on the Continent or in America. Ed Banbury wrote to Tom in France, offering him ten per cent of the profits, the loyal little group (now numbering only three, Bernard, Jeff and Ed) being the sole beneficiaries of Derwatt's sales. Tom had accepted, mainly because he considered it, his acceptance, rather a guarantee of his silence about the duplicity. But Bernard Tufts was painting like a demon.

Jeff and Ed bought the Buckmaster Gallery. Tom was not sure if Bernard owned any part of it. Several Derwatts were in a permanent collection of the gallery, and the gallery showed the paintings of other artists as well, of course. This was more Jeff's job than Ed's, and Jeff had hired an assistant, a sort of manager for the gallery. But this step up, the purchase of the Buckmaster Gallery, had come after Jeff and Ed had been approached by an art materials manufacturer called George Janopolos or some such, who wanted to start a line of goods to be labelled 'Derwatt', which would include everything from erasers to oil paint sets, and for which he offered Derwatt a royalty of one per cent. Ed and Jeff had decided to accept for Derwatt (presumably with Derwatt's consent). A company had then been formed called Derwatt Ltd.

All this Tom recollected at four in the morning, shivering a little despite his princely dressing-gown. Mme Annette always thriftily turned the central heating down at night. He held the cup of cold sweet tea between his hands and stared unseeing at a photograph of Heloise — long blonde hair on either side of a slender face, a pleasant and meaningless design to Tom just now rather than a face – and he thought of Bernard working in secret on his Derwatt forgeries in a closed, even locked room in his studio apartment. Bernard's place was pretty crummy, as it always had been. Tom had never seen the sanctum sanctorum where he painted his masterpieces, the Derwatts that brought in thousands of quid. If one painted more forgeries than one's own paintings, wouldn't the forgeries become more natural, more real, more genuine to oneself, even, than one's own painting? Wouldn't the effort finally go out of it and the work become second nature?

At last Tom curled up on the yellow sofa, slippers off and feet drawn under his robe, and slept. He did not sleep long before Mme Annette arrived and awaked him with a shriek, or a shrill gasp, of surprise.

'I must have fallen asleep reading,' Tom said, smiling, sitting up.

Mme Annette hurried off to make his coffee.

2

Tom booked a flight to London at noon on Tuesday. It would give him only a couple of hours to get made-up and to be briefed. Not enough time to grow nervous. Tom drove to Melun to pick up some cash – francs – at his bank.

It was eleven-forty, and the bank closed at twelve. Tom was third in the queue at the window where people received cash, but unfortunately a woman was delivering payroll money or some such at this window, heaving up bags of coins, while keeping her feet braced against the bags that remained on the floor. Behind the grille, a clerk with wetted thumb was counting stacks of banknotes as quickly as possible and making notations of their sums on two separate papers. How long would this go on, Tom wondered, as the clock crept towards twelve. Tom watched with amusement as the queue broke up. Three men now and two women pressed near the grille, staring glassy-eyed, like fascinated snakes, at all the dough, as if it were a heritage left them by a relative who had worked a lifetime for it. Tom gave it up and left the bank. He could manage without the cash, he thought, and in fact he had only been thinking of giving it or selling it to English friends who might be coming to France.

On Tuesday morning, when Tom was packing his bag, Mme Annette knocked on his bedroom door. 'I'm off for Munich,' Tom said cheerily. 'There's a concert.'

'Ah, Munich! Bavière! You must take warm clothing.' Mme Annette was used to his impromptu trips. 'For how long, M. Tome?'

'Two days, maybe three. Don't worry about messages. I may ring to see if any have come.'

Then Tom thought of something possibly useful, a Mexican ring that he had – he thought – in his studbox. Yes, there it was, among cufflinks and buttons, a heavy ring of silver whose design was two coiled snakes. Tom disliked it and had forgot how he acquired it, but at least it was Mexican. Tom blew on it, rubbed it against a trouser leg, and pocketed it.

The post at 10.30 A.M. brought three items, a telephone bill, lumpy in its envelope because of separate tabs for each non-Villeperce call; a letter from Heloise; and an American airmail letter addressed in a hand Tom didn't know. He turned the envelope over and was surprised to see the name Christopher Greenleaf on the back with a San Francisco return address. Who was Christopher? He opened Heloise's letter first.

11 octobre 19—

Chéri,

I am happy and very quite now. Very good repastes. We catch fishs off the boat. Zeppo sends love. [Zeppo was her swarthy Greek host and Tom could tell him what to do with his love.]

I learn better to mount a bicycle. We have made many voyages into the land which is dry. Zeppo makes photos. How goes it at Belle Ombre? I miss you. Are you happy? Many invites? [Did that mean guests or invitations?] Are you painting? I have received no word from Papa.

Kiss Mme A. I embrace you.

The rest was in French. She wanted him to send a red bathing-suit which he would find in a small *commode* in her bathroom. He should send it airmail. The yacht had a heated swimming-pool. Tom at once went upstairs where Mme Annette was still working in his room, and entrusted this task to her, giving her a hundred-franc note for it, because he thought she might be scandalized at the price of the airmail package and be tempted to send it slow post.

Then he went down and opened the Greenleaf letter hastily, because he had to leave for Orly in a few minutes.

Oct. 12 19—

Dear Mr Ripley,

I am a cousin of Dickie's and am coming to Europe next week, probably going to London first, though I cannot make up my mind whether to go to Paris first. Anyway, I thought it would be nice if we could meet. My uncle Herbert gave me your address, and he says you are not far from Paris. Haven't got your telephone number, but I can look it up.

To tell you a bit about myself, I am twenty and I go to Stanford University. I spent one year in military service, during which my college was interrupted. I'll return to Stanford for a degree in engineering but meanwhile I am taking a year off to see Europe and relax. Lots of fellows do this now. The pressure everywhere is quite something. I mean in America, but maybe you have been in Europe so long you don't know what I mean.

My uncle has told me a lot about you. He says you were a good friend of Dickie's. I met Dickie when I was 11 and he was 21. I remember a tall blond fellow. He visited my family in California.

Please tell me if you will be in Villeperce in late October, early November. Meanwhile here's hoping to meet you.

Sincerely

Chris Greenleaf

He would get out of that one politely, Tom thought. No use making closer contact with the Greenleaf family. Once in a blue moon Herbert Greenleaf wrote him, and Tom always replied, nice polite letters.

'Mme Annette, keep the home fires burning,' Tom said as he took off.

'What did you say?'

He translated it into French as best he could.

'Au revoir, M. Tome! Bon voyage!' Mme Annette waved to him from the front door.

Tom took the red Alfa-Romeo, one of the two cars in the garage. At Orly, he put the car in the indoor garage, saying it was for two or three days. He bought a bottle of whisky in the terminus to take to the gang. He had already a big bottle of Pernod in his suitcase (since he was permitted to enter London with only one bottle), because Tom had found that if he went through the green aisle and showed the visible bottle, the inspector never asked him to open his suitcase. On the plane he bought untipped Gauloises, always popular in London.

It was raining lightly in England. The bus crept along on the left side of the road, past the family houses whose names always amused Tom, though now he could hardly read them through the murk. Bide-a-wee. Unbelievable. Milford Haven. Dun Wandering. They hung on little signboards. Inglenook. Sit-Ye-Doon. Good God. Then came the stretch of jammed-together Victorian houses that had been converted into small hotels with grandiose names in neon lights between Doric doorway pillars: Manchester Arms, King Alfred, Cheshire House. Tom knew that behind the genteel respectability of those narrow lobbies some of the best murderers of the present day took refuge for a night or so, looking equally respectable themselves. England was England, God bless it!

The next thing that caught Tom's attention was a poster on a lamppost on the left side of the road. DERWATT was written in bold black script slanting downward – Derwatt's signature – and the picture reproduced in colour looked in the dim light dark purple or black and somewhat resembled the raised top of a grand piano. A new Bernard Tufts forgery, doubtless. There was another such poster a few yards on. It was odd to feel so 'announced' all over London, and to arrive so quietly, Tom thought as he stepped down from the bus at the West Kensington Terminal unnoticed by anyone.

From the terminal, Tom rang Jeff Constant at his studio. Ed Banbury answered.

'Hop in a taxi and come straight here!' Ed said, sounding wildly happy.

Jeff's studio was in St John's Wood. Second floor – first to the English – on the left. It was a proper neat little building, neither swank nor shabby.

Ed whipped the door open. 'My God, Tom, it's great to see you !'

They shook hands firmly. Ed was taller than Tom with lank blond hair that was apt to fall over his ears, so he was constantly shoving it aside. He was about thirty-five.

'And where's Jeff?' Tom fished out Gauloises and whisky from the red net bag, then the smuggled Pernod from his suit-case. 'For the house.'

'Oh, super ! Jeff's at the gallery. Listen, Tom, you'll *do* it? – Because I've got the stuff here and there isn't too much time.'

'I'll try it,' Tom said.

'Bernard's due. He'll help us. Briefing.' Ed looked hecticly at his wristwatch.

Tom had removed his topcoat and jacket. 'Can't Derwatt be a little late? Isn't the opening at five?'

'Oh, of course. No need to get there till six, anyway, but I do want to try the make-up. Jeff said to remind you you're not much shorter than Derwatt was – and who remembers those statistics? Assuming I ever wrote them anywhere? And Derwatt had bluish-grey eyes. But yours'll do.' Ed laughed. 'Want some tea?'

'No thanks.' Tom was looking at the dark-blue suit on Jeff's couch. It looked too wide, and it was unpressed. A pair of awful black shoes were on the floor by the couch. 'Why don't you have a drink?' Tom suggested to Ed, because Ed looked as jumpy as a cat. As usual, another person's nervousness was making Tom feel calm.

The doorbell rang.

Ed let Bernard Tufts in.

Tom extended a hand. 'Bernard, how are you?'

'All right, thank you,' Bernard said, sounding miserable. Bernard was thin and olive-skinned, with straight black hair and gentle dark eyes.

Tom thought it best not to try to talk to Bernard just now, but to be simply efficient.

Ed drew a basin of water in Jeff's tiny but modern bathroom, and Tom submitted to a hair rinse to make his hair darker. Bernard began to talk, but only after deliberate, then more importunate prodding from Ed.

'He walked with a slight stoop,' Bernard said. 'His voice — He was a little shy in public. It was a sort of monotone, I suppose. Like this, if I can illustrate,' Bernard said in a monotone. 'Now and then he laughed.'

'Don't we all!' Tom said, laughing nervously himself. Now Tom was sitting in a straight chair, being combed by Ed. On Tom's right was a platter of what looked like barbershop floor sweepings, but Ed shook this out, and it was a beard fastened to fine flesh-coloured gauze. 'Good God, I hope the lights are dim,' Tom murmured.

'We'll see to that,' said Ed.

While Ed worked with a moustache, Tom pulled off his two rings, one a wedding ring, one Dickie Greenleaf's ring, and pocketed them. He asked Bernard to bring him the ring from his left trouser pocket, and Bernard did. Bernard's thin fingers were cold and shaking. Tom wanted to ask him how Cynthia was, and remembered that Bernard was not seeing her any more. They had been going to marry, Tom remembered. Ed was snipping at Tom's hair with scissors, creating a bush in front.

'And Derwatt —' Bernard stopped, because his voice had cracked.

'Oh, shut up, Bernard!' Ed said, laughing hysterically.

Bernard laughed also. 'Sorry. Really, I'm sorry.' He sounded contrite, as if he meant it.

The beard was going on, with glue.

Ed said, 'I want you to walk around a bit here, Tom. Get used to it. At the gallery — You won't have to go in with the crowd, we decided against that. There's a back door, and Jeff will let us in. We'll invite some of the press to come into the office, you see, and we'll have just one standing lamp on across the room. We've removed a little lamp and the ceiling bulb, so that *can't* go on.'

The gluey beard felt cool on Tom's face. In the mirror in Jeff's loo, he looked a little like D. H. Lawrence, he thought. His mouth was surrounded by hair. It was a sensation Tom did not like. Below the mirror on a little shelf three snapshots of Derwatt were propped up – Derwatt reading a book in shirtsleeves in a deckchair, Derwatt standing with a man Tom did not know, facing the camera. Derwatt had glasses in all the pictures.

'The specs,' Ed said, as if he read Tom's thoughts.

Tom took the round-rimmed glasses Ed handed him, and put them on. That was better. Tom smiled, gently so as not to spoil the drying beard. The specs were plain glass, apparently. Tom walked with a stoop back into the studio, and said in what he hoped was Derwatt's voice, 'Now tell me about this man Murchison –'

'Deeper!' Bernard said, his skinny hands flailing wildly.

'This man Murchison,' Tom said.

Bernard said, 'M-Murchison, according to Jeff, thinks – Derwatt has returned to an old technique. In his painting "The Clock", you see. I don't know what he means – specifically – to tell you the truth.' Bernard shook his head quickly, pulled a handkerchief from somewhere and blew his nose. 'I was just looking at one of Jeff's shots of "The Clock". I haven't seen it in three years, you see. Not the picture itself.' Bernard was talking softly, as if the walls might be listening.

'Is Murchison an expert?' Tom asked, thinking, what was an expert?

'No, he's just an American businessman,' Ed said. 'He collects. He's got a bee in his bonnet.'

It was more than that, Tom thought, or they wouldn't all be so upset. 'Am I supposed to be prepared for anything specific?'

'No,' Ed said. 'Is he, Bernard?'

Bernard almost gasped, then tried to laugh, and for an instant he looked as he had looked years ago, younger, naïve. Tom realized that Bernard was thinner than when he had last seen him three or four years ago.

'I wish I knew,' Bernard said. 'You must only – stand by the fact that the picture, "The Clock", is Derwatt's.'

'Trust me,' Tom said. He was walking about, practising the stoop, assuming a slowish rhythm which he hoped was correct.

'But,' Bernard went on, 'if Murchison wants to continue whatever he's talking about, whatever it is – "Man in Chair" you've got, Tom –'

A forgery. 'He need never see that,' said Tom. 'I love it, myself.'

' "The Tub",' Bernard added. 'It's in the show.'

'You're worried about that?' Tom asked.

'It's in the same technique,' Bernard said. 'Maybe.'

'Then you know what technique Murchison is talking about? Why don't you take "The Tub" out of the show if you're worried about it?'

Ed said, 'It was announced on the programme. We were afraid if we removed it, Murchison might want to see it, want to know who bought it and all that.'

The conversation got nowhere, because Tom could not get a clear statement of what they, or Murchison, meant by the technique in these particular pictures.

'You'll never meet Murchison, so stop worrying,' Ed said to Bernard.

'Have you met him?' Tom asked Ed.

'No, only Jeff has. This morning.'

'And what's he like?'

'Jeff said about fifty or so, a big American type. Polite enough but stubborn. Wasn't there a belt in those trousers?'

Tom tightened the belt in his trousers. He sniffed at the sleeve of his jacket. There was a faint smell of mothballs, which probably wouldn't be noticed in all the cigarette smoke. And anyway, Derwatt could have been wearing Mexican clothes for the past few years, and his European clothes might have been put away. Tom looked at himself in a long mirror, under one of Jeff's very bright spotlights that Ed had put on, and suddenly doubled over with laughter. Tom turned around and said, 'Sorry, I was just thinking that considering Derwatt's fantastic earnings, he certainly hangs on to his old gear!'

'That's okay, he's a recluse,' Ed said.

The telephone rang. Ed answered, and Tom heard him assuring someone, no doubt Jeff, that Tom had arrived and was ready to go.

Tom did not feel quite ready to go. He felt sweaty from

nerves. He said to Bernard, trying to sound cheerful, 'How's Cynthia? Do you ever see her?'

'I don't see her any more. Not very often, anyway.' Bernard glanced at Tom, then looked back at the floor.

'What's she going to say when she finds out Derwatt's come back to London for a few days?' Tom asked.

'I don't think she'll say anything,' Bernard replied dully. 'She's not – going to spoil things, I'm sure.'

Ed finished his telephone conversation. 'Cynthia won't say anything, Tom. She's like that. You remember her, don't you, Tom?'

'Yes. Slightly,' Tom said.

'If she hasn't said anything by now, she's not going to,' Ed said. The way he said it made it sound like, 'She's not a bad sport or a babble-mouth.'

'She *is* quite wonderful,' Bernard said dreamily, to nobody. He suddenly got up and darted for the bathroom, perhaps because he had to go there, but it might have been to throw up.

'Don't worry about Cynthia, Tom,' Ed said softly. 'We live with her, you see. I mean, here in London. She's been quiet for three years or so. Well, you know – since she broke up with Bernard. Or he broke up with her.'

'Is she happy? Found somebody else?'

'Oh, she has a boy-friend, I think.'

Bernard was coming back.

Tom had a Scotch. Bernard took a Pernod, and Ed drank nothing. He was afraid to, he said, because he'd had a sedative. By five o'clock, Tom had been briefed or refreshed on several things: the town in Greece where Derwatt had officially last been seen nearly six years ago. Tom, in case he was queried, was to say he had left Greece under another name on a Greek tanker bound for Vera Cruz, working as oiler and ship's painter.

They borrowed Bernard's topcoat, which was older looking than Tom's or any of Jeff's in his closet. Then Tom and Ed set off, leaving Bernard in Jeff's studio, where they all were to meet later.

'My God, he's down in the mouth,' Tom said on the pavement. He was walking with a slump. 'How long can he go on like this?'

'Don't judge by today. He'll go on. He's always like this when there's a show.'

Bernard was the old workhorse, Tom supposed. Ed and Jeff were burgeoning on extra money, good food, good living. Bernard merely produced the pictures that made it possible.

Tom drew back sharply from a taxi, not having expected it to be bowling along on the left side of the road.

Ed smiled. 'That's great. Keep it up.'

They came to a taxi rank and got into a cab.

'And this – caretaker or manager at the gallery,' Tom said. 'What's his name?'

'Leonard Hayward,' Ed said. 'He's about twenty-six. Queer as Dick's hatband, belongs in a King's Road boutique, but he's okay. Jeff and I let him into the circle. Had to. It's really safer, because he can't spring any blackmail, if he signed a written agreement with us to caretake the place, which he did. We pay him well enough and he's amused. He also sends us some good buyers.' Ed looked at Tom and smiled. 'Don't forget a bit of woikin' class accent. You can do it quite well as I remember.'

3

Ed Banbury rang a bell at a dark-red door flush with the back of a building. Tom heard a key being turned, then the door opened and Jeff stood there, beaming at them.

'Tom ! It's *super* !' Jeff whispered.

They went down a short corridor, then into a cosy office with a desk and typewriter, books, cream-coloured wall-to-wall carpeting. Canvases and portfolios of drawings leaned against the wall.

'I can't tell you how right you look – Derwatt !' Jeff slapped Tom's shoulder. 'I hope that won't make your beard fall off.'

'Even a high wind wouldn't,' Ed put in.

Jeff Constant had gained weight, and his face was flushed –

or perhaps he had been using a sun-tan lamp. His shirt cuffs were adorned with square gold links, and his blue and black striped suit looked brand-new. Tom noticed that a toupee – what they called a hair-piece – covered the bald spot on the top of Jeff's head, which Tom knew must be quite barren by now. Through the closed door that led to the gallery came a hubbub of voices, lots of voices out of which a woman's laugh leapt like a porpoise over the surface of a troubled sea, Tom thought, though he was not in the mood for poetry now.

'Six o'clock,' Jeff announced, flashing more cuff to see his watch. 'I shall now quietly tell a few of the press that Derwatt is here. This being England, there will not be a –'

'Ha-ha! Not be a what?' Ed interrupted.

'– not be a *stampede*,' Jeff said firmly. 'I'll see to that.'

'You'll sit back here. Or stand, as you like,' Ed said, indicating the desk which was set at an angle and had a chair behind it.

'This Murchison chap is here?' Tom asked in Derwatt tones.

Jeff's fixed smile widened, but a little uneasily. 'Oh, yes. You ought to see him, of course. But after the press.' Jeff was jumpy, eager to be off, though he looked as if he might have said more, and he went out. The key turned in the lock.

'Any water anywhere?' Tom asked.

Ed showed him a small bathroom, which had been concealed by a section of bookshelf that swung out. Tom took a hasty gulp, and as he stepped out of the bathroom, two gentlemen of the press were coming in with Jeff, their faces blank with surprise and curiosity. One was fifty-odd, the other in his twenties, but their expressions were much alike.

'May I present Mr Gardiner of the *Telegraph*,' Jeff said. 'Derwatt. And Mr –'

'Perkins,' said the younger man. '*Sunday* . . .'

Another knock on the door before they could exchange greetings. Tom walked with a stoop, almost rheumatically, towards the desk. The single lamp in the room was near the door to the gallery, a good ten feet away from him. But Tom had noticed that Mr Perkins carried a flash camera.

Four more men and one woman were admitted. Tom feared a woman's eyes, under the circumstances, more than anything.

She was introduced to him as a Miss Eleanor Somebody of the *Manchester* Something or other.

Then the questions began to fly, although Jeff suggested that each reporter should ask his questions in turn. This was a useless proposal, as each reporter was too eager to get his own questions answered.

'Do you intend to live in Mexico indefinitely, Mr Derwatt?'

'Mr Derwatt, we're so surprised to see you here. What made you decide to come to London?'

'Don't call me *Mister* Derwatt,' Tom said grumpily. 'Just Derwatt.'

'Do you like the latest – group of canvases you've done? Do you think they're your best?'

'Derwatt – are you living alone in Mexico?' asked Eleanor Somebody.

'Yes.'

'Could you tell us the name of your village?'

Three more men came in, and Tom was aware of Jeff urging one of them to wait outside.

'One thing I will not tell you is the name of my village,' Tom said slowly. 'It wouldn't be fair to the inhabitants.'

'Derwatt, uh –'

'Derwatt, certain critics have said –'

Someone was banging with fists on the door.

Jeff banged back and yelled, 'No more just now, please!'

'Certain critics have said –'

Now the door gave a sound of splitting, and Jeff set his shoulder against it. The door was not giving, Tom saw, and turned his calm eyes from it to regard his questioner.

'– have said that your work resembles a period of Picasso's related to his cubist period, when he began to split faces and forms.'

'I have no periods,' Tom said. 'Picasso has periods. That's why you can't put your finger on Picasso – if anybody wants to. It's impossible to say "I like Picasso", because no one period comes to mind. Picasso plays. That's all right. But by doing this he destroys what might be a genuine – a genuine and integrated personality. What *is* Picasso's personality?'

The reporters scribbled diligently.

'What is your favourite painting in this show? Which do you think you like best?'

'I have no – No, I can't say that I have a favourite painting in this show. Thank you.' Did Derwatt smoke? What the hell. Tom reached for Jeff's Craven A's and lit one with a table lighter before two reporters could spring to his cigarette. Tom drew back to protect his beard from their fire. 'My favourites perhaps are the old ones – "The Red Chairs", "Falling Woman", maybe. Sold alas.' Out of nowhere, Tom had recalled the last title. It did exist.

'Where is that? I don't know that, but I know the name,' someone said.

Shyly, recluse-like, Tom kept his eyes on the leather-bound blotter on Jeff's desk. 'I've forgot. "Falling Woman". Sold to an American, I think.'

The reporters plunged in again: 'Are you pleased with your sales, Derwatt?'

(Who wouldn't he?)

'Does Mexico inspire you? I notice there are no canvases in the show with a Mexican settting.'

(A slight hurdle, but Tom got over it. He had always painted from imagination.)

'Can you at least describe the house where you live in Mexico, Derwatt?' asked Eleanor.

(This Tom could do. A one-storey house with four rooms. A banana tree out front. A girl came to clean every morning at ten, and did a little shopping for him at noon, bringing back freshly baked tortillas, which he ate with red beans – frijoles – for lunch. Yes, meat was scarce, but there was some goat. The girl's name? Juana.)

'Do they call you Derwatt in the village?'

'They used to, and they had a very different way of pronouncing it, I can tell you. Now it's Filipo. There's no need of another name but Don Filipo.'

'They have no idea that you're *Derwatt*?'

Tom laughed a little again. 'I don't think they're much interested in *The Times* or *Arts Review* or whatever.'

'Have you missed London? How does it look to you?'

'Was it just a whim that made you come back now?' young Perkins asked.

'Yes. Just a whim.' Tom smiled the worn, philosophic smile of a man who had gazed upon Mexican mountains, alone, for years.

'Do you ever go to Europe – incognito? We know you like seclusion –'

'Derwatt, I'd be most grateful if you could find ten minutes tomorrow. May I ask where you're –'

'I'm sorry, I haven't yet decided where I'm staying,' Tom said.

Jeff gently urged the reporters to take leave, and the cameras began to flash. Tom looked downward, then upward for one or two photographs on request. Jeff admitted a waiter in a white jacket with a tray of drinks. The tray was emptied in a trice.

Tom lifted a hand in a gesture of shy, gracious farewell. 'Thank you all.'

'No more, please,' Jeff said at the door.

'But I –'

'Ah, Mr Murchison. Come in, please,' Jeff said. He turned to Tom. 'Derwatt, this is Mr Murchison. From America.'

Mr Murchison was large, with a pleasant face. 'How do you do, Mr Derwatt?' he said, smiling. 'What an unexpected treat to meet you here in London!'

They shook hands.

'How do you do?' Tom said.

'And this is Edmund Banbury,' Jeff said. 'Mr Murchison.'

Ed and Mr Murchison exchanged greetings.

'I've got one of your paintings – "The Clock". In fact, I brought it with me.' Mr Murchison was smiling widely now, staring with fascination and respect at Tom, and Tom hoped his gaze was dazzled by the surprise of actually seeing him.

'Oh, yes,' Tom said.

Jeff again quietly locked the door. 'Won't you sit down, Mr Murchison?'

'Yes, thank you.' Murchison sat, on a straight chair.

Jeff quietly began gathering empty glasses from the edges of bookshelves and the desk.

'Well, to come to the point, Mr Derwatt, I – I'm interested in a certain change of technique that you show in "The Clock". You know, of course, the picture I mean?' Murchison asked.

Was that a casual or a pointed question, Tom wondered? 'Of course,' Tom said.

'Can you describe it?'

Tom was still standing up. A slight chill went over him. Tom smiled. 'I can never describe my pictures. It wouldn't surprise me if there were no clock in it. Did you know, Mr Murchison, I don't always make up my own titles? And how anyone got "Sunday Noon" out of the particular canvas is beyond me.' (Tom had glanced at the gallery programme of twenty-eight Derwatts now on exhibit, a programme which Jeff or someone had thoughtfully opened and placed on the blotter of the desk.) 'Is that your effort, Jeff?'

Jeff laughed. 'No, I think it's Ed's. Would you like a drink, Mr Murchison? I'll get you one from the bar.'

'No, thank you, I'm fine.' Then Mr Murchison addressed Tom. 'It's a bluish-black clock held by – Do you remember?' He smiled as if he were asking an innocent riddle.

'I think a little girl – who's facing the beholder, shall we say?'

'Hm-m. Right,' said Murchison. 'But then you don't do little boys, do you?'

Tom chuckled, relieved that he'd guessed right. 'I suppose I prefer little girls.'

Murchison lit a Chesterfield. He had brown eyes, light-brown wavy hair, and a strong jaw covered with just a little too much flesh, like the rest of him. 'I'd like you to see my picture. I have a reason. Excuse me a minute. I left it with the coats.'

Jeff let him out the door, then locked the door again.

Jeff and Tom looked at each other. Ed was standing against a wall of books, silent. Tom said in a whisper:

'Really, boys, if the damned canvas has been in the coat-room all this time, couldn't one of you've whisked it out and burnt it?'

'Ha-ha!' Ed laughed, nervously.

Jeff's plump smile was a twitch, though he kept his poise, as if Murchison were still in the room.

'Well, let us hear him out,' Tom said in a slow and confident Derwatt tone. He tried to shoot his cuffs, but they didn't shoot.

Murchison came back carrying a brown-paper-wrapped picture under one arm. It was a medium-sized Derwatt, perhaps two feet by three. 'I paid ten thousand dollars for this,' he said, smiling. 'You may think it careless of me to leave it in the cloakroom, but I'm inclined to trust people.' He was undoing the wrapping with the aid of a penknife. 'Do you know this picture?' he asked Tom.

Tom smiled at the picture. 'Of course I do.'

'You remember painting it?'

'It's my picture,' Tom said.

'It's the purples in this that interest me. The purple. This is straight cobalt violet – as you can probably see better than I.' Mr Murchison smiled almost apologetically for a moment. 'The picture is at least three years old, because I bought it three years ago. But if I'm not mistaken, you abandoned cobalt violet for a mixture of cad red and ultramarine five or six years ago. I can't exactly fix the date.'

Tom was silent. In the picture Murchison had, the clock was black and purple. The brushstrokes and the colour resembled those of 'Man in Chair' (painted by Bernard) at home. Tom didn't know quite what, in the purple department, Murchison was hammering at. A little girl in a pink-and-apple-green dress was holding the clock, or rather resting her hand on it, as the clock was large and stood on a table. 'To tell you the truth, I've forgot,' Tom said. 'Perhaps I did use straight cobalt violet there.'

'And also in the painting called "The Tub" outside,' Murchison said, with a nod towards the gallery. 'But in none of the others. I find it curious. A painter doesn't usually go back to a colour he's discarded. The cad red and ultramarine combination is far more interesting – in my opinion. Your newer choice.'

Tom was unworried. Ought he to be more worried? He shrugged slightly.

Jeff had gone into the little bathroom and was fussing about with glasses and ashtrays.

'How many years ago did you paint "The Clock"?' Murchison asked.

'That I'm afraid I can't tell you,' Tom said in a frank manner. He had grasped Murchison's point, at least in regard to time, and he added, 'It could have been four or five years ago. It's an old picture.'

'It wasn't sold to me as an old one. And "The Tub". That's dated only last year, and it has the same straight cobalt violet in it.'

The cobalt for the purpose of shadow, one might say, was not dominant in 'The Clock'. Murchison had an eagle eye. Tom thought 'The Red Chairs' – the earlier and genuine Derwatt – had the same straight cobalt, and he wondered if it had a fixed date? If he could say 'The Red Chairs' was only three years old, prove it somehow, Murchison could simply go to hell. Check with Jeff and Ed later on that, Tom thought.

'You definitely remember painting "The Clock"?' Murchison asked.

'I know it's my picture,' Tom said. 'I might have been in Greece or even Ireland when I painted it, because I don't remember dates, and the dates the gallery might have are not always the dates when I painted something.'

'I don't think "The Clock" is your work,' Murchison said with good-natured American conviction.

'Good heavens, why not?' Tom's good-nature matched Murchison's.

'I have a nerve sticking my neck out like this, I know. But I've seen some of your earlier work in a museum in Philadelphia. If I may say so, Mr Derwatt, you're –'

'Just call me Derwatt. I like it better.'

'Derwatt. You're so prolific, I think you might forget – I should say not remember a painting. Granted "The Clock" is in your style and the theme is typical of your –'

Jeff, like Ed, was listening attentively, and in this pause Jeff said, 'But after all this picture came from Mexico along with a few others of Derwatt's. He always sends two or three at a time.'

'Yes. "The Clock" has a date on the back. It's three years old, written in the same black paint as Derwatt's signature,' Murchison said, swinging his painting round so all could see it. 'I had the signature and the date analysed in the States. That's how carefully I've gone into this,' Murchison said, smiling.

'I don't quite know what the trouble is,' Tom said. 'I painted it in Mexico if the date's three years old in my own writing.'

Murchison looked at Jeff. 'Mr Constant, you say you received "The Clock" along with two others, perhaps, in a certain shipment?'

'Yes. Now that I recall – I think the other two are here now lent by London owners – "The Orange Barn" and – Do you recall the other, Ed?'

'I think it's "Bird Spectre" probably. Isn't it?'

From Jeff's nod, Tom could see it was true, or else Jeff was doing well at pretending.

'That's it,' said Jeff.

'They're not in this technique. There's purple in them, but made by mixed colours. The two you're talking about are genuine – genuinely later pictures at any rate.'

Murchison was slightly wrong, they were phoneys as well. Tom scratched his beard, but very gently. He kept a quiet, somewhat amused air.

Murchison looked from Jeff to Tom. 'You may think I'm being bumptious, but if you'll excuse me, Derwatt, I think you've been forged. I'll stick my neck out farther, I'll bet my life that "The Clock" isn't yours.'

'But Mr Murchison,' Jeff said, 'that's a matter of simply –'

'Of showing me a receipt for a certain number of paintings in a certain year? Paintings received from Mexico which might not be even titled? What if Derwatt doesn't give them a title?'

'The Buckmaster Gallery is the only authorized dealer for Derwatt's work. You bought that picture from us.'

'I'm aware of that,' said Murchison. 'And I'm not accusing you – or Derwatt. I'm just saying, I don't think this is a *Derwatt*. I can't tell you what *happened*.' Murchison looked at all of them in turn, a bit embarrassed by his own outburst, but still carried along by his conviction. 'My theory is that a painter never reverts to a single colour which he once used or any combination of colours once he has made a change to another colour as subtle and yet as important as lavender is in Derwatt's paintings. Do you agree, Derwatt?'

Tom sighed and touched his moustache with a forefinger. 'I can't say. I'm not so much of a theoretician as you, it seems.'

A pause.

'Well, Mr Murchison, what would you like us to do about "The Clock"? Refund your money?' Jeff asked. 'We'll be happy to do that, because – Derwatt has just verified it, and frankly it's worth more than ten thousand dollars now.'

Tom hoped Mr Murchison would accept, but he was not that kind of man.

Murchison took his time, pushed his hands into his trousers pockets and looked at Jeff. 'Thank you, but I'm more interested in my theory – my opinion, than in the money. And since I'm in London, where there're as good judges of painting as anywhere in the world, maybe the best, I intend to have "The Clock" looked at by an expert and compared with – certain indisputable Derwatts.'

'Very well,' said Tom amiably.

'Thank you very much for seeing me, Derwatt. A pleasure to meet you.' Murchison held out his hand.

Tom shook it firmly. 'A pleasure, Mr Murchison.'

Ed helped Murchison wrap up his painting, and provided more string, as Murchison's string would no longer tie.

'Can I reach you through the gallery here?' Murchison said to Tom. 'Say tomorrow?'

'Oh, yes,' Tom said. 'They'll know where I am.'

When Murchison had left the room, Jeff and Ed gave huge sighs.

'Well – how serious is it?' Tom asked.

Jeff knew more about pictures. He spoke first, with difficulty. 'It's serious if he drags in an expert, I suppose. And he will. He may have a point about the purples. One might call it a clue that could lead to worse.'

Tom said, 'Why don't we go back to your studio, Jeff? Can you whisk me out the back door again – like Cinderella?'

'Yep, but I want to speak to Leonard.' Jeff grinned. 'I'll drag him in to meet you.' He went out.

The hum from the gallery was less now. Tom looked at Ed, whose face was a bit pale. *I can disappear, but you can't*, Tom thought. Tom squared his shoulders, and lifted his fingers in a V. 'Chin up, Banbury. We'll see this one through.'

'Or that's what they'll do to *us*,' Ed replied, with a more vulgar gesture.

Jeff came back with Leonard, a smallish, neat young man in an Edwardian suit with many buttons and velvet facings. Leonard burst into laughter at the sight of Derwatt, and Jeff shushed him.

'It is marvellous, marvellous!' Leonard said, looking Tom over with a genuine admiration. 'I've seen so many pictures, you know! I haven't seen anything so good since I did Toulouse-Lautrec with my feet tied up behind me! That was last year.' Leonard stared at Tom. 'Who *are* you?'

'That,' Jeff said, 'you are not to know. Suffice it to say –'

'Suffice it to say,' Ed said, 'Derwatt has just given a brilliant interview to the press.'

'And tomorrow Derwatt is no more. He will return to Mexico,' Jeff said in a whisper. 'Now back to your duties, Leonard.'

'*Ciao*,' said Tom, raising a hand.

'*Hommage*,' said Leonard, bowing. He backed towards the door, and added, 'The crowd's nearly all gone. So's the booze.' He slipped out.

Tom was not quite so cheerful. He very much wanted out of his disguise. The situation was a problem, not yet solved.

Back at Jeff's studio, they found that Bernard Tufts had gone. Ed and Jeff seemed surprised. And Tom was a little uneasy, because Bernard ought to know what was going on.

'You can reach Bernard of course,' Tom said.

'Oh, sure,' said Ed. He was making some tea for himself in Jeff's kitchen. 'Bernard's always *chez lui*. He's got a telephone.'

It crossed Tom's mind that even the telephone might not be safe to use for long.

'Mr Murchison is going to want to see you again probably,' Jeff said. 'With the expert. So you've got to disappear. You'll

39

leave for Mexico tomorrow – officially. Maybe even tonight.'
Jeff was sipping a Pernod. He looked more confident, perhaps
because the press interview and even the Murchison interview
had gone reasonably well, Tom thought.

'Mexico my foot,' Ed said, coming in with his cup of tea.
'Derwatt will be somewhere in England staying with friends,
and even we won't know where. Let some days pass. *Then*
he'll go to Mexico. By what means? Who knows?'

Tom removed his baggy jacket. 'Is there a date for "The Red
Chairs"?'

'Yes,' Jeff said. 'It's six years old.'

'Printed here and there, I suppose?' Tom asked. 'I was thinking of updating it – to get over this purple business.'

Ed and Jeff glanced at each other, and Ed said quickly, 'No,
it's in too many catalogues.'

'There's one way out, have Bernard do several canvases – two
anyway – with the plain cobalt violet. Sort of prove that he uses
both kinds of purple.' But Tom felt discouraged as he said it,
and he knew why. Tom felt that it might be Bernard that they
couldn't count on any longer. Tom looked away from Jeff and
Ed. They were dubious. He tried standing up, straight, feeling
confident of his Derwatt disguise. 'Did I ever tell you about my
honeymoon?' Tom asked in Derwatt's monotone.

'No, tell us about your honeymoon!' Jeff said, ready for a
laugh and grinning already.

Tom assumed Derwatt's stoop. 'It was – most inhibiting –
the atmosphere. In Spain. We'd taken a hotel suite, you see,
and there I was with Heloise, and downstairs in the patio a
parrot sang *Carmen* – badly. And every time we – Well, there it
came: "Ah-ha-ha-ha-ha-ha-ha-haaaaaa! Ah-*ha*-ha-ha-ha-ha-ha-
ha-ha-ha-ha-*haaaaa*!" People leaned out windows yelling in
Spanish, "Shut your filthy beak! Who taught that – unmen-
tionable object to sing *Carmen*? Kill it! Boil it in soup!" It is
impossible to make love while laughing. Have you ever tried it?
Well – they say laughter distinguishes the human from the
animal. And – the other thing certainly doesn't. Ed, can you
get me out of this foliage?'

Ed was laughing, and Jeff rolling on the sofa in relief – which

Tom knew would be temporary – from the recent strain.

'Come in the loo.' Ed turned on the hot water in the basin.

Tom changed into his own trousers and shirt. If he could lure Murchison to his house somehow, before Murchison spoke to the expert he was talking about, perhaps something – Tom didn't know what – could be done about the situation. 'Where's Murchison staying in London?'

'Some hotel,' Jeff said. 'He didn't say which.'

'Can you ring a few hotels and see if you can find him?'

Before Jeff got to the telephone, it rang. Tom heard Jeff telling someone that Derwatt had taken a train north, and Jeff did not know where he was going. 'He's very much a loner,' Jeff said. 'Another gentleman of the press,' Jeff said when he had hung up, 'trying to get a personal interview.' He opened a telephone book. 'I'll try the Dorchester first. He looks like a Dorchester type.'

'Or a Westbury type,' Ed said.

It took a lot of delicately applied water to remove the gauze of the beard. Afterward came a shampoo to get the rinse out of his hair. Tom finally heard Jeff say in a cheerful tone, 'No, thank you, I'll ring back later.'

Then Jeff said, 'It's the Mandeville. That's off Wigmore Street.'

Tom put on his own pink shirt from Venice. Then he went to the telephone and booked a room at the Mandeville under the name Thomas Ripley. He would arrive by 8 p.m. or so, he said.

'What're you going to do?' Ed asked.

Tom smiled a little, 'I don't know just yet,' he said, which was true.

4

The Hotel Mandeville was rather plush, but by no means as expensive as the Dorchester. Tom arrived at 8.15 p.m. and registered, giving his address as Villeperce-sur-Seine. It had crossed his mind to give a false name and some English country address, because he might get into considerable difficulties with Mr Murchison and have to disappear quickly, but there was also the possibility of inviting Murchison to France, in which case Tom might need his real name. Tom asked a bellhop to take his suitcase to his room, and then he looked into the bar, hoping Mr Murchison might be there. Mr Murchison was not there, but Tom decided to have a lager and wait a few moments.

A ten-minute wait with a lager and an *Evening Standard* brought no Mr Murchison. The neighbourhood was full of restaurants, Tom knew, but he could hardly approach Murchison's table and strike up an acquaintance on the strength of saying he had seen Murchison at the Derwatt show that day. Or could he – saying he had also seen Murchison going into the back room to meet Derwatt? Yes. Tom was just about to venture out to explore the local restaurants, when he saw Mr Murchison coming into the bar, gesturing to someone to follow him.

And to Tom's surprise, horror even, he saw that the other person was Bernard Tufts. Tom slipped quickly out of the door on the other side of the bar, which opened onto the pavement. Bernard hadn't seen him. Tom was fairly sure. He looked around for a telephone booth, for another hotel from which to telephone, and, finding none, he went back into the Mandeville by the main entrance and took his key for his room, number four eleven.

In his room, Tom rang Jeff's studio. Three rings, four, five, then to Tom's relief, Jeff answered.

'Hello, Tom! I was just going down the stairs with Ed when I heard the phone. What's up?'

'Do you happen to know where Bernard is now?'

'Oh, we're leaving him alone tonight. He's upset.'

'He's having a drink with Murchison in the bar of the Mandeville.'

'*What*?'

'I'm ringing from my room. Now whatever you do, Jeff – Are you listening?'

'Yes-yes.'

'Don't tell Bernard I saw him. Don't tell Bernard I'm at the Mandeville. And don't get in a flap about anything. That's providing Bernard isn't spilling the beans now, I don't know.'

'Oh, my God,' Jeff groaned. 'No-no. Bernard wouldn't spill the *beans*. I don't *think* he would.'

'Are you in later tonight?'

'Yes, by – Oh, home before midnight, anyway.'

'I'll try to ring you. But don't be worried if I don't. Don't try to ring me because – I just might have somebody in my room,' Tom said with a sudden laugh.

Jeff laughed, but a bit sickly. 'Okay, Tom.'

Tom hung up.

He definitely wanted to see Murchison tonight. Would Murchison and Bernard have dinner? That would be a bore to wait out. Tom hung up a suit and stuck a couple of shirts in a drawer. He splashed some more water on his face and looked in the mirror to make sure every bit of glue was gone.

Out of restlessness, he left his room, his topcoat over his arm. He would take a walk, to Soho perhaps, and find a place for dinner. In the lobby, he looked through the glass doors of the Mandeville bar.

He was in luck. Murchison sat alone, signing the bill, and the street door of the bar was just closing, perhaps even with Bernard's departure. Still, Tom glanced around in the lobby, in case Bernard had slipped out to the men's room and might be coming back. Tom did not see Bernard, and he waited until Murchison was actually standing up to leave before he went into the bar. Tom looked depressed and thoughtful, and in fact he felt that way. He looked twice at Murchison, whose eyes met his once, as if he were recalling Murchison from somewhere.

Then Tom approached him. 'Excuse me. I think I saw you

43

at the Derwatt show today.' Tom had put on an American accent, mid-western with a hard *r* in Derwatt.

'Why, yes, I was there,' Murchison said.

'I thought you looked like an American. So am I. Do you like Derwatt?' Tom was being as naïve and straightforward as possible without seeming dim-witted.

'Yes, I certainly do.'

'I own two of his canvases,' Tom said with pride. 'I may buy one of the ones in the show today – if it's left. I haven't decided yet. "The Tub".'

'Oh? So do I own one,' Murchison said with equal candour. 'Y'do? What's it called?'

'Why don't you sit down?' Murchison was standing, but indicated the chair opposite him. 'Would you care for a drink?'

'Thanks, I don't mind if I do.'

Murchison sat down. 'My picture is called "The Clock". How nice to run into someone who owns a Derwatt, too – or a couple of them !'

A waiter came.

'Scotch for me, please. And you?' he asked Tom.

'A gin and tonic,' Tom said. He added, 'I'm staying here at the Mandeville, so these drinks are on me.'

'We'll argue about that later. Tell me what pictures you have.'

' "The Red Chairs",' Tom said, 'and –'

'Really? That's a gem ! "The Red Chairs". Do you live in London?'

'No, in France.'

'Oh,' with disappointment. 'And what's the other picture?'

' "Man in Chair".'

'I don't know that,' Murchison said.

For a few minutes, they discussed Derwatt's odd personality, and Tom said he had seen Murchison go into a back room of the gallery where he had heard Derwatt was.

'Only the press was let in, but I crashed the gate,' Murchison told Tom. 'You see, I've got a rather special reason for being here just now, and when I heard Derwatt was *here* this afternoon at the gallery, I wasn't going to let the opportunity slip.'

'Yes? What's your reason?' Tom asked.

Murchison explained. He explained his reasons for thinking Derwatt might be being forged, and Tom listened with rapt attention. It was a matter of Derwatt using a mixture of ultramarine and cadmium red now, for the past five years or so (since before his death, Tom realized, so Derwatt had begun this, not Bernard), and of having in 'The Clock' and in 'The Tub' gone back to his early simple cobalt violet. Murchison himself painted, he told Tom, as a hobby.

'I'm no expert, believe me, but I've read almost every book about painters and painting that exists. It wouldn't take an expert or a microscope to tell the difference between a single colour and a mixture, but what I mean is, you'll never find a painter going back to a colour that he has consciously or unconsciously discarded. I say unconsciously, because when a painter chooses a new colour or colours it is usually a decision made by his unconscious. Not that Derwatt uses lavender in every picture, no indeed. But my conclusion is that my "Clock" and possibly some other pictures including "The Tub" that you're interested in, by the way, are not Derwatts.'

'That's interesting. Very. Because as it happens my "Man in Chair" sort of corresponds to what you're saying. I think. And "Man in Chair" is about four years old now. I'd love you to see it. Well, what're you going to do about your "Clock"?'

Murchison lit one of his Chesterfields. 'I haven't finished my story yet. I just had a drink with an Englishman whose name is Bernard Tufts, a painter also, and he seems to suspect the same thing about Derwatt.'

Tom frowned hard. 'Really? It's pretty important if someone's forging Derwatts. What did the man say?'

'I have the feeling he knows more than he's saying. I doubt if he's in on any of it. He's not a crooked type, and he doesn't look as if he has much money, either. But he seems to know the London art scene. He simply warned me, "Don't buy any more Derwatts, Mr Murchison." Now what do you think of *that*?'

'Hm-m. But what's he got to go on?'

'As I say, I don't know. I couldn't get anything out of him. But he took the trouble to look me up here, and he said he called eight London hotels before he found me. I asked him how he knew my name, and he said, "Oh, word gets around." Very strange, since the Buckmaster Gallery people are the only people I've spoken to. Don't you think? I have an appointment with a man from the Tate Gallery tomorow, but even he doesn't know it's in regard to a Derwatt.' Murchison drank some of his Scotch and said, 'When paintings start coming from Mexico – Do you know what I'm going to do tomorrow besides showing "The Clock" to Mr Reimer at the Tate Gallery, I'm going to ask if I or he has the right to see the receipts or books of the Buckmaster Gallery people in regard to Derwatt paintings sent from Mexico. It's not the titles I'm so interested in, and Derwatt told me he doesn't always title them, it's the number of paintings. Surely they're let in by the customs or something, and if some paintings aren't recorded, there's a reason. Wouldn't it be amazing if Derwatt himself were being hoodwinked and a few Derwatts – well, some said to be four or five years old, for instance – were being painted right here in London?'

Yes, Tom thought. Amazing. 'But you said you spoke with Derwatt. Did you talk to him about your painting?'

'I showed it to him! He said it was his, but he wasn't dead sure of it in my opinion. He didn't say, "By God, that's mine!" He looked at it for a couple of minutes and said, "Of course, it's mine." It was maybe presumptuous of me, but I said to Derwatt I thought it was possible he could forget a canvas or two, an untitled canvas that he'd done years ago.'

Tom frowned as if he doubted this, which he did. Even a painter who did not give titles to his paintings would remember a painting, Tom thought, less a drawing, perhaps. But he let Murchison continue.

'And for another thing, I don't quite like the men at the Buckmaster Gallery. Jeffrey Constant. And the journalist Edmund Banbury, who's obviously a close friend of Constant's. They're old friends of Derwatt's, I realize that. I get *The Listener* and *Arts Review* and also the *Sunday Times* in Long

Island where I live. I see articles by Banbury quite often, usually with a plug for Derwatt, if the article isn't on Derwatt. And do you know what occurred to me?'

'What?' Tom asked.

'That – just maybe Constant and Banbury are putting up with a few forgeries in order to sell more Derwatts than Derwatt can produce. I don't go so far as to say Derwatt's in on it. But wouldn't that be a funny story, if Derwatt's so absent-minded he can't even remember how many pictures he's painted?' Murchison laughed.

It was funny, Tom supposed, but not hilarious. Not as funny as the truth, Mr Murchison. Tom smiled. 'So you're going to show your picture to the expert tomorrow?'

'Come up and see it now l'

Tom tried to take the bill, but Murchison insisted upon signing.

Tom went with him in the lift. Murchison had his painting in a corner of his closet, wrapped as Ed had wrapped it that afternoon. Tom looked at it with interest.

'It's a handsome picture,' Tom said.

'Ah, no one can deny that l'

'You know ?' Tom propped it on the writing-desk and was now looking at it from across the room with all the lights turned on. 'It does have a similarity to my "Man in Chair". Why don't you come over and look at my picture? I'm very near Paris. If you think my picture might be forged, too, I'll let you take it back with you to show in London.'

'Hum,' said Murchison, thinking. 'I could.'

'If you've been taken in, so have I, I think.' It would only be insulting to offer to pay for Murchison's flight, Tom thought, so he did not. 'I've a pretty big house and I'm alone at the moment, except for my housekeeper.'

'All right, I will,' said Murchison, who hadn't sat down.

'I intend to leave tomorrow afternoon.'

'All right, I'll postpone that Tate Gallery appointment.'

'I've lots of other paintings. Not that I'm a collector.' Tom sat down in the largest chair. 'I'd like you to have a look at them. A Soutine. Two Magrittes.'

'Really?' Murchison's eyes began to look a little dreamy. 'How far are you from Paris?'

Ten minutes later, Tom was in his own room one floor below. Murchison had proposed that they have dinner together, but Tom had thought it best to say he had an appointment at 10 p.m. in Belgravia, so there was hardly time. Murchison had entrusted Tom with booking their plane tickets for tomorrow afternoon to Paris, a round-trip for Murchison. Tom picked up the telephone and booked two seats on a flight that left tomorrow afternoon, Wednesday, at 2 p.m. for Orly. Tom had his own return ticket. He left a message downstairs for Murchison in regard to the flight. Then Tom ordered a sandwich and a half bottle of Médoc. After this, he napped until eleven, and put in a telephone call to Reeves Minot in Hamburg. This took nearly half an hour.

Reeves was not in, a man's German-accented voice said.

Tom decided to chance it, because he was fed up with Reeves, and said, 'This is Tom Ripley. Has Reeves any message for me?'

'Yes. The message is Wednesday. The Count arrives in Milan tomorrow. Can you come to Milan tomorrow?'

'No, I cannot come to Milan tomorrow. *Es tut mir leid*.' Tom didn't, as yet, want to say to this man, no matter who he was, that the Count already had an invitation to visit him when he next came to France. Reeves couldn't expect him to drop everything all the time – Tom had done so on two other occasions – to fly to Hamburg or Rome (much as Tom enjoyed little excursions), pretend to be in those cities by accident, and invite the 'host', as Tom always thought of the carrier, to his Villeperce house. 'I think there's no great complication,' Tom said. 'Can you tell me the Count's address in Milan?'

'Grand Hotel,' said the voice brusquely.

'Would you tell Reeves I'll be in touch, tomorrow probably. Where can I reach him?'

'Tomorrow morning at the Grand Hotel in Milan. He is taking a train to Milan tonight. He does not like aeroplanes, you know.'

Tom hadn't known. It was odd, a man like Reeves not liking

aeroplanes. 'I'll ring him. And I'm not in Munich now. I'm in Paris.'

'Paris?' with surprise. 'I know Reeves tried to ring you in Munich at the Vierjahreszeiten.'

That was too bad. Tom hung up politely.

The hands of his wristwatch moved towards midnight. Tom puzzled about what to tell Jeff Constant tonight. And what to do about Bernard. A speech of reassurance sprang full-blown to Tom's mind, and there was time to see Bernard before he left tomorrow afternoon, but Tom was afraid Bernard might be more upset and negative, if anybody made an obvious effort to reassure him. If Bernard had said to Murchison, 'Don't buy any more Derwatts,' it sounded as if Bernard wasn't going to paint any more Derwatts, and that, of course, was going to be very bad for business. A still worse possibility, which Bernard might be on the brink of, was a confession to the police or to one or several purchasers of phoney Derwatts.

What state of mind was Bernard really in, and what was he up to?

Tom decided he should not say anything to Bernard. Bernard knew that he, Tom, had proposed his forging. Tom took a shower and began to sing:

'Babbo non vuole
Mamma nemmeno
Come faremo
A far all' amor ...'

The Mandeville's walls gave a feeling – maybe an illusion – of being soundproof. Tom had not sung the song in a long time. He was pleased that it had come to him out of the blue, because it was a happy song, and Tom associated it with good luck.

He got into pyjamas and rang Jeff's studio.

Jeff answered at once. 'Hello. What's up?'

'I spoke with Mr M. tonight, and we got along fine. He's coming to France with me tomorrow. So that will delay things, you see.'

'And – you'll try to persuade him or something, you mean.'

'Yes. Something like that.'

'Want me to come to your hotel, Tom? You're probably too tired to pop over here. Or are you?'

'No, but there's no need. And you might just run into Mr M. if you came here, and we don't want that.'

'No.'

'Did you hear from Bernard?' Tom asked.

'No.'

'Please tell him –' Tom tried to find the right words. 'Tell him that you – not me – happen to know Mr M. is going to wait a few days before he does anything about his painting. I'm mainly concerned that Bernard doesn't blow up. Will you try to take care of that?'

'Why don't *you* speak to Bernard?'

'Because it would be wrong,' Tom said somewhat crossly. Some people had no inkling of psychology!

'Tom, you were marvellous today,' Jeff said. 'Thank you.'

Tom smiled, gratified by Jeff's ecstatic tone. 'Take care of Bernard. I'll ring you before I take off.'

'I expect to be in my studio all morning tomorrow.'

They said good night.

If he had told Jeff about Murchison's intention to ask for receipts, the records of paintings sent from Mexico, Jeff would have been in a tizzy, Tom thought. He must warn Jeff about that tomorrow morning, ring him from a pavement telephone booth, or from a post office. Tom was wary of hotel switchboard listeners. Of course, he hoped to dissuade Murchison from his theory, but if he couldn't, it would be just as well if Buckmaster Gallery made some records that looked authentic.

5

The next morning, breakfasting in bed – a privilege for which one paid a few Puritan shillings extra in England – Tom rang Mme Annette. It was only eight o'clock, but Tom knew she would have been up for nearly an hour, singing as she went about her chores of turning up the heat (a little gauge in the kitchen), making her delicate *infusion* (tea), because coffee in the morning made her heart beat fast, and adjusting her plants on various windowsills so they would catch the most sun. And she would be mightily pleased by a *coup de fil* from him in Londres.

'Allo! – Allo-*allo*!' Operator furious.

'Allo?' Quizzical.

'*Allo!*'

Three French operators were on the telephone at once, plus the woman at the Mandeville switchboard.

At last, Mme Annette came on. 'It is very beautiful here this morning. Sunlight!' Mme Annette said.

Tom smiled. He badly needed a voice of cheer. 'Mme Annette ... Yes, I am very well, thank you. How is the tooth? ... Good! I am telephoning to say I will be home this afternoon around four with an American gentleman.'

'Ah-h!' said Mme Annette, pleased.

'Our guest for tonight, perhaps for two nights, who knows? Will you prepare the guest-room nicely? With some flowers? And for dinner perhaps *tournedos* with your own delicious *béarnaise?*'

Mme Annette sounded delirious with joy that Tom would have a guest and she would have something definite to do.

Then Tom rang Mr Murchison, and they agreed to meet in the hotel lobby around noon and to take a taxi together to Heathrow.

Tom went out, intending to walk to Berkeley Square, off which was a haberdashery where he bought a pair of silk pyjamas as a small ritual nearly every time he came to London. It might also be his last chance this trip for a ride on the Underground. The Underground was a part of the atmosphere of London life, and Tom also was an admirer of Underground graffiti. The sun was struggling rather hopelessly through a wet haze, though it was not actually raining. Tom ducked into Bond Street station along with some last stragglers, perhaps, of the morning rush hour. What Tom admired about London graffiti-writers was their ability to scrawl things from moving escalators. Underwear posters abounded on the escalator routes, nothing but girls in girdles and panties, and they were adorned by anatomical additions male and female, sometimes whole phrases: I LOVE BEING HERMAPHRODITE! How did they do it? By running in an opposite direction from the escalator's while writing? WOGS OUT! was a favourite everywhere, varied WOGS OUT NOW! Down on the train platform, Tom spotted a poster for the Zeffirelli *Romeo and Juliet* with Romeo naked on his back and Juliet crawling over him with a shocking proposal coming out of her mouth. Romeo's reply in a balloon was 'Okay, why don't you?'

Tom had his pyjamas by 10.30. He bought a yellow pair. He had wanted purple, as he had none now, but he had heard enough about purple lately. Tom took a taxi to Carnaby Street. For himself, he bought a pair of narrow satin-like trousers, as he did not care for flared cuffs. And for Heloise flared hipsters of black wool, waist twenty-six. The booth where Tom tried on his own trousers was so tiny, he could not step back from the mirror to see if the length was right, but Mme Annette loved to adjust little things like that for him and Heloise. Besides, two Italians who kept saying '*Bellissimo!*' were pulling back the curtains every few seconds, wanting to come in and try on their own gear. When Tom was paying, two Greeks arrived and began discussing prices loudly in drachmas. The shop was about six feet by twelve, and no wonder there was only one assistant, because there would have been no room for two.

With his purchases in big crisp paper bags, Tom went to a pavement telephone booth and rang Jeff Constant.

'I spoke to Bernard,' Jeff said, 'and he's absolutely terrified of Murchison. I asked him what he said to Murchison, because Bernard told me he'd spoken with Murchison, you see. Bernard said he'd told Murchison not to buy any more – paintings. That's bad enough, isn't it?'

'Yes,' said Tom. 'And what else?'

'Well – I tried to tell Bernard he'd already said all he could or should. It's difficult to explain because you don't know Bernard, but he's got such a guilt thing about Derwatt's genius and all that. I tried to convince Bernard that he'd eased his own conscience by *saying* that to Murchison, and why not let well enough alone?'

'What did Bernard say to that?'

'He's so down in the mouth, it's hard to tell what he said. The show was a sell-out, you see, except for one picture. Imagine! And Bernard feels guilty about that!' Jeff laughed. ' "The Tub." It's one of the ones Murchison is picking on.'

'If he doesn't want to paint more just now, don't force him.'

'That's exactly my attitude. You're so right, Tom. But I think in about a fortnight, he'll be on his feet again. Painting. It's the strain of the show, and seeing you as Derwatt. He thinks more of Derwatt than most people do of Jesus Christ.'

Tom didn't have to be told that. 'One small thing, Jeff. Murchison may want to see the gallery's books for Derwatt's paintings. From Mexico. Do you keep some kind of record?'

'N-not from Mexico.'

'Can you fake something? Just in case I can't persuade him to drop the whole thing?'

'I'll try, Tom.' Jeff sounded a bit off balance.

Tom was impatient. 'Fake something. Age it. Regardless of Mr M., isn't it a good idea to have a few books to substantiate –?' Tom broke off. Some people didn't know how to run a business, even a successful business like Derwatt Ltd.

'All right, Tom.'

Tom detoured to the Burlington Arcade, where he stopped in a jewellery shop and bought a gold pin – a little crouched monkey – for Heloise, which he paid for with American travellers' cheques. Heloise's birthday was next month. Then he walked on towards his hotel, via Oxford Street, which was crowded as usual with shoppers, women with bulging bags and boxes, children in tow. A sandwich man advertised a passport photo studio, service fast and cheap. The old fellow wore an ancient overcoat, a limp hat, and a sordid unlit cigarette hung from between his lips. Get a passport for your cruise to the Greek islands, Tom thought, but this old guy was never going any-where. Tom removed the cigarette butt and stuck a Gauloise between the man's lips.

'Have a cigarette,' Tom said. 'Here's a light.' Tom lit it quickly with his matches.

'Ta,' said the man, through his beard.

Tom pushed the rest of the Gauloise pack, then his matches, into the torn pocket of the overcoat, and dashed away, his head ducked, hoping no one had seen him.

Tom rang Murchison from his room, and they met downstairs with their luggage.

'Been doing a little shopping for my wife this morning,' Murchison said in the taxi. He seemed in a good mood.

'Yes? So have I. A pair of Carnaby Street trousers.'

'For Harriet, it's Marks and Spencer sweaters. And Liberty scarves. Sometimes balls of wool. She knits, and she likes to think the wool came from old England, y'know?'

'You cancelled your appointment for this morning?'

'Yep. Made it for Friday morning. At the man's house.'

At the airport, they had a rather good lunch with a bottle of claret. Murchison insisted on paying. During lunch Murchison told Tom about his son who was an inventor working in a California laboratory. His son and daughter-in-law had just had their first baby. Murchison showed Tom a photograph of her, and laughed at himself for being a doting grandfather, but it was his first grandchild, named Karin after her grandmother on her maternal side. In answer to Murchison's questions, Tom said he had chosen to live in France because he had married a French girl three years ago. Murchison was not blunt enough to ask how Tom earned his living, but he did ask how he spent his time.

'I read history,' Tom said casually. 'I study German. Not to mention that my French still needs work. And gardening. I've got a pretty big garden in Villeperce. Also I paint,' he added, 'just for my amusement.'

They were at Orly by 3 p.m., and Tom went off in the little GASO bus to fetch his car from the garage, and then he picked up Murchison near the taxi rank with their suitcases. The sun was shining, and it was not so cold as in England. Tom drove to Fontainebleau and went past the château so that Murchison could see it. Murchison said he hadn't seen it in fifteen years. They reached Villeperce around 4.30 p.m.

'Where we buy most of our groceries,' Tom said, indicating a store on his left on the main village street.

'Very pretty. Unspoilt,' Murchison said. And when they came to Tom's house: 'Why this is terrific! Really beautiful!'

'You should see it in the summer,' Tom said, modestly.

Mme Annette, hearing the car, came out to greet them and to help with the luggage, but Murchison could not bear to see a woman carrying the heavy things, only the little bags of cigarettes and spirits.

'Everything goes well, Mme Annette?' Tom asked.

'Everything. Even the plumber came to repair the W.C.'

One of the W.C.s had been dripping, Tom remembered.

Tom and Annette showed Murchison up to his room which had an adjoining bath. It was actually Heloise's bath, and her room was on the other side of the bath. Tom explained that his wife was in Greece now, with friends. He left Murchison to wash and to open his suitcase, and said he would be downstairs in the living-room. Murchison was already gazing with interest at some drawings on the walls.

Tom went down and asked Mme Annette to make some tea. He presented her with a bottle of toilet water from England, 'Lake Mist' – which he had bought at Heathrow.

'Oh, M. Tome, *comme vous êtes gentil!*'

Tom smiled. Mme Annette always made him feel grateful for her gratitude. 'Good *tournedos* for tonight?'

'Ah, *oui!* And for dessert *mousse au chocolat.*'

Tom went into the living-room. Here were flowers, and Mme Annette had turned up the heat. There was a fireplace, and Tom loved fires, but he felt he had to watch them constantly, or he loved watching them so much he could not tear himself away, so he decided not to light one now. He stared at 'Man in Chair' over the fireplace, and bounced on his heels with satisfaction – satisfaction with its familiarity, its excellence. Bernard was good. He'd just made a couple of mistakes in his periods. Damn periods anyway. Logically, 'The Red Chairs,' a genuine Derwatt, should have the place of honour in the room over the fireplace. Typical of him that he had put the phoney in the choice spot, he supposed. Heloise didn't know that 'Man in Chair' was bogus, and knew nothing of the Derwatt forgeries, in fact. Her interest in painting was casual. If she had any passions, they were for travelling, sampling exotic food, and buying clothes. The contents of her two closets in her room looked like an international costume museum without the dummies. She had waistcoats from Tunisia, fringed sleeveless jackets from Mexico, Greek soldiers' baggy pants in which she looked quite charming, and embroidered coats from China that she had bought somehow in London.

Then Tom suddenly remembered Count Bertolozzi, and went to his telephone. He didn't particularly want Murchison to hear the Count's name, but on the other hand Tom was not going to do any harm to the Count, and perhaps maintaining his open manner was all to the good. Tom asked for inquiries for Milan, got the number, and gave it to the French operator. She told Tom the call might take half an hour.

Mr Murchison came down. He had changed his clothes, and wore grey flannel trousers and a green and black tweed jacket. 'The country life!' he said, beaming. 'Ah!' He had caught sight of 'The Red Chairs' facing him across the room, and went over for closer inspection. 'That's a masterpiece. That's the real McCoy!'

No doubt of that, Tom thought, and a thrill of pride went over him which made him feel slightly foolish. 'Yes, I like it.'

'I think I've heard about it. I remember the title from somewhere. I congratulate you, Tom.'

'And there's my "Man in Chair",' Tom said, nodding towards the fireplace.

'Ah,' Murchison said on a different note. He went nearer, and Tom saw his tall, sturdy figure grow tense with concentration. 'And how old is this?'

'About four years old,' Tom said truthfully.

'What did you pay, to ask a rude question?'

'Four thousand quid. Before devaluation. About eleven thousand two hundred dollars,' Tom said, calculating the pound at two eighty.

'I'm delighted to see this,' Murchison said, nodding. 'You see, the same purple turns up again. Very little of it here, but look.'

He pointed to the bottom edge of the chair. Due to the height of the picture and the width of the fireplace, Murchison's finger was inches away from the canvas, but Tom knew the streak of purple that he meant. 'Plain cobalt violet.' Murchison crossed the room and looked again at 'The Red Chairs', peering at it at a distance of ten inches. 'And this is one of the old ones. Plain cobalt violet too.'

'You really think "Man in Chair" is a forgery?'

'Yes, I do. Like my "Clock". The quality is different. Inferior to "The Red Chairs". Quality is something one can't measure with the aid of a microscope. But I can see it here. *And* – I'm also sure about the plain cobalt violet here.'

'Then,' Tom said in an unperturbed way, 'maybe it means Derwatt is using plain cobalt violet and the mixture you mentioned – alternately.'

Murchison, frowning, shook his head. 'I don't see it that way.'

Mme Annette was pushing the tea in on a cart. One wheel of the cart squeaked slightly. '*Voilà le thé*, M. Tome.'

Mme Annette had made flat brown-edged cookies, and they gave off a rosy smell of warm vanilla. Tom poured the tea.

Murchison sat on the sofa. He might not have seen Mme Annette come and go. He stared at 'Man in Chair' as if dazed or fascinated. Then he blinked at Tom, smiled, and his face was genial again. 'You don't believe me, I think. That's your privilege.'

'I don't know what to say. I don't see the difference in quality, no. Maybe I'm obtuse. If, as you say, you'll get an expert to look at yours, I'll abide by what an expert says. And by the way, "Man in Chair" is the picture you can take back to London with you, if you like.'

'I'd most certainly like. I'll write you a receipt for it and even insure it for you.' Murchison chuckled.

'It's insured. Don't worry.'

Over two cups of tea, Murchison asked Tom about Heloise, and what she was doing. Had they any children? No. Heloise was twenty-five. No, Tom didn't think Frenchwomen were more difficult than other women, but they had their own idea of the respect with which they should be treated. This subject did not make much progress, because every woman wanted to be treated with a certain respect, and though Tom knew Heloise's kind, he absolutely could not put it into words.

The telephone rang, and Tom said, 'Excuse me, I think I'll take that up in my room.' He dashed up the stairs. After all, Murchison might suppose it was Heloise, and that he wanted to speak with her alone.

'Hello?' Tom said. 'Eduardo! How are you? I'm in luck to get you ... Via the grapevine. A mutual friend in Paris rang today and told me you were in Milan ... Now you can pay me a visit? After all, you promised.'

The Count, a bon-vivant ever willing to be distracted from the swift pursuit of his business (export-import) showed a slight hesitation about changing his Paris plans, then agreed with enthusiasm to come to Tom. 'But not tonight. Tomorrow. Is that all right?'

That was quite soon enough for Tom, who wasn't quite sure what problems Murchison would present. 'Yes, even Friday would be –'

'*Thursday*,' said the Count, firmly, not getting the point.

'All right. I'll pick you up at Orly. At what time?'

'My plane is at – just a minute.' The Count took quite a time looking it up, came back to the telephone and said. 'Arriving at five fifteen. Flight three zero six Alitalia.'

Tom wrote this down. 'I'll be there. Delighted you can come, Eduardo!'

Then Tom went back downstairs to Thomas Murchison. By now they called each other Tom, though Murchison said his wife called him Tommy. Murchison said he was an hydraulic engineer with a pipe-laying company whose main office was in New York. Murchison was one of the directors.

They took a walk around Tom's back garden, which blended into virgin woods. Tom rather liked Murchison. Surely he could persuade him, convert him, Tom thought. What *should* he do?

During dinner, while Murchison talked about something brand-new in his plant, packaged transport by pipe of anything and everything in soup-tin-sized containers – Tom wondered if he should bother to ask Jeff and Ed to get Mexican letterheads from some shipping company on which to list Derwatt's paintings? And how quickly could this be done? Ed was the journalist, and couldn't he handle a clerical job like this, and have Leonard, the gallery manager, and Jeff walk all over them on the floor to make them look five or six years old? The dinner was excellent, and Murchison had praise for Mme Annette, which he delivered in quite passable French, for her *mousse* and even the Brie.

'We'll have coffee in the living-room,' Tom said to her. 'And can you bring the brandy?'

Mme Annette had lit the fire. Tom and Murchison settled themselves on the big yellow sofa.

'It's a funny thing,' Tom began, 'I like "Man in Chair" just as much as "The Red Chairs". If it's phoney. Funny, isn't it?' Tom was still talking in a mid-western accent. 'You can see it's got the place of honour in the house.'

'Well, you didn't know it was a forgery!' Murchison laughed a little. 'It'd be very interesting – very – to know who's forging.'

Tom stretched his legs out in front of him and puffed on a cigar. 'What a funny thing it would be,' he began, playing his last and best card, 'if a forger was doing all the Buckmaster Gallery Derwatts now, all the ones we saw yesterday. Someone as good as Derwatt, in other words.'

Murchison smiled. 'Then what's Derwatt doing? Sitting back and taking it? Don't be ridiculous. Derwatt was much as I'd thought he would be. Withdrawn and sort of old-fashioned.'

'Have you ever thought of collecting forgeries? I know a man in Italy who collects them. First as a hobby, and now he sells them to other collectors at quite high prices.'

'Oh, I've heard of that. Yes. But I like to know I'm buying a forgery when I buy one.'

Tom sensed that he was reaching a narrow and unpleasant spot. He tried again. 'I like to daydream – about absurd things like that. In a sense, why disturb a forger who's doing such good work? I intend to hang onto "Man in Chair".'

Murchison might not have heard Tom's remarks. 'And you know,' Murchison said, still gazing at the picture Tom was talking about, 'it's not merely the lavender, it's the soul of the painting. I wouldn't put it that way, if I weren't mellow on your good food and drink.'

They had finished a delicious bottle of Margaux, the best from Tom's cellar.

'Do you think the Buckmaster Gallery people might be crooks?' Murchison asked. 'They *must* be. Why would they be putting up with a forger? Shoving forgeries among the real ones?'

Murchison thought the other new Derwatts, all of them in the current show, except 'The Tub', were genuine, Tom realized. 'That's if these are really forgeries – your "Clock" and so forth. I suppose I'm not yet convinced.'

Murchison smiled with good humour. 'Just because you like your "Man in Chair". If your picture is four years old and mine's at least three, these forgeries have been going on quite a while. Maybe there's more in London that weren't lent for the show. Frankly, it's Derwatt I suspect. I suspect him of being in cahoots with the Buckmaster people to earn more money. Another thing – there've been no drawings by Derwatt for years now. That's odd.'

'Really?' Tom asked with a feigned surprise. He knew this, and he knew what Murchison was driving at.

'Drawings reveal an artist's personality,' Murchison said. 'I realized that myself, and then I read it somewhere – just to corroborate myself.' He laughed. 'Just because I manufacture pipe, people never give me credit for sensitivity! But a drawing is like a signature for a painter, a very complicated signature at that. You might say, you can forge a signature or a painting more easily than you can forge a drawing.'

'Never thought of that,' said Tom, and rolled his cigar end in the ashtray. 'You say Saturday you're going to speak to the Tate Gallery man?'

'Yes. There's a couple of old Derwatts at the Tate as you probably know. Then I'll speak to the Buckmaster people without giving them any warning – if Riemer corroborates me.'

Tom's mind began to make painful leaps. Saturday was the day after tomorrow. Riemer might want to compare 'The Clock' and 'Man in Chair' with the Tate Gallery Derwatts and those in the current show. Could Bernard Tufts's paintings stand up to it? And if they couldn't? He poured more brandy for Murchison and a bit for himself which he did not want. He folded his hands on his chest. 'You know, I don't think I'll sue – or whatever one does – if there's forging going on.'

'Hah! I'm a little more orthodox. Old-fashioned, maybe. My attitude. Suppose Derwatt's really in on it?'

'Derwatt's rather a saint, I hear.'

'That's the legend. He might've been more of a saint when he was younger and poorer. He's been in seclusion. His friends in London put him on the map, that's plain. A lot can happen to a poor man, if he suddenly becomes rich.'

Tom got no further during the evening. Murchison wanted to turn in early, because he was tired.

'I'll see about a plane in the morning. I should've booked one in London. That was stupid of me.'

'Oh, not in the morning, I hope,' Tom said.

'I'll book it in the morning. I'll take off in the afternoon, if that's all right with you.'

Tom saw his guest up to his room, made sure he had everything he needed.

It crossed his mind to ring Jeff or Ed. But what news had he, except that he wasn't getting anywhere in trying to persuade Murchison not to see the Tate Gallery man? And also Tom did not want Jeff's telephone number appearing too often on his bill.

6

Tom began the morning with a determined optimism. He put on old comfortable clothes – after having in bed Mme Annette's delicious coffee, one black cup to wake him up – and went down to see if Murchison was stirring as yet. It was a quarter to nine.

'Le m'sieur takes his breakfast in his room,' Mme Annette said.

While Mme Annette tidied his room, Tom shaved in his

bathroom. 'M. Murchison is leaving this afternoon, I think,' Tom said in answer to Mme Annette's question about the dinner menu for that evening. 'But today is Thursday. Do you think you could catch a nice pair of soles –' Tom gulped and thought of 'shoes, skates' in English '– from the fish merchant for lunch?' A fish van came to the village twice a week. There was no fish shop in the town, because Villeperce was too small.

Mme Annette was inspired by this suggestion. 'The grapes are lovely at the fruit merchant's,' she said. 'You wouldn't believe it . . .'

'Buy some.' Tom scarcely listened to her.

At 11 a.m. Tom and Murchison were walking in the woods behind Tom's property. Tom was in an odd mood, or state of mind. In a burst of bare-faced friendliness, honesty, or whatever one might call it, Tom had shown Murchison his own artistic efforts in the upstairs room where he painted. Tom painted landscapes and portraits mainly. He was ever trying to simplify, to keep the example of Matisse before him, but with little success, he thought. One portrait of Heloise, possibly Tom's twelfth, was not bad, and Murchison had praised it. *My God*, Tom thought, *I'll lay my soul bare, show him the poems I've written to Heloise, take my clothes off and do a sword dance, if he'll only – see things my way!* It was no use.

Murchison's plane was at 4 p.m. for London. Time for a decent lunch here, as Orly was about an hour away by car under good conditions. While Murchison had been changing his shoes for their little walk, Tom had wrapped 'Man in Chair' in three thicknesses of corrugated paper, string, brown paper and more string. Murchison was going to keep the painting with him on the plane, he had told Tom. Murchison said he had reserved a room at the Mandeville for this evening.

'But remember, no charges pressed on my part,' Tom said, 'about "Man in Chair".'

'That doesn't mean you'll deny it's a fake,' Murchison said with a smile. 'You're not going to insist it's genuine?'

'No,' Tom said. '*Touché*. I'll bow to the experts.'

The open woods was not the place for a conversation which had to get down to a pinpoint, Tom felt. Or did it have to expand into a huge grey cloud? Tom was not happy at any rate, talking to Murchison in the woods.

Tom asked Mme Annette to prepare the lunch rather early, because of M. Murchison's departure, and they began at a quarter to one.

Tom was determined to keep the conversation on the subject, because he did not want to abandon all hope. He brought up Van Meegeren, with whose career Murchison was acquainted. Van Meegeren's forgeries of Vermeer had finally achieved some value of their own. Van Meegeren may have started it first in self-defence, in bravado, but aesthetically there was no doubt that Van Meegeren's inventions of 'new' Vermeers had given pleasure to the people who had bought them.

'I cannot understand your total disconnection with the *truth* of things,' Murchison said. 'An artist's style is his truth, his honesty. Has another man the right to copy it, in the same way that a man copies another man's signature? And for the same purpose, to draw on his reputation, his bank account? A reputation already built by a man's talent?'

They were chasing the last morsels of sole and butter around their plates, with the last morsels of potato. The sole had been superb, the white wine still was. It was the kind of lunch that under any other circumstances would have given contentment, even happiness, would have inspired lovers to go to bed – perhaps after coffee – and make love and then sleep. The beauty of the lunch was today wasted on Tom.

'I speak for myself,' Tom said. 'I usually do. I don't mean to influence you. I'm sure I couldn't. But you have my permission to say to – who is it, Mr Constant, yes, that I'm rather happy with my forgery and I want to keep it.'

'I'll tell him that. But don't you think of the future? If there's somebody continuing to do this –'

There was a lemon soufflé. Tom struggled. He was convinced. Why couldn't he put it into words, put it well enough to convince Murchison? *Murchison was not artistic*. Or he wouldn't be talking like this. Murchison didn't appreciate Bernard. What the hell was Murchison doing dragging in truth and signatures and possibly even the police, compared to what Bernard was doing in his studio, which was undeniably the work of a fine painter? How had Van Meegeren put it (or had Tom himself put it that way, in one of his notebooks)? 'An artist does things naturally, without effort. Some power guides his hand. A forger struggles, and if he succeeds, it is a genuine achievement.' Tom realized it was his own paraphrase. But goddam it, that smug Murchison, holier-than-thou! At least Bernard was a man of talent, of more talent than Murchison with his plumbing, his pipe-laying, his packaging of transportable items, an idea which anyway had come from a young engineer in Canada, Murchison had said.

Coffee. Neither took brandy, though the bottle was at hand.

Thomas Murchison's face, full of flesh, somewhat ruddy – his face might have been stone to Tom. Murchison's eyes were bright, quite intelligent, and against him.

It was 1.30. They were to leave for Orly in half an hour or so. Should he go back to London as soon as possible after the Count left, Tom wondered? But what could he accomplish in London? Damn the Count, Tom thought. Derwatt Ltd was more important than the crap or the trinket that the Count was carrying. Tom realized that Reeves had not told him where to look in the Count's suitcase or briefcase or whatever. Tom supposed Reeves would telephone this evening. Tom felt wretched, and he simply had to move, now, from the chair where he had been squirming for the past ten minutes.

'I wanted you to take a bottle of wine from my cellar,' Tom said. 'Shall we go down and have a look?'

Murchison's smile became broader. 'What a marvellous idea! Thank you, Tom.'

The cellar was approachable from outdoors, down a few stone steps to a green door, or via a door in a downstairs spare loo, next to a little hall where guests hung their coats. Tom and Heloise had had the indoor stairs put in to avoid going outdoors in bad weather.

'I'll take the wine back to the States with me. It'd be a pity to crack it by myself in London,' Murchison said.

Tom put on the light in the cellar. The cellar was big, grey and as cool as a refrigerator, or so it seemed in contrast to the centrally heated house. There were five or six big barrels on stands, not all of them full, and many racks of wine bottles against all the walls. In one corner was the big fuel storage tank for the heating, and another tank that held hot water.

'Here are the clarets,' Tom said, indicating a wall of wine racks which were more than half full of dusty dark bottles.

Murchison whistled appreciatively.

It's got to be done down here, Tom thought, if anything has to be done. Yet he had not planned nearly enough, he had not planned anything. Keep moving, he told himself, but all he did was stroll about slowly, looking over his bottles, touching one or two of the red-tinfoil wrapped necks. He pulled one out. 'Margaux. You liked that.'

'Superb,' Murchison said. 'Thank you very much, Tom. I'll tell the folks about the cellar it came from.' Murchison took the bottle reverently.

Tom said, 'You won't possibly change your mind – just for the sake of sportsmanship – about speaking to the expert in London. About the forgeries.'

Murchison laughed a little. 'Tom, I can't. Sportsmanship! I can't for the life of me see why you want to protect them, unless –'

Murchison had had a thought, and Tom knew what that thought was, that Tom Ripley was in on it, deriving some kind of benefit or profit from it. 'Yes, I have an interest in it,' Tom said quickly. 'You see, I know the young man who spoke to you in your hotel the other day. I know all about him. He's the forger.'

'*What*? That – that –'

'Yes, that nervous fellow. Bernard. He knew Derwatt. It started out quite idealistically, you see –'

'You mean, Derwatt *knows* about it?'

'Derwatt is dead. They got someone to impersonate him.' Tom blurted it out, feeling he had nothing any longer to lose, and maybe something to gain. Murchison had his life to gain, but Tom could not quite put that into words, not plain words, as yet.

'So Derwatt's dead – since how long?'

'Five or six years. He really died in Greece.'

'So all the pictures –'

'Bernard Tufts – You saw what kind of fellow he is. He'd commit suicide if it came out he was forging his dead friend's paintings. He told you not to buy any more. Isn't that enough? The gallery asked Bernard to paint a couple of pictures in Derwatt's style, you see –' Tom realized *he* had suggested that, but no matter. Tom also realized that he was arguing hopelessly, not only because Murchison was adamant, but because there was a split in Tom's own reasoning, a split he was well acquainted with. He saw the right and the wrong. Yet both sides of himself were equally sincere: save Bernard, save the forgeries, save even Derwatt, was what Tom was arguing. Murchison would never understand. 'Bernard wants out of it, I know. I don't think you'd like to risk a man's killing himself out of shame just to prove a point, would you?'

'He might've thought of shame when he began!' Murchison looked at Tom's hands, his face, back to his hands again. 'Was it *you* impersonating Derwatt? Yes. I noticed Derwatt's hands.' Murchison smiled bitterly. 'And people think I don't notice little things!'

'You're very observant,' Tom said quickly. He suddenly felt angry.

'My God, I might've mentioned it yesterday. I thought of it yesterday. Your hands. You can't put a beard on those, can you?'

Tom said, 'Let them alone, would you? Are they doing much harm? Bernard's pictures are good, you can't deny that.'

'I'm damned if I'll keep my mouth shut about it! No! Not even if you or anybody else offers me a whacking lot of money to keep my mouth shut!' Murchison's face was redder, and his jowls trembled. He set the wine down rather hard on the floor, but it didn't break.

The rejection of his wine was a slight insult, or so Tom felt now, a minuscule but further insult and annoyance. Tom picked up the bottle almost at once and swung it at Murchison, hitting him on the side of the head. This time the bottle broke, wine splashed, and the base of the bottle fell to the floor. Murchison reeled against the wine racks, jiggling it all, but nothing else fell, except Murchison, who slumped down, bumping wine-bottle tops but not disturbing any. Tom seized the first thing to hand – which happened to be an empty coal scuttle – and swung it at Murchison's head. Tom struck a second blow. The base of the scuttle was heavy. Murchison was bleeding, lying sideways, his body somewhat twisted, on the stone floor. He wasn't moving.

What to do about the blood? Tom turned around in circles, looking for an old rag anywhere, even newspaper. He went over to the fuel tank. Under the tank was a large rag, stiff with age and dirt. He went back with it and mopped, but gave up the useless task after a moment, and looked around again. Put him under a barrel, he thought. He grabbed Murchison by the ankles, then at once dropped the ankles and felt Murchison's neck. There seemed to be no pulse. Tom took a huge breath, and got his hands under Murchison's arms. He pulled and jerked, dragging the heavy body towards the barrel. The corner behind the barrel was dark. Murchison's feet stuck out a little. Tom bent Murchison's knees so that the feet did not show. But since the barrel stood some sixteen inches above the floor on its stand, Murchison was more or less visible, if someone stood in the middle of the cellar and looked into that particular corner. By stooping, one had a view of Murchison's whole body. Of all times, Tom thought, not to find an old sheet, a piece of tarpaulin, newspaper, anything to cover something up with! That was Mme Annette's tidiness!

Tom kicked the bloodstained rag, and it landed on Murchison's feet. He kicked at a couple of pieces of broken bottle on the floor – the wine had mingled with the blood now – then quickly picked up the neck of the bottle, and hit the light bulb which hung on a cord from the ceiling. The bulb broke and tinkled to the floor.

Then, gasping a little, trying to get his breathing back to normal, Tom moved in the darkness towards the stairs and climbed them. He closed the door. The spare john had a basin, and here he washed his hands quickly. Some blood showed pink in the running water, and Tom thought it was Murchison's, until he saw that it kept coming, and that he had a cut at the base of his thumb. But it wasn't a bad cut, it could have been worse, so he considered himself lucky. He pulled toilet paper from the roll on the wall and wrapped it around his thumb.

Mme Annette was busy in the kitchen now, which was another piece of luck. If she came out, Tom thought, he would say that M. Murchison was already in the car – in case Mme Annette asked where he was. It was time to go.

Tom ran up to Murchison's room. The only things Murchison had not packed were his topcoat and toilet articles in the loo. Tom put the toilet articles into a pocket of Murchison's suitcase and closed it. Then he carried the suitcase and the topcoat down the stairs and out of the front door. He put these things into the Alfa-Romeo, then ran back upstairs for Murchison's 'Clock', which was still wrapped. Murchison had been so sure of himself, he hadn't bothered unwrapping 'The Clock' to compare it with 'Man in Chair'. Pride goeth before a fall, Tom thought. He took his wrapped 'Man in Chair' from Murchison's room into his own room, and stuck it in a back corner of his closet, then carried 'The Clock' downstairs. He grabbed his raincoat from a hook outside the spare loo, and went out to the car. He drove off for Orly.

Murchison's passport and airline ticket might be in the pocket of his jacket, Tom thought. He would take care of that later, burn them preferably, when Mme Annette was out of the house in the morning on her usual leisurely shopping tour. It also occurred to Tom that he had not told Mme Annette about the Count's arrival. Tom would ring her from somewhere, but not from Orly Airport, he thought, because he did not want to linger there.

The time was right, as if Murchison were actually going to make his plane.

Tom made for the departures doorway. Here taxis and private cars, as long as they did not pause too long, could deposit luggage and people or pick them up. Tom stopped, got Murchison's suitcase out, and set it on the pavement, then set 'The Clock' against the suitcase, and laid Murchison's coat on top. Tom drove off. There were a few other little assemblies of luggage on the pavement, he noticed. He drove out in the Fontainebleau direction, and stopped at a roadside bar-café, one of many medium-sized bar-cafés along the route between Orly and the beginning of the Autoroute du Sud.

He ordered a beer, and asked for a jeton to make a telephone call. No jeton was necessary, so Tom took the telephone on the bar near the cash register, and dialled the number of his house.

'Hello, it's me,' said Tom. 'M. Murchison had to hurry at the last moment, so he asked me to tell you good-bye and to thank you.'

'Oh, I understand.'

'*Alors* – there is another guest coming this evening, a Count Bertolozzi, an Italian. I shall find him at Orly, and we'll be home before six. Now can you buy perhaps some – calves' liver?'

'The butcher at the moment has beautiful *gigot*!'

Tom was not in the mood for anything with a bone in it, somehow. 'If it is not too much trouble, I think I prefer calves' liver.'

'And a Margaux? A Meursault?'

'Leave the wine to me.'

Tom paid – he said he had telephoned Sens, which was farther than his village – and went out to his car. He drove at a leisurely speed back to Orly, past the arrivals and departures section, and noticed that Murchison's things were still where he had left them. The coat would be the first to go, Tom thought, nicked by some enterprising young man. And if Murchison's passport were in the topcoat, the nicker might turn it to some advantage. Tom smiled a little as he drove into P-4, one of the one-hour parking lots.

Tom walked slowly through the glass doors which opened before him, bought a *Neue Züricher Zeitung* at the news-stand, then checked on the arrival time of Eduardo's plane. The flight was on time, and he had a few minutes to spare. Tom went to the crowded bar – it was always crowded – and at last got an elbow in and managed to order a coffee. After the coffee, he bought a ticket and went up to where people met the arrivals.

The Count was wearing a grey Homburg. He had a long thin black moustache and a bulging abdomen, which was visible even under his unbuttoned topcoat. The Count broke into a smile, a real spontaneous Italian smile, and he waved a greeting. The Count was presenting his passport.

Then they were shaking hands, giving each other a quick embrace, and Tom helped him with packages and carry-alls. The Count had also an attaché case. What was the Count carrying, and where? His suitcase was not even opened, only motioned through by the French official.

'If you'll wait here a minute, I'll fetch my car,' Tom said when they were on the pavement. 'It's just a few yards away.' Tom went off at a trot, and was back in five minutes.

He had to drive past the departures gate, and he noticed that Murchison's suitcase and painting were still there, but the coat was gone. One down and two to go.

On the drive homeward, they discussed, not very profoundly, Italian politics, French politics of the moment, and the Count inquired about Heloise. Tom scarcely knew the Count, and thought this was the second time they had seen each other, but in Milan they had talked about painting, which was a passionate interest of the Count's.

'At the moment, there is an *esposizione* of Derwatt in London. I look forward to that next week. And what do you think of Derwatt coming to London? I was *astound*! The first photographs of him in years!'

Tom had not bothered to buy a London newspaper. 'A big surprise. He hasn't changed much, they say.' Tom was not going to mention that he had been recently in London and had seen the show.

'I look forward to seeing your picture at home. What is it? The one with the little girls?'

'"The Red Chairs",' Tom said, surprised that the Count remembered. He smiled and gripped the wheel tighter. Despite the corpse in the cellar, despite the ghastly day, the nerve-racking afternoon, Tom was going to be very happy to get back home – to the scene of the crime, as they said. Tom didn't feel that it was a crime. Or was he due for a delayed reaction tomorrow, even tonight? He hoped not.

'Italy is producing worse espresso. In the cafés,' the Count announced in a solemn baritone. 'I am *convince*. Probably some

Mafia business at the bottom of it.' He mused sourly out the window for a few moments, then continued, 'And the hair-dressers in Italy, my goodness! I begin to wonder if I know my own country! Now in my old favourite barbershop off the Via Veneto, they have new young men who ask me what kind of shampoo I want. I say, "Just wash my hair, please – what's left of it!" "But is it oily or dry, signor? We have three kinds of shampoo. Have you dandruff?" "No!" I say. "Can't somebody have *normal* hair these days, or doesn't ordinary shampoo exist any more?" '

Like Murchison, the Count praised the sturdy symmetry of Belle Ombre. The garden, though there was hardly a rose left from summer, showed its handsome rectangular lawn sur-rounded by thick and formidable pines. It was home, and not exactly humble. Again Mme Annette met them on the doorstep, and was as helpful and welcoming as yesterday when Thomas Murchison had arrived. Again Tom showed his guest to his room, which Mme Annette had made ready. It was late for tea, so Tom said he would be downstairs when the Count wished to join him. Dinner was at eight.

Then Tom unwrapped 'Man in Chair' in his room, and took it downstairs and hung it in its usual place. Mme Annette might well have noticed its absence for a few hours, but if she asked him anything about it, Tom intended to say that Mr Murchison had taken it to his room, Tom's, to look at under a different light.

Tom parted the heavy red curtains of the french windows, and looked at his back garden. The dark green shadows were becom-ing black with the fall of night. Tom realized he was standing directly over Murchison in the cellar, and he edged away. He must, even if it had to be late tonight, go down and do what he could about cleaning up the wine and bloodstains. Mme Annette might have a reason to go to the cellar: she kept a good eye on the fuel supply. And then, how to get the body out of the house? There was a wheelbarrow in the toolshed. Could he wheel Mur-chison – covered by a tarpaulin which was in the toolshed also – into the woods behind the house and bury him? Primitive, un-pleasantly close to the house, but it might be the best solution.

The Count came down, spry and bouncing in spite of his bulk. He was a rather tall man.

'A-hah! A-*hah*!' Like Murchison he was struck by 'The Red Chairs' which hung on the other side of the room. But the Count turned at once, and looked towards the fireplace, and seemed even more impressed by 'Man in Chair'. 'Lovely! Delicious!' He peered at both pictures. 'You did not disappoint me. They are a pleasure. So is your entire house. I mean the drawings in my room.'

Mme Annette came in with the ice bucket and some glasses on the bar cart.

The Count, seeing Punt e Mes, said he would have that.

'Did the gallery in London ask you to lend your pictures for the *esposizione*?'

Murchison had asked that question twenty-four hours ago, but about 'Man in Chair' only, and had asked it because he was curious about the gallery's attitude to paintings they must know to be forgeries. Tom felt a little dizzy in the head, as if he were going to faint. He had been bending over the bar cart, and now he straightened up. 'They did. But it's such trouble, you know, shipping and insuring. I lent "The Red Chairs" for a show two years ago.'

'I may buy a Derwatt,' said the Count thoughtfully. 'That is if I can afford one. It will have to be a small one, at his prices.'

Tom poured a straight Scotch on ice for himself.

The telephone rang.

'Excuse me,' Tom said, and answered it.

Eduardo was walking about, looking at other things on the walls.

It was Reeves Minot. He asked if the Count had arrived, then if Tom were alone.

'No, I'm not.'

'It's in the —'

'I can't quite hear.'

'*Toothpaste*,' Reeves said.

'O-oh.' It was almost a groan from Tom, of fatigue, contempt, boredom even. Was this a child's game? Or something in a lousy film? 'Very good. And the address? Same as last time?' Tom had an address in Paris, three or four actually, where he had sent Reeves's items on other occasions.

'That'll do. The last one. Is everything all right?'

'Yes, I think so, thank you,' Tom said pleasantly. He might have suggested Reeves have a word with the Count, just to be friendly, but it was probably better the Count didn't know that Reeves had rung. Tom felt quite off his form, off on the wrong foot. 'Thanks for ringing.'

'No need to ring me if everything's okay,' said Reeves and hung up.

'Would you excuse me a second, Eduardo,' Tom said, and ran upstairs.

He went into the Count's room. One of his suitcases was open on the antique wood-box where guests and Mme Annette usually put suitcases, but Tom looked first in the bathroom. The Count had not put out his toilet articles. Tom went to the suitcase and found an opaque plastic bag with a zipper. He tried this and ran into tobacco. There was another plastic bag in which were shaving gear, toothbrush and toothpaste, and he took the toothpaste. The end of the tube was a little rough, but sealed. Reeves's man probably had some kind of clamp with which to seal the metal again. Tom squeezed the tube cautiously and felt a hard lump near the end of it. He shook his head in disgust, pocketed the toothpaste, replaced the plastic kit. He went to his own room and put the toothpaste at the back of his top left drawer which contained a stud box and a lot of starched collars.

Tom rejoined the Count downstairs.

During dinner they talked about Derwatt's surprising return, and his interview which the Count had read in the press.

'He's living in Mexico, isn't he?' Tom asked.

'Yes. And he won't say where. Like B. Traven, you know. Ha! Ha!'

The Count praised the dinner and ate heartily. He had the European faculty of being able to talk with his mouth full, which no American could manage without looking or feeling extremely messy.

After dinner, the Count, seeing Tom's gramophone, expressed

a desire for some music, and chose *Pelléas et Mélisande*. The Count wanted the third act – the duet, somewhat hectic, between soprano and deep male voice. While listening, even singing along, the Count managed to talk.

Tom tried to pay attention to the Count and to exclude the music, but Tom always found it hard to exclude music. He was in no mood for *Pelléas et Mélisande*. What he needed was the music from *A Midsummer Night's Dream*, the fabulous overture, and now as the other thing played on with its heavy drama, Mendelssohn's overture danced in Tom's inner ear – nervous, comic, full of invention. He desperately needed to be full of invention.

They were dipping into the brandy. Tom suggested that tomorrow morning they might take a drive and lunch at Moret-sur-Loing. Eduardo had said he wanted to take an afternoon train to Paris. But first he wanted to make sure he had seen all Tom's art treasures, so Tom took him on a tour of the house. Even in Heloise's room, there was a Marie Laurencin.

Then they said good night, and Eduardo retired with a couple of Tom's art books.

In his room, Tom got the tube of Vademecum toothpaste from his drawer, tried to open the bottom with a thumbnail, and failed. He went into the room where he painted, and got some pliers from his work-table. Back in his room, he cut the tube open, and out came a black cylinder. A microfilm, of course. Tom wondered if it could survive rinsing, decided against it, and merely wiped the thing with a Kleenex. It smelled of peppermint. He addressed an envelope to:

M. Jean-Marc Cahannier
16 Rue de Tison
Paris IX

then put the cylinder into a couple of sheets of writing-paper and stuck it all into the envelope. Tom swore to himself to pull out of this silly business, because it was degrading. He could tell Reeves without offending him. Reeves had a strange idea that the more an item changed hands, the safer it was. Reeves was fence-minded. But surely he lost money paying everybody, even paying them a little bit. Or did some people take it out in favours asked from Reeves?

Tom got into pyjamas and dressing-gown, looked into the hall, and was gratified to see that there was no light showing under Eduardo's door. He went quietly down to the kitchen. There were two doors between the kitchen and Mme Annette's bedroom, because there was a little hall with servants' entrance beyond the kitchen, so she was not likely to hear him or see the kitchen light. Tom got a sturdy grey cleaning rag and a container of Ajax, took a light bulb from a cabinet and put it in a pocket. He went down to the cellar. He shivered. Now he realized he had to have a torch and a chair to stand on, so he went back to the kitchen and took one of the wooden stools that belonged to the kitchen table, and picked up a torch from the hall table drawer.

He held the torch under his arm, and removed the shattered bulb and put in the new one. The cellar lit up. Murchison's shoes still showed. Then Tom realized to his horror that the legs had straightened with rigor mortis. Or he wasn't possibly still alive? Tom forced himself to make sure, or he knew he wouldn't be able to sleep that night. Tom put the back of his fingers against Murchison's hand. That was enough. Murchison's hand was cold and also stiff. Tom pulled the grey rag over Murchison's shoes.

There was a sink with cold water in a corner. Tom wet his cleaning rag and got to work. Some colour came off on the rag, which he washed out, but he could not see much improvement in the colour of the floor, though the dark of it might be due to its wetness now. Well, he could say to Mme Annette that he dropped a bottle of wine, in case she asked anything. Tom got up the last fragments of broken light bulb and wine bottle, rinsed the rag out in the sink cautiously, recovered the pieces of glass from the sink's drain, and put them into his dressing-gown pocket. He again worked on the floor with the rag. Then he went back upstairs, and in the better light of the kitchen made sure that the reddish tint in the rag was gone or almost gone. He laid the rag over the drainpipe under the sink.

But the blasted body. Tom sighed, and thought of locking the cellar until he returned tomorrow after seeing Eduardo off, but wouldn't this look pretty strange if Mme Annette wanted to go in? And she had her own key, and one to the outside door as well, which had a different lock. Tom took the precaution of bringing up a bottle of *rosé* and two of Margaux, and put them on the kitchen table. There were times when having a servant was annoying.

When Tom went to bed, more tired than the night before, he thought of putting Murchison into a barrel. But it would take a cooper to get the damned hoops back on it properly, he supposed. And Murchison would have to be in liquid of some sort or he would bump around in an empty barrel. And how could he manage Murchison's weight in a barrel by himself? Impossible.

Tom thought of Murchison's suitcase and 'The Clock' at Orly. Surely someone had removed them by now. Murchison would perhaps have an address book, some old envelope in his suitcase. By tomorrow, Murchison might be declared 'missing'. Or the day after tomorrow. The Tate Gallery man was expecting Murchison tomorrow morning. Tom wondered if Murchison had told anyone that he was going to stay with Tom Ripley. Tom hoped not.

7

Friday was sunny and cool, though not cool enough to be called crisp. Tom and Eduardo breakfasted in the living-room near the french windows through which the sun came. The Count was in pyjamas and dressing-gown, which he would not be wearing, he said, if there were a lady in the house, but he hoped Tom did not mind.

A little after 10 a.m., the Count went up to dress, and came downstairs with his suitcases, ready to take off for a drive before lunch. 'I wonder if I can borrow some toothpaste,' said Eduardo. 'I think I forgot mine in my hotel in Milano. Very stupid of me.'

Tom had been expecting the Count to ask this, and was rather glad that he had, at last. Tom went to speak with Mme Annette who was in the kitchen. Since the Count's toilet kit was in his suitcase downstairs, Tom supposed, Tom thought it best to show him the spare loo with the basin. Mme Annette brought some toothpaste to him.

The post arrived, and Tom excused himself to glance at it. A postcard from Heloise, saying nothing really. And another letter from Christopher Greenleaf. Tom tore this open. It said:

Oct. 15 19—

Dear Mr Ripley,

I just found out I can get a charter flight to Paris so I am coming earlier than I thought. I hope you are home just now. I am flying with a friend, Gerald Hayman, also my age, but I assure you I will not bring him to meet you because that might be a drag although he's a nice fellow. I am arriving in Paris Sat. 19th Oct. and will try to call you. Of course I will spend Saturday night in a Paris hotel somewhere, as the plane gets in 7 p.m. French time.

Meanwhile, greetings and yours sincerely,

Chris Greenleaf.

Saturday was tomorrow. At least Chris wasn't going to arrive here tomorrow. Good God, Tom thought, all he needed now was for Bernard to turn up. Tom thought of asking Mme Annette not to answer the telephone for the next two days, but that would seem strange, and would furthermore annoy Mme Annette, who received at least one telephone call a day from one of her friends, usually Mme Yvonne, another housekeeper in the village.

'Bad news?' asked Eduardo.

'Oh, no, not in the least,' Tom replied. He had to get Murchison's body out. Preferably tonight. And of course he could put Chris off, tell him he was busy at least until Tuesday. Tom had a vision of French police walking in tomorrow, looking for Murchison, and finding him within seconds in the most logical place, the cellar.

Tom went into the kitchen to say good-bye to Mme Annette. She was polishing a big silver tureen and a lot of soup spoons, all adorned with Heloise's family's initials P.F.P. 'I'm off for a little tour. M. the Count is leaving. Shall I bring anything back for the house?'

'If you find some really fresh parsley, M. Tome —'

'I'll remember it. *Persil*. I shall return before five o'clock, I think. Dinner tonight by myself. Something simple.'

'Shall I help with the valises?' Mme Annette stood up. 'I don't know where my mind is today.'

Tom assured her it was not necessary, but she came out to say good-bye to the Count — who bowed to her and paid compliments in French on her cooking.

They drove to Nemours, looked at the market-place with its fountain, then went northward along the Loing to Moret, whose one-way streets Tom negotiated very knowledgeably now. The town had splendid grey stone towers, formerly the town gates, on both sides of the bridge over the river. The Count was enchanted.

'It is not so *dusty* as Italy,' he remarked.

Tom did his best not to appear nervous during their slow lunch, and he gazed frequently out the window at the weeping willows on the river bank, wishing he could achieve within himself the easy rhythm of their branches that the breeze swung this way and that. The Count told a very long story of his daughter's second marriage to a young man of a titled family who had for a while been disowned by his Bologna family for marrying a girl who had been once married. Tom barely hung onto this story, because he was thinking about disposing of Murchison. Should he risk trying to dump him in some river? Could he manage Murchison's weight over a bridge parapet, plus the weight of stones? And not be seen? If he simply dragged him down the bank of a river, could he be sure Murchison would sink deep enough, even weighted? It had begun to rain slightly. That would make the earth easier to dig, Tom thought. The woods behind the house might be the best idea after all.

At the Melun station, Eduardo had only a ten-minute wait for his train to Paris. When he and Tom had said an affectionate good-bye, Tom drove to the nearest *tabac* and bought an excess of stamps to put on his envelope to Reeves's man, so that it would not be stopped by some petty post office clerk for want of five centimes.

Tom bought parsley for Mme Annette. *Persil*, French. *Peter-silie*, German. *Prezzemolo*, Italian. Tom then drove homeward. The sun was setting. Tom wondered if a torch or any kind of light in the woods would attract Mme Annette's attention if she looked out the window of her bathroom, which gave onto the back garden. If she would come up to his room (and find him gone) to tell him she had seen a light in the woods. The woods were never visited by anybody that Tom knew of, neither pic-nickers nor mushroom gatherers. Tom intended to go some dis-tance into the woods, however, and perhaps Mme Annette would not notice a light.

When he got home, Tom had a compulsion to put on levis at once and get the wheelbarrow out of the toolshed. He rolled the wheelbarrow near the stone steps that led down from the back terrace. Then, since there was still enough light, he trotted across the lawn to the shed again. If Mme Annette noticed anything, he would say that he was considering making a com-post heap in the woods.

Mme Annette's light was on in her bathroom, which had a clouded glass window, and he supposed she was taking her bath, as she did at this hour if there was not too much to do in the kitchen. Tom got a four-pronged fork from the shed and took it to the woods. He was in search of a likely spot, and he hoped to start a hole which would give him a bit of cheer when he really had to finish the job tomorrow, very early tomorrow morning. He found a place among a few slender trees, where hopefully there would not be too many big roots to get through. In the dimness, Tom believed it was the best spot, even though it was only some eighty yards from the edge of the woods, where his lawn began. Tom dug vigorously, releasing some of the nervous energy that had bothered him all day.

Next the garbage, he thought, and he stopped, panting, laughing out loud as he turned his face up to gulp air. Collect the potato peelings in the garbage bin now, and apple cores, and stick them all in with Murchison? And a big sprinkling of the powder that started the decomposition? There was a sack of it in the kitchen.

Now it was rather dark.

Tom went back with his fork, replaced it in the toolshed, and seeing that Mme Annette's bathroom light was still on – it was only seven – Tom went down to the cellar. Now he had more courage to touch Murchison, or *the thing* as they called it, and he reached at once into the inside pocket of Murchison's jacket. Tom was curious about the plane ticket and the passport. He found only a wallet, and two business cards fell out of it onto the floor. Tom hesitated, then shoved the wallet, with the cards replaced in it, back into the pocket. A side pocket of the jacket held a key on a ring, which Tom left. The other pocket, on which Murchison was lying, was more difficult, as Murchison was stiff as a piece of sculpture and seemed to weigh nearly as much. The left pocket yielded nothing. The trouser pockets had only some French coins mixed with English, which Tom let remain. Tom also left Murchison's two rings on his fingers. If Murchison was going to be found on his grounds, there would be no doubt who he was: Mme Annette had met him. Tom left the cellar and turned out the light at the top of the stairs.

Then Tom took a bath, and had just finished when the telephone rang. Tom lunged for it, hoping, expecting it was Jeff, perhaps with good news – but what *could* be good news?

' Ello, Tome! Jacqueline here. How are you?'

It was one of their neighbours, Jacqueline Berthelin, who with her husband Vincent lived in a town a few kilometres away. She wanted him to come for dinner Thursday. She was having les Clegg, a middle-aged English couple whom Tom knew, who lived near Melun.

'You know, my dear, it's bad luck for me. I have a guest coming. A young man from America.'

'Bring him. He is welcome.'

Tom tried to get out of it and couldn't completely. He said he would ring back in a couple of days and let her know, because he was not sure how long his American friend would be staying.

Tom was leaving his room when the telephone rang again.

This time it was Jeff, ringing from the Strand Palace Hotel, he said. 'How are things there?' Jeff asked.

'Oh all right, thanks,' Tom said with a smile, and pushed his fingers through his hair, as if he couldn't care less that there was a corpse in his cellar, a man Tom had killed for the protection of Derwatt Ltd. 'And how are things with you?'

'Where is Murchison? Is he still with you?'

'He left yesterday afternoon for London. But – I don't think he's going to talk to – you know, the Tate Gallery man. I'm sure of it.'

'You persuaded him?'

'Yes,' Tom said.

Jeff's sigh, or gasp of relief, was audible across the Channel. 'Super, Tom. You're a genius.'

'Tell them to calm down there. Especially Bernard.'

'Well – that's our problem. Sure, I'll tell him, with pleasure. He's – he's depressed. We're trying to get him to go somewhere, Malta, any damned place until the show's over. He's always like this with a show, but now it's worse because of – you know.'

'What's he doing?'

'Moping, frankly. We even rang up Cynthia – who still sort of likes him, I thought. Not that we told her about – about this scare,' Jeff hastened to add. 'We just asked her if she could spend some time with Bernard.'

'I gather she said no.'

'Right.'

'Does Bernard know you spoke with her?'

'Ed told him. I know, Tom, maybe it was a mistake.'

Tom was impatient. 'Will you just keep Bernard quiet for a few days?'

'We're giving him sedatives, mild ones. I slipped one in his tea this afternoon.'

'Would you tell him Murchison is – sedated?'

Jeff laughed. 'Yes, Tom. What's he going to do in London?'

'He said he had some things to do there. Then he's going back to the States. Listen, Jeff, no more rings for a few days, eh? I'm not sure I'm going to be home, anyway.'

Tom thought he could explain the few telephone calls he had made to Jeff, or received from Jeff, if the police bothered to look for them: he had considered buying 'The Tub', and had spoken to the Buckmaster Gallery about it.

That evening Tom went out to the toolshed and brought back a tarpaulin and a rope. While Mme Annette tidied in the kitchen, Tom wrapped Murchison's body and tied the rope so he could get a grip on it. The corpse was unwieldy, resembling a tree trunk and weighing more, Tom thought. He dragged it to the cellar steps. The fact that the body was covered made him feel slightly better, but now its nearness to the door, the steps, the front door, exacerbated his nerves all over again. What could he say if Mme Annette saw him, if one of the eternal doorbell-ringers – a gypsy selling baskets, Michel the town handyman asking if there was a job for him, a boy selling Catholic pamphlets – what would he say about the monstrous object that he was about to load on the wheelbarrow? People might not ask about it, but they would stare, and make a typical French comment in the negative:

'Not a very light weight, is it?' And they would remember.

Tom slept badly, and was curiously aware of his own snoring. He never quite fell asleep, so it was easy for him to get up at 5 a.m.

Downstairs, he pushed aside the mat before the front door, then went down to the cellar. Murchison went up half the steps very nicely, but Tom had spent a lot of energy on it, and had to pause. The rope was cutting his hands a bit, and he was too impatient to run to the toolshed for his gardening gloves. He took another grip and made it to the top. It was easier going across the marble floor. He varied his task by rolling the wheelbarrow round to the front and tipping it on its side. He would have preferred to get Murchison out via the french windows, but he couldn't cross the living-room with him without taking up the rug. Now Tom pulled the elongated lump down the four or five outside steps. He tried to put the thing sufficiently into the wheelbarrow, so that if he lifted one side of the wheelbarrow, he could right it. He did this, but the wheelbarrow tipped all the way over and spilled Murchison out the other side onto the ground again. It was almost funny.

The thought of having to drag the corpse back into the cellar was awful. Unthinkable. Tom spent a moment, thirty seconds, trying to recover his energies, staring at the damned thing on the ground. Then he flung himself at it as if it were a live, screaming dragon, or something supernatural that he had to kill before it killed him, and hoisted it into the upright barrow.

The front wheel of the barrow sank into the gravel. Tom knew at once it would be hopeless to take it across the lawn, already a bit soft from yesterday's showers. Tom ran and opened the big gates of his home. There were irregular flagstones between front steps and gate, and this went quite well, and then the wheelbarrow was on the hard sandy ground of the road. A lane to Tom's right led to the woods behind his house, a narrow lane that was more of a footpath or a way for carts than cars, though it was just wide enough for a car. Tom steered the barrow round little holes and puddles in the lane, and eventually he reached his woods – not his, certainly, but he rather felt they were his now, he was so glad to reach the concealment they offered.

Tom pushed the barrow some distance, then stopped and looked for the place where he had started to dig. He soon found it. There was a slope from the lane up to the woods, which Tom had not reckoned on, so he had to dump the corpse in the lane and drag it up. Then Tom pulled the wheelbarrow into the woods, so in case anyone passed along the lane, the wheelbarrow wouldn't be seen. By now there was a bit more light. Tom went off at a trot towards the toolshed for the fork. He also took a shovel – rusted, left behind by somebody when he and Heloise had bought the house. The shovel had a hole in it, but would still be of help. Tom went back and continued his digging. He struck roots. After fifteen minutes, it became obvious that he could not finish the hole that morning. By 8.30, Mme Annette would come upstairs to his bedroom with his coffee, for one thing.

Tom ducked as a man in faded blue came walking along the lane, pushing a wooden home-made wheelbarrow full of firewood. The man did not glance Tom's way. He was walking towards the road that ran in front of Tom's house. Where had he come from? Maybe he was pinching state wood, and was as glad to avoid Tom as Tom was to avoid him.

Tom dug until the trench was nearly four feet deep, traversed by roots that would take a saw to cut. Then he climbed out and looked around for a slope, any depression in which to hide Murchison temporarily. Tom found one fifteen feet away, and dragged the corpse by the ropes once more. He covered the grey tarpaulin with fallen branches and leaves. At least it would not catch the eye of someone in the lane, he thought.

Then he pushed the now feather-light barrow onto the lane, and for good measure returned the barrow to the shed, so that Mme Annette would not ask him a question about it if she saw it out.

He had to enter by the front door, because the french windows were locked. His forehead was wet with sweat.

Upstairs, he wiped himself with a hot wet towel, got back into pyjamas and went to bed. It was twenty to eight. He had done too much for Derwatt Ltd, he thought. Were they worth it? Curiously, Bernard was. If they could get Bernard past this *crise*.

But that wasn't the way to look at it. He wouldn't have killed someone just to save Derwatt Ltd or even Bernard, Tom supposed. Tom killed Murchison because Murchison had realized, in the cellar, that he had impersonated Derwatt. Tom had killed Murchison to save himself. And yet, Tom tried to ask himself, had he intended to kill Murchison anyway when they went down to the cellar together? Had he not intended to kill him? Tom simply could not answer that. And did it matter, much?

Bernard was the only one of the trio whom he could not understand perfectly, and yet Tom liked Bernard best. The motive of Ed and Jeff was so simple, to make money. Tom doubted that Cynthia had done the breaking off with Bernard. It would not have surprised Tom if Bernard (who certainly at one point had been in love with Cynthia) had broken it off, because he was ashamed of his forging. It would be interesting to sound Bernard out about this some time. Yes, in Bernard there was a mystery, and it was mystery that made people attractive, Tom thought, that caused people to fall in love, too. Despite the ugly, tarpaulin-bound lump in the woods behind his house, Tom felt his own thoughts bearing him away as if he were on a cloud. It was strange, and exceedingly pleasant, to daydream about Bernard's drives, fears, shames and possible loves. Bernard, like the real Derwatt, was a bit of a saint.

A pair of flies, insane as usual, were annoying Tom. He pulled one out of his hair. They were zooming around his night table. Late for flies, and he'd had quite enough of them this summer. The French countryside was famous for its variety of flies, which outnumbered the variety of cheeses, Tom had read somewhere. One fly jumped on the other's back. In plain view! Quickly Tom struck a match and held it to the bastards. Wings sizzled. *Buzz-buzz*. Legs stuck in the air and flailed their last. Ah, Liebestod, united even in death!

If it could happen in Pompeii, why not at Belle Ombre, Tom thought.

8

Tom spent Saturday morning lazily, writing a letter to Heloise c.o. American Express, Athens, and at 2.30 p.m. he listened to a comic programme on the radio, as he often did. Mme Annette, on Saturday afternoons, sometimes found Tom convulsed on the yellow sofa, and Heloise now and then asked him to translate, but much of it didn't translate, not the puns. At four, responding to an invitation that had come that noon by telephone, Tom went to take tea with Antoine and Agnès Grais, who lived on the other side of Villeperce, walking distance. Antoine was an architect who worked in Paris and spent weekdays there in his atelier. Agnès, a quiet blonde of about twenty-eight, stayed in Villeperce and took care of their two small children. There were four other guests at the Grais's, all Parisians.

'What have you been doing, Tome?' Agnès asked, bringing out her husband's speciality at the end of the tea, a bottle of strong old Holland gin, which the Grais recommended to be drunk neat.

'Painting a little. Wandering around the garden cleaning the wrong things, probably.' The French said cleaning for weeding.

'Not lonely? When is Heloise coming back?'

'Maybe in a month.'

The hour and a half at the Grais' was soothing to Tom. The Grais made no comment on his two guests, Murchison and Count Bertolozzi, and perhaps had not noticed them or heard of them via Mme Annette, who chatted freely in the food shops. Nor did the Grais notice his pink and almost bleeding palms, sore from the ropes around Murchison.

That evening, Tom lay with his shoes off on the yellow sofa, browsing in *Harrap's Dictionary*, which was so heavy he had to hold it against his thighs or rest it upon a table. He anticipated a telephone call, without being quite sure who would ring, and at a quarter past ten, one came. Chris Greenleaf in Paris.

'Is this – Tom Ripley?'

'Yes. Hello, Chris. How are you?'

'Fine, thanks. I just got here with my friend. I'm awfully glad you're in. I didn't have time to get a letter from you, in case you wrote. Well – look –'

'Where're you staying?'

'At the Hotel Louisiane. Highly recommended by the fellows back home! It's my first night in Paris. I haven't even opened my suitcase. But I thought I'd call you.'

'What're your plans? When would you like to visit?'

'Oh, any time. Of course I want to do some tourism. The Louvre first, maybe.'

'How about Tuesday?'

'Well – all right, but I was thinking of tomorrow, because my friend is busy all day tomorrow. He has a cousin living here, an older man, an American. So I was hoping . . .'

Somehow Tom couldn't turn him down, or think of a good excuse. 'Tomorrow. All right. In the afternoon? I'm a little busy in the morning.' Tom explained that he would have to take a train at Gare de Lyon for Moret-les-Sablons, and that he should ring again when he had chosen his train, so that Tom would know when to meet him.

Obviously Chris would stay overnight tomorrow. Tom realized that he would have to finish Murchison's grave and get him into it tomorrow morning. That was, in fact, probably why he had allowed Chris to come tomorrow. It was an added prod for himself.

Chris sounded naïve, but perhaps he had some of the Greenleaf good manners and would not outstay a welcome. Tom winced as this crossed his mind, because he had certainly outstayed his welcome at Dickie's in Mongibello in his callow youth, when he'd been twenty-five, not twenty. Tom had come from America, or rather had been sent by Dickie's father, Herbert Greenleaf, to bring Dickie back home. It had been a classic situation. Dickie hadn't wanted to go back to the United States. And Tom's *naïveté* at that time, was something that now made him cringe. The things he had had to learn! And then – well, Tom Ripley had stayed in Europe. He had learned a bit. After all he had some money – Dickie's – the girls had liked him well enough, and in fact Tom had felt a bit pursued. Heloise Plisson had been one of the ones who had liked him. And from Tom's point of view, she wasn't a piece of cement, orthodox, or far out, or another bore. Tom had not proposed marriage, nor had Heloise. It was a dark chapter in his life, a brief one. Heloise had said, in their rented bungalow in Cannes, 'Since we're living together, why not get married? ... *Apropos*, I am not sure Papa will countenance' (how had she said countenance in French? look that up) 'our living together much longer, whereas if we were really married – *ça serait un fait accompli*.' Tom had turned green at the wedding, even though it had been a civil wedding with no audience in a courtroom of some kind. Heloise had said later, laughing, 'You were green.' True. But Tom had at least gone through with it. He had hoped for a word of praise from Heloise, though he knew this was absurd on his part. It was for the bridegroom to say, 'Darling, you were gorgeous!' or 'Your cheeks were glowing with beauty and happiness!' or some such rot. Well, Tom's had been pale green. At least he hadn't collapsed going up the aisle – which had been a dingy passage between a few straight empty chairs in a magistrate's office in the South of France. Marriages ought to be secret, Tom thought, as private as the wedding night – which wasn't saying much. Since everybody's mind was frankly on the wedding night anyway at weddings, why was the affair itself so blatantly public? There was something rather vulgar about it. Why couldn't people surprise their friends by saying, 'Oh, but we've been married for three months now!' It was easy to see the reason for public weddings in the past – she's off our hands and you can't wriggle out of this one, old cock, or fifty relatives of the bride will boil you in oil – but why these days?

Tom went to bed.

On Sunday morning, again around 5 a.m., Tom donned his levis and went quietly down the stairs.

This time, he ran into Mme Annette, who opened the door from the kitchen into the hall, just as Tom was about to open the front door to go out. Mme Annette had a white cloth pressed to her cheek – no doubt the cloth contained hot salt of the coarse cooking type – and there was a dolorous expression on her face.

'Mme Annette – it's the tooth,' Tom said sympathetically.

'I could not sleep all night,' said Mme Annette. 'You are up early, M. Tome.'

'Damn that dentist,' Tom said in English. He continued in French, 'The idea of a nerve *falling* out! He doesn't know what he's doing. Now listen, Mme Annette, I have some yellow pills upstairs, I just remembered them. From Paris. Especially for toothache. Wait a second.' Tom ran back up the stairs.

She took one of the capsules. Mme Annette blinked as she swallowed. She had pale blue eyes. Her thin upper lids, drawn downward at the outer corners, looked Nordic. She was a Breton on her father's side.

'If you like, I can drive you to Fontainebleau today,' Tom said. Tom and Heloise had a dentist in Fontainebleau, and Tom thought he would see Mme Annette on a Sunday.

'Why are you up so early?' Mme Annette's curiosity was greater than her pain, it seemed.

'I'm going to work a little in the garden and go back to sleep for an hour or so. I also had a difficult time sleeping.'

Tom persuaded her gently back to her room, and left the bottle of capsules with her. Four in twenty-four hours were all right to take, he told her. 'Don't bother with breakfast or lunch for me, dear Madame. Repose yourself today.'

Then Tom went out to his task. He took it at a reasonable rate, or what he thought was reasonable. The trench ought to be five feet deep, and no nonsense about it. He had taken a rather rusty but still effective buck-saw from the tool shed, and with this he attacked the criss-crossing roots, heedless of the damp soil that stuck in the saw's teeth. He made progress. It was fairly light, though the sun was by no means up, when he finished the trench and hauled himself out, muddying the whole front of his sweater, unfortunately a beige cashmere. He looked around, but saw no one on the little lane that ran through the woods. A good thing, he thought, that the French tied up their dogs in the country, because a dog during last night might have snuffed up the branches that covered Murchison's corpse and barked an announcement that would have carried a kilometre. Again Tom tugged on the ropes that bound Murchison's tarpaulin. The body fell in with a thud positively delicious to Tom's ears. The shovelling in of earth was also a pleasure. There was soil to spare, and after stamping down the grave, Tom scattered the rest of the soil about in all directions. Then he walked slowly, but with a sense of achievement, back across his lawn and around to the front door.

He washed his sweater in some kind of delicate suds from Heloise's bathroom. Then he slept excellently till after 10 a.m.

Tom made some coffee in the kitchen, then went out to pick up his *Observer* and *Sunday Times* at the newspaper shop. Usually he stopped for a coffee somewhere while he glanced at the two newspapers – always a treasure to him – but today he wanted to be alone when he looked at the Derwatt write-ups. Tom almost forgot to buy Mme Annette's daily, the local edition of *Le Parisien*, whose headline was always in red. Today, something about a strangled twelve-year-old. The placards outside the shop touting various newspapers were equally bizarre but in a different way:

JEANNE AND PIERRE KISS AGAIN!

Who were they?

MARIE FURIOUS WITH CLAUDE!

The French were never merely annoyed, they were *furieux*.

ONASSIS FEARS THEY WILL STEAL JACKY FROM HIM!

Were the French lying awake worrying about that?

A BABY FOR NICOLE!

Nicole *who*, for Christ's sake? Tom never knew who most of these people were – film stars, pop singers, perhaps – but they evidently sold newspapers. The activities of the English Royal Family were unbelievable, Elizabeth and Philip on the brink of divorce three times a year, and Margaret and Tony spitting in each other's faces.

Tom put Mme Annette's paper on the kitchen table, then went up to his room. Both the *Observer* and the *Sunday Times* had a picture of him as Philip Derwatt on their arts review pages. In one, his mouth was open in the act of replying to questions, open in the disgusting beard. Tom looked quickly at the write-ups, not really wanting to read every word.

The Observer said: '... breaking his long retreat with a surprise appearance Wednesday afternoon at the Buckmaster Gallery, Philip Derwatt, who prefers to be called simply Derwatt, was reticent about his Mexican whereabouts but voluble enough when questioned about his work and that of his contemporaries. On Picasso: "Picasso has periods. I have no periods."' In the *Sunday Times* photograph, he stood behind Jeff's desk gesticulating with his left fist raised, an action Tom did not remember having made, but here it was. '... wearing clothes that had obviously been in a cupboard for years ... held his own against a battery of twelve reporters, which must have been a trial after six years of seclusion, we assume.' Was that 'we assume' a dig? Tom thought not, really, because the rest of the comment was favourable. 'Derwatt's current canvases maintain his high standards –

idiosyncratic, bizarre, even sick, perhaps? ... None of Derwatt's paintings is dashed off or unresolved. They are labours of love, though his technique appears quick, fresh and easy for him. This is not to be confused with facility or the look of it. Derwatt says he has never painted a picture in less than two weeks ...' Had he said that? '... and he works daily, often for more than seven hours per day. ... Men, little girls, chairs, tables, strange things on fire, these still predominate. ... The show is going to be another sell-out.' No mention was made of Derwatt's disappearance after the interview.

A pity, Tom thought, that some of these compliments couldn't be engraved upon Bernard Tufts's own tomb, wherever that might be finally. Tom was reminded of 'Here lies one whose name was writ in water', a line that had made Tom's eyes fill with tears on the three occasions he had seen it in the English Protestant Cemetery in Rome, and could sometimes make his eyes water when he merely thought of it. Perhaps Bernard, the plodder, the artist, would compose his own lines before he died. Or would he be anonymously famous because of one 'Derwatt', one splendid picture which he had yet to paint?

Or would Bernard ever paint another Derwatt? Good God, he didn't even know, Tom realized. And was Bernard painting any more of his own paintings, that might be called Tufts?

Mme Annette was feeling better before noon. And as Tom had foreseen, because of the anodynal pills, she did not want to be taken to the better dentist at Fontainebleau.

'Madame – I am inundated with *invités* just now, it seems. A pity Mme Heloise is not here. But tonight there is another for dinner, a young man called M. Christophe, an American. I can do all the shopping necessary in the village. ... *Non-non*, you repose yourself.'

And Tom did the shopping straight away and was back home before two. Mme Annette said an American had rung, but they could not understand each other, and the American would ring back.

Chris did, and Tom was to pick him up at 6.30 at Moret.

Tom put on old flannels, a turtleneck sweater, and desert boots, and left in the Alfa-Romeo. The menu tonight was *viande hâchée* – the French hamburger which was so red and delicious one could eat it raw. Tom had seen Americans swoon over hamburgers with onion and ketchup in the Paris Drugstores, when they had been away from America only twenty-four hours.

Tom recognized Chris Greenleaf at his first glimpse, as he had thought he might. Though Tom's view was obscured by several people, Christopher's blond head stuck a bit above them. His eyes and his brows had the same slight frown that Dickie's had had. Tom raised an arm in greeting, but Christopher was hesitant until their eyes actually met, and Tom smiled. The boy's smile was like Dickie's, but if there was a difference, it was in the lips, Tom thought. Christopher's lips were fuller, with a fullness unrelated to Dickie and no doubt from Christopher's mother's side.

They gripped hands.

'It's really like the country out here.'

'How do you like Paris?'

'Oh, I like it. It's bigger than I thought.'

Christopher took in everything, craning his neck at the most ordinary bar-cafés, plane trees, private houses along the way. His friend Gerald might go for two or three days to Strasbourg, Christopher told Tom. 'This is the first French village I've seen. It's real, isn't it?' he asked, as if it might be a stage-set.

Tom found it amusing, strangely nervous-making, Chris's enthusiasm. Tom remembered his own mad joy – though there'd been no one for him to speak to – at his first glimpse of the Leaning Tower of Pisa from a moving train, his first view of the curving lights of Cannes's shore.

Belle Ombre was not fully visible in the dark now, but Mme Annette had put the light on at the front door, and its proportions could be guessed from a light in the front left corner, where the kitchen was. Tom smiled to himself at Chris's ecstatic comments, but they pleased Tom nevertheless. Sometimes Tom felt like kicking Belle Ombre and the Plisson family, too, to pieces, as if they were a conglomerate sand castle that he could destroy with a foot. These times came when he was maddened by some incident of French bloodymindedness, greed, a lie that was not exactly a lie but a deliberate concealment of fact. When other people praised Belle Ombre, Tom liked it, too. Tom drove into the garage, and carried one of Chris's two suitcases. Chris said he had everything with him.

Mme Annette opened the front door.

'My housekeeper, faithful retainer, without whom I couldn't live,' Tom said, 'Mme Annette. M. Christophe.'

'How do you do? *Bonsoir*,' Chris said.

'Bonsoir, m'sieur. The room of m'sieur is ready.'

Tom took Chris upstairs.

'This is marvellous,' Chris said. 'It's like a museum!'

There was, Tom supposed, a considerable amount of satin and ormolu. 'It's my wife, I think – the decorating. She's not here just now.'

'I saw a picture of her with you. Uncle Herbert showed it to me in New York just the other day. She's blonde. Her name's Heloise.'

Tom left Christopher to wash up, and said he would be downstairs.

Tom's thoughts drifted to Murchison again: Murchison would be missing from his plane's passenger list. The police would check Paris hotels and find that Murchison had not been at any. An immigration check would show that Murchison had been at the Hotel Mandeville October 14th and 15th, and had said he would be back on the 17th. Tom's own name and address was on the Hotel Mandeville register for the night of 15 October. But he would not be the only resident of France in the Mandeville that night, surely. Would the police come to question him or would they not?

Christopher came downstairs. He had combed his wavy brown hair, and still wore his corduroy trousers and army boots. 'Hope you're not having guests for dinner. If you are, I'll change.'

'We're alone. It's the country, so wear what you like.'

Christopher looked at Tom's paintings, and paid more attention to a pinkish Pascin nude, a drawing, than to the paintings. 'You live here all year round? It must be a pleasure.'

He accepted a Scotch. Tom had to account for his time again, and mentioned his gardening and his informal study of languages, though in fact Tom's routine of study was stricter than he admitted. Tom loved his leisure, however, as only an American could, he thought – once an American got the hang of it, and so few did. It was not a thing he cared to put into words to anyone. He had longed for leisure and a bit of luxury when he had met Dickie Greenleaf, and now that he had attained it, the charm had not palled.

At the table, Christopher began to talk of Dickie. He said he had photographs of Dickie that someone had taken in Mongibello, and that Tom was in one of the photographs. Christopher spoke with a little difficulty of Dickie's death – his suicide, as everyone thought. Chris had something better than manners, Tom saw, which was sensitivity. Tom was fascinated by the candlelight through the irises of his blue eyes, because so often Dickie's eyes had looked the same late at night in Mongibello, or in some candlelit restaurant in Naples.

Christopher said, standing tall and looking at the french windows, and up at the cream-coloured coffered ceiling, 'It's fabulous to live in a house like this. And you have music besides – and paintings!'

Tom was reminded painfully of himself at twenty. Chris's family wasn't poor, Tom was sure, but their house wouldn't be quite like this one. While they drank coffee, Tom played *A Midsummer Night's Dream* music.

Then the telephone rang. It was about 10 p.m.

The French telephone operator asked him if his number was so-and-so, then told him not to quit for a call from London.

'Hello. This is Bernard Tufts,' said the tense voice, and there followed crackles.

'Hello? Yes. Tom here. Can you hear me?'

'Can you speak louder? I'm ringing to say . . .' Bernard's voice faded out as if drowned in a deep sea.

Tom glanced at Chris, who was reading the sleeve of a record. 'Is this *better*?' Tom roared into the telephone, and as if to spite him, the telephone gave a fart, then a crack like a mountain splitting beneath a stroke of lightning. Tom's left ear rang from the impact, and he switched to the right ear. He could hear Bernard struggling on slowly, loudly, but alas the words were quite unintelligible. Tom heard only 'Murchison'. *'He's in London!'* Tom shouted, glad to have something definite to convey. Now it was something about the Mandeville. Had the man from the Tate Gallery tried to reach Murchison at the Mandeville, then spoken to the Buckmaster Gallery, Tom wondered? 'Bernard, it is *hopeless* !' Tom yelled desperately. 'Can you write me?' Tom didn't know whether Bernard hung up or not, but a buzzing silence followed, and Tom assumed Bernard had given up, so he put the telephone down. 'To think one pays a hundred and twenty bucks just to *get* a telephone in this country,' Tom said. 'I'm sorry for all the shouting.'

'Oh, I've always heard French telephones are lousy,' Chris said. 'Was it important? Heloise?'

'No, no.'

Chris stood up. 'I'd like to show you my guide books. Can I?' He ran upstairs.

A matter of time, Tom thought, till the French police or the English – maybe even the American – questioned him about Murchison. Tom hoped Chris would not be here when it happened.

Chris came down with three books. He had the *Guide Bleu* for France, an art book on French châteaux, and a big book on the Rhineland, where he intended to go with Gerald Hayman when Gerald came back from Strasbourg.

Christopher sipped with pleasure at a single brandy, prolonging it. 'I have serious doubts about the value of democracy. That's a terrible thing for an American to say, isn't it? Democracy depends on a certain minimal level of education for everybody, and America tries to give it to everybody – but we really haven't got it. And it isn't even true that everybody wants it ...'

Tom half listened. But his occasional comments seemed to satisfy Chris, at least this evening.

The telephone rang again. Tom noticed that it was five to eleven by the little silver clock on the telephone table.

A man's voice said in French that he was an agent of police, and apologized for ringing at this hour, but was M. Ripley there? 'Good evening, m'sicur. Do you by any chance know an American named Thomas Murchison?'

'Yes,' Tom said.

'Did he by chance visit you recently? Wednesday? Or Thursday?'

'Yes, he did.'

'Ah *bon* ! Is he with you now?'

'No, he went back to London on Thursday.'

'No, he did not. But his suitcase was found at Orly. He did not take the sixteen hours plane he was supposed to.'

'Oh?'

'You are a friend of M. Murchison, M. Reeply?'

'No, not a friend. I have known him for only a short time.'

'How did he depart from your house to Orly?'

'I drove him to Orly – around three-thirty Thursday afternoon.'

'Do you know any friends of his in Paris – where he might be staying? Because he is not in any hotel in Paris.'

Tom paused, thinking. 'No. He did not mention anyone.'

This was evidently disappointing to the agent. 'You are at home in the next days, M. Reeply? ... We may wish to speak with you...'

This time Christopher was curious. 'What's that all about?'

Tom smiled. 'Oh – someone asking me where a friend is. I don't know.'

Who was making the fuss about Murchison, Tom wondered? The man at the Tate Gallery? The French police at Orly, had they started it? Or even Murchison's wife in America?

'What's Heloise like?' Christopher asked.

9

When Tom came downstairs the next morning, Mme Annette told him that M. Christophe had gone out for a walk. Tom hoped not into the woods behind the house, but it was more likely Chris would look around the village. Tom picked up the London Sundays, which he had barely glanced at yesterday, and looked through the news sections for any item, however small, about Murchison, or a disappearance at Orly. There was nothing.

Chris came in, pink-cheeked and smiling. He had bought a wire whisk, the kind the French beat eggs with, at the local *droguerie*. 'Little present for my sister,' Chris said. 'It doesn't weigh much in a suitcase. I'll tell her it came from your village.'

Tom asked if Chris would like to take a drive and have lunch in another town. 'Bring your *Guide Bleu* along. We'll drive along the Seine.' Tom wanted to wait a few minutes for the post.

The post brought only one letter addressed in a tall angular hand in black ink. Tom felt at once it was from Bernard, though he didn't know Bernard's writing. He opened the letter and saw from the signature at the bottom that he was correct.

127 Copperfield St
S.E.1.

Dear Tom,

Forgive this unexpected letter. I would like very much to see you. Can I come over? You do not need to put me up. It would be good for me to speak with you for a bit, providing you are willing.

Yours,
Bernard T.

P.S. I may try to ring you before you receive this.

He would have to cable Bernard at once. Cable him what? A refusal would depress Bernard further, Tom supposed, although Tom certainly did not want to see him – not just now. Perhaps he could cable Bernard from a small town post office this morning, and give a false last name and address for himself, since the sender's name and address were demanded at the bottom of French telegram forms. He must send Chris on his way as soon as possible, which he disliked doing. 'Shall we shove off?'

Chris got up from the sofa, where he had been writing a post-card. 'Fine.'

Tom opened the front door in the faces of two French police

officers who had been about to knock. In fact, Tom stepped back from the upraised fist in the white glove.

'Bonjour. M. Reeply?'

'Yes. Come in, please.' They must be from Melun, Tom thought, because the two police in Villeperce knew him, and Tom knew their faces, too, but not these faces.

The agents came in but declined to sit down. They removed their caps, stuck them under their arms, and the younger officer pulled a tablet and pencil from a pocket.

'I telephoned you last evening in regard to a M. Murchison,' said the older officer, who was a *commissaire*. 'We have spoken with London and after some telephone calls we ascertained that you and M. Murchison arrived at Orly on the same plane Wednesday and were also at the same hotel in London, the Mande-*veel*. So –' The *commissaire* smiled with satisfaction. 'You say you brought M. Murchison to Orly at three-thirty on Thursday afternoon?'

'Yes.'

'And you accompanied M. Murchison into the terminal?'

'No, because I couldn't park my car at the pavement, you see, so I let him out.'

'Did you see him go through the doors of the terminal?'

Tom thought. 'I did not look back as I drove away.'

'Because he left his suitcase on the pavement and he has simply disappeared. Was he expecting to meet someone at Orly?'

'He did not say anything about that.'

Christopher Greenleaf was standing some distance away, listening to all this, but Tom was sure he could not understand much.

'He mentioned friends in London he was going to see?'

'No. Not that I recall.'

'This morning we telephoned again to the Mande*veel*, where he was supposed to go, to ask if they had news. They informed us no, but a M. –' He turned to his colleague.

'M. Riemer,' the younger officer supplied.

'M. Riemer had telephoned to the hotel, because he had an appointment with M. Murchison on Friday. We also learned from the London police that M. Murchison is interested in verifying a painting in his possession. One by Derwatt. Do you know anything about this?'

'Oh, yes,' Tom said. 'M. Murchison had his painting with him. He wanted to see my Derwatts here.' Tom indicated them on his walls. 'That is why he came over from London with me.'

'Ah, I understand. How long have you known M. Murchison?'

'Since Tuesday last. I saw him at the art gallery, where the Derwatt exhibition is on, and then I saw him in my hotel that evening, and we began talking.' Tom turned and said, 'Excuse me, Chris, but this is important.'

'Oh, go ahead, I don't mind,' Chris said.

'Where is the painting of M. Murchison?'

'He took it with him,' Tom said.

'It was in his suitcase? It is not in his suitcase.' The *commissaire* looked at his colleague, and both men's faces showed some surprise.

It had been stolen at Orly, and thank God, Tom thought. 'It was wrapped in brown paper. M. Murchison was carrying it. I hope it wasn't stolen.'

'Ah, well – apparently it is. What was the picture called? And how big was it? Can you describe it?'

Tom replied to all this accurately.

'This is complicated for us, and perhaps is a matter for the London police, but we must tell them all we can. This is the picture – "L'Horloge" – of whose authenticity Murchison doubts?'

'Yes, he did doubt it at first. He is more of an expert than I am,' Tom said. 'I was interested in what he said, because of my own two Derwatts, so I invited him to come to see them.'

'And –' the *commissaire* frowned in a puzzled way, '– what did he say about yours?' It might have been a question inspired by simple curiosity.

'Certainly he thinks mine are genuine and so do I,' Tom replied. 'I think he began to think his own was genuine, too. He said he might cancel his appointment with M. Riemer.'

'Ah-hah.' The *commissaire* looked at the telephone, perhaps debating ringing Melun, but he did not ask to use the telephone.

'May I offer you a glass of wine?' Tom asked, including the two officers in his question.

They declined the wine, but they did wish to look at his paintings. Tom was pleased to show them. The two agents walked about, murmuring comments which might have been quite knowledgeable, judging from their fascinated faces and their gestures as they looked at canvases and drawings. They might have been visiting a gallery in their spare time.

'A famous painter in England, Derwatt,' said the younger officer.

'Yes,' Tom said.

The interview was over. They thanked Tom and took their leave.

Tom was glad Mme Annette had been out on her morning shopping round.

Christopher laughed a little when Tom had closed the door. 'Well, what was that all about? All I could understand was "Orly" and "Murchison".'

'It seems that Thomas Murchison, an American who visited me last week, didn't take his plane back to London from Orly. He seems to have disappeared. And they found his suitcase on the pavement at Orly – where I left him Thursday.'

'Disappeared? Gosh! – That's four days ago.'

'I didn't know anything about it till last night. That was the telephone call I had last night. From the police.'

'Gosh. How strange.' Chris asked a few questions, and Tom answered them, as he had answered the police. 'Sounds like he had a black-out, leaving his luggage like that. Was he sober?'

Tom laughed. 'Absolutely. I can't understand it.'

They rambled along the Seine in the Alfa-Romeo, and near Samois, Tom showed Chris the bridge where General Patton had crossed the Seine with his army, on the way to Paris in 1944. Chris got out and read the inscription on the grey little column, and came back as wet-eyed as Tom after the grave of Keats. Lunch in Fontainebleau, because Tom disliked the main restaurant in Bas Samois – Chez Bertrand or some such – where he and Heloise had never yet received an honest *addition*, and where the family who ran it had the habit of starting to mop the floors before people were finished eating, dragging metal-legged chairs across tiles with merciless unconcern for the human ear. Later, Tom did not forget his little chores for Mme Annette – *champignons à la grecque, céleri rémoulade*, and some sausages whose name Tom could not remember, because he did not care for them – things one could not buy in Villeperce. He got them in Fontainebleau, and also some batteries for his transistor.

On the way home, Chris burst out laughing and said, 'This morning in the woods I came across what looked like a fresh grave. Really fresh. I thought it was funny because of the police this morning. They're looking for a missing man who was at your house, and if they saw that *grave* shape in the woods –' He went off in guffaws.

Yes, it was funny, damned funny. Tom laughed at the crazy danger of it. But he made no comment.

10

The next day was overcast, and it began to rain around nine o'clock. Mme Annette went out to fasten a shutter that was banging somewhere. She had listened to her radio, and there were dire pronouncements of an *orage*, she warned Tom.

Wind made Tom jumpy. Tourism, that morning, was out for him and Chris. By midday, the storm was worse, and the wind bent the tops of the tall poplars like whips or sword-tips. Now and then a branch – small and dead, probably – was blown from a tree near the house and rattled as it hit the roof and rolled down.

'I really never saw anything like it – here,' Tom said at lunch.

But Chris, with the coolness of Dickie, or maybe of his whole family, smiled and enjoyed the disturbance.

The lights went out for half an hour, which Tom said happened all the time in the French countryside, even if the storm was a mild one.

After lunch, Tom went up to the room where he painted.

Sometimes painting helped when he was nervous. He painted standing up at his worktable, with the canvas propped against a heavy vice and a few thick art books and books on horticulture.

The bottom of the canvas rested on some newspapers plus a large paint rag which had been part of an old bed sheet. Tom bent zealously over his work, stepping back frequently to look at it. This was a portrait of Mme Annette done in – perhaps – rather a de Kooning style, which meant Mme Annette would never possibly recognize it as an attempted likeness. Tom was not consciously imitating de Kooning, and had not consciously thought of him when he began this opus, but there was no doubt the picture looked like a portrait in de Kooning's style. Mme Annette's pale lips were parted in a smile of slashing pink, her teeth decidedly off-white and irregular. She was in a pale purple dress with a white ruffle round the neck. All this was done with rather wide brushes and in long strokes. Tom's preliminary work for this had been several hasty cartoons of Mme Annette done on a pad on his knee in the living-room, when Mme Annette was unaware.

Now there was lightning. Tom straightened up and breathed, his chest aching from tension. On his transistor, *France Culture* was interviewing another uncomfortable-sounding author: 'Your book, M. Hublot (Heublein?) seems to me (crackle) . . . which is a departure from – as several critics have said – your up-to-now *challenge* to the concepts of anti-Sartrisme. But rather now it seems to be reversing . . .' Tom cut it off abruptly.

There was an ominous *crack* close by in the woods direction, and Tom looked out his window. The tops of pines and poplars still flexed, but if any tree had fallen in the woods, he could not see it from here in the grey-green murk of the forest. A tree might just fall, even a smallish tree, and cover the damned grave, Tom thought. He hoped so. Tom was mixing a reddish brown for Mme Annette's hair – he wanted to finish the painting today – when he heard voices, or thought he did, from downstairs. Men's voices.

Tom went into the hall.

The voices were speaking English, but he could not hear what they were saying. Chris and someone else. *Bernard*, Tom thought. An English accent. Yes, my God!

Tom laid his palette knife carefully across the turpentine cup. He closed the door behind him and trotted downstairs.

It was Bernard, standing bedraggled and wet on the mat just inside the front door. Tom was struck by his dark eyes which seemed deeper sunken under the straight black brows. Bernard looked terrified, Tom thought. Then in the next instant, Tom thought Bernard looked like death itself.

'Bernard!' Tom said. 'Welcome!'

'Hello,' Bernard said. He had a duffelbag at his feet.

'This is Christopher Greenleaf,' Tom said. 'Bernard Tufts. Maybe you've introduced yourselves.'

'Yes, we have,' said Chris, smiling, pleased to have company it seemed.

'I hope it's all right if I just arrived – like this,' Bernard said.

Tom assured him it was. Now Mme Annette came in, and Tom introduced them.

Mme Annette asked to take Bernard's coat.

Tom said to her in French, 'You might prepare the little room for M. Bernard.' This was a second guest-room, seldom used, with a single bed, which he and Heloise called 'the little bedroom'. 'And M. Bernard will dine with us tonight.' Then Tom said to Bernard, 'What did you do? Take a taxi from Melun? Or Moret?'

'Yes. Melun. I looked up the town on a map in London.' Thin and angular, like his writing, Bernard stood chafing his hands. Even his jacket looked wet.

'Want a sweater, Bernard? How about a brandy to warm you up?'

'Oh, no, no, thank you.'

'Come in the living-room! Some tea? I'll ask Madame to make some when she comes down. Sit down, Bernard.'

Bernard looked anxiously at Chris, as if expecting him to sit down first or something. But in the next minutes, Tom realized that Bernard looked anxiously at everything, even at an ashtray on the coffee-table. The exchange of words, such as it was, was extremely sticky, and Bernard plainly wished that Christopher were not here. But Chris did not seem to grasp this, Tom could see, and on the contrary thought his presence might be useful, because Bernard, obviously, was in a state. Bernard stuttered, and his hands shook.

'I really won't disturb you for long,' Bernard said.

Tom laughed. 'But you're not going back today! We're being treated to the worst weather I've seen in the three years I've been here. Did the plane have a hard time landing?'

Bernard didn't remember. His eyes drifted to the – his own – 'Man in Chair' over the fireplace, and away again.

Tom thought of the cobalt violet in the picture. Now it was like a chemical poison to Tom. To Bernard, too, Tom supposed. 'You haven't seen "The Red Chairs" in a long time,' Tom said, getting up. The picture was behind Bernard.

Bernard got to his feet and twisted around, his legs still pressed against the sofa.

Tom's effort was rewarded by a faint but genuine smile on Bernard's face. 'Yes. It's beautiful,' Bernard said in his quiet voice.

'Are you a painter?' asked Chris.

'Yes.' Bernard sat down again. 'But not as good as – as Derwatt.'

'Mme Annette, could you put on some water for tea?' Tom asked.

Mme Annette had come down from upstairs, carrying towels or something. 'At once, M. Tome.'

'Can you tell me,' Christopher began to Bernard, 'what makes a painter good – or not? For instance, it seems to me several painters are painting like Derwatt now. I can't remember their names off hand, because they're not as famous. Oh, yes, Parker Nunnally, for one. Do you know his work? What is it that makes Derwatt so good?'

Tom also tried for a correct answer, perhaps 'originality'. But the word 'publicity' flashed into his mind, too. He was waiting for Bernard to speak.

'It is personality,' Bernard said carefully. 'It is Derwatt.'

'You know him?' Chris asked.

A slight pang went through Tom, a twinge of sympathy for Bernard.

Bernard nodded. 'Oh, yes.' Now his bony hands were clasped around one knee.

'Do you feel this personality when you meet him? See him, I mean?'

'Yes,' Bernard said more firmly. But he writhed, perhaps in agony, at the conversation. At the same time his dark eyes seemed to be searching for something else he might say on the subject.

'That probably wasn't a fair question,' Chris said. 'Most good artists don't show their personalities or waste their fire in their personal life, I think. They seem perfectly ordinary on the surface.'

Tea was served.

'You have no suitcase, Bernard?' Tom asked. Tom knew he had no suitcase, and was worried about Bernard's general comfort.

'No, I just came over on a hop,' Bernard said.

'Don't worry. I've got everything you might want.' Tom felt Chris's eyes on him and Bernard, speculating probably as to how and how well they knew each other. 'Hungry?' Tom asked Bernard. 'My housekeeper loves to make sandwiches.' There were only petits fours with the tea. 'Her name's Mme Annette. Ask for anything you want.'

'No, thank you.' Bernard's cup made three distinct clicks against the saucer as he set it down.

Tom wondered if Jeff and Ed had so sedated Bernard that he was in need of something now? Bernard had finished his tea, and Tom took him upstairs to show him his room.

'You'll have to share the bath with Chris,' Tom said. 'You go across the hall here and through my wife's room.' Tom left the doors open. 'Heloise isn't here, she's in Greece. I hope you can rest a bit here, Bernard. What's the matter, really? What's worrying you?'

They were back in Bernard's 'little bedroom', and the door was shut.

Bernard shook his head. 'I feel as if I'm at the end. That's all.

The show was the end. It's the last show I can paint. The last picture. "The Tub." And now they're trying to bring – you know – bring him back to life.'

And I succeeded, Tom might have said, but his face remained as serious as Bernard's. 'Well – he's presumably *been* alive for the past five years. I'm sure they're not going to force you to go on painting if you don't want to, Bernard.'

'Oh, they're going to try, Jeff and Ed. But I've had enough, you see. Quite enough.'

'I think they know that. Don't worry about that. We can – Look, Derwatt can go into seclusion *again*. In Mexico. Let's say he's painting for the next many years, and refuses to show anything.' Tom walked up and down as he spoke. 'Years can pass. When Derwatt dies – we'll have him burn all his last paintings, something like that, so no one will ever see them!' Tom smiled.

Bernard's sombre eyes, staring at the floor, made Tom feel as if he had told a joke that his audience didn't get. Or worse, committed a sacrilege, cracked a bad joke in a cathedral.

'You need a rest, Bernard. Would you like a phenobarb? I have some mild ones, quarter grains.'

'No, thanks.'

'Want to wash up? Don't worry about Chris and me. We'll leave you in peace. Dinner at eight if you want to join us. Come down earlier if you want a drink.'

The wind just then made a '*Whoo-oo-oo*' and a huge tree bent – they both glanced at the window and saw it, it was in Tom's back garden – and it seemed to Tom as if the house bent, too, and he instinctively braced his feet. How could anyone be calm in this weather?

'Want me to close these curtains?' Tom asked.

'It doesn't matter.' Bernard looked at Tom. 'What did Murchison say when he saw "Man in Chair"?'

'He said he thought it was a forgery – at first. But I persuaded him it wasn't.'

'How could you? Murchison told me what he thought about – the lavenders. He's right. I made three mistakes, "Man in Chair", "The Clock" and now "The Tub". I don't know how it happened. I don't know why. I wasn't thinking. Murchison is right.'

Tom was silent. Then he said, 'Naturally it was a scare for all of us. Derwatt alive might have lived it down. It was the danger – the danger of his non-existence being exposed. But we're over that hump, Bernard.'

Bernard might not have followed this at all. He said, 'Did you offer to buy "The Clock" or something like that?'

'No. I persuaded him that Derwatt must've gone back – for a painting or two or maybe three – to a lavender he'd used before.'

'Murchison was even talking to me about the quality of the painting. Oh, Christ!' Bernard sat down on the bed and slumped back. 'What's Murchison doing now in London?'

'I don't know. But I know he's not going to see an expert, not going to do anything, Bernard – because I persuaded him our way,' Tom said soothingly.

'I can think of only one way you persuaded him, one wild way.'

'What do you mean?' Tom asked, smiling, a little frightened.

'You persuaded him to let me alone. As a thing of pity, a thing to be pitied. I don't wish to be pitied.'

'There was no mention of you – naturally.' *You're mad*, Tom felt like saying. Bernard was mad, or at least temporarily deranged. Yet what Bernard had said was exactly what Tom had tried to do in the cellar before he killed Murchison: persuade him to let Bernard alone, because Bernard would never paint any more 'Derwatts'. Tom had even tried to make Murchison understand Bernard's worship of Derwatt, his dead idol.

'I don't think Murchison could be persuaded,' Bernard said. 'You're not trying to make me feel better by lying to me, are you, Tom? Because I've had just about enough of *lies*.'

'No.' But Tom felt uncomfortable because he was lying to Bernard. It was seldom Tom felt uncomfortable, lying. Tom foresaw that he would have to tell Bernard at some time that Murchison was dead. It was the only way to reassure Bernard – reassure him partially, on the forgery score at least. But Tom couldn't tell him now, not in this nerve-racking storm, not in the state Bernard was in now, or Bernard would really go berserk. 'I'll be back in a minute,' Tom said.

Bernard got up from the bed at once and walked towards the window, just as the wind threw a hard spray of rain against the panes.

Tom winced at it, but Bernard did not. Tom went into his room, got some pyjamas and a Madras dressing-gown for Bernard, also house-slippers, and a new toothbrush still in its plastic box. He put the toothbrush in the bathroom in case Bernard had none, and brought the other things into Bernard's room. He told Bernard he would be downstairs if he wanted anything, and that he would leave him to rest for a while.

Chris had gone into his room, Tom saw from his light. The storm had made the house unnaturally dark. Tom went into his own room and got the Count's toothpaste from his top drawer. By rolling the bottom up, the tube was usable, and it was better that he use it than throw it away and run the risk of Mme Annette's seeing it in the garbage: inexplicable and wanton waste. Tom took his own toothpaste from the basin and put it in the bathroom used by Chris and Bernard.

What the hell would he do with Bernard, Tom wondered? And what if the police came back and Bernard was present, as Chris had been present? Bernard understood French pretty well, Tom thought.

Tom sat down and wrote a letter to Heloise. Writing to her always had a calming effect on him. When he was dubious about his French, he usually didn't bother running to the dictionary, because his errors amused Heloise.

Oct. 22 19—

Heloise chérie,

A cousin of Dickie Greenleaf, a nice boy named Christophe, is visiting for a couple of days. He is making his first visit to Paris. Imagine seeing Paris for the first time at the age of twenty? He is very astonished by its size. He is from California.

Today there is a terrible storm. Everyone is nervous. Wind and rain.

I miss you. Did you get the red bathing-suit? I told Mme Annette to airmail it and gave her lots of money, so if she did not send it airmail, I will hit her. Everyone asks when you are coming home. I had tea with the Grais. I feel myself very alone without you. Come back and we shall sleep in each other's arms.

Your solitary husband,

Tom

Tom stamped the letter and took it downstairs to put on the hall table.

Now Christopher was in the living-room, reading on the sofa. He jumped up. 'Listen –' He spoke quietly. 'What's the matter with your friend?'

'He's had a crisis. In London. He's depressed about his work. And I think he's had a – He's broken off with his girl-friend or she has with him. I don't know.'

'You know him well?'

'Not too. No.'

'I was wondering – since he's in such a funny state – if you'd like me to take off. Tomorrow morning. Even tonight.'

'Oh, certainly not tonight, Chris. In this weather? No, it doesn't bother me, your being here.'

'But I had the feeling it bothered him. Bernard.' Chris jerked his head towards the stairs.

'Well – there's plenty of room in this house for us to talk, Bernard and I, if he wants to. Don't worry.'

'All right. If you mean it. Till tomorrow then.' He shoved his hands in his back pockets and walked towards the french windows.

At any moment now, Mme Annette would come in and draw the curtains, Tom thought, which would at least be something calm in all this chaos.

'Look!' Chris pointed out towards the lawn.

'What is it?' A tree had fallen, Tom supposed, a minor matter. It took him a moment to see what Chris had seen, because it was so dark. Tom made out a figure walking slowly across the lawn, and his first thought was *Murchison's ghost*, and he jumped. But Tom didn't believe in ghosts.

'It's Bernard!' Chris said.

It was Bernard, of course. Tom opened the french windows and stepped out into the rain, which was now a cold spray blown

in all directions. 'Hey, Bernard! What're you doing?' Tom saw
that Bernard wasn't reacting, was still walking slowly, his head
lifted, and Tom dashed off towards him. Tom tripped on the top
step of his stone stairs, nearly fell down the rest of them, and
caught himself only at the bottom, turning an ankle at the same
time. 'Hey, Bernard, come in!' Tom yelled, limping towards
him now.

Chris ran down and joined Tom. 'You'll get soaking wet!'
Chris said with a laugh, and started to grab Bernard's arm, but
evidently didn't dare.

Tom took Bernard's wrist firmly. 'Bernard, are you trying to
catch a sensational cold?'

Bernard turned to them and smiled, and the rain dripped
down his black hair that was plastered to his forehead. 'I like it.
I really do. I *feel* like this!' He lifted his arms high, breaking
Tom's hold.

'But you're coming in now? Please, Bernard.'

Bernard smiled at Tom. 'Oh, all right,' he said, as if he were
humouring Tom.

The three walked back to the house together, but slowly, because Bernard seemed to want to absorb every drop. Bernard was
in good humour, and made some cheerful comment as he removed his shoes at the french windows, so as not to soil the rug.
He also removed his jacket.

'You've really got to change,' Tom said. 'I'll get something
for you.' Tom was taking off his own shoes.

'Very well, I'll change,' Bernard said, in the same tone of
condescension, and slowly climbed the stairs, shoes in hand.

Chris looked at Tom and frowned intently, like Dickie. 'That
guy's nuts!' he whispered. 'Really nuts!'

Tom nodded, strangely shaken – shaken as he always was
when in the presence of someone genuinely a bit off in the head.
It was a feeling of being shattered. The sensation was setting in
early: usually it took twenty-four hours. Tom stepped cautiously
on his ankle and worked it round. It was not going to be serious,
his ankle, he thought. 'You may be right,' he said to Chris. 'I'll
go up and find some dry clothes for him.'

11

Around ten o'clock that evening, Tom knocked on Bernard's door. 'It's me. Tom.'

'Oh, come in, Tom,' Bernard's voice said calmly. He was sitting at the writing-table, pen in hand. 'Please don't be alarmed by my walking in the rain tonight. I was myself in the rain. And that's become a rare thing.'

Tom understood, only too well.

'Sit down, Tom! Shut the door. Make yourself at home.'

Tom sat down on Bernard's bed. He had come to see Bernard as he had promised during dinner, in the presence of Chris, in fact. Bernard had been more cheerful during dinner. Bernard was wearing the Madras dressing-gown. There were a couple of sheets of paper covered with Bernard's black ink handwriting on the table, but Tom had the feeling Bernard was not writing a letter. 'I suppose a lot of the time you feel you're Derwatt,' Tom said.

'Sometimes. But who could be really him? And when I walk down a London street, no. Just sometimes when I paint, for seconds at a time, I've felt I'm him. And you know, I can talk easily now about it, and it's a pleasure, because I'm going to give it up, I hope.'

And that was perhaps a confession on the writing-table, Tom thought. A confession to whom?

Bernard put his arm over the back of his chair. 'And you know, my faking, my forgeries, have evolved in four or five years the way Derwatt's painting might have evolved. It's funny, isn't it?'

Tom didn't know what to say that would be correct, even respectful enough. 'Maybe it's not funny. You understood Derwatt. And critics have said the same thing, that the painting has developed.'

'You can't imagine how strange it is to paint like – Bernard Tufts. His painting hasn't developed as much. It's as if I'm faking Tufts now, because I'm painting the same Tufts as I did five years ago!' Bernard gave a real laugh. 'In a way, I have to make more of an effort to be myself than I do to be Derwatt. I *did*. And it was making me mad, you see. You can see that. I'd like to give myself a chance, if there's anything of me left.'

He meant give Bernard Tufts a chance, Tom knew. 'I'm positive that can be done. You should be the one that calls the tune.' Tom took his Gauloises from a pocket and offered Bernard one.

'I want to start with a clean slate. I intend to admit what I've done and start from there – or try to.'

'Oh, Bernard! You've got to get rid of *that* idea. You're not the only one involved. Think what it'd do to Jeff and Ed. All the pictures you've painted would – Really, Bernard, confess it to a priest, if you want to, but not the press. Or the English police.'

'You think I'm mad, I know. Well, I am sometimes. But I have only one life to lead. I've nearly ruined it. I don't intend to ruin the rest. And that's my affair, isn't it?'

Bernard's voice shook. Was he strong or weak, Tom wondered? 'I do understand,' Tom said gently.

'I don't mean to sound dramatic, but I have to see if people will accept me – see if they'll forgive me, if you like.'

They won't, Tom thought. The world absolutely wouldn't. Would it smash Bernard if he said this? Probably. Bernard might commit suicide instead of making a confession. Tom cleared his throat and tried to think, but nothing, nothing came to him.

'For another thing, I think Cynthia would like it if I made a clean breast of things. She loves me. I love her. I know she didn't want to see me just now. In London Ed told me. I don't blame her. Jeff and Ed presenting me like an invalid case: "Come to see Bernard, he needs you!"' Bernard said in a mincing voice. 'What woman would?' Bernard looked at Tom and opened his arms, smiling. 'You see how much good the rain did me, Tom? It did everything but wash away my sins.'

His laugh came again, and Tom envied him the carefreeness of it.

'Cynthia's the only woman I've ever loved. I don't mean – Well, she's had an affair or two since me, I'm sure. I was the one who more or less ended it. I got so – nervous, even scared in a way, when I began imitating Derwatt.' Bernard gulped. 'But I know she still loves me – if I'm *me*. Can you understand that?'

'I certainly can. Of course. Are you writing to Cynthia now?'

Bernard waved an arm at the sheets of paper and smiled. 'No, I'm writing – to anyone. It's just a statement. It's for the press or anyone.'

And that had to be stopped. Tom said calmly, 'I wish you'd think things over for a few days, Bernard.'

'Haven't I had enough time to think?'

Tom tried to think of something stronger, clearer to say to Bernard that would stop him, but half his mind was on Murchison, on the possibility of the police returning. How hard would they search here for clues? Would they look in the woods? Tom Ripley's reputation was already a bit – stained, perhaps, by the Dickie Greenleaf story. Though he'd been cleared of suspicion, he had for a time been under suspicion, there had been a story there, despite its happy ending. Why hadn't he put Murchison in the station wagon and driven him miles away to bury him, somewhere in the forest of Fontainebleau, camped out in the woods to get the job done, if he'd had to? 'Can we talk about it tomorrow?' Tom said. 'You might see things differently, Bernard.'

'Of course, we can talk about it any time. But I'm not going to feel any different tomorrow. I wanted to talk to you first, because you thought of the whole idea – of resurrecting Derwatt. I want to start with first things first, you see. I'm quite logical.' There was a touch of the insane in his dogmatic delivery of this, and Tom felt again a profound unease.

The telephone rang. There was a telephone in Tom's room, and the sound came clearly across the hall of the house.

Tom jumped up. 'You mustn't forget the others involved –'

'I won't drag you into it, Tom.'

'The telephone. Good night, Bernard,' Tom said quickly, and dashed across the hall to his room. He didn't want Chris to pick up the phone downstairs.

It was the police again. They apologized for ringing this late, but –

Tom said, 'I'm sorry, m'sieur, but could you ring back in perhaps five minutes? I am just now –'

The courteous voice said of course he could ring back.

Tom hung up and sank his face in his hands. He was sitting on the edge of the bed. He got up and shut his door. Events were getting a bit ahead of him. He'd been in a hurry about burying Murchison because of the damned Count. What a mistake! The Seine, the Loing were snaking around everywhere in the district, there were quiet bridges, quiet especially after one o'clock in the morning. The telephone call from the police could mean only bad news. Mrs Murchison – Harriet, had Murchison said her name was? – might have engaged an American or English detective to find her husband. She knew what Murchison's mission had been, to find out if a painting by an important artist was a forgery or not. Wouldn't she suspect foul play? If Mme Annette was questioned, wouldn't she say that she hadn't actually *seen* M. Murchison leave the house Thursday afternoon?

If the police wanted to see him tonight, Chris might volunteer the information about the grave-like patch in the woods. Tom envisaged Chris saying in English, 'Why don't you tell them about . . .' and Tom wouldn't be able to say something else to the police in French, because Chris would probably want to watch them digging.

The telephone rang again, and Tom answered it calmly.

'Hello, M. Reeply. The Prefecture of Melun here. We have had a telephone call from London. In the matter of M. Murchison, Mme Murchison has contacted the London Metropolitan Police, which wants us to provide all the information we can by tonight. The English Inspector will arrive tomorrow morning. Now, if you please, did M. Murchison make any telephone calls from your house? We should like to trace the numbers.'

'I can't remember,' Tom said, 'that he made a single telephone call. But I was not in the house all the time.' They could look at his telephone account, Tom thought, but let them think of that.

A moment later, they had hung up.

It was unfriendly, a little off-putting that the London police hadn't rung Tom direct to ask questions, Tom thought. He felt the London police were already treating him as suspect, and preferred to get information through official channels. Somehow

Tom feared an English detective more than a French detective, although for overall minutiae and sticklership, he had to give the French high marks.

He had to do two things, get the body out of the woods and Chris out of the house. And Bernard? Tom's brain almost boggled at the task.

He went downstairs.

Chris was reading, but he yawned and stood up. 'I was just going to turn in. How's Bernard? I thought he was better at dinner.'

'Yes, I think so, too.' Tom hated what he had to say, or hinting at it, which was worse.

'I found a time-table by the telephone. There's a train in the morning at nine fifty-two and one at eleven thirty-two. I can get a taxi from here to the station.'

Tom was relieved. There were earlier trains, but it was impossible for him to propose them. 'Whichever one you want. I'll take you to the station. I don't know what to make of Bernard, but I think he wants to be alone with me for a couple of days.'

'I only hope it's safe,' Chris said earnestly. 'You know, I thought of staying on a day or so just to give you a hand with him, in case you needed it.' Chris was speaking softly. 'There was a fellow in Alaska – I did my service there – who cracked up, and he acted a lot like Bernard. Just all of a sudden he turned violent, socking everybody.'

'Well, I doubt that Bernard will. Maybe you and your friend Gerald can visit after Bernard leaves. Or after you get back from the Rhineland.'

Chris brightened at this prospect.

When Chris had gone upstairs (he wanted the 9.52 a.m. train tomorrow), Tom walked up and down the living-room. It was five minutes to midnight. Something had to be done about Murchison's corpse tonight. Quite a task for one person to dig it up in the dark, load it in the station wagon and dump it – where? Off some little bridge, maybe. Tom pondered the idea of asking Bernard to help him. Would Bernard blow up or be co-operative – confronted by reality? Tom sensed that he wasn't going to be able to persuade Bernard not to confess, as things were. Mightn't the corpse shock him into a sense of the serious-ness of the situation?

It was a hell of a question.

Would Bernard take the leap into faith as Kierkegaard put it? Tom smiled as the phrase crossed his mind. But he had taken the leap when he had dashed to London to impersonate Der-watt. That leap had succeeded. He had taken another leap in killing Murchison. To hell with it. Nothing ventured, nothing gained.

Tom went to the stairway, but had to slow his pace because of the pain in his ankle. In fact, he paused with his bad foot on the first step, his hand on the gilt angel that formed the newel post. It had occurred to him that if Bernard balked tonight, Ber-nard would have to be disposed of, too. Killed. It was a sickening thought. Tom did not want to kill Bernard. Perhaps he would not even be able to. So if Bernard refused to help him, and added *Murchison* to his confession –

Tom climbed the stairs.

The hall was dark, except for the little light that came from Tom's own room. Bernard's light was off, and Chris's seemed to be too, but that didn't mean Chris was asleep. It was difficult for Tom to lift his hand and knock on Bernard's door. He knocked gently, because Chris's room was only eight feet away, and he did not want Chris to eavesdrop by way of protecting him from a possible assault by Bernard.

12

Bernard did not answer, and Tom opened the door and went in and closed it behind him.

'Bernard?'

'Hm-m? – Tom?'

'Yes. Excuse me. Can I put on the light?'

'Of course.' Bernard sounded quite calm, and found the bed-side light himself. 'What's the matter?'

'Oh, nothing. I mean, it's just that I've got to talk to you and quietly, because I don't want Chris to hear.' Tom pulled the straight chair rather close to Bernard's bed, and sat down. 'Bernard – I'm in trouble, and I'd like you to give me a hand, if you will.'

Bernard frowned with attention. He reached for his pack of Capstan Full-strength and lit one. 'What's the trouble?'

'Murchison is dead,' Tom said softly. 'That's why you don't have to worry about him.'

'Dead?' Bernard frowned. 'Why didn't you tell me?'

'Because – I killed him. Here in the cellar.'

Bernard gasped. '*You* did? You don't mean that, Tom !'

'Sh-h.' Oddly, Tom had the feeling Bernard was more sane than he at the moment. It made things more difficult for Tom, because he had anticipated a more bizarre reaction on Bernard's part. 'I had to kill him – here – and he's buried now in the woods behind the house. My problem is, I've got to get him away from here tonight. The police are already telephoning, you see. Tomorrow they may come and look around.'

'Killed him?' Bernard said, still incredulous. 'But why?'

Tom sighed, shuddering. 'First, need I point out, he was going to explode Derwatt? Derwatt Ltd. Second and worse, he recognized me down in the cellar. He recognized my hands. He said, "You pretended to be Derwatt in London." It was suddenly all up. I had no intention of killing him when I brought him here.'

'Dead,' Bernard repeated, stunned.

Tom was impatient as the minutes slipped by. 'Believe me. I did my best to make him let things alone. I even told him you were the forger, you the fellow he'd talked to in the bar of the Mandeville. Yes, I saw you there,' Tom said before Bernard could speak. 'I told you weren't going to paint any more Derwatts. I asked him to let you alone. Murchison refused. So – will you help me get the corpse off my grounds?' Tom glanced at the door. It was still closed, and there had been no sound from the hall.

Bernard got slowly out of bed. 'And what do you want me to do?'

Tom stood up. 'In about twenty minutes, I'd be grateful if you gave me a hand. I'd like to take it away in the station wagon.

It'll be much easier if there're two of us. I really can't do the whole thing alone. He's heavy.' Tom felt better, because he was talking the same way he often thought. 'If you don't want to help me, all right. I can try it alone, but –'

'All right, I'll help you.'

Bernard spoke in a resigned way, as if he meant it, yet Tom mistrusted it. Was Bernard going to have some unpredictable reaction later, in half an hour? Bernard's tone had been that of a saint saying to – well, someone superior to a saint, 'I will follow, wherever you lead.'

'Could you put some clothes on? Those trousers I gave you today. Try to be quiet. Chris mustn't hear us.'

'Right.'

'Can you be downstairs – outside the front steps in fifteen minutes?' Tom looked at his watch. 'Twelve twenty-seven now.'

'Yes.'

Tom went downstairs and unlocked the front door, which Mme Annette had locked for the night. Then he hobbled upstairs to his room where he took off his house-slippers and put on shoes and a jacket. He went back downstairs and picked up his car keys from the hall table. He turned off the living-room lights, except one: he often left one lamp burning all night. Then he took a raincoat and pulled on some rubber boots, which were on the floor in the spare loo, over the shoes. He took a torch from the hall-table drawer, and also a lantern which was in the spare loo. This light could stand upright on the ground.

He drove the Renault station wagon out, and into the lane that led to the woods. He used only his parking lights and having reached what he thought was the right spot, he cut them. He went into the woods with his torch, found the grave, then holding the torch so its beam was concealed as much as possible, he made his way to the toolshed, and got the shovel and the fork. These he took back to the muddy splotch which was Murchison's grave. Then he walked calmly, thinking of conserving strength, back along the lane to the house. Tom expected Bernard to be late, and was fully braced for him not to appear at all.

Bernard was there, standing like a statue in the dark hall, in his own suit that had been wet a few hours ago, but which Bernard had draped over the long radiator in his room, Tom had noticed.

Tom gestured, and Bernard followed him.

In the lane, Tom saw that Chris's window was still dark. Only Bernard's light was on. 'It's not far. That's the trouble!' Tom said, crazily amused suddenly. He handed Bernard the fork and kept the shovel, because he thought the shovel work was harder. 'I regret to say it's pretty deep.'

Bernard went at the task with his odd resignation, but his plunges with the fork were strong and effective. Bernard tossed the earth out, but soon he was merely loosening it, and Tom was standing in the trench shovelling out the soil as fast as he could.

'I'll take a break,' Tom said at last, but his break was carrying two big stones, each of which weighed over thirty pounds, to the back of the car. He had opened the drop-door, and Tom pushed the stones in.

Bernard had reached the body. Tom got down and tried to use his shovel to prise it up, but the trench was too narrow. They both, feet apart on either side of the body, hauled at the ropes. Tom's broke or came undone, and he cursed and tied it again, while Bernard held the torch. Something might have been sucking Murchison's body into the earth: it was like some force working against them. Tom's hands were muddy and sore, maybe bleeding.

'It's very heavy,' said Bernard.

'Yes. We'd better say "one, two, three", and really give it a heave.'

'Yes.'

'One – two – ' They were braced. '– three! *Oop!*'

Murchison went up onto ground level. Bernard had had the heavier end, the shoulders.

'The rest ought to be easier,' Tom said, just to be saying something.

They got the body into the car. The tarpaulin was still dripping clods, and the front of Tom's raincoat was a mess.

'Got to put the dirt back.' Tom's voice was hoarse with exhaustion.

Again this was the easiest part, and Tom for good measure pulled a couple of blown-down branches over it. Bernard casually dropped his fork to the ground, and Tom said, 'Let's put the tools back in the car.'

So they did. Then Tom and Bernard got into the car, and Tom drove in reverse, regretting the whine of the motor, towards the road. There was nowhere to turn in the lane. Then to Tom's horror, he saw Chris's light come on, just as he was backing into the road to start forward. Tom had glanced up at the dark window – Chris had a side window as well – and the light had blinked on then, as if in greeting. Tom said nothing to Bernard. There was no streetlight here, and Tom hoped that Chris could not make out the colour (dark green) of the car, though Tom's parking lights were on now, out of necessity.

'Where're we going?' Bernard asked.

'I know a spot eight kilometres from here. A bridge –'

There was not another car on the road just now, which was not unusual at the hour of 1.50 a.m. Tom had driven back from enough late dinner-parties to know that.

'Thanks, Bernard. Everything is fine,' Tom said.

Bernard was silent.

They came to the place Tom had thought of. It was beside a village called Voisy, a name Tom had never paid much attention to until tonight, when he had to pass the village marker and go through the village in order to get to the bridge he had recalled. The river was the Loing, Tom thought, which flowed into the Seine. Not that Murchison was going to flow very far with those stones on him. There was a dim and economical streetlight at this end of the bridge, but none at the other end which was black. Tom drove the car to the other end, and a few yards past the bridge. In the dark, with some aid from Tom's torch, they shoved the stones into the tarpaulin and re-tied the ropes.

'Now we drop it,' Tom said softly.

Bernard was moving with a calm efficiency, and seemed to know exactly what to do. The two of them carried the body, even with the stones, with fair ease. The wooden parapet of the bridge was four feet high. Tom, walking backward, looked all around, at the dark village behind him where only two street-lights showed, ahead where the bridge disappeared into blackness.

'I think we can risk the middle,' Tom said.

So they went to the middle of the bridge, and set the corpse down for a few moments until they gathered strength. Then they bent and lifted, and with a mutual heave they raised it high and over it went.

The splash was shattering – giving the effect of a *boom* in the silence, like a cannon that might awaken the village – and then came a hail of splatters. They walked back towards the car.

'Don't run,' Tom said, perhaps unnecessarily. Had they any energy left?

They got into the car and started off straight ahead, Tom neither knowing nor caring where they were going.

'It's finished !' Tom said. 'The damned thing's off our hands !' He felt wonderfully happy, light and free. 'I didn't tell you, I think, Bernard,' Tom said in a gay tone, his throat now not even dry, 'I've told the police I dropped Murchison at Orly on Thursday. I did drop his luggage there. So if Murchison didn't take his plane, it's not my fault is it? Ha !' Tom laughed, as he had often laughed alone, with similar relief after ghastly moments. 'By the way, "The Clock" was stolen at Orly. Murchison had it with his suitcase. I'd imagine anyone seeing Derwatt's signature would hang onto the picture and say nothing about it !'

But was Bernard exactly with him? Bernard said nothing.

It was starting to rain again ! Tom felt like cheering. The rain might, probably *would* erase his car tracks on the lane near his house, and would certainly aid the appearance of the now empty grave.

'I have to get out,' Bernard said, reaching for the door handle.

'What?'

'I feel sick.'

As soon as he could, Tom pulled closer to the edge of the road and stopped. Bernard got out.

'Want me to go with you?' Tom asked quickly.

'No, thanks.' Bernard went a couple of yards to the right,

where a dark bank rose abruptly a few feet high. He bent over.

Tom felt sorry for him. Himself so merry and well, and Bernard sick at his stomach. Bernard stayed two minutes, three, four, Tom thought.

A car was approaching from behind, moving at an easy speed. Tom had an impulse to douse his lights, but left them as they were, normal headlights on, but not the brightest. Due to a curve in the road, the car's headlights swept over Bernard's figure for a second. A police car, for God's sake! The roof had a blue light on it. The police car veered around Tom's car and went on, at the same easy speed. Tom relaxed. Thank goodness. They had no doubt thought Bernard was stopping to pee, and in France that was certainly not against the law at the edge of a country road, even in plain view in broad daylight. Bernard said nothing about the car when he got back in, and neither did Tom.

Back at the house, Tom drove quietly into the garage. He took out the shovel and fork and leaned them against a wall, then wiped out the back of the car with a rag. He closed the drop-door till it half-latched, not wanting to make a bang by closing it. Bernard was waiting. Tom gestured, and they went out of the garage. Tom closed the doors and gently snapped the padlock.

At the front door, they took off their shoes and carried them. Tom noticed that Chris's light had not been on when the car approached the house. Now Tom used his torch and they climbed the stairs. Tom motioned for Bernard to go to his own room, and signalled that he would be back in a moment.

Tom emptied his raincoat pockets and dropped the raincoat in the tub. He rinsed his boots under the tub tap, and stuck the boots in a closet. He could later wash his raincoat and hang it in the closet, too, so Mme Annette would not see it in the morning.

Then he went silently, in pyjamas and house-slippers now, to see Bernard.

Bernard was standing in stocking feet, smoking a cigarette. His soiled jacket was over a straight chair.

'Not much more can happen to that suit,' Tom said. 'Let me take care of it.'

Bernard moved slowly, but he moved. He took off his trousers and handed them to Tom. Tom took the trousers and jacket into his room. He could wipe off the mud later, and get it to a fast cleaners. It was not a good suit, which was typical of Bernard. Jeff or Ed had told Tom that Bernard did not accept all the money they wanted to give him from Derwatt Ltd. Tom went back to Bernard's room. It was the first time Tom appreciated the solidity of his parquet floors : they didn't creak.

'Can I bring you a drink, Bernard? I think you could use one.' Now he could afford to be seen downstairs, Tom thought, by Mme Annette or even Chris. He could even say he and Bernard had had a whim to take a little drive, and they'd just come back.

'No, thanks,' Bernard said.

Tom wondered if Bernard could get to sleep, but he was afraid to propose anything else, like a sedative or even hot chocolate, because he thought Bernard would say again, 'No, thanks.' Tom said, whispering, 'I'm sorry I let you in for this. Will you sleep all morning if you feel like it? Chris is leaving in the morning.'

'All right.' Bernard's face was a pale olive colour. He did not look at Tom. His lips had a firm line, like lips that seldom smiled or spoke – and now his mouth looked disappointed.

He looked betrayed, Tom thought. 'I'll take care of your shoes, too.' Tom picked them up.

In his bathroooom – his room door and bathroom door closed now, against Chris, possibly – Tom washed his own raincoat, and sponged Bernard's suit. He rinsed Bernard's desert boots and put them on a newspaper near the radiator in the loo. Mme Annette, though she brought his coffee and did his bed, did not go into his bathroom except perhaps once a week to give it a tidying, and the serious cleaning woman, a Mme Clusot, came once a week and was due today, in the afternoon.

At last, Tom took care of his own hands, which were not as bad as they felt. He put Nivea on them. In a curious way, he felt that he had dreamed the last hour or so – gone through the motions of it somewhere, which had made his hands sore – and that what had happened was not real.

The telephone gave an annunciatory *ping*. Tom leapt for it, catching it midway in its peal, which seemed shockingly loud.

It was nearly 3 a.m.

Beep-beep ... burr-r-r-r ... dup-dup-dup ... beep?

Submarine sounds. Where was this call coming from?

'*Vous êtes ... ne quittez pas ... Athènes vous appelle ...*'

Heloise.

'Ello, *Tome! ... Tome!*'

That was all Tom could understand for a maddening several seconds. 'Can you talk louder?' he said in French.

Heloise was telling him, he barely gathered, that she was unhappy and bored, *terriblement ennuyée*. Something else, maybe someone, was absolutely *disgusting* also.

'... this woman who is called Norita ...' Lolita?

'Come home, darling! I miss you!' Tom yelled in English. 'To hell with those stinks!'

'I know what I should do.' This came clearly. 'I was trying since two hours to reach you. Even the telephone does not work here.'

'It's not supposed to work anywhere. It's just a device to extort money.' Tom was pleased to hear her laugh a little – like a siren laughing beneath the sea.

'Do you love me?'

'Of course I love you!'

Just as audibility was improving, they were cut off. Tom was sure Heloise had not hung up.

The telephone did not ring again. It was 5 a.m. in Greece, Tom supposed. Had Heloise rung from an Athens hotel? From that crazy yacht? He wanted very much to see her. He had grown used to her, and he missed her. Was that loving someone? Or marriage? But he wanted to clear away the present débris first. Heloise was rather amoral, but she would not be able to take all this. And of course she knew nothing about the Derwatt forgeries.

13

Tom awakened groggily at Mme Annette's tap at his door. She brought his cup of black coffee.

'Good morning, M. Tome! It's a beautiful day today!'

The sun was indeed shining, a fantastic change from yesterday. Tom sipped his coffee, letting its black magic creep through him, then he got up and dressed.

Tom knocked on Chris's door. There was still time to catch the 9.52 train.

Chris was in bed with a large map spread against his knees. 'I decided to take the eleven thirty-two – if it's all right. I so enjoy loafing in bed like this for a few minutes.'

'Sure it's all right,' Tom said. 'You should've asked Mme Annette to bring you some coffee.'

'Oh, that's *too* much.' Chris sprang out of bed. 'I thought I'd take a quick walk.'

'Okay. See you later, then.'

Tom went downstairs. He reheated the coffee and poured another cup in the kitchen and stood looking out the window, sipping it. He saw Chris walking from the house, opening the big gates. He turned left in the direction of the town. He was probably going to pick up a café au lait and a croissant in a bar-café, French style.

Evidently Bernard was still sleeping, which was all to the good.

At ten past nine, the telephone rang. An English voice spoke carefully: 'This is Detective-Inspector Webster, London Metropolitan Police. Is Mr Ripley there?'

Was this the theme song of his existence? 'Yes, speaking.'

'I'm ringing from Orly. I'd like very much to see you this morning, if possible.'

Tom wanted to say that this afternoon would be more convenient, but his usual boldness was not with him just then, and he felt, too, that the Inspector might suspect he would spend the morning trying to hide something. 'This morning would be quite all right. Are you coming by train?'

'I thought I'd take a taxi,' the voice said casually. 'It doesn't seem all that far. How long should it take by taxi?'

'About an hour.'

'I'll see you in about an hour then.'

Chris would still be here. Tom poured another cup of coffee and took it up for Bernard. He would have preferred to keep Bernard's presence a secret from Inspector Webster, but under the circumstances, and also not knowing what Chris might blurt out, Tom thought it wisest not to try to conceal Bernard.

Bernard was awake, lying on his back, with his head propped on two pillows and his fingers interlaced under his chin. He might have been in the middle of some matutinal meditation.

'Morning, Bernard. Like some coffee?'

'Yes, thank you.'

'There's a man from the London police arriving in an hour. He may want to talk with you. It's about Murchison, of course.'

'Yes,' Bernard said.

Tom waited until Bernard had had a sip or two of coffee. 'I didn't put any suger in it. I didn't know if you liked it.'

'Doesn't matter. That's excellent coffee.'

'Now, Bernard, it's obviously best if you say you never met Murchison, never saw him. You never had that talk with him in the Mandeville bar. Do you understand?' Tom hoped it was penetrating.

'Yes.'

'And also, you never even *heard* of Murchison, even through Jeff and Ed. As you know, you're not supposed to be a very close friend of Jeff or Ed now. You all know one another, but Jeff and Ed wouldn't have troubled to tell *you* there was an American who – suspected "The Clock" wasn't genuine.'

'Yes,' Bernard said. 'Yes, of course.'

'And – the easiest thing to remember, because it's true,' Tom continued, as if he were talking to a class of schoolchildren who were not listening very carefully, 'is that you arrived here yesterday afternoon, a good twenty-four hours after Murchison left to go to London. Naturally, you never saw him or heard of him. All right, Bernard?'

'All right,' Bernard said. He was propped on one elbow.

'Want something to eat? Eggs? I can bring you a croissant. Mme Annette's been out and bought some.'

'No, thanks.'

Tom went downstairs.

Mme Annette was coming in from the kitchen. 'M. Tome, look.' She showed him the front page of her newspaper. 'Is this not the gentleman, the M. Murcheeson who visited Thursday? It says they are looking for M. Murcheeson!'

A la recherche de M. Murcheeson... Tom looked at the two-column-wide photograph of Murchison, full face, faintly smiling, in the lower left corner of *Le Parisien – Edition Seine et Marne.* 'Yes, it is,' Tom said. It read:

Thomas F. Murchison, 52, American, has been declared missing since Thursday afternoon, October 17th. His suitcase was found at the departure door at Orly Airport, but he did not board his airplane for London. M. Murchison is a business executive of New York, and had been visiting a friend in the region of Melun. His wife Harriet in America has begun inquiries with the aid of French and English police.

Tom was thankful that they had not mentioned his name.

Chris came in the front door, with a couple of magazines in his hand, but not a newspaper. 'Hello, Tom! Madame! It's a beautiful day!'

Tom greeted him, then said to Mme Annette, 'I had thought by now he would have been found. But in fact – an Englishman is coming this morning to ask me some questions.'

'Oh, yes? This morning?'

'In half an hour or so.'

'What a mystery!' she said.

'What's a mystery?' Chris asked Tom.

'Murchison. A picture of him in today's paper.'

Chris looked at the photograph with interest, and slowly read aloud some of the phrases underneath it, translating. 'Gosh! Still missing!'

'Madame Annette,' Tom said, 'I am not sure if the Englishman will stay for lunch. Could you manage four?'

'But yes, M'sieur Tome.' She went off to the kitchen.

'What Englishman?' Chris asked. 'Another one?'

Chris's French was improving rapidly, Tom thought. 'Yes, he's coming to ask about Murchison. You know – if you want the eleven-thirty train –'

'Well – could I stay? There's a train just after twelve, and of course some trains this afternoon. I'm curious about Murchison, what they've found out. Naturally – I wouldn't stay in the living-room when you spoke with him, if you want to be alone.'

Tom was irked, but he said, 'Why not? No secrets.'

The Detective-Inspector arrived by taxi around 10.30. Tom had forgot to tell him how to find the house, but he said he had asked at the post office for the house of M. Ripley.

'What a lovely place you have!' said the Inspector cheerfully. He was about forty-five, in plain clothes. He had black, thinning hair and a slight paunch, and wore black-rimmed glasses through which he peered alertly and courteously. In fact his pleasant smile appeared to be fixed. 'Been living here long?'

'Three years,' Tom said. 'Won't you sit down?' Tom had opened the door, since Mme Annette had not seen the taxi come up, and Tom now took the Inspector's coat.

The Inspector carried a neat slender black case of the kind that could hold a suit, and this he took with him to the sofa, as if he were not in the habit of parting with it. 'Well – first things first. When did you last see Mr Murchison?'

Tom sat down on a straight chair. 'Last Thursday. About three-thirty in the afternoon. I took him to Orly. He was going to London.'

'I know.' Webster opened his black case a little and took a notebook from it, then pulled a pen from his pocket. He wrote notes for a few seconds. 'He was in good spirits?' he asked, smiling. He reached for a cigarette from his jacket pocket, and lit it quickly.

'Yes.' Tom started to say he had just made him a present of a nice Margaux, but he didn't want to refer to his cellar.

'And he had his picture with him. Called "The Clock", I think.'

'Yes. Wrapped in brown paper.'

'Apparently stolen at Orly, yes. This was the picture Mr Murchison thinks is a forgery?'

'He said he suspected it – at first.'

'How well do you know Mr Murchison? For how long?'

Tom explained. 'I remembered seeing him go into the back office at the gallery, where Derwatt was, I'd heard. So – when I saw Mr Murchison in the bar of my hotel that evening, I spoke to him. I wanted to ask him what Derwatt was like.'

'I see. And then?'

'We had a drink together, and Murchison told me his idea that a few of Derwatt's paintings were being forged – lately. I said I had a couple of Derwatts in my house in France, and I asked if he wanted to come over and see them. So we came over together Wednesday afternoon and he spent the night here.'

The Detective-Inspector was making a note or two. 'You went over to London especially for the Derwatt show?'

'Oh, no.' Tom smiled a little. 'For two things. Half for the Derwatt show, I admit, and the other half because my wife's birthday is in November, and she likes things from England. Sweaters and trousers. Carnaby Street. I bought something in the Burlington Arcade –' Tom glanced at the stairway and thought of going up to fetch it, the gold monkey pin, but checked himself. 'I didn't buy a Derwatt this time, but I was thinking of buying "The Tub". Just about the only one not sold then.'

'Did you – uh – ask Mr Murchison over with an idea that your paintings could be forgeries also?'

Tom hesitated. 'I admit I was curious. But I never doubted mine. And after seeing my two, Mr Murchison thought they were genuine.' Tom certainly wasn't going to go into Murchison's lavender theory. And Inspector Webster did not seem much interested in Tom's Derwatts, not enough to do more than turn his head to look for a few seconds at 'The Red Chairs' behind him, and then at 'Man in Chair' in front of him.

'Not my forte, I'm afraid. Modern painting. You live by yourself, Mr Ripley? You and your wife?'

'Yes, except for my housekeeper Mme Annette. My wife's in Greece just now.'

'I'd like to meet your housekeeper,' said the Inspector, still smiling.

Tom made a start towards the kitchen to fetch Mme Annette, but just then Chris came down the stairs. 'Ah, Chris. This is Detective-Inspector Webster. From London. My guest Christopher Greenleaf.'

'How do you do?' Chris said, extending a hand and looking awed at meeting a member of the London Police.

'How do you do?' Webster said pleasantly, leaning forward to shake Chris's hand. 'Greenleaf. Richard Greenleaf. He was a friend of yours, was he not, Mr Ripley?'

'Yes. And Chris is his cousin.' Webster must have looked that up recently, Tom thought, must have delved into files to see if Tom Ripley had any record, because Tom couldn't imagine anyone remembering Dickie's name over a period of six years. 'If you'll excuse me, I'll call Mme Annette.'

Mme Annette was peeling something at the sink. Tom asked if she could come in and meet the gentleman from London. 'He probably speaks French.'

Then, as Tom went back into the living-room, Bernard was coming downstairs. He wore Tom's trousers, and a sweater without a shirt. Tom introduced him to Webster. 'Mr Tufts is a painter. From London.'

'Oh,' said Webster. 'Did you meet Mr Murchison while you were here?'

'No,' Bernard said, sitting on one of the straight yellow-upholstered chairs. 'I only arrived yesterday.'

Mme Annette came in.

Detective-Inspector Webster stood up, smiled, and said, 'Enchanté, madame.' He continued in perfect French though with a determined British accent, 'I am here to inquire about Mr Thomas Murchison who has disappeared.'

'Ah, yes! I read about it only this morning in the newspaper,' Mme Annette said. 'He has not been found?'

'No, madame.' Another smile, as if he were talking about something much more amusing. 'It seems that you and M. Ripley were the last people to see him. Or were you here, Mr Greenleaf?' he asked Chris in English.

Chris stammered, but was indisputably sincere. 'I never met Mr Murchison, no.'

'What time did M. Murchison leave the house on Thursday, Mme Annette? Do you remember?'

'Ooh, perhaps – It was just after lunch. I prepared lunch a little early. Let us say two-thirty he left.'

Tom remained silent. Mme Annette was correct.

The Inspector said to Tom, 'Did he mention any friends at all in Paris? Excuse me, madame, I can just as well speak in French.'

But the conversation went on in both languages, sometimes Tom, sometimes Webster translating for Mme Annette, because Webster wanted her contributions, if she had any.

Murchison had not mentioned anyone in Paris, and Tom said he did not think Murchison had intended to meet anyone at Orly.

'You see, the disappearance of Mr Murchison *and* his painting – this might be connected,' Inspector Webster said. (Tom explained to Mme Annette that a painting Murchison had had with him had been stolen at Orly, and Mme Annette, happily remembered seeing it standing against the gentleman's suitcase in the hall before he left. She must have had a very brief glimpse, Tom thought, but it was a piece of luck. Webster might have suspected that Tom had destroyed it.) 'The Derwatt corporation, as I think I have every reason to call it, is a large one. There's more to it than Derwatt himself, as a painter. Derwatt's friends, Constant and Banbury, own the Buckmaster Gallery as a sort of sideline to their own work, journalism and photography respectively. There's the Derwatt art supplies company. There's the Derwatt Art School in Perugia. If we throw forgery into all this, then we've really got something!' He turned to Bernard. 'I think you know Mr Constant and Mr Banbury, don't you, Mr Tufts?'

And Tom felt another sink of alarm, because Webster really must have dug for that one: for years Ed Banbury hadn't mentioned Bernard's name in his articles as being one of the original group of Derwatt's friends.

'Yes, I know them,' Bernard said in a somewhat dazed manner, but at least he was unruffled.

'Did you speak to Derwatt in London?' Tom asked the Inspector.

'He can't be found!' Inspector Webster said, positively beaming now. 'Not that I was particularly trying to find him, but one of my colleagues was – after Mr Murchison's disappearance. What is even more curious –' here he switched to French to include Mme Annette – 'there's no record that Derwatt entered England lately from Mexico or anywhere else. Not just in the last days, when presumably he arrived in England, but for years back. In fact the last record of the Emigration Bureau says that Philip Derwatt left the country six years ago bound for Greece. We have no record that he ever returned. As you perhaps know, Derwatt was believed to have drowned or committed suicide somewhere in Greece.'

Bernard sat forward, forearms on his knees. Was he rallying to the challenge, or about to blurt out all?

'Yes. I've heard that.' Tom said to Mme Annette, 'We speak about Derwatt the painter – his presumed suicide.'

'Yes, madame,' Webster said courteously, 'excuse us for a moment. Anything important, I shall say in French.' Then to Tom, 'So it means Derwatt entered and maybe even left England like the Scarlet Pimpernel or a ghost.' He chuckled. 'But you, Mr Tufts, you knew Derwatt in the old days, I understand. Did you see him in London?'

'No, I didn't.'

'But you went to his show, I suppose?' Webster's smile was in maniacal contrast to Bernard's gloom.

'No. I may go later,' Bernard said solmenly. 'I become – upset about anything to do with Derwatt.'

Webster seemed to look Bernard over with a new eye. 'Why?'

'I'm – very fond of him. I know he doesn't like publicity. I thought – when all the fuss is over, I'll go to see him before he goes back to Mexico.'

Webster laughed and slapped his thigh. 'Well, if you can find him tell us where he is. We'd like to speak to him on this matter of possible forgery. I've spoken to Mr Banbury and Mr

Constant. They saw "The Clock" and said it was genuine, but of course they might say that, if I may say so,' he added with a smiling glance at Tom, 'because they sold it. They also said Derwatt identified it positively as his own. But after all I've only – now – Mr Banbury's and Mr Constant's word for that, since I can't find Derwatt or Mr Murchison. It would be interesting if Derwatt had disowned it, or maybe was doubtful about it, and – Oh, well, I'm not writing mystery stories, even in my imagination!' Webster gave a hearty laugh, the corners of his mouth went up merrily, and he rolled a little on the sofa. His laugh was infectious and attractive, despite Webster's oversized and somewhat stained teeth.

Tom knew that Webster had been going to say: the Buckmaster Gallery people might have seen fit to shut Derwatt up somehow, or spirit him away. Shut Murchison up, too. Tom said, 'But Mr Murchison told me about his conversation with Derwatt. He said Derwatt acknowledged the painting. What worried Mr Murchison is that he thought Derwatt might've forgotten painting it. Or should I say *not* painting it. But Derwatt seems to have remembered it.' Now Tom laughed.

Detective-Inspector Webster looked at Tom and blinked, and kept what Tom felt was a polite silence. It was the same as saying, 'And now I have *your* word, which might not be worth much.' Webster finally said, 'I'm fairly sure someone for some reason thought it worth while to get rid of Thomas Murchison. What else can I think?' He translated this politely to Mme Annette.

Mme Annette said, *'Tiens!'* and Tom sensed her *frisson* of horror, though he did not glance at her.

Tom was glad that Webster didn't know that he knew Jeff and Ed, even slightly. It was funny Webster hadn't asked directly if he knew them, Tom thought. Or had Jeff and Ed already told him they knew Tom Ripley *slightly*, because he'd bought two pictures from them? 'Mme Annette, perhaps we might have some coffee. Can I offer you some coffee, Inspector, or a drink?'

'I saw some Dubonnet on your cart. I'd love some with a little ice and a lemon peel, if it's not too much trouble.'

Tom conveyed this to Mme Annette.

Nobody wanted coffee. Chris, leaning on the back of a chair near the french windows, did not want anything. He seemed rapt by the goings on.

'Exactly why,' Webster said, 'did Mr Murchison think his painting was a forgery?'

Tom sighed thoughtfully. The question had been addressed to him. 'He spoke about the spirit of it. Something also about the brushstrokes.' All vague.

'I'm quite sure,' Bernard said, 'that Derwatt would not countenance any forgery of his work. It's out of the question. If he thought "The Clock" was a forgery, he would've been the first to say so. He would've gone straight to the – I don't know – the police, I suppose.'

'Or the Buckmaster Gallery people,' said the Inspector.

'Yes,' said Bernard firmly. He stood up suddenly. 'Would you excuse me a minute?' He went off towards the stairs.

Mme Annette served Webster's drink.

Bernard came down with a thick brown notebook, quite worn, in which he was trying to find something as he walked across the room. 'If you want to know a little about Derwatt – I copied several things from his journals here. They were left in a suitcase in London when he went to Greece. I borrowed them for a while. His journals are chiefly about painting, the difficulties he had from day to day, but there's one entry – Yes, here it is. It's seven years old. This is really Derwatt. May I read it?'

'Yes, please do,' said Webster.

Bernard read, ' "There is no depression for the artist except that caused by a return to the Self." He spells Self with a capital, "The Self is that shy, vainglorious, egocentric, conscious magnifying glass which should never be looked at or through. A glimpse of it occurs in midstream sometimes, when it is a real horror, and between paintings, and on vacations – which should never be taken." ' Bernard laughed a little. ' "Such a depression consists in, besides wretchedness, vain questions such as what is it all about? And the exclamation, how badly I've fallen short! And the even worse discovery which I should have noticed long ago, I can't even depend on the people who are supposed to love me at a time when I need them. One doesn't need them when working well. I mustn't show myself in this moment of weakness. It will be, might be, thrown at me at some later date, like a crutch that should have been burnt – tonight. Let the memory of the black nights live only in me." Next paragraph,' said Bernard with reverence. ' "Do people who can really talk to each other without fear of reprisals have the best marriages? Where has kindness, forgiveness gone in the world? I find more in the faces of children who sit for me, gazing at me, watching me with innocent wide eyes that make no judgement. And friends? In the moment of grappling with the enemy Death, the potential suicide calls upon them. One by one, they are not at home, the telephone doesn't answer, or if it does, they are busy tonight – something quite important that they can't get away from – one is too proud to break down and say, 'I've got to see you tonight or else!' This is the last effort to make contact. How pitiable, how human, how noble – for what is more godlike than communication? The suicide knows that it has magical powers." ' Bernard closed the notebook. 'Of course he was rather young when he wrote that. Still not thirty.'

'Very moving,' said the Inspector. 'When did you say he wrote that?'

'Seven years ago. In November,' Bernard replied. 'He tried a suicide in London in October. He wrote this when he recovered. It wasn't a – bad bout. Sleeping pills.'

Tom listened uneasily. He hadn't heard of Derwatt's attempted suicide.

'Perhaps you think it melodramatic,' Bernard said to the Inspector. 'His journals weren't meant for anyone to read. The Buckmaster Gallery has the others. Unless Derwatt asked for them.' Bernard had begun to stammer, to look uncomfortable, probably because he was carefully trying to lie.

'He's the suicide type, then?' asked Webster.

'Oh, no! He has ups and downs. Perfectly normal. I mean, normal for a painter. At the time he wrote this, he was broke. A mural assignment had fallen through, and Derwatt had even finished the mural. The judges turned it down because there

were a couple of nudes in it. It was for a post office somewhere.'
Bernard laughed as if it were of no importance now.

And oddly, Webster's face was serious and thoughtful.

'I read this to show you that Derwatt is an honest man,' Bernard continued, undaunted. 'No dishonest man could have written this – or anything else that's in this book on the subject of painting – or simply life.' Bernard thumped the book with the back of his fingers. 'I was one of the ones who was too busy to see him when he needed me. I had no idea he was in such a bad state, you see. None of us did. He even needed money, and he was too proud to ask for any. Such a man doesn't steal, doesn't commit – I mean permit forgery.'

Tom thought Inspector Webster was going to say, with the solemnity proper to the occasion, 'I understand,' but he only sat with splayed knees, still thoughtful, with one hand turned inward on his thigh.

'I think that's great – what you read,' Chris said in the long silence. When no one said anything, Chris ducked his head, then lifted it again, as if ready to defend his opinion.

'Any more later entries?' Webster asked. 'I'm quite interested in what you read, but –'

'One or two,' Bernard said, leafing through the notebook. 'But again six years ago. For instance, "The eternal falling short is the only thing that takes the terror out of the act of creation." Derwatt has always been – respectful of his talent. It's very hard for me to put into words.'

'I think I understand,' said Webster.

Tom sensed at once Bernard's severe, almost personal disappointment. He glanced at Mme Annette, standing discreetly mid-distance from the arched doorway and the sofa.

'Did you speak with Derwatt at all in London, even by telephone?' Webster asked Bernard.

'No,' Bernard said.

'Or with Banbury or Constant either – while Derwatt was there?'

'No. I don't often see them.'

No one, Tom thought, could suspect Bernard of lying. He looked the essence of probity.

'But you're on good terms with them?' Webster asked, cocking his head, looking a little apologetic for the question. 'I understand you knew them years ago when Derwatt lived in London?'

'Oh, yes. Why not? But I don't go out much in London.'

'Do you know if Derwatt has any friends,' Webster continued to Bernard in his rather gentle voice, 'with a helicopter or a boat or a couple of boats who could've whisked him into England and out again – like a Siamese cat or a Pakistani?'

'I don't know. I certainly don't know of any.'

'Another question, surely you wrote to Derwatt in Mexico when you learned he was alive, didn't you?'

'No, I didn't.' Bernard gulped, and his rather large Adam's apple seemed in distress. 'As I said, I have little contact with – Jeff and Ed at the Buckmaster. And they don't know Derwatt's village, I know that, because the paintings are sent from Vera Cruz by boat. I thought Derwatt could've written to me, if he wanted to. Since he didn't, I didn't try to write to him. I felt –'

'Yes? You felt?'

'I felt Derwatt had been through enough. In his spirit. Maybe in Greece or before Greece. I thought it might have changed him and even soured him on his past friends, and if he didn't want to communicate with me – that was his way of doing things, seeing things.'

Tom could have wept for Bernard. He was doing his painful best. Bernard was as miserable as someone, who was not an actor, trying to act on a stage and hating every minute of it.

Inspector Webster glanced at Tom, then looked at Bernard. 'Strange – You mean Derwatt was in such –'

'I think Derwatt was really fed to the back teeth,' Bernard interrupted, 'fed up with people when he went to Mexico. If he wanted seclusion, I didn't make any effort to break it. I could have gone to Mexico and looked for him for ever – until I found him, I suppose.'

Tom almost believed the words he had just heard. He must believe them, he told himself. So he began to believe them. Tom went to the bar to refresh Webster's glass of Dubonnet.

'I see. And now – when Derwatt leaves again for Mexico, and perhaps he's already left, you won't know where to write to him?' asked Webster.

'Certainly not. I'll only know that he's painting and – I suppose, happy.'

'And the Buckmaster Gallery? They won't know where to find him either?'

Bernard shook his head again. 'As far as I know, they won't.'

'Where do they send the money that he earns?'

'I think – to a bank in Mexico City which forwards it to Derwatt.'

For this smooth reply, much thanks, thought Tom, as he bent to pour the Dubonnet. He left room in the glass for ice, and brought the bucket from the cart. 'Inspector, will you stay for lunch with us? I've told my housekeeper I expected you would stay.'

Mme Annette had slipped away to the kitchen.

'No, no, thank you very much,' Inspector Webster said with a smile. 'I've a lunch appointment with the police of Melun. The only time I could speak with them at leisure, I think. That's very French, isn't it? I'm due in Melun at a quarter to one, so the next thing I should do is ring for a taxi.'

Tom rang a Melun taxi service for a cab.

'I would like to look around your grounds,' said the Inspector. 'They look lovely!'

This might have been a change of mood, Tom thought, like someone asking to have a look at the roses by way of escaping a deadly tea conversation, but Tom didn't think it was that.

Chris would have followed them, so fascinated was he by the British police, but Tom gave him a negative glance, and went out with the Inspector alone. Down the stone steps where Tom had nearly fallen yesterday, only yesterday, in pursuit of the rain-soaked Bernard. The sun was half-hearted, the grass almost dry. The Inspector shoved his hands into his baggy trousers. Webster might not definitely suspect him of wrong-doing, Tom thought, but he sensed that he was not entirely in the clear. *I have done the State some disservice and they know't.* It was an odd morning for Shakespeare to be in his head.

'Apple trees. Peach. You must have a wonderful life here. Have you a profession, Mr Ripley?'

The question was sharp as that of an Immigration Inspector, but Tom was used to it by now. 'I garden, paint and study what I please. I have no occupation in the sense of having to go to Paris daily or even weekly. I seldom go to Paris.' Tom picked up a stone that was marring his lawn, and aimed it at a tree trunk. The stone hit the tree with a *tock*, and Tom suffered a twinge in his turned ankle.

'And woods. Are these yours?'

'No. As far as I know, they're communal. Or State. I sometimes get a bit of firewood from them, kindling, from trees that've already fallen. Do you want to take a little walk?' Tom indicated the lane.

Inspector Webster did go five or six steps farther towards the lane, into it, but having glanced down the lane, he turned. 'Not just now, thank you. I'd better be looking out for my taxi, I think.'

The taxi was at the door when they got back.

Tom said good-bye to the Inspector, and so did Chris. Tom wished him 'Bon appétit'.

'Fascinating!' Chris said. 'Really! Did you show him the grave in the woods? I wasn't looking out the windows, because I thought it would be rude.'

Tom smiled. 'No.'

'I started to mention it, then I thought I'd be an idiot if I did. Bringing in false clues.' Chris laughed. Even his teeth were like Dickie's, sharp eye-teeth and the rest set rather narrowly in his mouth. 'Imagine the Inspector digging it up looking for Murchison?' Chris went off again.

Tom laughed, too. 'Yes, if I dropped him at Orly, how'd he get back here?'

'Who killed him?' Chris asked.

'I don't think he's *dead*,' said Tom.

'Kidnapped?'

'I dunno. Maybe. Along with his painting. I dunno what to think. Where's Bernard?'

'He went upstairs.'

Tom went upstairs to see him. Bernard's door was closed. Tom knocked and heard a mumble in response.

Bernard was sitting on the edge of the bed with his hands clasped. He looked defeated and exhausted.

Tom said as cheerfully as he could, or as he dared, 'That went well, Bernard. *Tout va bien.*'

'I failed,' Bernard said, with miserable eyes.

'What're you talking about? You were marvellous.'

'I failed. That's why he asked all those questions about Derwatt. About how to find him in Mexico. Derwatt failed and so did I.'

14

It was one of the worst lunches Tom had ever sat through, matching almost the lunch with Heloise and her parents after Heloise had told them they were already married. But at least this lunch did not last so long. Bernard was in the hopeless depression of an actor, Tom supposed, who had just given a performance that he believed was rotten, so no words of comfort helped. Bernard was suffering the exhaustion – Tom had known it – of the player who has given his all.

'You know, last night,' Chris said, finishing the last of a glass of milk which he drank along with wine, 'I saw a car backing out of that lane in the woods. Must've been about one. I don't suppose it's important. The car was backing with the minimum of lights on, like someone who didn't want to be seen.'

Tom said, 'Probably – lovers.' He was afraid Bernard would react somehow – how? – to this, but Bernard might not have heard it.

Bernard excused himself and got up.

'Gosh, it's a shame he's so upset,' Chris said when Bernard was out of earshot. 'I'll take off right away. I hope I haven't stayed too long.'

Tom wanted to check on the afternoon trains, but Chris had a different idea. He preferred to hitch-hike to Paris. There was no dissuading him. Chris was convinced it would be an adventure. The alternative was a train close to five, Tom knew. Chris came downstairs with his suitcases, and went into the kitchen to say good-bye to Mme Annette.

Then they went out to the garage.

'Please,' Chris said, 'say good-bye for me to Bernard, would you? His door was shut. I had the feeling he doesn't want to be disturbed, but I don't want him to think I'm rude.'

Tom assured him he would make things all right with Bernard. Tom took the Alfa-Romeo.

'You can drop me anywhere, really,' Chris said.

Tom thought Fontainebleau was the best bet, the highway to Paris by the Monument. Chris looked like what he was, a tall American boy on vacation, neither rich nor poor, and Tom thought he would have no trouble getting a lift into Paris.

'Shall I call you in a couple of days?' Chris asked. 'I'll be interested in what's happening. I'll look at the papers, too, of course.'

'Yes,' Tom said. 'Let me ring you. Hotel Louisiane, rue de Seine, isn't it?'

'Yes. I can't tell you how wonderful it's been for me – just seeing the inside of a French house.'

Yes, he could. Or rather, he didn't have to tell him, Tom thought. On the way home, Tom drove faster than usual. He felt very worried, but he did not know exactly what he ought to be worried about. He felt out of touch with Jeff and Ed, and for him or them to try to communicate would be unwise. He thought it best to try to persuade Bernard to stay on. It might be difficult. But going back to London would mean the Derwatt show in Bernard's face again, posters on the streets, perhaps seeing Jeff and Ed who were frightened and off-balance now themselves. Tom put the car in the garage and went directly up to Bernard's room and knocked.

No answer.

Tom opened the door. The bed was made as it had been made that morning when Bernard sat on it, and now Tom saw the faint depression in the bedspread where Bernard had sat. But everything of Bernard's was gone, his duffelbag, his unpressed suit which Tom had put in the closet. Tom took a quick look in his own room. Bernard was not there. And there was no note anywhere. Mme Clusot was vacuuming in his room, and Tom said, 'Bonjour, madame,' to her.

Tom went downstairs. 'Mme Annette!'

Mme Annette was not in the kitchen, she was in her bedroom. Tom knocked and, hearing a word from her, opened the door. Mme Annette was reclining on her bed under a mauve knitted coverlet, reading *Marie-Claire*.

'Don't disturb yourself, madame!' Tom said. 'I only wanted to ask where is M. Bernard?'

'Is he not in his room? Perhaps he has gone out for a walk.'

Tom did not want to tell her that he appeared to have taken his things and left. 'He didn't say anything to you?'

'No, m'sieur.'

'Well –' Tom managed a smile. 'Let's not worry about it. Were there any telephone calls?'

'No, m'sieur. And how many will there be for dinner this evening?'

'Two, I think, thank you, Mme Annette,' Tom said, thinking that Bernard might be back. He went out and closed the door.

My God, Tom thought, plunge into a couple of soothing Goethe poems. *Der Abschied* or some such. A little German solidity. Goethian conviction of superiority and – maybe genius. That was what he needed. Tom pulled the book down – *Goethes Gedichte* – from a shelf, and as fate or the unconscious would have it, he opened the book at *Der Abschied*. Tom knew it by heart almost, though he would never have dared recite it to anyone, being afraid his accent was not perfect. Now the first lines upset him:

> *Lass mein Aug' den Abschied sagen,*
> *Den mein Mund nicht nehmen kann!*
>   Let my eyes say the adieu that my mouth cannot.
> *Schwer, wie schwer ist er zu tragen!*
> *Und ich bin –*

Tom was startled by the closing of a car door. Someone was arriving. Bernard had taken a taxi back, Tom thought.

But no, it was Heloise.

She stood bareheaded, her long blonde hair blowing in the breeze, fumbling with her purse.

Tom bolted for the door and flung it open. 'Heloise!'

'Ah, *Tome*!'

They embraced. Ah, Tome, ah, Tome! Tom had grown used to his bookish name, and from Heloise, he liked it.

'You're all sunburnt!' Tom said in English, but he meant suntanned. 'Let me get rid of this guy. How much is it?'

'One hundred forty francs.'

'Bastard. From Orly he's –' Tom repressed, even in English, the words he had been going to use. Tom paid the bill. The driver did not assist with the luggage.

Tom took everything into the house.

'Ah, how good to be home!' Heloise said, stretching her arms. She flung a big tapestry-like bag – a Greek product – onto the yellow sofa. She was wearing brown leather sandals, pink, bell-bottomed trousers, an American Navy pea-jacket. Tom wondered where and how she had acquired the pea-jacket?

'All is well. Mme Annette is at ease in her bedroom,' Tom said, switching to French.

'What a terrible vacation I had!' Heloise plopped on the sofa and lit a cigarette. She would take several minutes to calm down, so he started to carry her suitcases upstairs. She screamed at one of them, because there was something in it which belonged downstairs, so Tom left that and took something else. 'Must you be so American and so efficient?'

What was the alternative? Standing and waiting for her to unwind? 'Yes.' He took the other things to her room.

When he came down, Mme Annette was in the living-room, and she and Heloise were talking about Greece, the yacht, the house there (evidently in a small fishing village), but not, Tom noticed, about Murchison as yet. Mme Annette was fond of Heloise, because Mme Annette liked to be of service to people, and Heloise liked to be served. Heloise did not want anything now, though at Mme Annette's insistence, she agreed to a cup of tea.

Then Heloise told him about her vacation on the *Princesse*

de Grèce, the yacht of the oaf called Zeppo, a name which re-called the Marx Brothers to Tom. Tom had seen pictures of this hairy beast, whose self-esteem matched that of any of the Greek shipping tycoons, from what Tom could gather, and Zeppo was only the son of a minor real estate shark, small potatoes. A businessman screwing his own people, himself already screwed by the Fascist colonels there, according to Zeppo and Heloise, yet still making so much money that his son could cruise around on a yacht throwing caviare to the fish and filling the yacht's swimming-pool with champagne, which they later heated so they could swim in it. 'Zeppo had to hide the champagne, so he put it in the pool,' Heloise explained.

'And who was in bed with Zeppo? Not the wife of the President of the United States, I trust?'

'Any-body,' Heloise said in English, with disgust, and blew her smoke out.

Not Heloise, Tom was sure. Heloise was sometimes – not even too often – a tease, but Tom was sure she had not jumped into bed with anyone but him since they were married. Thank God, not Zeppo, who was a gorilla. Heloise would never go for that. Zeppo's treatment of women sounded repellent, but Tom's atti-tude to that – which he had never dared express to a woman – was that if women put up with it from the start, in order to get a diamond bracelet or a villa in the south of France, why should they complain about it later? Heloise's main irritation seemed to be due to the jealousy of one woman named Norita, because a certain man on the yacht had been paying attention to Heloise. Tom scarcely listened to this gossip-column drivel, because he was wondering how to tell Heloise some of his news in a manner that wouldn't upset her.

Tom was also half-expecting Bernard's gaunt figure to appear at the front door at any moment. He walked up and down the floor slowly, glancing at the front door at each turn. 'I went to London.'

'Yes? How was it?'

'I brought you something.' Tom ran up the stairs – his ankle was much better – and returned with the Carnaby Street trou-sers. Heloise put them on in the dining-room. They fitted well.

'I love them !' Heloise said, and gave Tom a hug and a kiss on his cheek.

'I came back with a man called Thomas Murchison,' Tom said, and proceeded to tell her what had happened.

Heloise had not heard of his disappearance. Tom explained Murchison's suspicion of his 'Clock' as a forgery, and Tom said he was convinced there was no forgery being done of Derwatt's paintings, and so, like the police, he could not account for Murchison's disappearance. Just as Heloise did not know about the forging, she did not know how much of an income Tom derived from Derwatt Ltd, about $12,000 per year, about the same as the income from the stocks he had acquired from Dickie Greenleaf. Heloise was interested in money, but not particularly in where it came from. She knew her family's money contributed as much to their household as Tom's, but she had never thrown this up to Tom, and Tom knew she couldn't have cared less, which was another thing he appreciated in Heloise. Tom had told her that Derwatt Ltd insisted on giving him a small percentage of their profits, because he had helped them organize their business years ago, before he and Heloise met. Tom's Derwatt Ltd income was sent to him, or handled by the New York company which was a distributor of the Derwatt-labelled art supplies. Some of this Tom invested in New York, and some he had sent to France to be turned into francs. The head of the Derwatt art supply company (who also happened to be a Greek) was aware that Derwatt did not exist and was being falsified.

Tom continued : 'Another matter. Bernard Tufts — I don't think you ever met him — was visiting for a couple of days, and just this afternoon he appears to have taken a walk — with his things. I don't know if he's coming back or not.'

'Bernard Toofts? *Un Anglais?*'

'Yes. I don't know him well. He's a friend of friends. He's a painter, a little upset now because of his girl-friend. He's probably gone off to Paris. I thought I should tell you about him in case he comes back.' Tom laughed. He felt more and more convinced that Bernard would not come back. Had he taken a taxi perhaps, to Orly to hop the first plane he could back to London? 'And — my other news is we're invited tomorrow night to the Berthelins for dinner. They'll be *enchanted* that you're back! Oh, I almost forgot. I had still another guest – Christopher Greenleaf, a cousin of Dickie's. He was here two nights. Didn't you get my letter about him?' But she hadn't, because he had sent it only Tuesday.

'Mon dieu, you have been busy!' Heloise said in English, with a funny edge of jealousy in it. 'Did you miss me, Tome?'

He put his arms around her. 'I missed you – really I did.'

The item Heloise had for the downstairs was a vase, short and sturdy with two handles, and two black bulls on it lowering their heads at each other. It was attractive, and Tom did not ask if it was valuable, very old, or anything else, because at that moment he did not care. He put on Vivaldi's *Four Seasons*. Heloise was upstairs unpacking, and she said she wanted to take a bath.

By 6.30 p.m. Bernard had not arrived. Tom had a feeling Bernard was in Paris, not London, but it was only a feeling, something he shouldn't count on. During dinner, which he and Heloise took at home, Mme Annette chatted with Heloise about the English gentleman who had come that morning to ask about M. Murchison. Heloise was interested but only slightly, and certainly she wasn't worried, Tom saw. She was more interested in Bernard.

'You expect him back? Tonight?'

'In fact – now I don't,' Tom said.

Thursday morning came and went tranquilly, without even a telephone call, though Heloise rang up three or four people in Paris, including her father at his Paris office. Now Heloise wore faded levis and she went barefoot in the house. There was nothing in Mme Annette's *Parisien* today about Murchison. When Mme Annette went out in the afternoon – ostensibly to shop, but probably to call on her friend Mme Yvonne and inform her of Heloise's arrival and of the visit of an *agent* of the London police – Tom lay with Heloise on the yellow sofa, drowsily, his head against her breast. They had made love that morning. Amazing. It was supposed to be a dramatic fact. It was not so important to Tom as having fallen asleep with Heloise the night before, with Heloise in his arms. Heloise often said, 'You are nice to sleep with, because when you turn over it is not like an earthquake shaking the bed. Really I don't know when you turn over.' That pleased Tom. He had never even asked who the earthquakes had been. Heloise existed. It was odd for Tom. He could not make out her objectives in life. She was like a picture on the wall. She might want children, some time, she said. Meanwhile, she existed. Not that Tom could boast of having any objectives himself, now that he had attained the life he had now, but Tom had a certain zest in seizing the pleasures he was now able to seize, and this zest seemed lacking in Heloise, maybe because she had had everything she wished since birth. Tom felt odd sometimes making love with her, because he felt detached half the time, and as if he derived pleasure from something inanimate, unreal, from a body without an identity. Or was this some shyness or puritanism on his part? Or some fear of (mentally) giving himself completely, which would be to say to himself, 'If I should not have, if I should lose Heloise, I couldn't exist any longer.' Tom knew he was capable of believing that, even in regard to Heloise, but he did not like to admit it to himself, did not permit it, and had certainly never said it to Heloise, because it would (as things were now) be a lie. The condition of utter dependence on her he sensed merely as a possibility. It had little to do with sex, Tom thought, with any dependence on that. Usually Heloise was disrespectful of the same things he was. She was a partner, in a way, though a passive one. With a boy or a man, Tom would have laughed more – maybe that was the main difference. Yet Tom remembered one occasion with her parents, when he'd said, 'I'm sure every member of the Mafia is baptized, and what good does it do *them*?' and Heloise had laughed. Her parents hadn't. They (the parents) somehow ferreted out of Tom the fact that he hadn't been baptized in the United States – a point Tom actually was vague about, but certainly his Aunt Dottie had never mentioned it. Tom's parents had been drowned when he was very small, so he'd never heard anything on the subject from them. Impossible to explain to the Plissons, who were Catholics, that in the United States baptism and mass and confession and pierced ears and Hell and the Mafia were sort of, somehow, Catholic and not

Protestant, not that Tom was anything, but if he was sure of anything, he was sure he wasn't Catholic.

The times that Heloise came most alive to Tom were when she flew into a temper. She had tempers and tempers. Tom did not count the tempers over a delayed delivery of something from Paris, when Heloise swore (untruthfully) that she would never patronize such-and-such a shop again. The more serious tempers were caused by boredom or a minor assault upon her ego, and could occur if a guest had bested or contradicted her in a discussion at the table. Heloise would control herself until the guest or guests had departed – which was something – but once the people had gone, she would walk up and down the floor ranting, throwing pillows at the walls, shouting, *'Fous-moi la paix! – Salauds!'* ('Get the hell out of here! – Slobs!') with Tom as her only audience. Tom would say something soothing and irrelevant, Heloise would go limp, a tear would roll out of each eye, and she could be laughing a moment later. Tom supposed that was Latin. It certainly wasn't English.

Tom worked for an hour or so in the garden, then read a bit in *Les Armes Secrètes* by Julio Cortazar. Then he went up and did the last work on his portrait of Mme Annette – this was her day off, Thursday. At 6 p.m. Tom asked Heloise to come in and look at it.

'It's not bad, you know? You have not worked too much on it. I like that.'

Tom was pleased by this. 'Don't mention it to Madame.' He put it in a corner to dry, face to the wall.

Then they got ready to go to the Berthelins. Dress was informal. Levis would do. Vincent was another husband who worked in Paris and came to his country house at weekends.

'What has Papa to say?' Tom asked.

'He is glad I am back in France.'

Papa didn't like him much, Tom knew, but Papa had a vague feeling that Heloise neglected him. Bourgeois virtue was at war with a nose for character, Tom supposed. 'And Noëlle?' Noëlle was a favourite friend of Heloise who lived in Paris.

'Oh, the same. Bored, she says. She never likes the autumn.'

The Berthelins, though quite well off, deliberately roughed it in the country, with an outside john, and no hot water in the kitchen sink. Hot water was made in a kettle on the stove which burnt wood. Their guests, the Cleggs, the English couple, were about fifty, the same age as the Berthelins. Vincent Berthelin's son, whom Tom had not met before, was a dark-haired young man of twenty-two (Vincent told Tom his age in the kitchen, when he and Tom were drinking Ricards, and Vincent was doing the cooking), living with a girl-friend now in Paris, and on the brink of abandoning his architectural studies at the Beaux Arts, which had Vincent in a tizzy. '*The girl is not worth it!*' Vincent stormed at Tom. 'It is the English influence, you know?' Vincent was a Gaullist.

The dinner was excellent, chicken, rice, salad, cheese, and apple tart made by Jacqueline. Tom's mind was on other things. But he was pleased, pleased to the point of smiling, because Heloise was in good spirits, talking about her Greek adventures, and at the last they all sampled the ouzo Heloise had brought.

'Disgusting taste, that ouzo! Worse than Pernod!' said Heloise at home, brushing her teeth at the basin in her bathroom. She was already in her nightdress, a short blue thing.

In his bedroom, Tom was putting on his new pyjamas from London.

'I'm going down to get some champagne!' Heloise called.

'I'll get it,' Tom hurried into his slippers.

'I have to get this taste out. Besides I want some champagne. You would think the Berthelins were paupers, the things they serve to drink. *Vin ordinaire!*' She was going down the stairs.

Tom intercepted her.

'I shall get it,' Heloise said. 'Get some ice.'

Tom somehow didn't want her to go into the cellar. He went on to the kitchen. He had just pulled an ice tray out, when he heard a scream — a muffled scream because of the distance, but Heloise's scream, and a terrible one. Tom dashed across the front hall.

There was a second scream, and he collided with her in the spare loo.

'Mon dieu! Someone has hanged himself down there!'

'Oh, Christ!' Tom half supported Heloise and guided her up the stairs.

'Don't go down, Tome! It is horrible!'

It was Bernard, of course. Tom was trembling as he walked up the stairs with her, she talking in French and he in English.

'Promise me you won't go down! Call the police, Tome!'

'All right, I'll call the police.'

'Who is it?'

'I don't know.'

They went into Heloise's bedroom.

'Stay here!' Tom said.

'No, don't leave me!'

'I insist!' Tom said in French, and ran out, and down the stairs. A straight Scotch was the best thing, he thought. Heloise hardly drank spirits, so it ought to help her at once. Then a sedative. Tom ran back upstairs with the bottle and a glass from the bar cart. He poured half a glassful, and when Heloise hesitated, drank some himself, then put the glass between her lips. Her teeth were chattering.

'You will call the police?'

'Yes!' At least this was suicide, Tom thought. That ought to be provable. It wasn't murder. Tom sighed, shuddering, almost as shaky as Heloise. She was sitting on the edge of the bed. 'How about the champagne? A lot of it.'

'Yes. *Non!* You must not go down there! Telephone the police!'

'Yes.' Tom went down the stairs.

He went into the spare loo, hesitated just an instant at the open doorway – the cellar light was still on – then started down the steps. A shock went through him at the sight of the dark, hanging figure, head askew. The rope was short. Tom blinked. There seemed to be no feet. He went closer.

It was a dummy.

Tom smiled, then he laughed. He slapped the limp legs—which were nothing but empty trousers, the trousers of Bernard Tufts. '*Heloise!*' he yelled, running back up the stairs, not caring if he might waken Mme Annette. 'Heloise, it's a *dummy*!' he said in English. 'It's not real! *C'est un mannequin!* You mustn't be afraid!'

It took a few seconds to convince her. It was a joke that perhaps Bernard had played – perhaps even Christopher, Tom added. At any rate, he had felt the legs, and he was sure.

Gradually, Heloise became angry, which was a sign of recovery. 'What stupid jokes these English play! Stupid! Imbecilic!'

Tom laughed with relief. 'I'm going down to get the champagne! And the ice!'

Tom went down again. The dummy hung from a belt which Tom recognized as one of his own. A hanger supported the dark grey jacket, the trousers were buttoned onto a button on the jacket, and the head was a grey rag, tied at the neck with a string. Tom got a chair quickly from the kitchen – happily Mme Annette had not awakened in all this – and returned to the cellar and took the thing down. The belt had hung from a nail in a rafter. Tom dropped the empty clothes on the floor. Then he chose a champagne quickly. He removed the hanger from the jacket, and also took the belt with him. He managed to take the ice bucket from the kitchen also, and to turn out the lights, and then he went upstairs.

15

Tom awakened just before seven. Heloise was sleeping soundly. Tom got gently out of bed, and took his dressing-gown which was hanging in Heloise's bedroom.

Mme Annette might be up. Tom went quietly down the stairs. He wanted to remove Bernard's suit from the cellar before Mme Annette found it. The stain of the spilt wine and Murchison's blood, Tom saw now, was not serious. If a technician examined it for blood, he would no doubt find traces, but Tom was optimistic enough to think this would not happen.

He unbuttoned the jacket from the trousers. A piece of white paper fluttered down, a note from Bernard, written in his tall pointed hand:

I hang myself in effigy in your house. It is Bernard Tufts that I hang, not Derwatt. For D. I do penance in the only way I can, which is to kill the self I have been for the last five years. Now to continue and try to do my work honestly in what is left of my life.

B.T.

Tom had an impulse to crumple the note and destroy it. Then he folded it, and stuck it in a pocket of his dressing-gown. He might need it. Who knew? Who knew where Bernard was and what he was doing? He shook out Bernard's crumpled suit, and tossed the rag in a corner. He'd send the suit to the cleaners. No harm in that. Tom started to take it up to his room, then decided to leave it on the hall table where he put clothes for Mme Annette to take to the cleaners.

'Bonjour, M. Tome!' Mme Annette said from the kitchen. 'Again you are up early! Mme Heloise also? Would she like her tea?'

Tom went to the kitchen. 'I think she wants to sleep this morning. She should sleep as late as she wishes. But I'd like some coffee now, please.'

Mme Annette said she would bring it up to him. Tom went upstairs and dressed. He wanted to take a look at the grave in the woods. Bernard might have done something odd – opened it partly, God knew what – maybe even buried himself in it.

After his coffee, he went downstairs. The sun was hazy and hardly up, the grass wet with dew. Tom idled by his shrubs, not wanting to make a bee-line for the grave, in case Heloise or Mme Annette was looking out a window. Tom did not look back at the house, because he believed one person's eye attracted the eye of another.

The grave was just as he and Bernard had left it.

Heloise did not awaken until after ten, and Mme Annette told Tom, who was in his workroom then, that Mme Heloise wanted to see him. Tom went into her bedroom. She was having her tea in bed.

She said, chewing grapefruit, 'I do not like the jokes of your friends.'

'There won't be any more. I removed the clothes – from the cellar. Don't think any more about that. Would you like to go to a nice place for lunch? Somewhere along the Seine? A late lunch?'

She liked this idea.

They found a restaurant new to them in a small town to the south, not on the Seine as it happened.

'Shall we go away somewhere? To Ibiza?' Heloise asked.

Tom hesitated. He would love to go somewhere by boat, take all the luggage he wanted, books, a record player, paints and drawing-pads. But it would look like an evasion, he felt, to Bernard, to Jeff and Ed, and to the police – even if they knew where he was going. 'I will think about it. Maybe.'

'Greece left an unpleasant taste. Like the ouzo,' Heloise said.

Tom was in the mood for a lovely snooze after lunch. So was Heloise. They would sleep in her bed, she said, until they woke up, or until time for dinner. Unplug the telephone in Tom's room, so it would only ring downstairs, and Mme Annette would answer it. It was at moments like these, Tom thought, as he drove lazily back through the woods towards Villeperce, that he enjoyed being jobless, rather well-off, and married.

Tom was certainly not prepared for what he saw as soon as he opened the front door with his key. Bernard was sitting in one of the yellow straight chairs, facing the door.

Heloise did not see Bernard at once, and said, 'Tome, chéri, can you bring me some Perrier and ice? Oh, I am so sle-epy!' Heloise fell into Tom's arms, and was surprised to find him tense.

'Bernard's here. You know, the Englishman I mentioned.' Tom walked into the living-room. 'Hello, Bernard. How are you?' Tom could not quite extend a hand, but he tried to smile.

Mme Annette came in from the kitchen. 'Ah, M. Tome! Mme Heloise! I did not hear the car. I must be growing deaf. M. Bernard has returned.' Mme Annette seemed flustered.

Tom said as calmly as he could, 'Yes. Good. I was expecting him,' though he had told Mme Annette he wasn't sure Bernard would come back, he remembered.

Bernard stood up. He needed a shave. 'Pardon me for returning unannounced.'

'Heloise, this is Bernard Tufts — a painter who lives in London. My wife, Heloise.'

'How do you do?' Bernard said.

Heloise stood where she was. 'How do you do?' she replied in English.

'My wife's a little tired.' Tom walked towards her. 'Want to go upstairs – or stay with us?'

With a motion of her head, Heloise asked Tom to come with her.

'Back in a moment, Bernard,' Tom said, and followed her.

'Is that the one who played the trick?' Heloise asked when they were in her bedroom.

'I'm afraid so. He's rather eccentric.'

'What is he doing here? I don't like him. Who is he? You never mentioned him before. And he's wearing your clothes?'

Tom shrugged. 'He's a friend of some friends of mine in London. I'm sure I can persuade him to take off this afternoon. He probably needs some extra money. Or clothes. I'll ask him.' Tom kissed her cheek. 'Get into bed, darling. I'll see you soon.'

Tom went to the kitchen and asked Mme Annette to take up Heloise's Perrier.

'M. Bernard will be here for dinner?' asked Mme Annette.

'I don't think so. But we shall be in. Something simple. We had a big lunch.' Tom went back to Bernard. 'Were you in Paris?'

'Yes, Paris.' Bernard was still standing.

Tom didn't know what tack to take. 'I found your effigy downstairs. It gave my wife quite a shock. You shouldn't play tricks like that – with women in the house.' Tom smiled. 'By the way, my housekeeper took your suit to be cleaned and I'll see that you get it in London – or wherever you are. Sit down.' Tom sat down on the sofa. 'What're your plans?' It was like asking an insane man how he felt, Tom thought. Tom was uneasy, and he felt worse when he realized that his heart was beating rather fast.

Bernard sat down. 'Oh –' Long pause.

'Not going back to London?' In desperation, Tom took a cigar from the box on the coffee-table. It was enough to gag him just now, but did it matter?

'I came to talk to you.'

'All right. What about?'

Another silence, and Tom was afraid to break it. Bernard might have been groping in clouds, infinite clouds of his own thoughts in the last days. It was as if he were trying to hunt down one fleecy little sheep amid a gigantic flock, Tom felt. 'I have all the time you want. You're among friends, Bernard.'

'It's quite simple. I must start my life over again. Cleanly.'

'Yes, I know. Well, you can.'

'Does your wife know – about my forging?'

Tom welcomed this logical question. 'No, of course not. No one knows. No one in France.'

'Or about Murchison?'

'I told her Murchison was missing. And that I dropped him at Orly.' Tom spoke softly, in case Heloise might be in the hall upstairs, listening. But he knew voices did not carry well from the living-room, up the faraway curve of the stairs.

Bernard said somewhat irritably, 'I really can't talk with other people in the house. Like your wife. Or the housekeeper.'

'All right, we can go somewhere.'

'No.'

'Well, I can hardly ask Mme Annette to leave. She runs this place. Want to take a walk? There's a quiet café –'

'No, thanks.'

Tom leaned back on the sofa with his cigar, which now smelled like a house burning down. Usually he liked the smell. 'By the way, I've heard nothing from the English Inspector since I saw you. Or the French.'

Bernard showed no reaction. Then he said, 'All right, let's take a walk.' He stood up and looked at the french windows. 'Out the back way, perhaps.'

They walked out, onto the lawn. Neither had put on a top-coat and it was chilly. Tom let Bernard go where he wished, and Bernard drifted towards the woods, towards the lane. Bernard walked slowly, a bit unsteadily. Was he weak from not having eaten, Tom wondered? Soon they were passing the spot where

Murchison's corpse had been. Tom felt fear, a fear that made the hair on his neck and behind his ears prickle. It was not a fear of that spot, Tom realized, but a fear of Bernard. Tom kept his hands free, and walked a little to one side of Bernard.

Then Bernard slowed and turned around, and they began walking back towards the house.

'What's on your mind?' Tom asked.

'Oh, I – I don't know where this thing's going to end. It's already caused a man's death.'

'Well – regrettable, yes. I agree. But really nothing to do with you, is it? Since you're not painting any more Derwatts, the new Bernard Tufts can start over – cleanly.'

No reply from Bernard.

'Did you ring Jeff or Ed when you were in Paris?'

'No.'

Tom hadn't troubled to buy any English newspapers, and Bernard perhaps hadn't troubled, either. Bernard's anxieties were within himself. 'If you'd like to, you can ring Cynthia from the house. You can do it from my room.'

'I spoke to her from Paris. She doesn't want to see me.'

'Oh.' That was the trouble. That was the last straw, Tom supposed. 'Well, you can always write her. That may be better. Or see her when you go back to London. Storm her door!' Tom laughed.

'She said no.'

Silence.

Cynthia wanted to keep clear of it, Tom supposed. Not that she mistrusted Bernard's intention of stopping the forgeries – no one could doubt Bernard when he stated something – but she'd had enough. Bernard's hurt was beyond Tom's grasp, for the moment. They were standing on the stone terrace outside the french windows. 'I've got to go in, Bernard. I'm freezing. Come in.' Tom opened the doors.

Bernard came in, too.

Tom ran up to see Heloise. He was still rigid with cold, or fear. Heloise was in her bedroom, sitting on her bed, sorting snapshots and postcards.

'When is he leaving?'

'Darling – it's his girl-friend in London. He rang her from Paris. She doesn't want to see him. He's unhappy and I can't just ask him to leave. I don't know what he's going to do. Darling, would you like to visit your parents for a few days?'

'*Non!*'

'He wants to talk to me. I'm only hoping he'll get at it soon.'

'Why can't you put him out? He is not your friend. Also he is mad!'

Bernard stayed.

*

They had not finished dinner when the front doorbell sounded. Mme Annette answered it, and returned and said to Tom:

'It is two *agents* of police, M. Tome. They would like to speak with you.'

Heloise gave a sigh of impatience, and threw her napkin down. She had detested sitting at the table, and now she stood up. 'Again some intrusions!' she said in French.

Tom had stood up, too.

Only Bernard seemed unperturbed.

Tom went into the living-room. It was the same pair of agents who had visited him Monday.

'We are sorry to disturb you, m'sieur,' said the older man, 'but your telephone is not working. We have reported it.'

'Really?' The telephone's non-functioning happened, in fact, every six weeks or so, inexplicably, but now Tom wondered if Bernard had done something odd, like cut the line. 'I was not aware of it. Thank you.'

'We have been in touch with the English investigator. Rather he has been in touch with us.'

Heloise came in, out of both curiosity and anger, Tom supposed. Tom introduced her, and the officers gave their names again, Commissaire Delaunay, and the other name Tom missed.

Delaunay said, 'Now it is not merely M. Murchison but the painter Derwatt who is missing. The English investigator Webstair, who also tried to ring you this afternoon, would like to know if you have heard from either of them?'

Tom smiled, actually a little amused. 'I have never met

Derwatt, and he certainly doesn't know me,' Tom said, just as Bernard came into the room. 'And I have had no word from M. Murchison, I regret to say. May I present Bernard Tufts, an English friend. Bernard, two gentlemen of the police force.'

Bernard mumbled a greeting.

Bernard's name did not mean anything to the French police, Tom noticed.

'Even the people who own the gallery where Derwatt now has an exhibition do not know where Derwatt is,' said Delaunay. 'It is astounding, this.'

It was indeed odd, but Tom could not help them at all.

'Do you by any chance know the American, M. Murchison?' Delaunay asked Bernard.

'No,' Bernard said.

'Or you, madame?'

'No,' Heloise said.

Tom explained that his wife had just returned from Greece, but he had told her about M. Murchison's visit and his disappearance.

The officers looked as if they did not know what move to make next. Delaunay said, 'Because of the circumstances, M. Reeply, we have been asked by Inspector Webstair to make a search of your house. A formality, you understand, but necessary. We might come across a clue. I speak of M. Murchison, of course. We must aid our English *confrères* all we can!'

'But certainly! Would you like to begin now?'

It was rather dark, as far as the outdoors was concerned, but the police said they would begin now, and continue tomorrow morning. Both officers stood on the stone terrace, looking longingly, Tom felt, at the dark garden and the woods beyond.

They went over the house, under Tom's guidance. They were first interested in Murchison's bedroom, the one Chris had used afterwards. Mme Annette had emptied the waste-basket. The officers looked into drawers, all of which were empty except for two bottom drawers of a chest, or *commode* as the French called it, which contained bedspreads and a couple of blankets. There was no sign of Murchison or Chris. They looked into Heloise's bedroom. (Heloise was downstairs in a repressed fury, Tom knew.) They looked into Tom's atelier, even picked up one of his saws. There was an attic. The light had burnt out, and Tom had to get a lightbulb and a torch from downstairs. The attic was dusty. There were chairs under cloth covers, and an old sofa that Tom and Heloise had not removed from previous tenants. The policemen also looked behind things with the aid of their own torches. They were looking for something larger than a clue. Tom supposed, absurd as the idea might be that he would leave a corpse behind a sofa.

Then it was the cellar. Tom showed it with the same ease, standing right on the stain, and shining his torch into the corners, though the light was good. Tom was a bit afraid Murchison might have bled onto the cement floor behind the wine cask. Tom had not looked at that spot carefully enough. But if there was any blood, the officers did not see it, and gave the floor only a glance. This did not mean they would not make a more thorough search tomorrow, Tom thought.

They said they would be back at eight in the morning, if that was not too early for Tom. Tom told them that eight would be quite all right.

'Sorry,' Tom said to Heloise and Bernard, when he had closed the front door. Tom had the feeling Heloise and Bernard had been sitting in silence with their coffee the whole time.

'Why do they want to search the house?' Heloise demanded.

'Because this so-and-so American is still missing,' Tom said. 'M. Murchison.'

Heloise stood up. 'Can I speak to you upstairs, Tome?'

Tom excused himself to Bernard and went with her.

Heloise went into her bedroom. 'If you don't put this *fou* out, I am leaving the house tonight!'

That was a dilemma. He wanted Heloise to stay, and yet if she did, Tom knew he would get nowhere with Bernard. And like Bernard, he couldn't think with Heloise's indignant eyes glaring at him. 'I'll try again to get him out,' Tom said. He kissed Heloise on the neck. At least she permitted this.

Tom went downstairs. 'Bernard – Heloise is upset. Would you mind going back to Paris tonight? I could drive you to – Why not Fontainebleau? A couple of good hotels there. If you want to talk to me, I could come tomorrow to Fontainebleau –'

'No.'

Tom sighed. 'Then she'll take off tonight. I'll go and tell her.' Tom went back up the stairs and told Heloise.

'What is this, another Dickie Granelafe? You can't tell him to get out of your house?'

'I never – Dickie wasn't in *my* house.' Tom stopped, wordless. Heloise looked angry enough to oust Bernard herself, but she wouldn't be able to, Tom thought, because Bernard's adamance was beyond convention or etiquette.

She dragged a small leather suitcase down from the top of a closet and began to pack. Useless to say he felt responsible for Bernard, Tom supposed. Heloise would wonder why.

'Heloise, darling, I am sorry. Are you taking the car or do you want me to drive you to the station?'

'I take the Alfa to Chantilly. By the way, there is nothing wrong with the telephone. I just tried it in your room.'

'Maybe the word from the *flics* got it fixed.'

'I think maybe they lied. They wanted to surprise us.' She paused in the act of putting a shirt into her suitcase. 'What have you done, Tome? Did you do something to this Murchison?'

'No!' Tom said, startled.

'You know, my father is not going to support any more nonsense, any more scandal.'

She referred to the Greenleaf business. Tom had cleared his name there, to be sure, but there were always suspicions. The Latins made wild jokes, and the jokes in a curious way became Latin truths. Tom might have killed Dickie. And everyone knew that he derived some money from Dickie's death, much as Tom had tried to hide this. Heloise knew he had an income from Dickie, and so did Heloise's father, whose own hands were not immaculate in his business activities, but Tom's had, perhaps, blood on them. *Non olet pecunia, sed sanguis* . . .

'There won't be any more scandal,' Tom said. 'If you only knew, I'm trying my best to avoid scandal. That's my objective.'

She closed her suitcase. 'I never know what you are doing.'

Tom took the suitcase. Then he set it down and they embraced. 'I would like to be with you tonight.'

Heloise would have liked to be with him, too, and she did not have to say it in words. This was the other side of her *fous-moi-le-camp!* Now she was leaving. Frenchwomen had to leave a room, a house, or ask someone else to change his room, or go somewhere, and the more inconvenient it was for the other person, the better they liked it, but it was still less inconvenient than their screaming. Tom called it 'The Law of French Displacement.'

'Did you telephone your family?' Tom asked.

'If they are not there, the servants are there.'

It would take her nearly two hours to drive. 'Will you ring me when you get there?'

'Au revoir, Bernard!' Heloise shouted from the front door. Then to Tom, who walked out with her, *'Non!'*

Tom watched bitterly as the red lights of the Alfa-Romeo turned left at the gates and disappeared.

Bernard sat smoking a cigarette. From the kitchen came the faint clatter of the garbage pail's lid. Tom took his torch from the hall table, and went into the spare loo. He went down to the cellar and looked behind the wine cask where Murchison had been. Very luckily there was no bloodstain there. Tom went back upstairs.

'You know, Bernard, you're welcome here tonight, but tomorrow morning the police arrive to look the house over more thoroughly.' He suddenly thought, the woods, too. 'They might ask you questions. It'll be annoying to you. Do you want to leave before they arrive – at eight?'

'Possibly, possibly.'

It was nearly 10 p.m. Mme Annette came in to ask if they would like more coffee. Tom and Bernard declined.

'Mme Heloise has gone out?' Mme Annette asked.

'She decided to go and see her parents,' said Tom.

'At this hour! Ah, Mme Heloise!' She collected the coffee things.

Tom sensed that she disliked Bernard, or mistrusted him, in the same way Heloise did. It was regrettable, Tom thought, that Bernard's character did not come through, that it had such an off-putting surface for most people. Tom realized that neither Heloise nor Mme Annette could like him, because they knew nothing about him really, nothing about his devotion to Derwatt – which they would probably consider 'putting Derwatt to use'. Above all, neither Heloise nor Mme Annette, with their quite different backgrounds, would ever understand Bernard Tufts's progress from rather working-class origin (according to Jeff and Ed) to what might be called the edge of greatness by virtue of his talent – though he signed his work with another name. Bernard did not even care about the money side of it – which would again be incomprehensible to Mme Annette and Heloise. Mme Annette left the room rather quickly, and in what Tom felt was as much of a huff as she dared.

'There's something I'd like to tell you,' Bernard said. 'The night after Derwatt died – We all heard about his death twenty-four hours after it happened in Greece – I-I had a vision of Derwatt standing in my bedroom. There was moonlight coming through the window. I'd broken a date with Cynthia, I remember, because I wanted to be alone. I could *see* Derwatt there and feel his presence. He was even smiling. He said, "Don't be alarmed, Bernard, I'm not badly off. I'm feeling no pain." Can you imagine Derwatt saying something as predictable as that? Yet I heard him.'

Bernard had heard his inner ear. Tom listened respectfully.

'I sat up in bed watching him for maybe a minute. Derwatt sort of drifted around my room, the room where I paint sometimes – and sleep.'

Bernard meant painted Tufts, not Derwatts.

Bernard continued, 'He said, "Carry on Bernard, I'm not sorry." I gathered he meant he wasn't sorry he'd killed himself. He meant, just go on living. That is –' Bernard looked at Tom for the first time since he had begun speaking '– for as long as it's supposed to last. It's hardly something one has control over, is it? Destiny does it for you.'

Tom hesitated. 'Derwatt had a sense of humour. Jeff says he might've appreciated your forging his work with such success.' Thank God, this went down not badly.

'To a point. Yes, the forging might have been a professional joke. Derwatt wouldn't have liked the business side of it. Money might have made him commit suicide as easily as being broke.'

Tom felt Bernard's thoughts starting to turn again, in a disorganized and hostile way, hostile to him. Should he make a move to call it a night? Or would Bernard take that as an insult? 'The blasted *flics* are arriving so early, I think I'll turn in.'

Bernard leaned forward. 'You didn't understand what I meant the other day when I said I'd failed. With that detective from London, when I was trying to explain Derwatt to him.'

'Because you didn't fail. Look, Chris knew what you meant. Webster said it was very moving, I remember.'

'Webster was still considering the possibility of forgery, of Derwatt's permitting it. I couldn't even convey Derwatt's character. I did my best and I failed.'

Tom said, trying desperately to get Bernard on the rails again, 'Webster is looking for Murchison. That's his assignment. Not Derwatt at all. I'm going upstairs.'

Tom went to his room and put on pyjamas. He opened the window a crack at the top, and got into bed – which Mme Annette had not turned down this evening – but he felt shaky and had an impulse to lock his door. Was that silly? Was it sensible? It seemed cowardly. He did not lock the door. He was midway in a volume of Trevelyan's *English Social History*, and started to pick it up, then took his *Harrap's Dictionary* instead. *To forge*. Old French *forge*, a workshop. *Faber*, a workman. *Forge* in French had only to do with a worshop for metal. The French for forgery was *falsification* or *contrefaire*. Tom already knew this. He closed the book.

He lay for an hour without falling asleep. Every few moments, the blood sang in his ears in a crescendo, loud enough to startle him, and he kept having sensations of falling from a height.

By the radium hands of his wristwatch, Tom saw that it was 12.30 a.m. Should he ring Heloise? He wanted to ring her, but he did not want to incur further disapproval of Papa by ringing at a late hour. Damn other people.

Then Tom was aware of being flung over by the shoulders, and of hands around his throat. Tom threshed his legs free of the covers. He was pulling ineffectively at Bernard's arms to get his hands from his throat, and at last Tom got his foot against Bernard's body and pushed. The hands left his throat. Bernard dropped with a thud to the floor, gasping. Tom turned on his lamp, nearly knocked it over, and did knock over a glass of water which spilt on the blue oriental rug.

Bernard was getting his breath back painfully.

So was Tom, in a sense.

'My God, Bernard,' Tom said.

Bernard didn't reply, or couldn't. He sat on the floor, propped on one arm, in the position of The Dying Gaul. Was he going to attack again as soon as he recovered his strength, Tom wondered? Tom stood up from his bed, and lit a Gauloise.

'Really, Bernard, what a stupid thing to do!' Tom burst out laughing, and coughed on his smoke. 'You wouldn't have had a chance! Even trying to escape! Mme Annette knows you're here, so do the police.' Tom watched as Bernard got to his feet. It was not often, Tom thought, that a near-victim could smoke a cigarette and walk around bare-foot, smiling at someone who had just tried to kill him. 'You shouldn't do that again.' Tom knew his words were absurd. Bernard didn't care what happened to himself. 'Aren't you going to say anything?'

'Yes,' Bernard said. 'I detest you – because all this is entirely your fault. I should never have agreed to it – true. But you're the origin.'

Tom knew. He was a mystic origin, a font of evil. 'We're all trying to wind the thing up, not continue it.'

'And I am finished. Cynthia –'

Tom puffed on his cigarette. 'You said you felt like Derwatt sometimes when you painted. Think what you've done for his name! Because he wasn't famous at all when he died.'

'It has been corrupted,' Bernard said like the voice of doom or judgement or hell itself. He went to the door and went out, with more of a look of purpose than usual.

Where was he going, Tom wondered? Bernard was still dressed, though it was after 3 a.m. Was he going to wander out in the night? Or go downstairs and set the house on fire?

Tom turned the key in his door. If Bernard came back, he'd

have to bang to get in, and of course Tom would let him in, but it was only fair to have a bit of warning.

Bernard would be no asset tomorrow morning with the police.

16

At 9.15 a.m., Saturday October 26th. Tom stood at his french windows looking out towards the woods, where the police had begun to dig up Murchison's old grave. Behind Tom, Bernard paced the living-room floor quietly and restlessly. And in his hand, Tom held a formal letter from Jeffrey Constant asking on behalf of the Buckmaster Gallery if he knew the whereabouts of Thomas Murchison, because they didn't.

Three police agents had arrived that morning, two new to Tom, and the other the Commissaire Delaunay, who Tom thought was not going to do any digging. 'Do you know what is the recently dug place in the woods?' they had asked. Tom said he knew nothing about it. The woods did not belong to him. The gendarme had gone across the lawn to speak to his con-frères. They had been over the house again.

Tom also had a letter from Chris Greenleaf which he had not opened.

The police had now been digging for perhaps ten minutes.

Tom read Jeff's letter more carefully. Jeff had written it either with an idea that Tom's post was being looked at, or Jeff was in a mood to be droll, but Tom believed the first idea.

The Buckmaster Gallery
Bond Street W1
Oct. 24 19—

Thomas P. Ripley, Esq.
Belle Ombre
Villeperce 77

Dear Mr Ripley,

We have been informed that Detective-Inspector Webster visited you recently with regard to Mr Thomas Murchison, who accompanied you last Wednesday to France. This is to inform you that we have heard nothing from Mr Murchison since Thursday 15th inst. when he came to our gallery.

We know that Mr Murchison wished to see Derwatt before he (Mr Murchison) returned to the United States. At the moment we do not know where Derwatt is in England, but we expect he will get in touch with us before returning to Mexico. It may be that Derwatt has arranged a meeting with Mr Murchison of which we know nothing. [A ghostly tea, perhaps, Tom thought.]

We as well as the police are concerned about the disappearance of the painting by Derwatt called 'The Clock'.

Please ring us and reverse the charges if you have information.

Yours sincerely,
Jeffrey Constant.

Tom turned around, in arrogant good spirits now – at least for the moment, and at any rate Bernard's sullenness bored him. Tom wanted to say, 'Listen, old crud, clot or cock, what the hell are you doing hanging around here anyway?' But Tom knew what Bernard was doing, waiting to have another go at him. So Tom only held his breath for a moment, smiling at Bernard who wasn't even looking at him, and Tom listened to blue tits twittering over some suet that Mme Annette had hung from a tree, heard Mme Annette's transistor faintly from the kitchen, and he heard also the *clink* of a police agent's spade, distant in the woods.

Tom said with the dead-pan coolness of Jeff's letter: 'Well, they're not going to find any signs of Murchison out there.'

'Let them drag the river,' Bernard said.

'Are you going to *tell* them to do that?'

'No.'

'Anyway, what river? I can't even remember which it was.' Tom was sure Bernard couldn't.

Tom was waiting for the police to return from the woods, and to say they hadn't found anything. Or maybe they would not bother saying that, maybe they would say nothing. Or they might go farther into the woods, searching. It might be an all-day affair. It was not a bad way, on a nice day, for the police to kill time. Lunch in the village or some village near by, or more likely their own homes in the district, then a return to the woods.

Tom opened Chris's letter.

Oct. 24, 19—

Dear Tom,

Thank you once more for the elegant days I spent with you. They are quite a contrast to my squalid abode here, but I sort of like it here. Last evening I had an adventure. I met a girl called Valerie in a St-Germain-des-Prés café. I asked her if she would like to come to my hotel for a glass of wine. (Ahem!) She accepted. I was with Gerald, but he tactfully disappeared like the gentleman he sometimes is. Valerie came upstairs a few minutes after me, her idea, though I don't think it would have mattered with the desk downstairs. She asked if she could wash up. I told her I had no bathroom, only a basin, so I offered to go out of the room while she washed up. When I knocked on the door again, she asked was there a bathroom with a tub. I said of course but I would have to get the key. This I did. Well, she disappeared in the bathroom for at least fifteen minutes. Then she came back and again wanted me to leave the room while she washed. Okay, so I did, but by this time I was wondering what on earth she could still be washing. I waited downstairs on the sidewalk. When I went up again, she was gone, the room was empty. I looked in the halls, everywhere. Gone! I thought, there's a girl who has washed herself right out of my life. Maybe I didn't do the right thing. Better luck next time, Chris!

I may go to Rome next with Gerald . . .

Tom looked out of the window. 'I wonder when they'll be finished? Ah, here they come! Look! Swinging their empty shovels.'

Bernard did not look.

Tom sat down comfortably on the yellow sofa.

The French knocked at the back windows, and Tom gestured for them to come in, then jumped up to open the windows for them.

'Nothing in the trench except this,' said the Commissaire Delaunay, holding up a small coin. It was a 20-centime piece, gold-coloured. 'The date is nineteen hundred sixty-five.' He smiled.

Tom smiled, too. 'Funny you found that.'

'Our treasure for today,' said Delaunay, pocketing the coin. 'Yes, the hole was recently dug. Very strange. Just the size for a corpse, but no corpse. You saw no one digging there recently?'

'I certainly did not. But – one can't see the place from the house. It is concealed by trees.'

Tom went to speak with Mme Annette in the kitchen, but she was not there. Probably she was out shopping, a tour that would be longer than usual, because she would tell three or four acquaintances about the arrival of the police who searched the house for M. Murchison, whose picture was in the newspaper. Tom prepared a tray of cold beer and a bottle of wine, and brought it into the living-room. The French officer was chatting with Bernard. It was about painting.

'Who makes use of the woods there?' asked Delaunay.

'Oh, now and then some farmers, I think,' Tom replied, 'who get wood. I seldom see anybody in that lane.'

'And recently?'

Tom thought. 'I can't remember anybody.'

The three agents departed. They had ascertained a few matters: his telephone was working; his *femme de ménage* was out shopping just now (Tom said he thought they might find her in the village, if they wished to speak with her); Heloise had gone to visit her parents in Chantilly. Delaunay had not bothered to take her address.

'I want to open the windows,' Tom said when they had gone. He did, the front door and the french windows.

The chill did not bother Bernard.

'I'm going to see what they did out there,' Tom said, and walked across the lawn towards the woods. What a relief to have the men of the law out of the house !

They had filled in the hole. It stood a bit high, reddish-brown earth, but they had been quite tidy about it. Tom walked back to the house. Good God, he thought, how many more discussions, repetitions, could he bear? One thing, perhaps, he should be grateful for, Bernard was not self-pitying. Bernard accused him. That was at least active and positive and definite.

'Well,' Tom said, entering the living-room, 'a tidy job they did. And twenty centimes for their trouble. Why don't we leave before –'

Just then, Mme Annette opened the door from the kitchen –

Tom heard it without seeing it – and Tom advanced to speak with her.

'Well, Mme Annette, the agents have departed. No clues for them, I'm afraid.' He was not going to mention the grave in the woods.

'It is very strange, is it not?' she said quickly, often a protocol in French for something else more important. 'It is a mystery here, is it not?'

'It is a mystery at Orly or Paris,' Tom replied. 'Not here.'

'Will you and M. Bernard be here for lunch?'

'Not today,' Tom said. 'We shall go out somewhere. And as for this evening, don't trouble yourself. If Mme Heloise telephones, would you tell her I shall ring back tonight? In fact –' Tom hesitated, 'I'll definitely ring back by five this afternoon. In any case, why don't you take the rest of the day off?'

'I bought some cutlets just in case. Yes, I have a rendezvous with Mme Yvonne at –'

'That's the spirit!' Tom interrupted. He turned to Bernard. 'Shall we take off somewhere?'

But they could not leave at once. Bernard wanted to do something in his room, he said. Mme Annette (Tom thought) left the house, possibly to have lunch with a friend in Villeperce. Tom at last knocked on Bernard's closed door.

Bernard was writing at the table in his room.

'If you want to be left alone –'

'In fact, I don't,' Bernard said, getting up readily enough.

Tom was mystified. What do you want to talk about? Tom wanted to ask. Why are you here? Tom could not bring himself to ask these questions. 'Let's go downstairs.'

Bernard came with him.

Tom wanted to ring Heloise. It was now 12.30 p.m. Tom could catch her before lunch. At home, the family ate on the hour, at 1 p.m. The telephone rang as Tom and Bernard entered the living-room. 'Maybe Heloise,' Tom said, and picked the telephone up.

'*Vous êtes ... blur-r-p ... Ne quittez pas. Londres vous appelle ...*'

Then Jeff came on. 'Hello, Tom. I'm ringing from a post office. Can you come over again – possibly?'

Tom knew he meant come over as Derwatt. 'Bernard is here.'

'We thought so. How is he?'

'He's – taking it easy,' Tom said. Tom did not think Bernard – gazing out the french windows – even cared to listen, but Tom was not sure. 'I *can't* just now,' Tom said. Didn't they realize, after all, that he had killed Murchison?

'Can't you think it over – please?'

'But I have a few obligations here, too, you know. What's happening?'

'That Inspector was here. He wanted to know where Derwatt was. He wanted to look at our books.' Jeff gulped, his voice had become perhaps unconsciously lower for reasons of secrecy, but at the same time he sounded so desperate that he might not have cared who heard or understood him. 'Ed and I – we made a few lists, recent ones. We said we'd always had an informal arrangement, that no pictures had ever been lost. I think that went down all right. But they are curious about Derwatt himself, and if you could carry it off again –'

'I don't think it's wise,' Tom said, interrupting.

'If you could confirm our books –'

Damn their books, Tom thought. Damn their income. What about Murchison's murder, was that his responsibility only? And what about Bernard and Bernard's life? In one strange instant, while he was not even thinking, Tom realized that Bernard was going to kill himself, was going to be a suicide somewhere. And Jeff and Ed were worried about *their* income, *their* reputation, and about going to prison! 'I have certain responsibilities here. It's impossible for me to go to London.' In Jeff's disappointed silence, Tom asked, 'Is Mrs Murchison coming over, do you know?'

'We haven't heard anything about that.'

'Let Derwatt stay where he is, wherever that is. Maybe he's got a friend with a private plane, who knows?' Tom laughed.

'By the way,' Jeff said, slightly more cheerful, 'what happened to "The Clock?" Was it really stolen?'

'Yes. Amazing, isn't it? I wonder who's enjoying that treasure?'

The note on which Jeff hung up was still a disappointed one: Tom was not coming over.

'Let's take a walk,' Bernard said.

So much for ringing Heloise, Tom thought. Tom started to ask if he might take ten minutes up in his room to ring her, then thought it better to humour Bernard. 'I'll get a jacket.'

They walked around the village. Bernard did not want a coffee, or a glass of wine, or lunch. They walked nearly a kilometre on two of the roads that led out of Villeperce, then turned back, stepping aside sometimes for wide farm trucks, for wagons pulled by Percheron horses. Bernard talked of Van Gogh and Arles, where Bernard had been twice.

'... Vincent like all the others had a certain span of life and no more. Can anybody imagine Mozart living to be eighty? I'd like to see Salzburg again. There's a café there, the Tomaselli. Marvellous coffee. ... Can you imagine Bach dying at twenty-six, for example? Which proves a man is his work, nothing more or less. It's never a man we're talking about, but his work ...'

It was threatening to rain. Tom had long ago turned his jacket collar up.

'... Derwatt had a certain decent span, you see. It was absurd that I prolonged it. But of course I didn't. All that can be rectified,' Bernard said like a judge pronouncing sentence, a wise sentence – in the opinion of the judge.

Tom took his hands from his pockets and blew on them, and stuffed them back in his pockets.

Back at the house, Tom made tea and brought out the whisky and brandy. The drink would either calm Bernard or bring matters to a crisis by making Bernard angry, and something would happen.

'I must ring my wife,' Tom said. 'Help yourself to anything.' Tom fled up the stairs. Heloise, even if angry still, would be a voice of sanity.

Tom said the Chantilly number to the operator. The rain began to fall. It was gentle against the windowpanes. There was no wind just now. Tom sighed.

'Hello, Heloise!' She had answered. '*Yes*, I am all right. I wanted to ring you last evening, but it became too late. ... I was just out walking. (She had tried to ring him.) With Bernard ... Yes, he is still here but I think he's leaving this afternoon, maybe tonight. When will you come home?'

'When you get rid of that *fou*!'

'Heloise, *je t'aime*. I may come to Paris. With Bernard, because I think it will help him to leave.'

'Why are you so nervous? What is happening?'

'Nothing!'

'Will you tell me when you are in Paris?'

Tom went back downstairs, and put on some music. He chose jazz. It was not good, not bad jazz, and as he had noticed in other crucial moments in his life, the jazz did nothing for him. Only classical music did something – it soothed or it bored, gave confidence or took confidence quite away, because it had order, and one either accepted that order or rejected it. Tom dumped a lot of sugar into his tea, now cold, and drank it off. Bernard had not shaved in two days, it seemed. Was he going to affect a Derwatt beard?

A few minutes later, they were strolling over the back lawn. One of Bernard's shoelaces was untied. Bernard wore desert boots, rather flattened with wear, their soles against the uppers like the beaks of newborn birds, which had a curious way of looking ancient. Was Bernard going to tie his shoelace or not?

'The other night,' Tom said, 'I tried to compose a limerick.

> There once was a match by computer.
> A nought was wed to a neuter.
> Said the neuter to nought,
> "I'm not what I ought,
> But our offspring will be even mooter."

The trouble is, it's clean. But maybe you can think of a better last line.' Tom had two versions of middle part and last line, but was Bernard even listening?

They were going into the lane now, into the woods. The rain had stopped, and now it was merely drippy.

'Look at the little frog!' Tom said, bending to scoop it up, because he had almost trod on it, a little thing no bigger than a thumbnail.

The blow hit Tom on the back on the head, and might have been Bernard's fist. Tom heard Bernard's voice saying something, was aware of wet grass, a stone against his face, then he passed out – for all practical purposes, though he felt a second blow on the side of his head. *This is too much*, Tom thought. He imagined his empty hands groping stupidly over the ground, but he knew he was not moving.

Then he was being rolled over and over. Everything was silent, except for a ringing in his ears. Tom tried to move and could not. Was he face down or face up? He was thinking, in a way, without being able to see. He blinked his eyes, and they were gritty. He began to realize, to believe, that weights or a weight was descending on his spine, his legs. Through the ringing in his ears came the whispering sound of a shovel driving into soil. Bernard was burying him. Tom was sure now that his eyes were open. How deep was the hole? It was Murchison's grave, Tom was sure. How much time had passed?

Good God, Tom thought, he couldn't allow Bernard to bury him several feet under, or he'd never get out. Dimly, even with dim humour, Tom thought that there could be a limit to placating Bernard, and the limit was his own life. *Listen! Okay!* Tom imagined, believed that he had yelled this, but he hadn't.

'. . . not the first,' Bernard's voice said, thick and muffled by the earth that surrounded Tom.

What did that mean? Had he even heard it? Tom was able to turn his head a little, and he realized he was face down. He could turn his head to a very small degree.

And the weight had stopped falling. Tom concentrated on breathing, partly through his mouth. His mouth was dry, and he spat out gritty soil. If he didn't move, Bernard would leave. Now Tom was awake enough to realize that Bernard must have got the shovel from the toolshed, while he was knocked out. Tom felt a warm trickle on the back of his neck. That was blood, probably.

Maybe two, maybe five minutes passed, and Tom wanted to

173

bestir himself, or at least try to, but was Bernard standing there watching him?

Impossible to hear anything, such as footfalls. Maybe Bernard had departed minutes ago. And anyway, would Bernard attack again if he saw him struggling out of the grave? It was a bit amusing. Later, if there was any later, Tom would laugh, he thought.

Tom risked it. He worked his knees. He got his hands in a position to push himself upward, and then found he had no strength. So he began to dig upward with his fingers like a mole. He cleared a space for his face, and tunnelled upward for air, without reaching any air. The earth was wet and loose but very clinging. The weight on his spine was formidable. He began to push with his feet and to work upward with his hands and arms, like someone trying to swim in unhardened cement. It couldn't be more than three feet of earth on top of him, Tom thought optimistically, maybe not even that. It took a long time to excavate three feet, even soft earth like this, and Bernard surely hadn't been at work very long. Tom felt sure he was now stirring the top of his prison, and if Bernard were standing there not reacting, not tossing more earth on or digging him up to hit him on the head again, he could afford to give a big heave and relax for a few seconds. Tom gave a big heave. It gained him more breathing space. He took some twenty inhalations of tomblike wet air, then went at it again.

Two minutes later, he was standing reeling like a drunk, beside Murchison's – now his own – grave, covered from head to foot with mud and clods.

It was growing dark. There was no light on in the house, Tom saw when he staggered into the lane. Automatically, Tom thought of the appearance of the grave, thought of covering it back, wondered where the shovel was that Bernard had used, and then thought the hell with it all. He was still wiping dirt out of his eyes and ears.

Maybe he would find Bernard sitting in the more or less dark of the living-room, in which case Tom would say, 'Boo!' Bernard's had been a rather ponderous practical joke. Tom took his shoes off on the terrace and left them. The french windows were ajar. 'Bernard!' Tom called. He was really in no state to withstand another attack.

No answer.

Tom walked into his living-room, then turned and walked dazedly out again and dropped his muddy jacket on the terrace, also his trousers. In his shorts now, he put on lights and went upstairs to his bathroom. A bath refreshed him. He put a towel around his neck. The cut on his head was bleeding. Tom had touched it only once with his washcloth to get the mud out, and then tried to forget it, because there was nothing he could do about it alone. He put on his dressing-gown and went down to the kitchen, made a sandwich of sliced ham and poured a big glass of milk, and had this snack at the kitchen table. Then he hung his jacket and trousers in his bathroom. Brush them and send them to the cleaners, the redoubtable Mme Annette would say, and what a blessing she was not here now, but she'd be back by 10 p.m., Tom thought, maybe 11.30 p.m. if she'd gone to the cinema in Fontainebleau or Melun, but he shouldn't count on that. It was now ten minutes to eight.

What would Bernard do now, Tom wondered? Drift to Paris? Somehow Tom could not see Bernard going back to London, so he ruled that idea out. But Bernard was so deranged at the moment as to be really unpredictable by any standards. Would Bernard, for instance, inform Jeff and Ed that he had killed Tom Ripley? Bernard might as well shout anything from the housetops now. In fact, Bernard was going to kill himself, and Tom sensed this the way he might have sensed a murder, because suicide was after all a form of murder. And in order for Bernard to go through, or carry out, whatever it was he intended, Tom knew that he himself had to continue to be dead.

And what a bore that was, in view of Mme Annette, Heloise, his neighbours, the police. How could he make all of them believe he was dead?

Tom put on levis and went back to the lane with the lantern from the spare loo. Sure enough, the shovel lay on the ground between the much used grave and the lane. Tom used it to fill in the grave. A beautiful tree ought to grow there at some time, Tom thought, because the ground was so well loosened. Tom even dragged back some of the old branches and leaves with which he had originally covered Murchison.

R.I.P. Tom Ripley, he thought.

Another passport might be useful, and who but Reeves Minot should he call on for it? It was high time he asked Reeves for a small favour.

Tom wrote a note to Reeves on his typewriter, and enclosed two, for safety, of his current passport photographs. He should ring Reeves tonight from Paris. Tom had decided to go to Paris, where he could hide out for a few hours and think. So Tom now took his muddy shoes and clothes up to the attic, where Mme Annette would probably not go. Tom changed clothes again, and took the estate wagon to the Melun railway station.

He was in Paris by 10.45 p.m., and he dropped the note to Reeves in a Gare de Lyon post box. Then he went to the Hotel Ritz, where he took a room under the name Daniel Stevens, wrote a made-up American passport number, saying he did not have his passport with him. Address: 14 rue du Docteur Cavet, Rouen, a street which as far as Tom knew did not exist.

17

Tom telephoned Heloise from his room. She was not in. The maid said she had gone out to dinner with her parents. Tom put in a call to Reeves in Hamburg. This came through in twenty minutes, and Reeves was in.

'Greetings, Reeves. Tom here. I'm in Paris. How goes everything? ... Can you pop me a passport *tout de suite*? I've already sent you photographs.'

Reeves sounded flustered. Good heavens, was this a real request at last? A passport? Yes, those essential little things that were pinched all the time, everywhere. How much would Reeves want for it, Tom was polite enough to ask.

Reeves couldn't say just now.

'Put it on the bill,' Tom said with confidence. 'The point is to get it to me at once. If you get my pictures Monday morning, can you finish by Monday night? ... Yes, it is urgent. Have you got a friend flying to Paris late Monday night, for example?' If not, find one, Tom thought.

Yes, Reeves said, a friend could fly to Paris. Not another carrier (or host), Tom insisted, because he would not be in any position to pick someone's pockets or suitcase.

'Any American name,' Tom said. 'American passport preferred, English will do. Meanwhile I'm at the Ritz, Place Vendôme ... Daniel Stevens.' Tom gave the Ritz's telephone number for Reeves's convenience, and said he would meet Reeves's messenger personally, once he knew the time the man could get to Orly.

By this time, Heloise was back in Chantilly, and Tom spoke with her. '*Yes*, I am in Paris. Do you want to come in tonight?'

Heloise did. Tom was delighted. He had a vision of sitting across a table from Heloise, drinking champagne, in another hour or so, if Heloise wanted champagne, and she usually did.

Tom stood on the grey pavement, looking out at the round Place Vendôme. Circles annoyed him. What direction should he take? Left towards l'Opéra, or right towards the rue de Rivoli? Tom preferred to think in squares or rectangles. Where was Bernard? Why do you want a passport, he asked himself? As an ace in the hole? An added measure of potential freedom? *I can't draw like Derwatt*, Bernard had said this afternoon. *I simply don't draw any more – seldom for myself even*. Was Bernard at this moment in some Paris hotel, cutting his wrists in a basin? Leaning over the Seine on one of the bridges about to jump over – gently – when no one was looking?

Tom walked in a straight line towards the rue de Rivoli. It was dull and dark at this time of night, and shop windows were barred with steel bands and chains against the theft of the tourist-aimed crap they displayed – silk handkerchiefs with 'Paris' printed on them, overpriced silk ties and shirts. He thought of taking a taxi to the sixth *arrondissment*, strolling about in that more cheerful atmosphere and having a beer at Lippe's. But he did not want possibly to run into Chris. He went back to his hotel, and put in a call to Jeff's studio.

This call (the operator said) would take forty-five minutes, the lines were crowded, but it came through in half an hour.

'Hello? – Paris?' Jeff's voice came like that of a drowning dolphin.

'*It's Tom in Paris!* Can you hear me?'

'*Badly!*'

It was not bad enough for Tom to attempt a second call. He pursued: 'I don't know where Bernard *is*. Have you heard from him?'

'Why are you in Paris?'

Rather useless, under the circumstances of near inaudibility, to explain that. Tom managed to learn that Jeff and Ed had not heard anything from Bernard.

Then Jeff said, 'They're trying to find *Derwatt* ...' (Muttered English curses.) 'My God, if I can't hear *you*, I doubt if anybody in between can hear a bloody ...'

'*D'accord!*' Tom responded. 'Tell me all your troubles.'

'Murchison's wife may ...'

'What?' Good God, the telephone was a maddening device. People should revert to pen and paper and the packet-boat. 'Can't hear a damned word!'

'We sold "The Tub" ... They are asking ... for Derwatt! Tom, if you'd only ...'

They were suddenly cut off.

Tom banged the telephone down in anger, gripped it and lifted it again, ready to blast at the operator downstairs. But he put the telephone down. It wasn't her fault. It was nobody's fault, nobody who could be found.

Well, Mrs Murchison was coming over, as Tom had foreseen. And maybe she knew about the lavender theory. And 'The Tub' was sold, to whom? And Bernard was – where? Athens? Would he repeat Derwatt's act and drown himself off a Greek island? Tom saw himself going to Athens. What was that island of Derwatt's? Icaria? Where was it? Find out tomorrow in a tourist agency.

Tom sat down at the writing-table and dashed off a note:

Dear Jeff,

In case you see Bernard, I am supposed to be dead. Bernard thinks he has killed me. I will explain later. Don't pass this on to anyone, it is *only* in case you see Bernard and he says he has killed me – pretend to believe him and don't do anything. Stall Bernard, please.

All the best,
Tom

Tom went downstairs and posted the letter with a seventy-centime stamp bought at the desk. Jeff probably wouldn't get it till Tuesday. But it was not the kind of message he dared send by cable. Or did he? *I must lie low even under ground re Bernard.* No, that wasn't clear enough. He was still pondering when Heloise came in the door. Tom was glad to see that she had her small Gucci valise with her.

'Good evening, Mme Stevens,' Tom said in French. 'You are Mme Stevens this evening.' Tom thought of steering her to the desk to register, then decided not to bother, and led Heloise to the lift.

Three pairs of eyes followed them. Was she really his wife?

'Tome, you are pale!'

'I've had a busy day.'

'Ah, what is that –'

'Sh-h.' She meant the back of his head. Heloise noticed everything. Tom thought he could tell her a few things, but not everything. The grave – that would be too horrible. Besides, it would make Bernard out a killer, which he wasn't. Tom tipped the lift man, who insisted on carrying Heloise's valise.

'What happened to your head?'

Tom took off the dark green and blue muffler that he had been wearing high around his neck to catch the blood. 'Bernard hit me. Now don't be worried, darling. Take off your shoes. Your clothes. Make yourself comfortable. Would you like some champagne?'

'Yes. Why not?'

Tom ordered it by telephone. Tom felt light-headed, as if he had a fever, but he knew it was only fatigue and loss of blood. Had he checked over the house for blood drops? Yes, he remembered going upstairs at the last minute especially to look for blood anywhere.

'Where is Bernard?' Heloise had slipped off her shoes and was barefoot.

'I really don't know. Maybe Paris.'

'You had a fight? He wouldn't leave?'

'Oh – a slight fight. He is very nervous just now. It is nothing serious, nothing.'

'But why did you come to Paris? Is he still at the house?'

That was a possibility, Tom realized, though Bernard's things had been gone from the house. Tom had looked. And Bernard couldn't get back into the house without breaking a french window. 'He's not at the house, no.'

'I want to see your head. Come into the bathroom where there is more light.'

A knock came at the door. They were quick with the champagne. The portly, grey-haired waiter grinned as the cork popped. The bottle crunched pleasantly into a bucket of ice.

'Merci, m'sieur,' said the waiter, taking Tom's banknote.

Tom and Heloise lifted their glasses, Heloise a little uncertainly, and drank. She had to see his head. Tom submitted. He took off his shirt, and bent over and closed his eyes, as Heloise washed the back of his head in the basin with a face towel. He closed his ears, or tried to, to her exclamations which he had anticipated.

'It isn't a big cut, or it would've kept on bleeding!' Tom said. The washing was making it bleed again, of course. 'Get another towel – get something,' Tom said, and returned to the bedroom, where he sank gently to the floor. He was not out, so he crawled to the bathroom where the floor was of tile.

Heloise was talking about adhesive tape.

Tom fainted for a minute, though he didn't mention it. He crawled to the toilet and threw up briefly. He used some of Heloise's wet towels for his face and forehead. Then a couple of minutes later, he was standing at the basin, sipping champagne, while Heloise made a bandage out of a small white handkerchief. 'Why do you carry adhesive tape?' Tom asked.

'I use it for my nails.'

How, Tom wondered? He held the tape while she cut it. 'Pink adhesive tape,' Tom said, 'it is a sign of racial discrimination. Black Power in the States ought to get onto that – and stop it.'

Heloise didn't understand. Tom had spoken in English.

'I will explain it tomorrow – maybe.'

Then they were in bed, in the luxurious wide bed with four thick pillows, and Heloise had donated her pyjamas to put under Tom's head, in case he bled any more, but he thought it had almost stopped. Heloise was naked, and she felt unbelievably smooth, like something of polished marble, only of course she was soft, and even warm. It was not an evening for making love, but Tom felt very happy, and not at all worried about tomorrow – which was perhaps unwise of him, but that night, or rather early morning, he indulged himself. In the darkness, he heard the hiss of champagne bubbles as Heloise sipped her glass, and the click as she set it down on the night-table. Then his cheek was against her breast. Heloise, you're the only woman in the world who has ever made me think of *now*, Tom wanted to say, but he was too tired, and the remark was probably not important.

In the morning, Tom had some explaining to do to Heloise, and he had to do it subtly. He said that Bernard Tufts was upset because of his English girl-friend, that he might kill himself, and Tom wanted to find him. He might be in Athens. And since the police wanted to keep Tom in their sight because of Murchison's disappearance, it was best that the police thought he was in Paris, staying with friends, perhaps. Tom explained that he was awaiting a passport which could come only by Monday evening at best. Tom and Heloise were breakfasting in bed.

'I don't understand why you bother about this *fou* who even hit you.'

'Friendship,' Tom said. 'Now, darling, why don't you go back to Belle Ombre and keep Mme Annette company? Or – we can ring her and you can spend today and tonight with me,' Tom said more cheerfully. 'But we'd better change hotels today, just for safety.'

'Oh, Tome –' But Heloise didn't mean her disappointed tone,

Tom knew. She liked doing things that were a little sly, keeping secrets when secrets were unnecessary. The stories she'd told Tom about her adolescent intrigues with girl schoolmates, and boys, too, to evade her parents' surveillance, matched the inventions of Cocteau.

'We'll have another name today. What name would you like? Got to be something American or English, because of me. You're just my French wife, you see?' Tom was speaking in English.

'Hm-m. Gladstone?'

Tom laughed.

'Is there something funny about Gladstone?'

How Heloise hated the English language, because she thought it was full of dirty double meanings that she could never master. 'No, it's just that he invented a suitcase.'

'He invented the *suitcase*! I don't believe you! Who could invent a suitcase? It is too *simple*! Really, Tome!'

They moved to the Hotel Ambassadeur, in the boulevard Haussmann, in the ninth *arrondissement*. Conservative and respectable. Here, Tom registered as William Tenyck, with wife Mireille. Tom made a second call to Reeves, and left his new name, address and telephone number, PRO 72–21, with the man with the German accent who frequently answered Reeves's telephone.

Tom and Heloise went to a film in the afternoon, and returned to the hotel at 6 p.m. No message as yet from Reeves. Heloise rang Mme Annette, at Tom's suggestion, and Tom spoke with Madame also.

'Yes, we are in Paris,' Tom said. 'I am sorry I didn't leave you a note . . . Perhaps Mme Heloise will return late tomorrow night, I am not sure.' He handed the phone back to Heloise.

Bernard had certainly not been in evidence at Belle Ombre, or Mme Annette would have mentioned him.

They went to bed early. Tom had unsuccessfully tried to persuade Heloise to cut away the silly strips of adhesive on the back of his head, and she had even bought some lavender-coloured French antiseptic with which she soaked the patch of bandage. She had rinsed his muffler out at the Ritz, and it had been dry by morning. Just before midnight, their telephone rang. Reeves said that a friend would bring him what he needed tomorrow night Monday on Lufthansa flight 311 due at Orly at 12.15 a.m.

'And his name?' Tom asked.

'It's a woman, Gerda Schneider. She knows what you look like.'

'Okay,' Tom said, quite pleased with the service in view of the fact Reeves hadn't yet received his photographs. 'Want to come with me tomorrow night to Orly?' Tom asked Heloise when he had hung up.

'I will drive you. I want to know if you are safe.'

Tom told her that the station wagon was at the Melun station. She perhaps could get André, a gardener they sometimes used, to go with her to fetch it.

They decided to stay another night at the Ambassadeur, in case there was any hitch about the passport on Monday night. Tom thought of catching a night-flight to Greece in the small hours of Tuesday, but this couldn't be determined until he had the passport in hand. There was also the matter of acquainting himself with the signature on the passport. All this, he realized, to save Bernard's life. Tom wished he could share his thoughts, his feelings, with Heloise, but he was afraid he could not make her understand. Would she understand if she knew about the forgeries? Yes, she might, intellectually, if he could use such a word. But Heloise would say, 'Why is it all on your shoulders? Can't Jeff and Ed look for their friend – their breadwinner?' Tom did not begin the story to her. It was best to be alone, stripped for action, in a sense. Stripped of sympathy, even of tender thoughts from home.

And all went well. Tom and Heloise arrived at Orly at midnight Monday, and the flight came in on time, and Gerda Schneider – or a woman who used that name – accosted Tom at the upstairs gate where he waited.

'Tom Ripley?' she said, smiling.

'Yes. Frau Schneider?'

She was a woman of about thirty, blonde, quite handsome and intelligent looking, and quite unmade up, as if she had just washed her face in cold water and put on some clothes. 'Mr

Ripley, I am indeed honoured to meet you,' she said in English. 'I have heard so much about you.'

Tom laughed out loud at her polite and amused tone. It was a surprise to him that Reeves could muster such interesting people to work for him. 'I'm with my wife. She's downstairs. You're staying the night in Paris?'

She was. She even had a hotel room booked, at the Pont-Royal in the rue Montalembert. Tom introduced her to Heloise. Tom fetched the car, while Heloise and Frau Schneider waited for him not far from where Tom had deposited Murchison's suitcase. They drove all the way to Paris, to the Pont-Royal, before Frau Schneider said:

'I shall give you the package here.'

They were still in the car. Gerda Schneider opened her large handbag and removed a white envelope which was rather thick.

Tom was parked, and it was somewhat dark. He took out the green American passport and stuck it in his jacket pocket. The passport had been wrapped in apparently blank sheets of paper. 'Thank you,' Tom said. 'I'll be in touch with Reeves. How is he? ...'

A few minutes later, Tom and Heloise were driving towards the Hotel Ambassadeur.

'She is quite pretty, for a German,' Heloise said.

In their room, Tom took a look at the passport. It was a well-worn thing, and Reeves had abrased his photograph to match it. *Robert Fiedler Mackay* was his name, age 31, born in Salt Lake City, Utah, occupation engineer, dependants none. The signature was slender and high, all the letters connected, a hand-writing Tom associated with a couple of boring characters, American men, he had known.

'Darling – Heloise – I am now *Robert*,' Tom said in French. 'If you'll excuse me, I have to practise my signature for a while.'

Heloise was leaning against the *commode*, watching him.

'Oh, darling! Don't worry! ' Tom put his arms around her. 'Let's have champagne! All goes well!'

*

By 2 p.m. on Tuesday, Tom was in Athens – more chromed,

cleaner than the Athens he had seen last, five or six years ago. Tom registered at the Hotel Grande Bretagne, tidied up a little in his room which gave onto Constitution Square, then went out to look around and to inquire at a few other hotels for Bernard Tufts. Impossible to believe Bernard had registered at the Grande Bretagne, Tom thought, the most expensive hotel in Athens. Tom was even sixty per cent sure Bernard was *not* in Athens, but he had made his way to Derwatt's island, or to some island; even so Tom felt it would be stupid not to ask at a few Athens hotels.

Tom's story was that he had been separated from a friend whom he was supposed to meet – Bernard Tufts. No, his own name didn't matter, but when asked it, Tom gave it – Robert Mackay.

'What is the situation now with the islands?' Tom asked at one reasonably decent hotel where he thought they might know something about tourism. Tom spoke in French here, though in other hotels, English had been spoke, a little. 'Icaria in particular.'

'Icaria?' with surprise.

It was considerably east, one of the northernmost of the Dodecanese. No airport. There were boats, but the man was not sure how frequently they went.

Tom got there on Wednesday. He had to hire a speedboat with a skipper from Mykonos. Icaria – after Tom's brief and instantaneous optimism about it – was a crashing disappointment. The town of Armemisti (or something like that) was sleepy-looking, and Tom saw no Westerners at all, only sailors mending nets, and locals sitting in tiny cafés. From here, after inquiring if there had been an Englishman named Bernard Tufts, dark-haired, slender, etc. Tom made a telephone call to another town on the island called Agios Kirycos. A hotel-keeper there checked for him, and said he would check at another hostelry and ring back. He did not ring back. Tom gave it up. A needle in a haystack, Tom thought. Maybe Bernard had chosen another island.

Still, *this* island, because it had been the scene of Derwatt's suicide, had a faint and filtered mystery for Tom. On these yellow-white beaches, somewhere, Philip Derwatt had taken a walk out to sea and had never returned. Tom doubted that any inhabitant of Icaria would react to the name Derwatt, but Tom tried it with the café proprietor, without success. Derwatt had been here scarcely a month, Tom thought, and that six long years ago. Tom refreshed himself at a little restaurant with a plate of stewed tomato and rice and lamb, then extricated the skipper from another bar-restaurant where the skipper had said he would be until 4 p.m., in case Tom wanted him.

They sped back to Mykonos, where the skipper was based. Tom had his suitcase with him. Tom felt restless, exhausted and frustrated. He decided to go back to Athens tonight. He sat in a café, dejectedly drinking a cup of sweet coffee. Then he went back to the dock where he had met the Greek skipper, and found him after going to his house, where he was having supper.

'How much to take me to Piraeus tonight?' Tom asked. Tom still had some American travellers' cheques.

Much to-do, a recitation of difficulties, but money solved everything. Tom slept part of the way, tied onto a wooden bench in the small cabin of the boat. It was 5 a.m. or so when they got to the Piraeus. The skipper Antinou was giddy with joy or money or fatigue, or maybe ouzo, Tom didn't know. Antinou said he had friends in Piraeus who were going to be happy to see him.

The dawn cold was cutting. Tom bludgeoned a taxi-driver, verbally, by promising handfuls of money, to take him to Constitution Square in Athens, and to the door of the Grande Bretagne.

Tom was given a room, not the same one he had had. They had not finished cleaning that, the night porter told him quite honestly. Tom wrote Jeff's studio number on a piece of paper and asked the porter to put the call through to London.

Then he went upstairs to his room and had a bath, listening all the while for the telephone's ringing. It was a quarter to 8 a.m. before the call came through.

'This is Tom in Athens,' Tom said. He had been almost asleep in his bed.

'Athens?'

'Any news of Bernard?'

'No, nothing. What're you –'

'I'm coming over to London. By tonight, I mean. Get the make-up ready. All right?'

18

On impulse on Thursday afternoon, Tom bought a green rain-coat in Athens, a raincoat of a style he would never have chosen himself – that was to say, Tom Ripley would never have touched it. It had a lot of flaps and straps, some of which fastened with double rings, some of which had little buckles, as if the raincoat had been meant to be weighted down with dispatches, military water-bottles, cartridges, a mess kit, bayonet and a baton or two. It was in bad taste, and Tom thought it would help him on entering London – just in case one of the immigration inspectors actually remembered what Thomas Ripley looked like. Tom also changed the parting in his hair from left to right, though the parting did not show in the straight-on photographs. Luckily, his suitcase bore no initials. Money was now the problem, as Tom had only travellers' cheques in the name Ripley, which he couldn't hand out in London the way he had to the Greek skipper, but Tom had enough drachmas (obtained with French francs from Heloise) for a one-way ticket to London, and in London Jeff and Ed could finance him. Tom removed cards and anything identifying from his billfold, and stuck these things into the buttoned back pocket of his trousers. But he really was not expecting a search.

He survived the Heathrow Immigration Control desk. 'How long are you here for?' 'Not more than four days, I think.' 'A business trip?' 'Yes.' 'Where will you be staying?' 'The Londoner Hotel – Welbeck Street.'

Once more, the bus ride to the London Terminus, and Tom went to a booth and rang Jeff's studio. It was 10.15 p.m.

A woman answered.

'Is Mr Constant there?' Tom asked. 'Or Mr Banbury?'

'They're both out just now. Who is that, please?'

'Robert – Robert Mackay.' No reaction, because Tom had not

given his new name to Jeff. Tom knew that Jeff and Ed must have left someone, someone who was an ally, in the studio to await Tom Ripley. 'Is this Cynthia?'

'Y-yes,' said the rather high voice.

Tom decided to risk it. 'This is Tom,' he said. 'When is Jeff coming back?'

'Oh, Tom! I wasn't sure it was you. They're due back in half an hour. Can you come here?'

Tom caught a taxi to the St John's Wood studio.

Cynthia Gradnor opened the door. 'Tom – hello.'

Tom had almost forgotten how she looked: medium height, brown hair that hung straight to her shoulders, rather large grey eyes. Now she looked thinner than he recalled. And she was nearly thirty. She seemed a trifle jumpy.

'You saw Bernard?'

'Yes, but I don't know where he went to.' Tom smiled. He assumed Jeff (and Ed) had obeyed him and not told anyone of Bernard's attempt on his life. 'He's probably in Paris.'

'Do sit down, Tom! Can I get you a drink?'

Tom smiled, and offered the parcel he had acquired at the Athens airport, White Horse Scotch. Cynthia was quite friendly – on the surface. Tom was glad.

'Bernard's always upset during a show,' said Cynthia, fixing the drinks. 'So I'm told. I haven't seen him much lately. As you may know.'

Tom emphatically wasn't going to mention that Bernard had told him Cynthia had rejected him – didn't want to see him. Maybe Cynthia didn't really mean that. Tom couldn't guess. 'Well,' Tom said cheerfully, 'he says he's not going to paint any more – Derwatts. That's one good thing for him, I'm sure. He's hated it, he says.'

Cynthia handed Tom his drink. 'It's a ghastly business. *Ghastly!*'

It was, Tom knew. Ghastly. Cynthia's visible shudder brought it home to Tom. A murder, lies, fraud – yes it was a ghastly business. 'Well – unfortunately it's gone this far,' Tom said, 'but it won't go further. This is Derwatt's final appearance, you might say. Unless Jeff and Ed have decided they – they don't want me to play him any more. Even now, I mean.'

Cynthia seemed to pay no attention to this. It was odd. Tom had sat down, but Cynthia walked slowly up and down the floor, and seemed to be listening for the footsteps of Jeff and Ed on the stairs. 'What happened to the man called Murchison? His wife is arriving tomorrow, I think. Jeff and Ed think.'

'I don't know. I can't help you,' Tom said quite calmly. He could not afford to let Cynthia's questions upset him. He had work to do. Good God, the wife arriving tomorrow.

'Murchison knows the paintings are being forged. What did he base that on, exactly?'

'*His* opinion,' Tom said, and shrugged. 'Oh, he talked about the spirit of a painting, the personality – I doubt if he could have convinced a London expert. Who knows where the line divides between Derwatt and Bernard now frankly? Tedious bastards, these self-appointed art critics. Just about as amusing to listen to as art reviews are to read – spatial concepts, plastic values and all that jazz.' Tom laughed, shot his cuffs, and this time they shot. 'Murchison saw mine at home, one genuine and one of Bernard's. Naturally, I tried to discourage him, and if I may say so, I think I did. I don't think he was going to keep his appointment with – with the man at the Tate Gallery.'

'But where did he disappear to.'

Tom hesitated. 'It's a mystery. Where did Bernard disappear to? I don't know. Murchison may have had ideas of his own. Personal reasons for disappearing. Or else it's a mysterious shanghaiing at Orly!' Tom was nervous, and hated the subject.

'It doesn't simplify things here. It looks as if Murchison was eliminated or something, because he knew about the forging.'

'That is what I'm trying to correct. And then bow out. The forging has not been proven. Ah, yes, Cynthia, it's a nasty game, but having gone this far, we have to see it through – to a certain extent.'

'Bernard said he wanted to admit it all – to the police. Maybe he's doing that.'

That *was* a horrible possibility, and Tom shuddered a little at the thought, as Cynthia had shuddered. He tossed off his drink. Yes, if the British police crashed in tomorrow with amused smiles, while he was in the middle of his second Derwatt performance, that would be rather a catastrophe. 'I don't think Bernard's doing that,' Tom said, but he wasn't sure of what he said.

Cynthia looked at him. 'Did you try to persuade Bernard, too?'

Tom was suddenly stung by her hostility, a hostility of years' standing, Tom knew. *He* had dreamed up this whole mess. 'I did,' Tom said, 'for two reasons. One – it would finish Bernard's own career, and second –'

'I think Bernard's career is finished, if you mean Bernard Tufts as a painter.'

'Second,' Tom said as gently as he could, 'Bernard is not the only person involved, unfortunately. It would ruin also Jeff and Ed, the – whoever they are making the art supplies, unless they deny knowing about the fraud, which I doubt they could do successfully. The art school in Italy –'

Cynthia gave a tense sigh. She seemed unable to speak. Perhaps she did not want to say any more. She walked around the square studio again, and looked at a blown-up photograph of a kangaroo that Jeff had leaned against a wall. 'It's been two years since I was in this room. Jeff gets more posh all the time.'

Tom was silent. To his relief, he heard faint footsteps, a blur of male voices.

Someone knocked. 'Cynthia? It's us!' Ed called.

Cynthia opened the door.

'Well, *Tom*!' Ed yelled, and rushed to grip his hand.

'Tom! Greetings!' Jeff said, as merry as Ed.

Jeff carried a small black suitcase which contained the make-up, Tom knew.

'Had to call on our Soho friend for the make-up again,' Jeff said. 'How are you, Tom? How was Athens?'

'Gloomy,' Tom said. 'Have a drink, boys. The colonels, you know. Didn't hear any bouzoukis. Look, I hope there's no show tonight.' Jeff was opening the suitcase.

'No. Just checking to see if everything is here. Did you hear anything from Bernard?'

'What a question,' Tom said. 'No.' He glanced uneasily at Cynthia, who was leaning with folded arms against a cabinet across the room. Did she know he had gone to Greece especially to look for Bernard? Was it of any importance to tell her? No.

'Or Murchison?' Ed asked over his shoulder. He was helping himself to a drink.

'No,' Tom said. 'I understand Mrs Murchison is coming tomorrow?'

'She *may*,' Jeff replied. 'Webster rang us up today and said that. You know, Webster the Inspector.'

Tom simply could not speak with Cynthia in the room. He didn't speak. He wanted to say something casual, such as, 'Who bought "The Tub"?' but he couldn't even do this. Cynthia was hostile. She might not betray them, but she was anti.

'By the way, Tom,' Ed said, bringing Jeff a drink (Cynthia still had her drink), 'you can stay here tonight. We're hoping you will.'

'With pleasure,' Tom said.

'And tomorrow – morning, Jeff and I thought we'd ring Webster around ten-thirty, and if we can't get him, we'll leave a message, that you arrived by train in London this morning – tomorrow, and rang us up. You've been staying with friends near Bury St Edmunds, something like that and you hadn't – uh –'

'You didn't consider the search for you serious enough for you to inform the police of your whereabouts,' Jeff put in, as if he were reciting a Mother Goose rhyme. 'Matter of fact they weren't combing the streets for you. They just asked us a couple of times where Derwatt was, and we said you were probably with friends in the country.'

'*D'accord*,' Tom said.

'I think I'll push off,' Cynthia said.

'Oh, Cynthia – not the other half of your drink?' Jeff asked.

'No.' She was putting on her coat, and Ed helped her. 'I really only wanted to know if there was news of Bernard, you know.'

'Thanks, Cynthia, for holding the fort for us here,' Jeff said.

An unfortunate metaphor, Tom thought. Tom stood up. 'I'll be sure to let you know if I hear anything, Cynthia. I'll be going back to Paris soon – maybe even tomorrow.'

Mumbled good-byes at the door among Cynthia, Jeff and Ed. Jeff and Ed came back.

'Is she really still in love with him?' Tom asked. 'I didn't think so. Bernard said —'

Both Jeff and Ed had vaguely pained expressions.

'Bernard said what?' Jeff asked.

'Bernard said he rang her from Paris last week and she said she didn't want to see him. Or maybe Bernard was exaggerating, I don't know.'

'Neither do we,' Ed said, and shoved his lank blond hair back. He went for another drink.

'I thought Cynthia had a boy-friend,' Tom said.

'Oh, it's the same one,' Ed said in a bored tone from the kitchen.

'Stephen something,' Jeff said. 'He hasn't set her on fire.'

'He's not the fireball type!' Ed said, laughing.

'She still has the same job,' Jeff went on. 'It pays well and she's Number One girl for some sort of a big shot.'

'She is *settled*,' Ed put in, with finality. 'Now where *is* Bernard, and what did you mean by he's supposed to think you're dead?'

Tom explained, briefly. Also about the burial, which he managed to make funny so that Jeff and Ed were enthralled, maybe morbidly fascinated, and laughing at the same time. 'Just a small tap on the head,' Tom said. He had stolen Heloise's scissors and cut off the adhesive tape in the loo of the plane going to Athens.

'Let me touch you!' Ed said, seizing Tom's shoulder. 'Here's a man who's climbed out of the grave, Jeff!'

'More than we'll do. More than I'll do,' said Jeff.

Tom removed his jacket and seated himself more comfortably on Jeff's rust-coloured couch. 'I suppose you have guessed,' Tom said, 'that Murchison is dead?'

'We did *think* that,' Jeff said solemnly. 'What happened?'

'I killed him. In my cellar — with a wine bottle.' At this odd moment, it occurred to Tom that he might, that he ought to send Cynthia some flowers. She could toss them in the waste-basket or the fireplace, if she wished. Tom reproached himself for having been ungallant with Cynthia.

Jeff and Ed were still speechlessly recovering from what he had said.

'Where's the body?' asked Jeff.

'At the bottom of some river. Near me. I think the Loing,' Tom said. Should he tell them that Bernard assisted him? No. Why bother? Tom rubbed his forehead. He was tired, and he slumped on one elbow.

'My God,' Ed said. 'Then you took his stuff to Orly?'

'His stuff, yes.'

'Haven't you got a housekeeper?' Jeff asked.

'Yes. I had to do all this secretly. Around her,' Tom said. 'Early in the morning and all that.'

'But you spoke about the burial place in the woods – that Bernard used.' This from Ed.

'Yes, I – had Murchison buried in the woods first, then the police came investigating, so before they got to the woods, I thought I should get him – out of the woods, so I –' Tom gestured, a vague dumping motion. No, best not to mention that Bernard had helped him. If Bernard wanted to – what did he want to do, redeem himself? – the less complicity Bernard had, the better.

'Gosh,' Ed said. 'My God. Can you face his wife?'

'Sh-h,' said Jeff quickly, with a nervous smile.

'Of course,' Tom said. 'I had to do it, because Murchison got onto me – down in the cellar, matter of fact. He realized that I'd been playing Derwatt in London. So it was all up if I didn't get rid of him. You see?' Tom walked about trying to feel less sleepy.

They did see, and they were impressed. At the same time, Tom could sense their brains grinding: Tom Ripley had killed before. Dickie Greenleaf, no? And maybe the other fellow named Freddie something. That was a suspicion merely, but wasn't it true? How seriously was Tom taking this killing, and in fact how much gratitude was he going to expect from Derwatt Ltd? Gratitude, loyalty, money? Did it all come down to the same thing? Tom was idealistic enough to think not, to hope not. Tom hoped for a higher calibre in Jeff Constant and Ed Banbury. After all, they had been friends of the great Derwatt, even his best friends. How great was Derwatt? Tom dodged this question. How great was Bernard? Well, pretty great as a painter, if the truth be told. Tom stood up straighter, because of Bernard (who had avoided Jeff and Ed for years from the point of view of friendship), and said, 'Well, my friends – how about briefing me on tomorrow? Who else is turning up? I admit I'm tired and I wouldn't mind going to bed soon.'

Ed was standing facing him. 'Any clues against you about Murchison, Tom?'

'Not that I know of.' Tom smiled. 'Nothing except the facts.'

'Was "The Clock" really stolen?'

'The picture was with Murchison's suitcase – wrapped separately – at Orly. Somebody swiped it, that's plain,' Tom said. 'I wonder who's hanging it now? I wonder if they know what they've got? In which case it might not be hanging. Let's get on with the briefing, shall we? Can we have some music?'

To souped-up Radio Luxembourg, Tom submitted to a semi-dress rehearsal. The beard, on gauze, was still in one piece, and they tested it but did not glue it. Bernard had not taken back Derwatt's old dark-blue suit, and Tom put on the jacket.

'Do you know anything about Mrs Murchison?' Tom asked.

They didn't really, though they volunteered fragments of information which showed her, as far as Tom could see, neither aggressive nor timid, intelligent nor stupid. One datum cancelled out the other. Jeff had spoken with her by telephone at the Buckmaster Gallery, where she had rung by a cabled pre-arrangement.

'A miracle she didn't ring me,' Tom said.

'Oh, we said we didn't know your telephone number,' said Ed, 'and considering it was France, I suppose it gave her pause.'

'Mind if I ring my house tonight?' Tom asked, putting on Derwatt's voice. 'By the way, I'm broke here.'

Jeff and Ed could not have been more obliging. They had plenty of cash on hand. Jeff put in the call at once to Belle Ombre. Ed made Tom a small strong coffee, which Tom asked for. Tom showered and got into pyjamas. That was better – in a pair of Jeff's house-slippers as well. Tom was to sleep on the studio couch.

'I hope I've made it clear,' Tom said, 'Bernard wants to call it quits. Derwatt will go into permanent retirement and – maybe get eaten by ants in Mexico or devoured by fire, and presumably any future paintings along with him.'

Jeff nodded, started to nibble a fingernail, and whipped it out of his mouth. 'What have you told your wife?'

'Nothing,' Tom said. 'Nothing important, really.'

The telephone rang.

Jeff beckoned Ed to come into his bedroom with him.

'Hello, darling, it's *me*!' Tom said. 'No, I'm in London... Well, I changed my mind...'

When was he coming home? ... And Mme Annette's tooth was hurting again.

'Give her the dentist's name in *Fontainebleau*!' Tom said.

It was surprising how comforting a telephone call could be in the circumstances in which he was now. It almost made Tom love the telephone.

19

'Is Detective Inspector Webster there, please?' Jeff asked. 'Jeffrey Constant of the Buckmaster Gallery. ... Would you tell the Inspector that I had a ring from Derwatt this morning, and we expect to see him this morning at the gallery. ... I'm not sure of the exact time. Before twelve.'

It was a quarter to ten.

Tom stood in front of the long mirror again, examining his beard and the reinforcement of his eyebrows. Ed was looking at his face under one of Jeff's strongest lamps, which was glaring in Tom's eyes. His hair was lighter than the beard, but darker than his own, as before. Ed had been careful with the cut on the back of his head, and happily it was not bleeding. 'Jeff, old man,' Tom said in Derwatt's taut voice. 'Can you cut that music and get something else?'

'What would you like?'

'*A Midsummer Night's Dream*. Have you got a record?'

'No-o,' Jeff said.

'Can you get it? That's what I'm in the mood for. It inspires me, and I need inspiration.' Imagining the music this morning was not quite enough.

Jeff didn't know anyone, even, who he was sure had it.

'Can't you go out and get it, Jeff? Isn't there a music shop between here and St John's Wood Road?'

Jeff ran out.

'You didn't speak with Mrs Murchison, I suppose,' Tom said, relaxing for a moment with a Gauloise. 'I must buy some English cigarettes. I don't want to push my luck too much with these Gauloises.'

'Take these. If you run out, people'll offer you fags,' Ed said quickly, shoving a packet of something into Tom's pocket. 'No, I didn't speak with her. At least she hadn't sent over an American detective. That might be pretty rough if she did.'

She might be flying over with one, Tom thought. He removed his two rings. He had not, of course, the Mexican ring now. Tom picked up a ball-point pen and tried duplicating the bold DERWATT signature stamped on a blue pencil eraser on Jeff's table. Tom did the signature three times, then crumpled the paper on which he had written it, and dropped it into a basket.

Jeff arrived back, panting as if he had run.

'Turn it up loud – if you can,' Tom said.

The music began – rather loud. Tom smiled. It was *his* music. An audacious thought, but this was the time for audacity. Tom felt aglow now, stood up taller, then remembered Derwatt didn't stand tall. 'Jeff, can I ask another favour? Ring up a florist and have some flowers sent to Cynthia. Put it on my bill.'

'Are you talking about bills? Flowers – to Cynthia. Okay. What kind?'

'Oh, gladioli, if they have them. If not, two dozen roses.'

'Flowers, flowers, florists –' Jeff was looking in his telephone directory. 'From whom? Just signed "Tom"?'

'With love from Tom,' Tom said, and held still while Ed went over his upper lip again with pale pink lipstick. Derwatt's upper lip was fuller.

They left Jeff's studio while the first half of the record was still playing. It would turn off automatically, Jeff said. Jeff took the first taxi by himself. Tom felt sure enough to have gone on his own, but he sensed that Ed did not want to risk that, or didn't want to leave him. They went in a taxi together, and got out a street away from Bond Street.

'If somebody speaks to us, I happened to meet you walking to the Buckmaster,' Ed said.

'Relax. We shall carry the day.'

Again, Tom went in by the red-painted back door of the gallery. The office was empty, except for Jeff who was on the telephone. He motioned for them to sit down.

'Would you put that through as quickly as possible?' Jeff said. He hung up. 'I'm making a courtesy call to France. The police in Melun. To tell them Derwatt has turned up again. They did ring us, you know – Derwatt, and I promised to let them know if you got in touch with us.'

'I see,' Tom said. 'I suppose you haven't told any newspapers?'

'No, and I don't see why I should, do you?'

'No, let it go.'

Leonard, the blithe spirit who was the front manager, poked his head in the door. 'Hello! May I come in?'

'No-o!' Jeff whispered, not meaning it.

Leonard came in and closed the door, beaming at the second resurrection of Derwatt. 'I couldn't believe my eyes, if I weren't looking at it! Who're we expecting this morning?'

'Inspector Webster of the Metropolitan Police for a start,' said Ed.

'Am I to let anyone –'

'No, not just anyone,' Jeff said. 'Knock first, and I'll open the door, but I won't lock the door today. Now shoo!'

Leonard went out.

Tom was sunk in the armchair when Inspector Webster arrived.

Webster smiled like a happy rabbit with his big stained front teeth. 'How do you do, Mr Derwatt? Well! I never expected I'd have the pleasure of meeting you!'

'How do you do, Inspector?' Tom did not quite get up. Remember, he told himself, you are a little older, heavier, slower, more stooped than Tom Ripley. 'I am sorry,' Tom said easily, as if he were not very sorry and certainly not disturbed, 'that you were wondering where I was. I was with some friends down in Suffolk.'

'So I was told,' said the Inspector, taking a straight chair which was some two yards from Tom.

The venetian blind of the window was three-quarters down, partly closed, Tom had noticed. The light was adequate, even for writing a letter, but not bright.

'Well, your whereabouts were incidental, I think, to those of Thomas Murchison,' Webster said, smiling. 'It's my job to find him.'

'I read something or – Jeff said something about his disappearing in France.'

'Yes, and one of your pictures disappeared with him. "The Clock".'

'Yes. Probably not the first – theft,' Tom said philosophically. 'I understand his wife may come to London?'

'Indeed she has come.' Webster looked at his watch. 'She's due at 11 a.m. After a night flight, I dare say she'll want to rest for a couple of hours. Will you be here this afternoon, Mr Derwatt? Can you be here?'

Tom knew he had to say yes to be courteous. He said, with only a hint of reluctance, that he could be, of course. 'About what time? I have a few errands to do this afternoon.'

Webster stood up, like a busy man. 'Shall we say three-thirty? And in case of a change, I'll let you know through the gallery.' He turned to Jeff and Ed. 'Thank you so much for informing me about Mr Derwatt. Bye-bye, gentlemen.'

'Bye-bye, Inspector.' Jeff opened the door for him.

Ed looked at Tom and smiled a satisfied smile, with his lips closed. 'A little more lively for this afternoon. Derwatt was a little more – energetic. Nervous energy.'

'I have my reasons,' Tom said. He put his finger-tips together and stared into space, in the manner of Sherlock Holmes reflecting, an unconscious gesture perhaps, because he had been thinking of a certain Sherlock Holmes story which resembled this situation. Tom hoped his disguise would not be seen through so easily. At any rate, it was better than some of those exploded by Sir Arthur – when a nobleman forgot to remove his diamond ring or some such.

'What's your reason?' Jeff asked.

Tom jumped up. 'Tell you later. Now I could use a Scotch.'

They lunched at Norughe's, an Italian restaurant in the Edgware Road. Tom was hungry, and the restaurant was just to his taste – quiet, pleasant to look at, and the pasta was excellent. Tom had gnocchi with a delicious cheese sauce, and they drank two bottles of Verdicchio. A near-by table was occupied by some notables of the Royal Ballet, who plainly recognized Derwatt, as Tom recognized them, but in the English style, the exchanged glances soon stopped.

'I'd rather arrive at the gallery alone and through the front door this afternoon,' Tom said.

They all had cigars and brandy. Tom felt fit for anything, even Mrs Murchison.

'Let me out here,' Tom said in the taxi. 'I feel like walking.' He spoke in Derwatt's voice, which he had used throughout lunch, too. 'I know it's a bit of a walk, but at least there're not so many hills as in Mexico. Ah-hum.'

Oxford Street looked busy and inviting. Tom realized he had not asked Jeff or Ed if they had concocted any more receipts for paintings. Maybe Webster would not ask for them again. Maybe Mrs Murchison would. Who knew? Some of the crowd on Oxford Street glanced at him twice, perhaps recognizing him – though Tom really doubted that – or perhaps their eyes were caught by his beard and his intense eyes. Tom supposed his eyes looked intense because of his brows, and because Derwatt frowned a little, though this had not meant ill-temper, Ed had assured him.

This afternoon is either success or failure, Tom thought. It would be, it had to be a success. Tom began to imagine what would happen if the afternoon were a failure, and his mind stopped when he came to Heloise – and her family. It would be the end of all that, the end of Belle Ombre. Of Mme Annette's kind services. In plain words, he would go to prison, because it would be more than obvious that he had eliminated Murchison. Perish the thought of going to prison.

Tom came head-on with the old bloke with the sandwich boards advertising quick passport photos. As if he were blind, the old man didn't step aside. Tom did. Tom ran in front of him again. 'Remember me? Greetings!'

'Eh? Um-m?' An unlighted half-cigarette again hung from between his lips.

'Here's for luck!' Tom said, and stuck what was left of his packet of cigarettes into the old tweed overcoat pocket. Tom hurried on, remembering to stoop.

Tom walked quietly into the Buckmaster Gallery, where all Derwatt's pictures, except those on loan, were graced with a little red star. Leonard gave him a smile and a nod that was almost a bow. There were five other people in the room, a young couple (the girl barefoot on the beige carpet), one elderly gentleman, two men. As Tom made his way towards the red door at the rear of the gallery, he could feel all eyes turn and follow him – until he was out of sight.

Jeff opened the door. 'Derwatt, hello. Come in. This is Mrs Murchison – Philip Derwatt.'

Tom bowed slightly to the woman seated in the armchair. 'How do you do, Mrs Murchison?' Tom nodded also to Inspector Webster, who was sitting on a straight chair.

Mrs Murchison looked about fifty, with short razor-cut hair that was red-blonde, bright blue eyes, a rather wide mouth – a face, Tom thought, that might have been cheerful if the circumstances had been different. She wore a good tweed suit of graceful cut, a necklace of jade, a pale green sweater.

Jeff had gone behind his desk, but was not seated.

'You saw my husband in London. Here,' Mrs Murchison said to Tom.

'Yes, for a few minutes. Yes. Perhaps ten minutes.' Tom moved towards the straight chair that Ed was offering. He felt Mrs Murchison's eyes on his shoes, the nearly cracked shoes that had actually belonged to Derwatt. Tom sat down gingerly, as if he had rheumatism, or worse. Now he was some five feet away from Mrs Murchison, who had to turn her head a little to her right to see him.

'He was going to visit a Mr Ripley in France. He wrote me that,' said Mrs Murchison. 'He didn't make an appointment to see you later?'

'No,' Tom said.

'Do you happen to know Mr Ripley? I understand he has some of your pictures.'

'I've heard his name, never met him,' Tom said.

'I'm going to try to see him. After all – my husband may still be in France. What I would like to know, Mr Derwatt, is if you think there is any *ring* of your paintings – It's hard for me to put in words. Any people who would think it worth their while to do away with my husband to keep him from exposing a forgery? Or maybe several forgeries?'

Tom shook his head slowly. 'Not to my knowledge.'

'But you've been in Mexico.'

'I've talked with –' Tom looked up at Jeff, then at Ed who was leaning against the desk. 'This gallery knows of no group or ring and what is more, don't know of any forgeries. I saw the picture your husband brought, you know. "The Clock".'

'And that's been stolen.'

'Yes, so I'm told. But the point is, it's my picture.'

'My husband was going to show it to Mr Ripley.'

'He did,' Webster put in. 'Mr Ripley told me about their conversation –'

'I know, I know. My husband had his theory,' Mrs Murchison said with an air of pride or courage. 'He might be wrong. I admit I'm not such a connoisseur of paintings as my husband. But supposing he *is* right.' She waited for an answer, from anybody.

Tom hoped she didn't know about her husband's theory, or didn't understand it.

'What was his theory, Mrs Murchison?' Webster asked with an eager expression.

'Something about the purples in Mr Derwatt's later paintings – some of them. Surely he discussed it with you, Mr Derwatt?'

'Yes,' Tom said. 'He said the purples of my earlier paintings were darker. That may be so.' Tom smiled slightly. 'I hadn't noticed. If they're lighter now, I think there're more of 'em. Witness "The Tub" out there.' Tom had mentioned, without thinking, a painting Murchison had considered quite as obvious a forgery as 'The Clock' – the purples in both paintings being pure cobalt violet, in the old style.

No reaction from this.

'By the way,' Tom said to Jeff, 'you were trying to ring the French police this morning to say I was back in London. Did the call go through?'

Jeff started. 'No. No, by George, it didn't.'

Mrs Murchison said, 'Did my husband mention anyone besides Mr Ripley he was going to see in France, Mr Derwatt?'

Tom pondered. Start a small wild-goose chase? Or be honest. Tom said very honestly, 'Not that I recall. He didn't mention Mr Ripley to me, for that matter.'

'May I offer you some tea, Mrs Murchison?' Ed asked amiably.

'Oh, no thank you.'

'Anyone for tea? Or a spot of sherry?' Ed asked.

No one wanted or dared to accept anything.

It seemed to be a signal, in fact, for Mrs Murchison to take her leave. She wanted to ring Mr Ripley – she had his telephone number from the Inspector – and make an appointment to see him.

Jeff, with a coolness that was right up Tom's alley, said, 'Would you like to ring him from here, Mrs Murchison?' indicating the telephone on his desk.

'No, thanks very much, but I'll do it from my hotel.'

Tom stood up as Mrs Murchison left.

'Where're you staying in London, Mr Derwatt?' Inspector Webster asked.

'I'm staying at Mr Constant's studio.'

'May I ask how you arrived in England?' A big smile. 'The Immigration Control has no record of your entering.'

Tom looked deliberately vague and thoughtful. 'I have a Mexican passport now.' Tom had expected the question. 'And I have another name in Mexico.'

'You flew?'

'By boat,' Tom said. 'I don't much like aeroplanes.' Tom expected Webster to ask if he had landed at Southampton or where, but Webster said only:

'Thanks, Mr Derwatt. Good-bye.'

If he looked that up, Tom thought, what would he find? How many people from Mexico had entered London a fortnight ago? Probably not many.

Jeff closed the door once more. There were a few seconds of silence while their visitors moved out of hearing distance. Jeff and Ed had heard his last words.

'If he wants to look that up,' Tom said, 'I'll manufacture something else.'

'What?' asked Ed.

'Oh – a Mexican passport, for instance,' Tom replied. 'I did know – that I'd have to hop it back to France at once.' He spoke like Derwatt, but in almost a whisper.

'Not tonight, do you think?' Ed said. '*Surely* not.'

'No. Because I said I'd be at Jeff's. Don't yer know?'

'Good God,' said Jeff with relief, but he wiped the back of his neck with a handkerchief.

'We have succeeded,' Ed said, mock solemn, pulling a hand down the front of his face.

'Christ, I wish we could celebrate!' Tom said suddenly. 'How can I celebrate in this bloody beard? Out of which I had to keep the cheese sauce this *noon*? I've got to wear this beard all evening!'

'And sleep with it!' Ed yelped, falling all over the room with laughter.

'Gentlemen –' Tom drew himself up, and promptly slumped again. 'I must risk, because of need, a ring to Heloise. May I, Jeff? Subscriber Trunk Dialling, so I hope it isn't conspicuous on your bill. Too bad if it is, because I feel this is necessary.' Tom took the telephone.

Jeff made tea, and reinforced the tray with a whisky bottle.

Mme Annette answered, as Tom had hoped she wouldn't. He put on a woman's voice and asked in worse French than his own if Mme Ripley was there. 'Hush!' Tom said to Jeff and Ed who were laughing. 'Hello, Heloise.' Tom spoke in French. 'I must be brief, my darling. If anyone telephones to speak to me, I am staying in Paris with friends ... I expect a woman may ring you, a woman who speaks only English, I don't know. You must give a false number for me in Paris ... Invent one ... Thank you, darling ... I think tomorrow afternoon, but you must not say this to the American lady ... And don't tell Mme Annette I am in London ...'

When Tom hung up, he asked Jeff if he could have a look at the books Jeff said they had made, and Jeff got them out. They were two ledgers, one a bit worn, the other newer. Tom bent over them for a few minutes, reading titles of canvases and dates. Jeff was generous with space, and the Derwatts did not predominate, as the Buckmaster Gallery dealt with other painters. Jeff had entered some titles in different inks after some dates, because Derwatt did not always give his pictures titles.

'I like this page with the tea stain,' Tom said.

Jeff beamed. 'Ed's contribution. Two days old.'

'Speaking of celebrating,' Ed said, bringing his hands together with a subdued clap, 'what about Michael's party tonight? Ten thirty, he said. Holland Park Road.'

'We'll think about that,' Jeff said.

'Look in for twenty minutes?' Ed said hopefully.

'The Tub' was correctly listed as one of the later pictures, Tom saw, there probably had been no avoiding that. The ledgers were mainly filled with purchasers' names and addresses, the prices they had paid, the purchases genuine, the arrival times sometimes faked, Tom supposed, but all in all, he thought Jeff and Ed had done quite a good job. 'And the Inspector looked at these?'

'Oh, yes,' Jeff said.

'He didn't raise any questions, did he, Jeff?' Ed said.

'No.'

Vera Cruz ... Vera Cruz ... Southampton ... Vera Cruz ...
If it had passed muster, it had passed, Tom supposed.

They said good-bye to Leonard – it was near closing time anyway – and took a taxi to Jeff's studio. Tom felt they both looked at him as if he were some sort of magical personage: it amused

Tom, yet in a way he did not like it. They might have imagined him a saint, able to cure a dying plant by touching it, able to erase a headache by waving a hand, able to walk on water. But Derwatt hadn't been able to walk on water, or maybe hadn't wanted to. Yet Tom was Derwatt now.

'I want to ring Cynthia,' Tom said.

'She works till seven. It's a funny office,' Jeff said.

Tom rang Air France first and booked a 1 p.m. flight for tomorrow. He could pick up his ticket at the terminus. Tom had decided to be in London tomorrow morning, in case any difficulties arose. It mustn't look again as if Derwatt were fleeing the scene posthaste.

Tom drank sugared tea and reclined on Jeff's couch, without jacket and tie now, but still with the bothersome beard. 'I wish I could make Cynthia take Bernard back,' Tom said musingly, as if he were God having a weak moment.

'Why?' asked Ed.

'I'm afraid Bernard may destroy himself. I wish I knew where he was.'

'You mean really? Kill himself?' Jeff asked.

'Yes,' Tom said. 'I told you that – I thought. I didn't tell Cynthia. I thought it wasn't fair. It'd be like blackmail – to make her take him back. And I'm sure Bernard wouldn't like that.'

'You mean commit suicide somewhere?' Jeff said.

'Yes, I do mean that.' Tom hadn't been going to mention the effigy in his house, but he thought, why not? Sometimes the truth, dangerous as it was, could be turned to advantage to reveal something new, something more. 'He hanged himself in my cellar – in effigy. I should say he hung himself, since he was a batch of clothes. He labelled it "Bernard Tufts". The old Bernard, you see, the forger. Or maybe the real one. It's all muddled in Bernard's mind.'

'Wow! He's off his rocker, eh?' Ed said, looking at Jeff.

Both Jeff and Ed were wide-eyed, Jeff in his somewhat more calculating fashion. Were they only now realizing that Bernard Tufts was not going to paint any more Derwatts?

Tom said, 'I am speculating. No use getting upset before it's happened. But you see –' Tom got up. He started to say, *the important thing is that Bernard thinks he has killed me*. But Tom wondered, *was* it important? If so, how? Tom realized he had been glad no journalists had been on hand to write, tomorrow, 'Derwatt is back', because if Bernard saw it in any newspaper, he would know that Tom was out of the grave, somehow, alive. That, in a sense, might be good for Bernard, because Bernard might be less inclined to kill himself, if he thought he had not killed Tom Ripley. Or would this really count, in Bernard's confused thinking just now? What was right and what was wrong?

After seven, Tom rang Cynthia at a Bayswater number. 'Cynthia – before I leave, I wanted to say – in case I see Bernard again, anywhere, can I tell him one small thing, that –'

'That what?' Cynthia asked, brisk, so much more on the defensive, or at least on the protective, than Tom.

'That you'll agree to see him again. In London. It'd be wonderful, you see, if I could just say something positive like that to him. He's very depressed.'

'But I see no use in seeing him again,' Cynthia said.

In her voice, Tom heard the bulwarks of castles, churches, the middle-class. Grey and beige stones, impregnable. Decent behaviour. 'Under any circumstances, you just don't want to see him again?'

'I'm afraid I don't. It's much easier if I don't prolong things. Easier on Bernard, too.'

That was final. Stiff upper-lip stuff. But it was also petty, bloody petty. Tom at least understood where he was now. A girl had been neglected, jilted, ousted, abandoned – three years ago. It was Bernard who had broken it off. Let Bernard, under the best of circumstances, try to remedy that. 'All right, Cynthia.'

Would it do her pride any good, Tom wondered, to know Bernard would hang himself again because of her?

Jeff and Ed had been in Jeff's bedroom talking, and had not heard any of the conversation, but they asked Tom what Cynthia had said.

'She doesn't want to see Bernard again,' Tom said.

Neither Jeff nor Ed seemed to see the consequences of this.

Tom said, to bring the matter to a conclusion, 'Of course, I may never see Bernard again myself.'

20

They went to Michael's party. Michael who? They arrived around midnight. Half the guests were tiddly, and Tom could not see anyone who looked of any importance, as far as he was concerned. Tom sat in a deep chair, actually rather under a lamp, with a long Scotch and water, and chatted with a few people who seemed a little in awe of him, or at least respectful. Jeff was keeping an eye on him from across the room.

The décor was pink and full of huge tassels. Chairs resembled white meringues. Girls wore skirts so short that Tom's eye – unused to such gear – was drawn to intricate seaming of tights of various colours – then repelled. Goony, Tom thought. Absolutely nuts. Or was he seeing them as Derwatt would? Was it possible for anybody to imagine approachable flesh under those tights that showed nothing but fortified seams and sometimes more panties under them? Breasts were visible when the girls bent for cigarettes. Which half of the girl was one supposed to look at? Looking higher, Tom was startled by brown-rimmed eyes. A colourless mouth below the eyes said:

'Derwatt – can you tell me where you live in Mexico? I don't expect a real answer, but a half-real answer will do.'

Through his undistorting glasses, Tom regarded her with contemplative puzzlement, as if he were devoting half his great brain to the question she had asked, but in fact he was bored. How he preferred, Tom thought, Heloise's skirts to just above the knee, no make-up at all, and eyelashes that didn't look like a handful of spears pointed at him. 'Ah, well,' Tom said, ruminating on nothing. 'South of Durango.'

'Durango, where is that?'

'North of Mexico City. No, of course I can't tell you the name of my village. It's a long Aztec name. Ah-hah-hah.'

'We're looking for something unspoilt. We meaning my husband Zach, and we have two kids.'

'You might try Puerto Vallarta,' Tom said, and was rescued, or at least beckoned by Ed Banbury from a distance. 'Excuse me,' said Tom, and hauled himself up from the white meringue.

Ed thought it was time they slipped out. So did Tom think so. Jeff was circulating smoothly, maintaining his easy smile, chatting. Commendable, Tom thought. Young men, older men regarded Tom, perhaps not daring to approach, perhaps not wanting to.

'Shall we blow?' Tom said as Jeff joined them.

Tom insisted on finding his host, whom he had not met or seen for the hour he had been there. Michael the host was the one in a black bear parka with the hood not pulled over his head. He was not very tall and had crew-cut black hair. 'Derwatt, you've been the jewel in my carcanet tonight! I can't tell you how pleased I am and how grateful I am to these old ...'

The rest was lost in noise.

Handshakes, and at last the door closed.

'Well,' Jeff said over his shoulder when they were safely down a flight of stairs. He whispered the rest. 'The only reason we went to the party is because the people are of no importance.'

'And yet they are, somehow,' Ed said. 'They're still people. Another success tonight!'

Tom let it go. It was true, nobody had ripped off his beard.

They dropped Ed off somewhere in their taxi.

In the morning, Tom breakfasted in bed, Jeff's idea of a small consolation for having to eat through the beard. Then Jeff went out to pick up something from a photographer's supply shop, and said he would be back by 10.30 – though of course he couldn't accompany Tom to the West Kensington Terminal. It became 11. Tom went into the bathroom and started carefully removing the gauze of his beard.

The telephone rang.

Tom's first thought was not to answer it. But wouldn't that look just a little odd? Maybe evasive?

Tom braced himself for Webster and answered it, in Derwatt's voice. 'Yes? Hello?'

'Is Mr Constant there? ... Or is that Derwatt? ... Oh, good. Inspector Webster. What are your plans, Mr Derwatt?' Webster asked in his usual pleasant voice.

Tom had no plans, for Inspector Webster. 'Oh – I expect to leave this week. Back to the salt mines.' Tom chuckled. 'And quietude.'

'Could you – perhaps give me a ring before you go, Mr Derwatt?' Webster gave his number, plus an extension, and Tom wrote it down.

Jeff came back. Tom had almost his suitcase in his hand, so eager was he to be off. Their good-byes were brief, even perfunctory on Tom's part, though they knew, each knew, that their welfare depended on each other.

'Good-bye. God bless.'

'Good-bye.'

To hell with Webster.

Soon, Tom was in the cocoon of the aeroplane, the synthetic, strapped-in atmosphere of smiling hostesses, stupid yellow and white cards to fill out, the unpleasant nearness of elbows in business suits, which made Tom twitch away. He wished he had travelled first class.

Would he have to say to anyone where, as Tom Ripley, he had been in Paris? At least last night, for instance? Tom had a friend who would vouch, but he didn't want to involve another person, because there were enough people already involved.

The plane took off, standing on its tail. How boring, Tom thought, to be jetting at a few hundred miles an hour, hearing very little, letting the unfortunate people who lived below suffer the noise. Only trains excited Tom. The non-stop trains from Paris rocketing by on smooth rails past the platform in Melun – trains going so fast, one couldn't read the French and Italian names on their sides. Once Tom had almost crossed a track where it was forbidden to cross. The tracks had been empty, the station silent. Tom had decided not to risk it, and fifteen seconds later, two chromium express trains had passed each other going like hell, and Tom had imagined being chewed up between them, his body and his suitcase strewn for yards in either direction, unidentifiable. Tom thought of it now and winced in the jet aeroplane. He was glad, at least, that Mrs Murchison was not on the plane. He had even glanced around for her when he boarded.

21

France now, and as the plane descended, the tops of trees began to look like dark green and brown knots embroidered in a tapestry, or like the ornate frogs on Tom's dressing-gown at home. Tom sat in his ugly new raincoat. At Orly, the passport control glanced at him and at the picture in his Mackay passport, but did not stamp anything – nor had they when he had left Orly for London before. Only London inspectors stamped, it seemed. Tom went through the 'nothing to declare' aisle, and hopped into a taxi for home.

He was at Belle Ombre just before 3 p.m. In the taxi, he had put the parting in his hair back in its usual place, and he carried the raincoat over his arm.

Heloise was home. The heat was working. The furniture and floors gleamed with wax. Mme Annette took his bag upstairs. Then Tom and Heloise kissed.

'What did you do in Greece?' she asked a bit anxiously. 'And then in London?'

'I looked around,' Tom said, smiling.

'For that *fou*. Did you see him? How is your head?' She turned him around by the shoulders.

It was barely hurting. Tom was much relieved that Bernard hadn't turned up to alarm Heloise. 'Did the American woman telephone?'

'Ah, yes. Mme Murchison. She speaks some French, but very fon-ny. She telephoned this morning from London. She arrives at Orly this afternoon at three, and she wants to see you. Ah, *merde*, who *are* these people?'

Tom looked at his wristwatch. Mrs Murchison's plane should be touching down in ten minutes.

'Darling, do you want a cup of tea?' Heloise led him towards the yellow sofa. 'Did you see this Bernard anywhere?'

'No. I want to wash my hands. Just a minute.' Tom went into the downstairs loo and washed his hands and face. He hoped Mrs Murchison would not want to come to Belle Ombre, that she would be satisfied with seeing him in Paris, although Tom hated the idea of going to Paris today.

Mme Annette was coming downstairs as Tom went into the living-room. 'Madame, how goes the famous tooth? Better, I hope?'

'Yes, M. Tome. I went to the dentist in Fontainebleau this morning and he took out the nerve. He *really* took it out. I must go again on Monday.'

'Would we could all have our nerves taken out! All of them! No more pain now, you can count on that!' Tom was hardly aware of what he was saying. Should he have rung Webster? It had seemed to Tom a better idea *not* to ring him before leaving, because ringing might have looked too much as if he were trying to obey police orders. An innocent man wouldn't have rung, had been Tom's reasoning.

Tom and Heloise had tea.

'Noëlle wants to know if we can come to a party Tuesday night,' Heloise said. 'Tuesday is her birthday.'

Noëlle Hassler, Heloise's best friend in Paris, gave delightful parties. But Tom had been thinking about Salzburg, about going there at once, because he had decided that Bernard might have chosen Salzburg to go to. The home of Mozart, another artist who had died young. 'Darling, you must go. I am not sure I'll be here.'

'Why?'

'Because – now I may have to go to Salzburg.'

'In *Austria*? Not to look for this *fou* again! Soon it will be China!'

Tom glanced nervously at the telephone. Mrs Murchison was going to ring. When? 'You gave Mrs Murchison a telephone number in Paris where she could ring me?'

'Yes,' Heloise said. 'An invented number.' She was still speaking French, and becoming a bit annoyed with him.

Tom wondered how much he could dare explain to Heloise? 'And you told her I would be home – when?'

'I said I did not know.'

The telephone rang. If it was Mrs Murchison, she was ringing from Orly.

Tom stood up. 'The important thing,' he said quickly in English, because Mme Annette was coming in, 'is that I was not in London. Very important, darling. I was only in Paris. Don't mention London, if we have to see Mrs Murchison.'

'Is she coming *here*?'

'I hope not.' Tom picked the telephone up. 'Hello ... Yes ... How do you do, Mrs Murchison?' She wanted to come to see him. 'That would be quite all right, of course, but wouldn't it be easier for you if I came to Paris? ... Yes, it is *some* distance, farther than from Orly to Paris ...' He was having no luck. He might have discouraged her with difficult directions, but he didn't want to inconvenience the unfortunate woman any further. 'Then the easiest is to take a taxi.' Tom gave her the directions to the house.

Tom tried to explain to Heloise. Mrs Murchison would arrive in an hour, and would want to talk to him about her husband. Mme Annette had left the room, so Tom was able to speak in French to Heloise, though Mme Annette could have listened for all he cared. It had crossed Tom's mind, before Mrs Murchison rang, to tell Heloise why he had gone to London, to explain to her that he had twice impersonated Derwatt the painter, who was now dead. But this moment was not the time to spring all that on her. If they got through Mrs Murchison's visit successfully, that was all Tom could demand of Heloise.

'But what happened to her husband?' Heloise asked.

'I don't know, darling. But she has come to France and naturally she wants to speak to –' Tom didn't want to say to the last person who had seen her husband. 'She wants to see the house, because her husband was last here. I took him to Orly from here.'

Heloise stood up with a twist of impatience in her body. But she was not stupid enough to make a scene. She was not going to be uncontrollable, unreasonable. That might come later.

'I know what you're going to say. You don't want her here

for the evening. All right. She will not be invited for dinner. We can say we have an engagement. But I must offer her tea or a drink or both. I would estimate – she will be here not more than an hour, and I'll handle everything politely. And correctly.'

Heloise subsided.

Tom went upstairs to his room. Mme Annette had emptied his suitcase and put it away, but there were some things not quite in their usual place, so Tom put them back as they were when he stayed at Belle Ombre for weeks on end. Tom had a shower, then put on grey flannels, a shirt and sweater, and he took a tweed jacket from his closet, in case Mrs Murchison might want to take a stroll on the lawn.

Mrs Murchison arrived.

Tom went to the front door to meet her, and to make sure the taxi was settled correctly. Mrs Murchison had French currency and overtipped the driver, but Tom let it go.

'My wife, Heloise,' Tom said. 'Mrs Murchison – from America.'

'How do you do?'

'How do you do?' said Heloise.

Mrs Murchison agreed to a cup of tea. 'I hope you'll excuse me for inviting myself so abruptly,' she said to Tom and Heloise, 'but it's a matter of importance – and I wanted to see you as soon as possible.'

They were all seated now, Mrs Murchison on the yellow sofa, Tom on a straight chair, like Heloise. Heloise had a marvellous air of not being much interested in the situation, but of being polite enough to be present. But she was quite interested, Tom knew.

'My husband –'

'Tom, he told me to call him,' Tom said, smiling. He stood up. 'He looked at these pictures. Here on my right "Man in Chair". Behind you "The Red Chairs". It's an earlier one.' Tom spoke boldly. Carry it off or not, and to hell with propriety, ethics, kindness, truth, the law, or even fate – meaning the future. Either he brought it off now, or he did not. If Mrs Murchison wanted a tour of the house, it could even include the cellar as far as Tom was concerned. Tom waited for Mrs Murchison to ask a question, perhaps, about what her husband had thought about the validity of the paintings.

'You bought these from the Buckmaster?' Mrs Murchison asked.

'Yes, both of them.' Tom glanced at Heloise, who was smoking an unaccustomed Gitane *maïs*. 'My wife understands English,' Tom said.

'Were you here when my husband visited?'

'No, I was in Greece,' Heloise replied. 'I did not meet your husband.'

Mrs Murchison stood up and looked at the paintings, and Tom turned on two lamps in addition to the other light, so she could see them better.

'I'm fondest of "Man in Chair",' Tom said. 'That's why it's over the fireplace.'

Mrs Murchison seemed to like it, too.

Tom was expecting her to say something with regard to her husband's theory about Derwatt being forged. She did not. She did not make a comment on the lavenders or the purples in either of the paintings. Mrs Murchison asked the same questions that Inspector Webster had, whether her husband had been feeling well when he left, whether he had an appointment with anyone.

'He seemed in very good spirits,' Tom said, 'and he didn't mention any appointment, as I said to Inspector Webster. What is strange is that your husband's painting was stolen. He had it with him at Orly, very well wrapped.'

'Yes, I know.' Mrs Murchison was smoking one of her Chesterfields. 'The painting hasn't been found. But neither has my husband or his passport.' She smiled. She had a comfortable, kindly face, a little plump, which precluded any creases of age as yet.

Tom poured another cup of tea for her. Mrs Murchison was looking at Heloise. An assessing glance? Wondering what Heloise thought of all this? Wondering how much Heloise knew? Wondering if there was anything to know in the first place? Or which side Heloise would be on if her husband were guilty of anything?

'Inspector Webster told me that you were a friend of Dickie

Greenleaf who was killed in Italy,' Mrs Murchison said.

'Yes,' Tom said. 'He wasn't killed, he was a suicide. I'd known him about five months – maybe six.'

'If he was not a suicide – I think Inspector Webster seems doubtful about it – then who might have killed him? And why?' asked Mrs Murchison. 'Or have you any ideas on the subject?'

Tom was standing up, and he planted his feet firmly on the floor, and sipped the tea. 'I have no ideas on the subject. Dickie killed himself. I don't think he could find his way – as a painter, and certainly not in his father's business. Shipbuilding or boat-building. Dickie had lots of friends, but not sinister friends.' Tom paused, and so did everyone else. 'Dickie had no reason to have enemies,' Tom added.

'Nor did my husband – except possibly if there is some forging of Derwatts going on.'

'Well – that I wouldn't know about, living here.'

'There may be a ring of some kind.' She looked at Heloise. 'I hope you understand what we're saying, Mme Ripley.'

Tom said to Heloise in French, 'Mme Murchison wonders if there might be a gang of dishonest people – in regard to Der-watt's paintings.'

'I understand,' Heloise said.

Heloise was dubious about the Dickie affair, Tom knew. But Tom knew he could count on her. Heloise was that curious bit of a crook herself. At any rate, before a stranger, Heloise would not appear doubtful of what Tom said.

'Would you like to see the upstairs of the house?' Tom asked Mrs Murchison. 'Or the grounds before it gets dark?'

Mrs Murchison said she would.

She and Tom went upstairs. Mrs Murchison wore a light grey woollen dress. She was well-built – perhaps she rode horseback or golfed – though no one could have called her fat. People never did call these sturdy sportswomen fat, though what else were they? Heloise had declined to come with them. Tom showed Mrs Murchison his guest-room, opening the door widely and putting on the light. Then in a free and easy manner, he showed her the rest of his upstairs rooms, including

Heloise's, whose door he opened, without turning the light on, because Mrs Murchison did not seem much interested in seeing it.

'I thank you,' said Mrs Murchison, and they went downstairs.

Tom felt sorry for her. He felt sorry that he had killed her husband. But, he reminded himself, he could not afford to reproach himself for that now: if he did, he would be exactly like Bernard, who wanted to tell all at the expense of several other people. 'Did you see Derwatt in London?'

'I saw him, yes,' said Mrs Murchison, seating herself on the sofa again, but rather on the edge of it.

'What's he like? I came within an inch of meeting him the day of the opening.'

'Oh, he has a beard – Pleasant enough but not talkative,' she finished, not interested in Derwatt. 'He did say he didn't think there was any forgery of his work going on – and that he'd said that to Tommy.'

'Yes, I think your husband told me that, too. And you believe Derwatt?'

'I think so. Derwatt seems sincere. What else can one say?' She leaned back on the sofa.

Tom stepped forward. 'Some tea? How about a Scotch?'

'I think I'd like a Scotch, thank you.'

Tom went to the kitchen for ice. Heloise joined him and helped him.

'What is this about Dickie?' Heloise asked.

'Nothing,' Tom said. 'I would tell you if it were something. She knows I was a friend of Dickie's. Would you like some white wine?'

'Yes.'

They carried the ice and glasses in. Mrs Murchison wanted a taxi. To Melun. She excused herself for asking for it just then, but she did not know how long it would take.

'I can drive you to Melun,' Tom said, 'if you want a train to Paris.'

'No, I wanted to go to Melun to speak with the police there. I called them from Orly.'

'Then I'll take you,' Tom said. 'How's your French? Mine's not perfect, but –'

'Oh, I think I can get along. Thank you very much.' She smiled a little.

She wanted to speak with the police without him, Tom supposed.

'Was there anyone else at the house when my husband was here?' Mrs Murchison asked.

'Only our housekeeper, Mme Annette. Where is Mme Annette, Heloise?'

She was perhaps in her room, perhaps out for some last minute shopping, Heloise thought, and Tom went to Mme Annette's room and knocked. Mme Annette was sewing something. Tom asked if she could come in for a moment and meet Mme Murchison.

In a moment or two, Mme Annette came in, and her face showed interest because Mme Murchison was the wife of the man who was missing. 'The last time I saw him,' said Mme Annette, 'm'sieur had lunch and then he left with M. Tome.'

Mme Annette had evidently forgot, Tom thought, that she had not actually seen M. Murchison walking out of the house.

'Is there something you wish, M. Tome?' Mme Annette asked.

But they didn't need anything, and Mrs Murchison apparently had no more questions. Mme Annette a bit reluctantly left the room.

'What do you think happened to my husband?' Mrs Murchison asked, looking at Heloise, then back at Tom.

'If I were to guess anything,' Tom said, 'it would be that someone knew he was carrying a valuable painting. Not a very valuable painting, to be sure, but a Derwatt. I gather that he spoke to a few people about it in London. If someone tried to kidnap him and the painting, they might have gone too far and killed him. Then they would have to hide his body somewhere. Or else – he's being held alive somewhere.'

'But that sounds as if my husband is right in thinking "The Clock" is a forgery. As you say, the picture wasn't very valuable, maybe because it isn't very big. But maybe they're trying to hush up the whole idea of Derwatt's being forged.'

'But I don't believe your husband's picture was a forgery. And *he* was dubious when he left. As I said to Webster, I don't think Tommy was going to bother showing "The Clock" to the expert in London. I didn't ask him, as I recall. But I had the idea he had second thoughts after seeing my two. I may be wrong.'

A silence. Mrs Murchison was wondering what to say or ask next. The only important thing was the people around the Buckmaster Gallery, Tom supposed. And how could she ask him about them?

The taxi arrived.

'Thank you, Mr Ripley,' Mrs Murchison said. 'And Madame. I may see you again if –'

'Any time,' Tom said. He saw her out to the taxi.

When he came back into the living-room, Tom walked slowly to the sofa and sank down in it. The Melun police couldn't tell Mrs Murchison anything new, or they would certainly have told him something by now, Tom thought. Heloise had said they had not rung while he had been gone. If the police had found Murchison's body in the Loing or wherever it was –

'Chéri, you are so nervous,' Heloise said. 'Take a drink.'

'I might,' Tom said, pouring it. There had been no item in the London papers that Tom had seen on the plane about Derwatt turning up again in London. The English didn't think it important apparently. Tom was glad, because he did not want Bernard, wherever he was, to know that he had somehow climbed out of the grave. Just why Tom didn't want Bernard to know this was hazy in Tom's mind. But it had something to do with what Tom felt was Bernard's destiny.

'You know, Tome, the Berthelins want us to come for an apéritif tonight at seven. It would do you good. I said you might be here tonight.'

The Berthelins lived in a town seven kilometres away. 'Can I –' The telephone interrupted Tom. He motioned for Heloise to answer it.

'Shall I say to anyone that you are here?'

He smiled, pleased at her concern. 'Yes. And maybe it's

Noëlle asking your advice about what to wear Tuesday.'

'Oui. Yes. Bonjour.' She smiled at Tom. 'One moment.' She handed him the telephone. 'An English trying to speak French.'

'Hello, Tom, this is Jeff. Are you all right?'

'Oh, perfectly.'

Jeff wasn't, quite. His stutter had come back, and he was talking quickly and softly. Tom had to ask him to speak up.

'I said Webster is asking about Derwatt again, where he is. If he's left.'

'What did you tell him?'

'I said we didn't know if he'd left or not.'

'You might say to Webster that – he seemed depressed and might want to be by himself for a while.'

'I think Webster might want to see you again. He's coming over to join Mrs Murchison. That's the reason I'm ringing.'

Tom sighed. 'When?'

'It could be today. I can't tell what he's up to. . . .'

When they had hung up, Tom felt stunned, and also angry, or irritated. Face Webster again for what? Tom preferred to leave the house.

'Chéri, what is it?'

'I can't go to the Berthelins,' Tom said, and laughed. The Berthelins were the least of his problems. 'Darling, I must go to Paris tonight, to Salzburg tomorrow. Maybe Salzburg tonight, if there is a plane. The English Inspector Webster may telephone this evening. You must say I went to Paris on business, to talk to my accountant, anything. You don't know where I'm staying. At some hotel, you don't know which hotel.'

'But what are you running from, Tome?'

Tom gasped. Running? Running from? Running to? 'I don't know.' He had begun to sweat. He wanted another shower, but was afraid to take the time. 'Tell Mme Annette also that I had to dash up to Paris.'

Tom went upstairs and took his suitcase out of the closet. He would wear the ugly new raincoat again, repart his hair and become Robert Mackay again. Heloise came in to help him.

'I'd love a shower,' Tom said, and at that instant heard Heloise turn on the shower in his bathroom. Tom jumped out of his clothes and stepped under the shower, which was lukewarm, just right.

'Can I come with you?'

How he wished she could! 'Darling, it's the passport thing. I can't have Mme Ripley crossing the French–German or Austrian border with Robert Mackay. Mackay, *that* swine!' Tom got out of the shower.

'The English Inspector is coming because of Murchison? Did you kill him, Tome?' Heloise looked at him, frowning, anxious, but far from hysteria, Tom saw.

She knew about Dickie, Tom realized. Heloise had never said it in so many words, but she knew. He might as well tell her, Tom thought, because she might be of help, and in any case the state of affairs was so desperate that if he lost, or tripped anywhere, everything was up, including his marriage. It occurred to him, couldn't he go as Tom Ripley to Salzburg? Take Heloise with him? But much as he would have liked to, he didn't know what he would have to do in Salzburg, or where the trail would lead from there. He should take both passports, however, his own and Mackay's.

'You killed him, Tome? Here?'

'I had to kill him to save a lot of other people.'

'The Derwatt people? Why?' She began to speak in French. 'Why are those people so important?'

'It's Derwatt who is dead – for years,' Tom said. 'Murchison was going to – to expose that fact.'

'He is *dead*?'

'Yes, and I impersonated him twice in London,' Tom said. The word in French sounded so innocent and gay: he had 'représenté' Derwatt twice in London. 'Now they are looking for Derwatt – maybe not desperately just now. But nothing falls into place just yet.'

'You have not been forging his paintings, too?'

Tom laughed. 'Heloise, you do me credit. It is Bernard the *fou* who has been forging. He wants to stop it. Oh, it is very complicated to explain.'

'Why must you look for the *fou* Bernard? Oh, Tome, stay away from it. . . .'

Tom did not listen to the rest of what she said. He suddenly knew he must find Bernard. He had suddenly a vision. Tom picked up his suitcase. 'Good-bye, my angel. Can you drive me to Melun? And avoid the police station, please?'

Downstairs, Mme Annette was in the kitchen, and Tom said a hasty good-bye from the front hall, averting his head so she might not notice the different parting in his hair. The ugly, but perhaps lucky, raincoat was over his arm.

Tom promised to keep in touch with Heloise, though he said he would sign a different name to any telegram that he sent. They kissed good-bye in the Alfa-Romeo, and Tom left the comfort of her arms and boarded a first-class carriage for Paris.

In Paris, he discovered that there was no direct plane for Salzburg, and only one daily flight of use, on which one had to change planes at Frankfurt to get to Salzburg. The plane to Frankfurt left at 2.40 p.m. every day. Tom stayed in a hotel not far from the Gare de Lyon. Just before midnight, he risked a telephone call to Heloise. He could not bear to think of her there at the house alone, possibly facing Webster, not knowing where he was. She had said she was not going to the Berthelins.

'Darling, hello. If Webster is there, say I have got the wrong number, and hang up,' Tom said.

'M'sieur, I think you have made a mistake,' Heloise's voice said, and the telephone was hung up.

Tom's spirit sank, his knees sank, and he sat down on his hotel room bed. He reproached himself for having rung her. It was better to work alone, always. Surely Webster would realize, or very much suspect, that it was he who had rung.

What was Heloise going through now? Was it better that he had told her the truth or not?

22

In the morning, Tom bought his airline ticket, and by 2.20 p.m.
was at Orly. If Bernard were not in Salzburg, where then?
Rome? Tom hoped not. It would be difficult to find anyone in
Rome. Tom kept his head down and did not look around at
Orly, because it was possible that Webster had called someone
over from London to look out for him. That depended on how
hot things were, and Tom didn't know. Why was Webster
calling on *him* again? Did Webster suspect he had impersonated
Derwatt? If so, his second impersonation with a different passport to enter and leave England was a slight point in his favour:
at least Tom Ripley hadn't been in London during the second
impersonation.

There was a wait of an hour in the Frankfurt terminus, then
Tom boarded a four-engined plane of the Austrian Airlines with
the charming name of *Johann Strauss* on its fuselage. At the
Salzburg terminus, he began to feel safer. Tom rode in on the
bus to Mirabeleplatz, and since he wanted to stay at the Goldener
Hirsch, he thought it best to ring first, because it was the best
hotel and often full. They had a room with bath to offer. Tom
gave his name as Thomas Ripley. Tom decided to walk to the
hotel, because the distance was short. He had been to Salzburg
twice before, once with Heloise. On the pavements, there were a
few men in Lederhosen and Tyrolian hats, their costume complete down to the hunting knives in their knee-high stockings.
Rather large old hotels, which Tom recalled vaguely from his
other trips, displayed their menus on big placards propped beside their front doors: full meals featuring Wienerschnitzel at
twenty-five and thirty Schillings.

Then there was the River Salzach and the main bridge – the
Staatsbrücke was it called? – and a couple of smaller bridges in
view. Tom took the main bridge. He was watching everywhere
for the gaunt and probably stooping figure of Bernard. The grey
river flowed quickly, and there were sizeable rocks along either
green bank over which the water frothed. It was dusk, just after

6 p.m. Lights began to come on irregularly in the older half of the city that he was approaching, lights that jumped higher like constellations onto the great hill of the Feste Hohensalzburg and onto the Mönchsberg. Tom entered a narrow short street that led to the Getreidegasse.

Tom's room had a view on the Sigmundsplatz at the rear of the hotel: to the right was the 'horse bath' fountain backed by a small rocky cliff, and in front was an ornate well. In the morning, they sold fruit and vegetables from push-carts here, Tom remembered. Tom took a few minutes to breathe, to open his suitcase, and walk in socked feet on the immaculately polished pinewood floors of his room. The furnishings were predominantly Austrian green, the walls white, the windows double-glazed with deep embrasures. Ah, Austria! Now to go down and have a Doppelespresso at the Café Tomaselli just a few steps away. And this might not be a bad idea, as it was a big coffee house and Bernard might be there.

But Tom had a slivowitz instead at Tomaselli's, because it wasn't the hour for coffee. Bernard was not there. Newspapers in several languages hung on rotating racks, and Tom browsed in the London *Times* and the Paris *Herald-Tribune*, without finding anything about Bernard (not that he expected to in the *Herald-Tribune*) or about Thomas Murchison or his wife's visit to London or France. Good.

Tom wandered out, crossed the Staatsbrücke again, and went up the Linzergasse, the main street that led from it. It was now after 9 p.m. Bernard, if he were here, would be at a medium-priced hotel, Tom thought, and as likely this side of the Salzach as the other. And he would have been here two or three days. Who knew? Tom stared into windows that displayed hunting knives, garlic presses, electric razors, and windows full of Tyrolian clothes – white blouses with ruffles, dirndl skirts. All the shops were closed. Tom tried the back streets. Some were not streets, but unlighted narrow alleys with closed doorways on either side. Towards ten, Tom was hungry, and went into a restaurant up and to the right of the Linzergasse. Afterwards, he walked back by a different route to the Café Tomaselli, where he intended to spend an hour. In the street of his hotel, the

Getreidegasse, was also the house where Mozart had been born. Perhaps Bernard, if he was lingering in Salzburg, frequented this area. Give the search twenty-four hours, Tom told himself.

No luck at Tomaselli's. The clientèle now seemed to be the regulars, the Salzburgers, families enjoying huge pieces of cake with espressos-with-cream, or glasses of pink Himbeersaft. Tom was impatient, bored by the newspapers, frustrated because he did not see Bernard, angry – because he was tired. He went back to his hotel.

Tom was out on the streets again by 9.30 a.m., and on the 'right bank' of Salzburg, the newer half, he rambled in a zigzag, watching out for Bernard, pausing sometimes to look into shop windows. Tom started back towards the river, with the idea of visiting the Mozart Museum in the street of his hotel. Tom walked through the Dreifaltigkeitsgasse into the Linzergasse, and as he approached the Staatsbrücke, Tom saw Bernard stepping off the bridge on the other side of the street.

Bernard's head was down, and he was almost hit by a car. Tom, who wanted to follow him, was held up by a long traffic light, but that didn't matter, because Bernard was in plain view. Bernard's raincoat was dirtier, and its belt hung out of one strap nearly to the ground. He looked almost like a tramp. Tom crossed the street and kept some thirty feet behind, ready to dash forward if Bernard turned a corner, because he did not want Bernard to vanish into a small hotel in a little street where there were perhaps a couple of hotels.

'Are you busy this morning?' asked a female voice in English.

Startled, Tom glanced into the face of a blond floozy who was standing in a doorway. Tom walked on quickly. My God, did he look that desperate, or that kooky in his green raincoat? At ten in the morning!

Bernard kept walking up the Linzergasse. Then Bernard crossed the street and half a block farther went into a doorway over which there was a sign: *Zimmer und Pension*. A drab doorway. Tom paused on the opposite pavement. Der Blaue something, the place was called. The sign was worn off. At least Tom knew where Bernard was staying. And he'd been right! Bernard was in Salzburg! Tom congratulated himself on his intuition. Or was Bernard only now engaging a room?

No, evidently he was staying at the Blaue Something, because he did not appear in the next minutes, and he had not been carrying his duffelbag. Tom waited it out, and a dreary wait it was, because there was no café near by from which he might watch the doorway. And at the same time, Tom had to keep himself hidden, in case Bernard might look out a front window of the establishment and see him. But somehow people who looked like Bernard never got a room with a view. Still, Tom hid himself, and he had to wait until nearly eleven.

Then out came Bernard, shaven now, and Bernard turned right as if he had a destination.

Tom followed discreetly, and lit a Gauloise. Over the main bridge again. Through the street Tom had taken last evening, and then Bernard turned right in the Getreidegasse. Tom had a glimpse of his sharp, rather handsome profile, his firm mouth – and of a hollow that made a shadow in his olive cheek. His desert boots had collapsed. Bernard was going into the Mozart Museum. Admission twelve Schillings. Tom pulled his raincoat collar up and went in.

One paid admission in a room at the top of the first flight of steps. Here were glass cases full of manuscripts and opera programmes. Tom looked into the main front room for Bernard, and not seeing him, assumed he had gone up to the next floor, which as Tom recalled had been the living quarters of the Mozart family. Tom climbed the second flight.

Bernard was leaning over the keyboard of Mozart's clavichord, a keyboard protected by a panel of glass from anyone who might wish to press a key. How many times had Bernard looked at it, Tom wondered?

There were only five or six people drifting about in the museum, or at least on this floor, so Tom had to be careful. In fact, at one point he stepped back behind a door jamb, so Bernard would not see him if he looked his way. Actually, Tom realized, he wanted to watch Bernard to try to see what state of mind he was in. Or – Tom tried to be honest with himself – was he merely curious and amused, because for a short time he could observe someone whom he knew slightly, someone in a crisis, who was not aware of him? Bernard drifted into a front room on the same floor.

Eventually, Tom followed Bernard up the next and last stairs. More glass cases. (In the clavichord room had been the spot, a labelled corner, where Mozart's cradle had rested, but no cradle. A pity they hadn't put at least a replica there.) The stairs had slender iron banisters. Windows were set at angles in some corners, and Tom, awed as always by Mozart, wondered on what view the Mozart family had looked out? Surely not the cornice of another building just four feet away. The miniature stage models – *Idomeneo* ad infinitum, *Così Fan Tutte* – were dull and rather clumsily done, but Bernard drifted through them, staring.

Bernard turned his head unexpectedly towards Tom – and Tom stood still in a doorway. They stared at each other. Then Tom fell back a step and moved to the right, which put him behind a doorway and in another room, a front room. Tom began to breathe again. It had been a funny instant, because Bernard's face –

Tom did not dare pause to think any more, and made for the stairway down at once. He was not comfortable, and even then not much, until he was in the busy Getreidegasse, in the open air. Tom took the little short street towards the river. Was Bernard going to try to follow him? Tom ducked his head and walked faster.

Bernard's expression had been one of disbelief, and after a split-second fear, as if Bernard had seen a ghost.

Tom realized that that was exactly what Bernard had thought he had seen: a ghost. A ghost of Tom Ripley, the man he had killed.

Tom turned suddenly and started back towards the Mozarthaus, because it had occurred to him that Bernard might want to leave the town, and Tom did not want this to happen without his knowing where Bernard was going. Should he hail Bernard now, if he saw him on a pavement? Tom waited a few minutes across the street from the Mozart museum, and when Bernard did not appear, Tom started walking towards Bernard's pension. Tom did not see Bernard along the way, and then as Tom drew nearer the pension, he saw Bernard walking rather quickly on the other side, the pension side, of the Linzergasse. Bernard went into his hotel-pension. For nearly half an hour, Tom waited, then decided Bernard was not going out for a time. Or perhaps Tom was willing to risk Bernard's leaving, Tom himself didn't know. He much wanted a coffee. He went into a hotel which had a coffee bar. He also made a decision, and when he left the bar, he went straight back to Bernard's pension with an idea of asking the desk to tell Herr Tufts that Tom Ripley was downstairs and would like to speak with him.

But Tom could not get past the modest, drab entrance. He had one foot on the doorstep, then he drifted back onto the pavement, feeling for an instant dizzy. It's indecision, he told himself. Nothing else. But Tom went back to his hotel on the other side of the river. He walked into the comfortable lobby of the Goldener Hirsch, where the grey-and-green uniformed porter at once handed him his key. Tom took the self-operating lift to the third floor and entered his room. He removed the awful raincoat and emptied its pockets – cigarettes, matches, Austrian coins mingled with French. He separated the coins, and tossed the French into a top pocket of his suitcase. Then he took off his clothes and fell into bed. He had not realized how tired he was.

When he awakened, it was after 2 p.m. and the sun was shining brightly. Tom went for a walk. He did not look for Bernard, but rambled around the town like any tourist, or rather not like a tourist, because he had no objective. What was Bernard doing here? How long was he going to stay? Tom felt now wide awake, but he did not know what he should do. Approach Bernard and try telling him that Cynthia wanted to see him? Should he talk to Bernard and try to persuade him – of what?

Between four and five in the afternoon, Tom suffered a depression. He had had coffee and a Steinhäger somewhere. He was far up (as the river flowed, up the river) beyond Hohensalzburg but still on the quay on the old side of town. He was thinking of the changes in Jeff, Ed and now Bernard since the Derwatt fraud. And Cynthia had been made unhappy, the course of her life had been changed because of Derwatt Ltd – and this seemed to Tom more important than the lives of the three men involved. Cynthia by now would have married Bernard and might have had a couple of children, though since Bernard would have been equally involved, it was impossible for Tom to say why he thought the alteration of Cynthia's life of more importance than that of Bernard's. Only Jeff and Ed were pink-cheeked and affluent, their lives outwardly changed for the better. Bernard looked exhausted. At thirty-three or thirty-four.

Tom had intended to dine in the restaurant of his hotel, which was considered the best restaurant of Salzburg also, but he found himself not in the mood for such fine food and surroundings, so he wandered up the Getreidegasse, past the Bürgerspitalplatz (Tom saw by a streetmarker) and through the Gstättentor, a narrow old gateway wide enough for a single lane of traffic, one of the original gates of the town at the foot of the Mönchsberg which loomed darkly beside it. The street beyond was almost equally narrow and rather dark. There'd be a small restaurant somewhere, Tom thought. He saw two places with almost identical menus outside: twenty-six Schillings for soup-of-the-day, Weiner schnitzel with potatoes, salad, dessert. Tom went into the second, which had a little lantern-shaped sign out in front, the Café Eigler or some such.

Two Negro waitresses in red uniforms were sitting with male customers at one table. There was a juke box playing, and the light was dim. Was it a whorehouse, a pick-up joint, or just a cheap restaurant? Tom had taken only a step into the place, when he saw Bernard in a booth by himself, bending over his bowl of soup. Tom hesitated.

Bernard lifted his eyes to him.

Tom looked like himself now, in a tweed jacket, with his muffler round his neck against the chill – the muffler that Heloise had washed the blood from in the Paris hotel. Tom was on the brink of going closer, of extending his hand, smiling, when Bernard half stood up with a look of terror on his face.

The two plump coloured waitresses looked from Bernard to Tom. Tom saw a waitress get up with what seemed like the slowness of Africa, with an obvious intention of going to

Bernard to ask, eventually, if something was the matter, because Bernard looked as if he had swallowed something that was going to kill him.

Bernard waved his hand negatively, rapidly – against the waitress or him, Tom wondered?

Tom turned and went through the inside door (the place had a storm door), then walked out onto the pavement. He pushed his hands into his pockets and ducked his head, much like Bernard, as he walked back through the Gstättentor, towards the more lighted part of town. Had he done wrong, Tom asked himself. Should he have simply – advanced? But Tom had felt that Bernard would let out a scream.

Tom went past his hotel and on to the next corner, where he turned right. The Tomaselli was a few yards on. If Bernard was following him – Tom was sure Bernard was going to leave the restaurant – if Bernard wanted to join him here, very well. But Tom knew it was something different. Bernard thought he was seeing a vision, really. So Tom sat at a conspicuous middle table, ordered a sandwich and a carafe of white wine, and read a couple of newspapers.

Bernard did not come in.

The big wood-framed doorway had an arched brass curtain rod which supported a green curtain, and every time the curtain moved, Tom glanced up, but the person entering was never Bernard.

If Bernard did come in and walk towards him, it would be because Bernard wanted to make sure he was real. That was logical. (The trouble was, Bernard was not doing anything logical, probably.) Tom would say, 'Sit down and have some wine with me. I'm not a ghost, you see. I spoke with Cynthia. She'd like to see you again.' *Pull Bernard out of it*.

But Tom doubted that he could.

23

By the next day, Tuesday, Tom made another decision: to speak to Bernard by hook or by crook, even if he had to tackle him. He would try also to make Bernard go back to London. Bernard must have some friends there, apart from Jeff and Ed whom he would probably shun. Didn't Bernard's mother still live there? Tom wasn't sure. But he felt he had to do something, because Bernard's air of misery was pitiable. Each glimpse of Bernard sent a weird pain through Tom: it was as if he were seeing someone already in the throes of death, yet walking about.

So at 11 a.m., Tom went to the Blaue Something, and spoke to a dark-haired woman of about fifty at the downstairs desk. 'Excuse me, there is a man called Bernard Tufts – ein Englischer – staying here?' Tom asked in German.

The woman's eyes went wider. 'Yes, but he has just checked out. About an hour ago.'

'Did he say where he was going?'

Bernard had not. Tom thanked her, and he felt her eyes following him as he left the hotel, staring at him as if he were just as odd as Bernard, simply because he knew Bernard.

Tom took a taxi to the railway station. There were probably few planes out of Salzburg airport, which was small. And trains were cheaper than planes. Tom did not see Bernard at the railway station. He looked on platforms and in the buffet. He then walked back towards the river and the centre of town, watching for Bernard, for a man in a limp beige raincoat carrying a duffelbag. Around 2 p.m. Tom took a taxi to the airport, in case Bernard was flying to Frankfurt. No luck there, either.

It was just after 3 p.m. when Tom saw him. Bernard was on a bridge over the river, one of the smaller bridges that had a handrail and one-way traffic. Bernard leaned on his forearms, gazing down. His duffelbag was at his feet. Tom had not started across the bridge. He had seen Bernard from quite a distance. Was he thinking about jumping in? Bernard's hair lifted and fell over his forehead with the wind. He was going to kill himself, Tom realized. Maybe not this instant. Maybe he would walk around and come back in an hour, in two hours. Maybe this evening. Two women, walking past Bernard, glanced at him with a brief curiosity. When the women had gone by, Tom walked towards Bernard, neither fast nor slowly. Below, the river foamed quickly over the rocks that bordered its banks. Tom had never seen a boat on the river, that he could recall. The Salzach was perhaps rather shallow. Tom, at a distance of four yards, was ready to say Bernard's name, when Bernard turned his head to the left and saw him.

Bernard straightened up suddenly, and Tom had the feeling that his staring expression did not change at the sight of him, but Bernard picked up his duffelbag.

'Bernard!' Tom said, just as a noisy motorcycle pulling a trailer passed by them, and Tom was afraid Bernard hadn't heard him. *'Bernard!'*

Bernard ran off.

'Bernard!' Tom collided with a woman, and would have knocked her down, except that she struck the handrail instead. 'Oh! – I'm *terribly* sorry!' Tom said. He repeated it in German, picking up a parcel the woman had dropped.

She replied something to him, something about a 'football player'.

Tom trotted on. Bernard was in sight. Tom frowned, embarrassed and angry. He felt a sudden hatred for Bernard. It made him tense for a moment, then the emotion passed away. Bernard was walking briskly, not looking behind him. There was a madness in the way Bernard walked, with nervous but regular strides that Tom felt he could keep up for hours until he simply dropped. Or would Bernard ever simply drop? It was curious, Tom thought, that he felt Bernard was as much a kind of ghost as Bernard apparently thought he was.

Bernard began to zigzag meaninglessly in the streets, but he stayed rather close to the river. They walked for half an hour, and now they had left the town proper behind them. The streets were thin now, with an occasional florist's shop, woods, gardens, a residence, a tiny *Konditorei* with a now empty terrace giving a view of the river. Bernard at last went into one of these.

Tom slowed his steps. He was not tired or out of breath after all his fast walking. He felt odd. Only the pleasant coolness of the wind on his forehead reminded him that he was still among the living.

The little square café had glass walls, and Tom could see that Bernard was seated at a table with a glass of red wine in front of him. The place was empty, save for a skinny and rather elderly waitress in black uniform with a white apron. Tom smiled, relieved, and without thinking or pondering anything, he opened the door and went in. Now Bernard looked at him as if he were a bit surprised, puzzled (Bernard was frowning), but there was not the same terror.

Tom smiled a little and nodded. He didn't know why he nodded. Was it a greeting? Was it an affirmation? If so, an affirmation of what? Tom imagined pulling out a chair, sitting down with Bernard and saying, 'Bernard, I'm not a ghost. There wasn't much earth on top of me and I dug my way out. Funny, isn't it? I was just in London and I saw Cynthia and she said ...' And he imagined lifting a glass of wine also, and he would slap Bernard on the sleeve of his raincoat and Bernard would know that Tom was real. But it was not happening. Bernard's expression changed to one of weariness and, Tom thought, hostility. Tom felt again a slight pique of anger. Tom stood up straighter, and opened the door behind him and stepped smoothly and gracefully out, though he did it backwards.

That had been rather deliberate on his part, Tom realized.

The waitress in the black uniform had not glanced at Tom, because presumably she had not seen him. She had been doing something at the counter on Tom's right.

Tom crossed the road, walking away from the café where Bernard was, and farther away from Salzburg. The café was on the land side, not the river side of the street, so Tom was now quite near the river and its embankment. There was a telephone booth full of glass panels near the kerb, and Tom took refuge behind this. He lit a French cigarette.

Bernard came out of the café, and Tom walked slowly around

the booth, keeping it between him and Bernard. Bernard was looking for him, but his glances seemed merely nervous, as if he did not really expect to see Tom. At any rate, Bernard did not see him, and kept on walking rather quickly in a direction away from the town of Salzburg and on the land side of the street. Tom eventually followed him.

The mountains rose up ahead, cut by the narrowing Salzach, mountains covered with dark-green trees, mainly pine. It was still a pavement that they walked on, but Tom could see where it finished ahead, and the road became a two-lane country road. Was Bernard going to walk straight up some mountain with his crazy energy? Bernard glanced behind him once or twice, so Tom stayed out of sight — at least from a glance — and Tom could tell from Bernard's behaviour that he had not seen him.

They must be eight kilometres from Salzburg, Tom thought, and paused to wipe his forehead, to loosen his tie under his muffler. Bernard moved out of sight around a curve in the road, and Tom walked on. Tom ran, in fact, thinking as he had thought in Salzburg that Bernard might walk right or left and disappear somewhere that Tom could not find him.

Tom saw him. Bernard looked behind him in that instant, and Tom stopped and held both his arms out sideways — to be better seen. But Bernard turned away as quickly as he had turned away several times before, and Tom was left with a feeling of doubt: had Bernard seen him or not? Did it even matter? Tom walked on. Bernard had again disappeared around a curve, and again Tom trotted. When Tom came to the next straight section of road, Bernard was not in sight, so Tom stopped and listened, in case Bernard had gone into the woods. All Tom heard was the twittering of a few birds, and from afar the bells of a church.

Then on his left, Tom heard a faint crackling of branches, which soon stopped. Tom walked a few feet into the woods, and listened.

'*Bernard!*' Tom yelled, his voice hoarse. Surely Bernard heard that.

There seemed to be complete silence. Was Bernard hesitating?

Then there was a remote thud. Or had Tom imagined it?

Tom walked farther into the woods. Some twenty yards in, there was a slope down towards the river, and beyond this a cliff of light grey rock, which went down thirty or forty feet, it seemed, and perhaps more. At the top of this cliff was Bernard's duffelbag, and Tom knew at once what had happened. Tom went closer, listening, but even the birds seemed silent just now. At the edge of the cliff, Tom looked down. It was not sheer, and Bernard would have had to walk or start falling down a slope of rocks before he jumped or simply toppled over.

'Bernard?'

Tom moved to the left, where it was safer to look down. By clinging to a small tree, and with another tree in sight in case he slipped and had to catch hold of something, Tom looked down and saw a grey, elongated form on the stones below, one arm flung out. It was something like a four-storey drop, and onto rocks. Bernard was not moving. Tom made his way back to safer ground.

He picked up the duffelbag, a pitiably light weight.

It was a few moments before Tom could think of anything at all. He was still holding the duffelbag.

Was anyone going to find Bernard? From the river, could anyone see him? But who was ever on the river? It was not likely that a hiker would see him or come across him, not soon, anyway. Tom could not face going closer to Bernard now, looking at him. Tom knew he was dead.

It had been a curious murder.

Tom walked back along the downward sloping road towards Salzburg, and he encountered no one. Somewhere, down near the town, Tom saw a bus and hailed it. He had not much idea where he was, but the bus seemed to be going in the Salzburg direction.

The driver asked Tom if he were going to a certain place, a name which Tom did not know.

'Nearer Salzburg,' Tom said.

The driver took a few Schillings from him.

Tom got off as soon as he recognized something. Then he

walked. Finally, he was trudging across Residenzplatz, then into the Getreidegasse, carrying Bernard's duffelbag.

He entered the Goldener Hirsch, breathed suddenly the pleasant scent of furniture wax, the aroma of comfort and tranquillity.

'Good evening, sir,' said the porter, and handed Tom his key.

24

Tom awakened from a dream of frustration in which some eight people (only one of whom was recognizable, Jeff Constant) in some house, mocked him and chuckled, because nothing went right for him, he was late for something, he had difficulty settling a bill he owed, he was in shorts when he should have been in trousers, he had forgotten an important engagement. The depression caused by the dream lingered for minutes after he had sat up. Tom put out his hand and touched the thick, polished wood of his night-table.

Then he ordered a Kaffee Komplett.

The first sips of coffee helped. He had been vacillating between doing something about Bernard – what? – and ringing Jeff and Ed to tell them what had happened. Jeff might be more articulate, but Tom doubted if either he or Ed could come up with an idea about the next move he should make. Tom felt anxious, with the kind of anxiety that got him nowhere. The reason he had to speak with Jeff and Ed was simply that he felt scared and alone.

Rather than wait in a noisy, crowded post office, Tom lifted his telephone and gave Jeff's number in London. The next half hour or so while he waited for the call was a curious but not unpleasant limbo. Tom began to realize that he had willed or wished Bernard's suicide, while at the same time, since he had known Bernard was going to kill himself, Tom could hardly accuse himself of forcing suicide upon Bernard. On the contrary, Tom had showed himself pretty clearly alive several times – unless Bernard had preferred to see a ghost. Also Bernard's suicide had not much and maybe nothing to do with Tom's belief that he had killed him. Hadn't Bernard hanged himself as a dummy already in Tom's cellar, days before Bernard attacked him in the woods?

Tom also realized that he wanted Bernard's corpse, and that this had been in the back of his mind. If he used the corpse as Derwatt's, this would leave the question of what happened to Bernard Tufts. Settle that problem later, Tom thought.

The telephone rang and Tom leapt for it. Jeff spoke.

'This is Tom. In Salzburg. Can you hear me?'

The connection was excellent.

'Bernard – Bernard's dead. Down a cliff. He jumped.'

'You don't mean it. He's killed himself?'

'Yes. I saw him. What's happening in London?'

'They're – The police are looking for Derwatt. They don't know where he is in London or – or elsewhere,' Jeff said, stuttering.

'We've got to make an end of Derwatt,' Tom said, 'and this is a good chance to. Don't mention Bernard's death to the police.'

Jeff didn't understand.

The next exchanges were awkward, because Tom could not tell Jeff what he intended to do. Tom conveyed that he would somehow get Bernard's remains out of Austria and possibly into France.

'You mean – Where is he? He's still lying there?'

'Nobody's seen him. I'll simply have to do it,' Tom said with laborious and painful patience, trying to reply to Jeff's blunt or half-formed questions, 'as if he incinerated himself or wanted to be incinerated. There's no other way, is there?' Not if he tried once more to help Derwatt Ltd.

'No.' Helpful as usual, Jeff.

'I will soon notify the French police, and Webster if he's still there,' Tom said more firmly.

'Oh, Webster's back. They're looking for Derwatt *here* and one man – a plain-clothes man yesterday suggested that Derwatt could have been impersonated by someone.'

'Are they onto *me* about it?' Tom asked anxiously, but with a rush of defiance.

'No, they're not, Tom. I don't think so. But somebody – I'm not sure if it was Webster – said they were wondering where you were in Paris.' Jeff added, 'I think they've checked the Paris hotels.'

'Just now,' Tom said, 'you don't know where *I* am, naturally, and you must say that Derwatt seemed depressed. You have no idea where he might have gone.'

Seconds later, they had hung up. If the police investigated at some later date Tom's doings in Salzburg, and found this call on his bill, Tom would say he had rung because of Derwatt. He would have to create a story that he followed Derwatt to Salzburg, for some reason. Bernard would have to figure in the story, too. If Derwatt for instance –

Derwatt, depressed and disturbed by Murchison's disappearance and possible death, might have rung Tom Ripley at Belle Ombre. Derwatt could also have known, through Jeff and Ed, that Bernard had visited Belle Ombre. Derwatt might have proposed that they meet in Salzburg, where Derwatt wanted to go. (Or Tom might attribute to Bernard that suggestion of Salzburg.) Tom would say that he saw Derwatt at least two or three times in Salzburg, probably with Bernard. Derwatt was depressed. Why, particularly? Well, Derwatt had not told Tom everything. Derwatt had spoken little about Mexico, but had asked about Murchison, and had said that his trip to London had been a mistake. In Salzburg, Derwatt had insisted on going to out-of-the-way places to drink coffee, to have a bowl of gulyassuppe, or a bottle of Grinzing. True to his character, Derwatt had not told Tom where he was stopping in Salzburg, had always left Tom and walked off alone when they had said goodbye. Tom had assumed he was staying somewhere under another name.

Tom would say that he had not wished to tell even Heloise that he was going to Salzburg in order to meet Derwatt.

The story, so far as it went, began to fall into place.

Tom opened his window onto Sigmundsplatz, which was now filled with pushcarts displaying huge white radishes, bright oranges and apples. People stood dipping long sausages into mustard on paper plates.

Perhaps now he could face Bernard's duffelbag. Tom knelt on the floor and opened the zipper. A soiled shirt was on top. Below were shorts and a singlet. Tom tossed them onto the floor. Then he turned the key in his door – though unlike the staff of many hotels, the maids did not come plunging in without knocking here. Tom continued. A *Salzburger Nachrichten* two days old, a London *Times* of the same age. Toothbrush, razor, a much-used hairbrush, a pair of beige chino pants rolled up, and at the bottom the worn brown notebook that Bernard had produced to read from at Belle Ombre. Below this was a drawing-pad with a spiral binding, on its cover the Derwatt signature that was the trademark of the art supply company. Tom opened it. Baroque churches and towers of Salzburg, some rather leaning, embellished with extra curlicues. Birds resembling bats flew above some of them. Shadows had been achieved here and there by a wetted thumb moved across the paper. One sketch had been heavily crossed out. In a corner of the duffelbag was a bottle of India ink, the top of its cork broken off, but still the cork was holding, and a bundle of drawing-pens and a couple of brushes held together by a rubber band. Tom dared to open the brown notebook to see if there were any late entries. Nothing since October 5th of this year, but Tom could not read it now. He detested reading other people's letters or personal papers. But he recognized the folded notepaper of Belle Ombre, two sheets. This was what Bernard had written the first evening at Tom's house, and at a glance Tom saw that it was an account of Bernard's forging, beginning six years ago. Tom did not want to read it, and tore the pages into small bits which he dropped into the wastebasket. Tom put the things back into the duffel-bag, zipped it, and set it into his closet.

How to buy gasoline, petrol, to burn the corpse?

He could say his car had run out. It couldn't all be done today, certainly, because the only plane was at 2.40 p.m. going towards Paris. He had a return ticket. He could, of course, take a train, but would the luggage inspection be more severe? Tom didn't want a customs inspector to open a suitcase and find a parcel of ashes.

Would a corpse burn enough, in the open, to become ashes?

Didn't it require a sort of oven? To augment the heat?

Tom left his hotel shortly before noon. Across the river, he bought a smallish pigskin suitcase at a shop in the Schwarz-strasse, and bought also several newspapers and put them into the suitcase. It was a cool, gusty day, though there was sunlight. Tom caught a bus going up the river on the old side of the town, in the direction of Mariaplain and Bergheim, two towns on the way which he had looked up. Tom got off in what he thought was the right area, and began to look for a petrol station. It took him twenty minutes to find one. He left the new suitcase in the woods before approaching the station.

The attendant was courteous and offered to drive him to his car, but Tom said it was not far, and could he purchase the container also, because he didn't want to come back? Tom bought ten litres. He did not look back as he walked up the road. He picked up his suitcase. He was, at least, on the right road, but it was a long walk, and he twice investigated areas in the woods which were not the right ones.

At last he found the spot. He saw the grey rocks ahead. Tom left the suitcase and descended with the petrol in a roundabout way. Blood had run in wild little veins to right and left below Bernard. Tom looked around. He needed a cave, a recess, some-thing overhanging to increase the heat. It would take a lot of wood. He recalled pictures of Indian corpses on high burning ghats. That took a lot of wood, apparently. Tom found a suitable place below the cliff, a sort of cavity among the rocks. The easiest thing would be to roll the body down.

First Tom removed the one ring that Bernard wore, a gold ring with what looked like a worn-out crest on it. He started to hurl it into the woods, but reflected that there was always a chance it would be found at some time, so he pocketed it with an idea of dropping it into the Salzach from a bridge. Next the pockets. Nothing but a few Austrian coins in the raincoat, cigarettes in a jacket pocket which Tom left, billfold in a trousers pocket, and Tom took the contents out and crumpled them, money and papers, and put them in his own pocket to start the fire with, or to toss on the fire later. Then he lifted the sticky body and rolled it. It tumbled down the rocks. Tom

239

climbed down, and pulled the body towards the recess he had found.

Then, glad to turn away from the thing, he began gathering wood energetically. He made at least six trips to the pale little vault he had discovered. He avoided looking at Bernard's face and head, all of which was of a general darkness now. At last he gathered handfuls of dried leaves and twigs, such as he could find, and stuck the papers and money from Bernard's billfold among them. Then he dragged the body onto the heap of wood, holding his breath as he pushed the legs, shoved one arm with his foot, into place. The body was stiff, with one arm extended. Tom got the gasoline, and poured half of it over the raincoat, soaking it. He decided to gather more wood to put on top, before he lit the whole thing.

Tom struck one match and from a distance tossed it.

The flames sprang up at once, yellow and white. Tom – with eyes half shut – found a spot away from the smoke. There was a lot of crackling. He did not look.

Nothing alive was in sight, not even a flying bird.

Tom gathered more wood. There couldn't be too much, he thought. The smoke was pale but abundant.

A car went by on the road, a truck, judging from the grinding sound of its motor. It was out of sight to Tom because of the trees. Its sound faded, and Tom hoped it had not stopped to investigate. But for three or four minutes nothing happened, and Tom assumed the driver had gone on. Without looking at the remains of Bernard, Tom poked branches nearer the flames. He was using a long stick. He felt he was doing things clumsily, that the fire was not hot enough – nowhere near the intense heat needed to cremate a body properly. The only thing he could do, therefore, was make the fire burn as long as possible. It was now 2.17 p.m. Quite a heat came from the fire, because of the overhang, and Tom had to toss branches finally. He did this steadily for several minutes. When the flames died down a little, he could approach the fire, pick up the half burnt branches, and throw them back again. There was still half the can of gasoline left.

With some method in mind, Tom gathered still more wood,

from a greater distance, for a final effort. When he had a heap of wood, he tossed the gasoline tin onto the body – which still had a discouragingly bodylike shape. The raincoat and trousers were burnt, but not the shoes, and the flesh, what he could see of it, was black, but not burnt, evidently only smoked. The gasoline tin made a drumlike boom, not an explosion. Tom was constantly listening for footfalls, or twigs crackling, in the woods. It was possible that someone might come because of the smoke. Finally, Tom withdrew a few yards, took off his raincoat and held it over his arm as he sat down on the ground, his back to the burning. Let a good twenty minutes pass, he thought. The bones were not going to burn, not going to collapse, he knew. It would mean another grave. He'd have to get a shovel somewhere. Buy one? To steal one would be wiser.

When Tom faced the pyre again, it was black, ringed by red embers. Tom poked these back. The body remained a body. As a cremation, it had failed, Tom knew. He debated whether to finish the job today or to come back tomorrow, and decided to finish today, if there remained enough light for him to see what he was doing. What he needed was something to dig with. He poked with the same long stick at the body, and found it jelly-like. Tom put the suitcase flat on the ground, in a little clump of trees.

Then he almost ran up the slope towards the road. The smell of the smoke was awful, and in fact he had not been breathing much for several minutes. He could give the search for the shovel an hour, he thought, if it would take an hour. He liked to have *some* plan, because he felt quite lost and inexpert just now. He walked down the road, free of suitcase, empty-handed. After several minutes, he arrived at the stretch of thinly scattered houses, not far from the café where Bernard had had his glass of red wine. There were a few neat gardens, there were glass-enclosed greenhouses, but there was no shovel leaning conveniently against a brick wall.

'Grüss' Gott!' said one man, digging in his garden with the kind of narrow, sharp spade Tom could have used.

Tom returned his greeting casually.

Then Tom saw a bus-stop, one he hadn't noticed yesterday,

and a young girl, or woman, was walking towards it, towards Tom. A bus must be due. Tom wanted to take it when it came, to forget about the corpse, the suitcase. Tom walked past the girl without glancing at her, hoping she would not remember him. Then Tom saw a metal wheelbarrow full of leaves beside the kerb, and across the wheelbarrow lay a shovel. He couldn't believe it. A small gift of God – except that the shovel was blunt. Tom slowed his steps, and glanced into the woods, thinking that the workman to whom these things belonged might have disappeared for a moment.

The bus came. The girl got on it, and the bus went on.

Tom took the shovel, and walked back as casually as he had come, holding the shovel as nonchalantly as he might have held an umbrella, except that he had to carry the shovel horizontally.

Back at the spot, Tom dropped the shovel and went in search of more wood. The time was getting on, and while it was still light enough to see quite well, Tom ventured farther into the woods for fuel. He would have to demolish the skull, he realized, above all get rid of the teeth, and he did not want to come back tomorrow. Tom stoked the fire once more, then took up the shovel and began to dig in an area of damp leaves. It was not so easy as with a fork. On the other hand, the remains of Bernard would not be of interest to any wandering animal, so the grave did not have to be deep. When he grew tired, he turned back to the fire, and without pausing brought the shovel down on the skull. It wasn't going to work, he saw. But another couple of strokes removed the jawbone, and Tom raked it out with the shovel. He pushed more wood near the skull.

Then he went to the suitcase and deployed the newspapers over its interior. He would have to take something from the corpse. He recoiled at the idea of a hand or foot. Some of the flesh from the corpse, perhaps. Flesh was flesh, this was human and could not be mistaken for the flesh of a cow, for instance, Tom supposed. For a few moments, he suffered nausea and crouched, leaning against a tree. Then he went directly to the fire with his shovel, and raked out some of the flesh at Bernard's waist. The stuff was dark and a little damp. Tom carried it in the shovel to the suitcase and dropped it in. He left the suitcase open. Then he lay down on the ground, exhausted.

Perhaps an hour passed. Tom did not sleep. He was aware of the dusk closing in around him, and realized that he had no torch. He got to his feet. Another try with the shovel at the head brought no results. Nor would his foot if he stamped on it, Tom knew. It would have to be a rock. Tom found a rock, and rolled it towards the fire. Then he lifted it with a new-found, and perhaps brief energy, and let it drop on the skull. The rock lay there. The skull was crushed under it. Tom pushed the rock off with his shovel, stepping back quickly to avoid the heat of the rosy red fire. Tom poked, and brought forth with his shovel a strange mess of bones and what should have been the upper teeth.

This activity brought a relief, and Tom now began tidying the fire. Optimistically, he felt that the elongated form bore no resemblance even to a human thing. He returned to his digging. It was a narrow trench, and soon it was nearly three feet deep. Tom worked with his shovel, and rolled the smoking form towards the grave he had dug. Now and again he smacked out little flames on the ground with his shovel. He checked, before burying the skeleton, to see if he had got the upper teeth, and he had. He buried the remains, and covered it over with earth. Some wreaths of smoke rose up through the leaves that he scattered on at the last. He tore some newspaper from those of the suitcase, and wrapped the bit of bones that contained the upper teeth, picked up the lower jaw also and put it in.

He pushed the fire together and made as sure as he could that embers were not going to pop out and start a fire amid the trees. He dragged leaves back from the fire, so that this would not happen. But he could not afford to spend more time here, because of the growing dark. Tom folded the newspapers in the suitcase around the small parcel, and walked back up the slope, with suitcase and shovel.

When he reached the bus-stop, the wheelbarrow was not where it had been. Tom left the shovel on the kerb, however.

At the next bus-stop, quite a way on, Tom waited. A woman joined him in the wait. Tom did not glance at her.

As the bus rolled and bumped springily, letting passengers off and on with a wheeze of its door, Tom tried to think, and he thought in erratic jumps, as usual. How would it be for all of them – Bernard, Derwatt and himself – to have met here in Salzburg, to have spoken together several times? Derwatt had spoken of suicide. He had said he wanted to be cremated, not in a crematory, but in the open. He had asked Bernard and Tom to do it. Tom had tried to persuade both men out of their depression, but Bernard had been depressed because Cynthia (Jeff and Ed could vouch for that), and Derwatt –

Tom got off the bus, not caring where he was, because he wanted to think while walking.

'Take your bag, sir?' It was the bellhop at the Goldener Hirsch.

'Oh, it's very light,' Tom said. 'Thank you.' He went up to his room.

Tom washed his hands and face, then took off his clothes and bathed. He was imagining conversations with Bernard and Derwatt in various Salzburg Bier- and Weinstübl. It would have been the first time Bernard had seen Derwatt since Derwatt had gone off to Greece five or more years ago, because Bernard had avoided seeing him on Derwatt's return to London, and Bernard had not been in London during Derwatt's second brief visit. Bernard had already been in Salzburg. Bernard had spoken to Tom in Belle Ombre about Salzburg (true), and when Derwatt had rung Heloise in Belle Ombre, she had told Derwatt that Tom had gone to Salzburg to see Bernard, or to try to find him, therefore Derwatt had gone, too. Under what name had Derwatt come? Well, that would have to remain a mystery. Who knew what name Derwatt was using in Mexico, for example? It remained for Tom to tell Heloise (but only when and if someone asked her) that Derwatt had telephoned Belle Ombre.

Maybe that wasn't all perfect and ironed out as yet, but it was a beginning.

For the second time, he faced Bernard's duffelbag, and now he looked for recent notes by Bernard. The October 5th note said, 'I sometimes feel I am already dead. There is curiously enough of me to realize that my identity, my self has disintegrated and somehow vanished. I never was Derwatt. But now am I really Bernard Tufts?'

Tom couldn't let that last pair of sentences stand, so he tore out the whole page.

Some of the drawings had notes on them. A few about colours, the greens of Salzburg buildings. 'Mozart's noisy public shrine – not a single portrait of him that one feels is any good.' Then, 'I gaze often at the river. It's a fast river and that's nice. That's perhaps the best way to go, off a bridge one night hopefully when no one is around to shout "Save him!" '

That was what Tom needed, and he closed the drawing-pad quickly and dropped it back into the duffel.

Were there any entries about him? Tom looked again through the pad for his name or initials. Then he opened the brown notebook. Most of this was the copied excerpts from Derwatt's journals, and the last few entries at the end, made by Bernard, were all dated, all during the time Bernard had been in London. Nothing about Tom Ripley.

Tom went down to the restaurant in the hotel. It was late, but he could still order something. After a few bites of food, he began to feel better. The cool, light white wine was inspiring. He could afford to leave on tomorrow afternoon's plane. If his telephone call to Jeff yesterday was questioned, Tom would say he had rung Jeff on his own initiative to tell him that Derwatt was in Salzburg and that Tom was worried about him. Tom would also have to say he had asked Jeff not to tell anyone where he was – least of all 'the public'. And Bernard? Tom might have mentioned to Jeff that Bernard was also in Salzburg, because why not? The police were not looking for Bernard Tufts. Bernard's disappearance, surely a suicide and probably in the River Salzach, must have taken place the night of the day Tom and Bernard cremated Derwatt's body. Best to say Bernard had helped him with that.

He was going to be censured for aiding and abetting a suicide, Tom foresaw. What did they do to people who did that? Derwatt had insisted on taking a massive dose of sleeping pills, Tom would say. The three of them had spent the morning in the woods, walking. Derwatt had taken a few pills before they joined one another. It had been impossible for them to prevent his taking the rest and – Tom would have to confess it – he had not wished to interfere with a desire so strong on Derwatt's part. Nor had Bernard.

Tom returned to his room, opened his window, then opened the pigskin suitcase. He removed the smaller newspaper-wrapped bundle, and added more newspaper. It was still hardly bigger than a grapefruit. Then he closed the suitcase lest a maid come in (though the bed had already been turned down), left his window slightly open, and went downstairs with his little parcel. He took the bridge to the right, the bridge with the handrail, where he had seen Bernard leaning yesterday. Tom leaned on the rail in the same fashion. And when there were no passers-by, Tom opened his hands and let the thing drop. It dropped lightly, and was lost to sight soon in the darkness. Tom had brought Bernard's ring, and he dropped this in the same manner.

The next morning, Tom made his flight reservation, and then went out to buy some things, mostly for Heloise. He bought a green waistcoat for her and a Wolljanker of clear blue like the colour of the Gauloise packet, a white ruffled blouse, and for himself a darker green waistcoat and a couple of hunting knives.

This time, his little plane was called the *Ludwig van Beethoven*.

Orly by 8 p.m. Tom presented his own passport. A glance at him and his photograph, and no stamping was done. He took a taxi to Villeperce. He had been afraid Heloise would have visitors, and he was right, he saw from the slumping dark red Citroën in front of the house. The Grais' car.

They were finishing dinner. There was a comfortable little fire going.

'Why didn't you telephone?' Heloise complained, but she was happy to see him.

'Don't let me interrupt you,' Tom said.

'But we are finished!' said Agnès Grais.

It was true. They were about to have coffee in the living-room.

'Have you had dinner, M. Tome?' Mme Annette asked.

Tom said he had, but he would like some coffee. Tom, in

quite a normal way, he thought, told the Grais he had been in Paris to see a friend who was in some personal difficulties. The Grais were not inclined to pry. Tom asked why Antoine, the busy architect, was home in Villeperce on a Thursday evening?

'Self-indulgence,' said Antoine. 'The weather is good, I convince myself I am making notes for a new building, and what is more important, I am designing a fireplace for our guest-room.' He laughed.

Only Heloise, Tom thought, noticed that he was not quite as usual. 'How was Noëlle's party Tuesday?' Tom asked.

'Lots of fun!' said Agnès. 'We missed you.'

'What about the mysterious Mur-*chee*-son?' asked Antoine. 'What is happening?'

'Well – they still can't find him. Mrs Murchison came here to see me – as Heloise might have told you.'

'No, she didn't,' said Agnès.

'I couldn't help her very much,' Tom said. 'Her husband's painting, one by Derwatt, was stolen at Orly also.' No harm in telling that, Tom thought, because it was true and it had been in the papers.

After his coffee, Tom excused himself, saying he wanted to open his suitcase, and he would be back in a moment. To his annoyance, Mme Annette had carried his suitcases up, and his casual request to leave them downstairs had gone unheeded. Upstairs, Tom was relieved to see that Mme Annette had not opened either of the suitcases, probably because she had enough to do downstairs. Tom set the new pigskin suitcase into a closet, and opened the lid of the other suitcase, which was full of his new purchases. Then he went downstairs.

The Grais were early risers, and left before eleven.

'Did Webster ring again?' Tom asked Heloise.

'No.' She said softly in English, 'Is it all right if Mme Annette knows you were in Salzburg?'

Tom smiled, a smile of relief because of Heloise's efficiency. 'Yes. In fact now you must say I was there.' Tom wanted to explain, but he couldn't tell Heloise about Bernard's remains tonight, or maybe any night. The ashes of Derwatt-Bernard. 'I'll explain later. But now I must ring London.' Tom took the telephone and put in a call to Jeff's studio.

'What happened in Salzburg? Did you see the *fou*?' Heloise demanded, with more concern for Tom than annoyance with Bernard.

Tom glanced towards the kitchen, but Mme Annette had said good night and closed the door. 'The *fou* is dead. A suicide.'

'*Vraiment!* You are not joking, Tome?'

But Heloise knew he wasn't joking. 'The important thing – to tell anybody – is that I went to Salzburg.' Tom knelt on the floor beside her chair, put his head in her lap for a second, then stood up and kissed her on both cheeks. 'Darling, I've got to say Derwatt is dead, too, also in Salzburg. And – in case you are asked, Derwatt rang Belle Ombre from London, and asked if he could see me. So you told him, "Tom went to Salzburg." All right? It's easy to remember, because it is the truth.'

Heloise looked at him askance, a little mischievously. 'What is true, what is not true?'

Her tone sounded oddly philosophic. It was indeed a question for philosophers, and why should he and Heloise bother about it? 'Come upstairs and I'll prove I was in Salzburg.' He pulled Heloise up from her chair.

They went up to Tom's room and looked at the things in his suitcase. Heloise tried on the green waistcoat. She embraced the blue jacket. She tried it on, and it fitted.

'And you've bought a new suitcase!' she said, seeing the brown pigskin in his closet.

'That's quite ordinary,' Tom said in French, as the telephone rang. He waved her away from the suitcase. Tom was told that Jeff's telephone did not answer, and Tom asked the operator to keep trying. It was nearing midnight.

Tom took a shower, while Heloise talked to him. 'Bernard is *dead*?' she asked.

Tom was rinsing soap off, delighted to be home, to feel a tub he was acquainted with under his feet. He put on silk pyjamas. He did not know where to begin explaining. The telephone rang. 'If you listen,' Tom said, 'you will understand.'

'Hello?' Jeff's voice said.

Tom stood up straight and tense, and his voice was serious. 'Hello. Tom here. I'm ringing to say that Derwatt is dead ... He died in Salzburg ...'

Jeff stammered, as if his telephone were being tapped, and Tom continued like an ordinary honest citizen:

'I haven't yet told the police anywhere. The death – it was in circumstances I don't care to describe over the telephone.'

'Are you – c-coming to London?'

'I am not, no. But would you speak to Webster and tell him I rang you, that I went to Salzburg to find Bernard ... Well, never mind Bernard just now, except for one important thing. Can you get into his studio and destroy every sign of Derwatt?'

Jeff understood. He and Ed knew the superintendent. They could get the keys. They could say that Bernard needed something. And this would account, Tom hoped, for sketches, the unfinished canvases possibly, that they might have to carry out.

'Do a thorough job,' Tom said. 'To continue, Derwatt is supposed to have rung my wife a few days ago. My wife told him I'd gone to Salzburg.'

'Yes, but why did –'

Why did Derwatt want to go to Salzburg, Tom supposed Jeff was going to ask. 'I think the important thing is that I'm ready to see Webster here. In fact I want to see him. I have news.'

Tom hung up and turned to Heloise. He smiled, hardly daring to smile. And yet, wasn't he going to succeed?

'What do you mean,' Heloise asked in English, 'Derwatt died in Salzburg, when he died three years ago in Greece, you told me?'

'He's got to be proven to be dead. You know, darling, I did all this to preserve the – the honour of Philip Derwatt.'

'How can one kill a man already dead?'

'Can you leave that to me? I have –' Tom looked at his wrist-watch on his night-table. 'I have thirty minutes' work to do tonight and after that I would love to join in –'

'Work?'

'Little things to do.' Goodness, if a woman couldn't understand little things to do, who could? 'Little duties.'

'Can't they wait until morning?'

'The Inspector Webster *might* arrive tomorrow. Even in the morning. And by the time you get undressed, almost, I shall be with you.' He pulled her up. She got up willingly, so he knew she was in a good mood. 'Any news from Papa?'

Heloise burst into French saying something like, 'Oh, the hell with Papa on an evening like this! ... Two men dead in Salzburg! You must mean one, chéri. Or do you mean any at all?'

Tom laughed, delighted with Heloise's irreverent attitude, because it resembled his own. Her propriety was a veneer only, Tom knew, or surely she'd never have married him.

When Heloise went across the hall, Tom went to his suitcase and took out Bernard's brown notebook and the drawing-pad, and put them neatly on his writing-table. He had disposed of Bernard's chino pants and his shirt in a rubbish bin in a Salzburg street, and of the duffelbag itself in another rubbish bin. Tom's story was going to be that Bernard had asked him to keep his duffelbag while he went off to look for another hotel. Bernard had never returned, and Tom had kept only what was of value. Then from his stud-box, Tom took his Mexican ring that he had worn in London the first time he had impersonated Derwatt. He went downstairs with it, silent and barefoot. Tom put the ring in the centre of what was left of the embers. It might melt to a glob, he supposed, because Mexican silver was pure and soft. Something would remain, and he would add this to Derwatt's — rather Bernard's ashes. He must get up early tomorrow, before Mme Annette cleaned the ashes out of the fireplace.

Heloise was in bed, smoking a cigarette. He did not like to smoke her blond cigarettes, but he liked the smell of the smoke when she smoked them. Tom held Heloise more tightly, when they had turned the light out. A pity he hadn't tossed Robert Mackay's passport into the fire tonight. Was there ever a moment's peace?

25

Tom extricated himself from the sleeping Heloise, withdrawing an arm from under her neck, daring to turn her over and kiss one breast before he eased himself from the bed. She hadn't wakened much, and would probably think he was off to the loo. Tom went on bare feet to his room and got the Mackay passport from a pocket of his jacket.

He went downstairs. A quarter to seven by the clock near the telephone. The fire looked like white ashes, but was no doubt still warm. Tom took a twig and scraped for the silver ring, prepared at the same time to conceal the green passport in his hand – he had bent the passport in half – in case Mme Annette came in. Tom found the ring, blackened and somewhat out of shape, but not the collapsed thing he had expected. He put the ring on the hearth to cool, stirred up the embers, and tore apart the passport. He used a match to hasten the burning of the passport, and watched until it was done. Then he went upstairs with the ring, and put it with the indescribable black and red stuff in the pigskin suitcase from Salzburg.

The telephone rang, and Tom caught it at once.

'Oh, Inspector Webster, hello! ... That's quite all right, I was up.'

'If I understand Mr Constant – Derwatt is *dead*?'

Tom hesitated an instant, and Webster added that Mr Constant had rung his office late last night to leave a message. 'He killed himself in Salzburg,' Tom said. 'I was just in Salzburg.'

'I'd like to see you, Mr Ripley, and the reason I ring so early is because I find I can take a nine o'clock plane. Can I come to see you this morning round eleven?'

Tom agreed readily.

Tom then went back to Heloise's bedroom. They would be awakened – in case Tom slept – in another hour by Mme Annette with her tray of tea for Heloise and coffee for him. Mme

Annette was used to finding them both in one or the other's bedroom. Tom did not sleep, but some repose, such as he had with Heloise, was just as restorative.

Mme Annette arrived around 8.30 a.m., and Tom signalled that he would take his coffee but Heloise would prefer to sleep longer. Tom sipped his coffee and thought what he must do, how he must behave. Honest above all, Tom thought, and he went over the story in his mind. Derwatt ringing because he was distressed about Murchison's disappearance (over distressed, oddly, just the sort of illogical thing that would ring true, an unexpected reaction that would sound real), and could he come to see Tom? And Heloise telling him that Tom had gone to Salzburg to look for Bernard Tufts. Yes, best if Heloise mentioned Bernard to Webster. To Derwatt, Bernard Tufts was an old friend whose name he would have responded to at once. In Salzburg, he and Derwatt had been more concerned over Bernard than Murchison.

When Heloise stirred, Tom got out of bed and went downstairs to ask Mme Annette to make fresh tea. It was about 9.30 a.m.

Tom went out to look at the former grave of Murchison. Some rain had fallen since he had last seen it. He left the few branches over it as they were, because they looked natural, not as if someone had tried to conceal the spot, and Tom had no reason anyway to conceal the policemen's digging.

Around ten, Mme Annette went out to do the shopping.

Tom told Heloise that Inspector Webster was due and that he would like her to be present. 'You can say quite frankly I went to Salzburg to try to find Bernard.'

'Is M. Webster going to accuse you of anything?'

'How could he?' Tom replied, smiling.

Webster arrived at a quarter to eleven. He came in with his black attaché case, looking as efficient as a doctor.

'My wife – whom you've met,' Tom said. He took Webster's coat and asked him to sit down.

The Inspector sat on the sofa. First he went through the times of things, making notes. Tom had heard from Derwatt when? November the third, Sunday, Tom thought.

'My wife spoke to him when he rang,' Tom said. 'I was in Salzburg.'

'You spoke to Derwatt?' Webster asked Heloise.

'Oh, yes. He would like to speak with Tome, but I told him Tome was in Salzburg – to look for Bernard.'

'Um-m. At what hotel did you stop?' Webster asked Tom. He had his usual smile, and from his jolly expression, there might have been no death involved.

'The Goldener Hirsch,' Tom said. 'I went first to Paris, look-ing for Bernard Tufts on a hunch, then I went to Salzburg be-cause Bernard had mentioned Salzburg. He hadn't said he was going there, but he said he'd like to see it again. It's a small town and it's not difficult to find someone you're looking for. Anyway, I found Bernard on the second day.'

'Whom did you see first, Bernard or Derwatt?'

'Oh, Bernard, because I was looking for him. I didn't know Derwatt was in Salzburg.'

'And – go on,' said Webster.

Tom sat forward on his chair. 'Well – I suppose I spoke to Bernard alone once or twice. With Derwatt the same. Then we were a few times together. They were old friends. I thought it was Bernard who was the more depressed. His friend Cynthia in London doesn't want to see him again. Didn't Derwatt –' Tom hesitated. 'Derwatt seemed more concerned with Bernard than himself. I have by the way a couple of notebooks of Bernard's that I think I ought to show you.' Tom stood up, but Webster said:

'I'll just get a few facts down first. Bernard killed himself how?'

'He disappeared. This was just after Derwatt's death. From what he wrote in his notebook, I think he might have drowned himself in the river in Salzburg. But I wasn't sure enough to report that to the police there. I wanted to speak with you first.'

Webster looked a bit puzzled, or benumbed, which didn't sur-prise Tom. 'I'm most interested in seeing Bernard's notebooks, but Derwatt – what happened there?'

Tom glanced at Heloise. 'Well, on Tuesday, we all had an

appointment to meet around ten in the morning. Derwatt had taken sedatives, he said. He'd talked before of killing himself and said he wanted to be cremated – by us, Bernard and me. I at least hadn't taken it too seriously until he turned up groggy Tuesday and sort of – making jokes. He took more pills as we walked. We were in the woods, where Derwatt wanted to go.' Tom said to Heloise, 'If you don't want to listen, dear, you should go upstairs. I have to tell it as it happened.'

'I will listen.' Heloise put her face in her hands for a moment, then took her hands down and stood up. 'I shall ask Mme Annette for some tea. All right, Tome?'

'A good idea,' Tom said. He continued to Webster, 'Derwatt jumped off a cliff onto rocks. You could say he killed himself in three ways, by the pills, by jumping over – and by being burnt, but he was certainly dead when we burnt him. He died from the jump. Bernard and I returned – the next day. We burnt what we could. We buried the rest.'

Heloise came back.

Webster said, writing, 'The next day. November the sixth, Wednesday.' Where had Bernard been staying? Tom was able to say Der Blaue Something in the Linzergasse. But after Wednesday, Tom was not sure. Where and when had they bought the petrol? Tom was vague about the place, but it was Wednesday noon. Where had Derwatt been staying? Tom said he had never tried to find out.

'Bernard and I had promised to meet around nine-thirty Thursday morning in the Alter Markt. Wednesday night, Bernard gave me his duffelbag and asked me to keep it while he found another hotel that night. I asked him to stay at my hotel, but he didn't want to. Then – he didn't keep our date Thursday. I waited an hour or so. I never saw him again. He had left no message at my hotel. I felt Bernard didn't want to keep that date, that he'd destroyed himself probably – probably by drowning himself in the river. I came home.'

Webster lit a cigarette, more slowly than usual. 'You were to keep his duffelbag overnight on Wednesday?'

'Not necessarily. Bernard knew where I was, and I rather expected him to pick the bag up later that night. I did say,

"If I don't see you tonight, we'll meet tomorrow morning." '

'You asked at hotels for him yesterday morning?'

'No, I didn't. I think I'd lost all hope. I was upset and discouraged.'

Mme Annette served the tea, and exchanged a *'Bonjour'* with Inspector Webster.

Tom said, 'Bernard hung a dummy downstairs in our cellar a few days ago. It was meant to be himself. My wife found it and it gave her quite a scare. Bernard's trousers and jacket hanging from a belt from the ceiling with a note attached.' Tom glanced at her. 'Heloise, sorry.'

Heloise bit her lip and shrugged. Her reaction was indisputably genuine. What Tom had said had happened had happened, and she did not enjoy recalling it.

'Have you got the note he wrote?' Webster said.

'Yes. It must be still in the pocket of my dressing-gown. Shall I get it?'

'In a moment.' Webster almost smiled again, but not quite. 'May I ask why you went to Salzburg exactly?'

'I was worried about Bernard. He'd mentioned wanting to see Salzburg. I felt Bernard might be going to kill himself. And I wondered – why should he have looked me up after all? He knew I had two Derwatt paintings, true, but he didn't know me. Yet he talked very freely on his first visit here. I thought perhaps I could help. Then as it turned out, both Derwatt and Bernard killed themselves, Derwatt first. One doesn't want to meddle somehow – with a man like Derwatt, anyway. One feels one is doing the wrong thing. I don't really mean *that*, but I mean, to tell somebody not to kill himself when one knows it won't be accepted by the other person who's determined to kill himself. That's what I mean. It's wrong and it's hopeless, and why should someone be reproached for *not* saying something, when he knows it's no good to say it?' Tom paused.

Webster was listening attentively.

'Bernard went off – probably to Paris – after hanging himself in effigy here. Then he came back. That's when Heloise met him.'

Webster wanted the date Bernard Tufts had returned to Belle

Ombre. Tom did the best he could. October twenty-fifth, he thought.

'I tried to help Bernard by telling him his girl-friend Cynthia might see him again. Which I don't think was true, not from what I could gather from Bernard. I was simply trying to pull him out of his depression. I think Derwatt tried even harder. I'm sure they saw each other alone a few times in Salzburg. Derwatt was fond of Bernard.' Tom said to Heloise. 'Are you understanding this, darling?'

Heloise nodded.

It was probably true that she understood all of it.

'Why was Derwatt so depressed?'

Tom thought for a moment. 'He was depressed about the whole world. Life. I don't know if there was something personal – in Mexico – contributing to it. He mentioned a Mexican girl who had married and gone away. I don't know how important this was. He seemed disturbed because he'd come back to London. He said it was a mistake.'

Webster stopped taking notes at last. 'Shall we go upstairs?'

Tom took the Inspector into his room, and went to the closet for his suitcase.

'I don't want my wife to see this,' Tom said, and opened the suitcase. He and Webster stooped beside it.

The small remains were wrapped in Austrian and German newspapers that Tom had bought. Tom noticed that Webster looked at the dates of the newspapers before he lifted the bundle out and set it on the rug. He put more newspaper under the bundle, but Tom knew it was not damp. Webster opened it.

'Um-m. Dear me. What did Derwatt want you to do with this?'

Tom hesitated, frowning. 'Nothing.' Tom went to the window, and opened it a little. 'I don't know why I took it. I was upset. So was Bernard. If Bernard said we should take some back to England, I don't remember. But I took that. We'd expected ashes. It wasn't.'

Webster was poking in the stuff with the end of his ballpoint pen. He came upon the ring and fished it out with the pen. 'A silver ring.'

'I took that on purpose.' Tom knew the two snakes on the ring were still visible.

'I'll take this back to London,' Webster said, standing up. 'If you have a box, perhaps –'

'Yes, certainly,' Tom said, starting for the door.

'You spoke of Bernard Tufts's notebooks.'

'Yes.' Tom turned back, and pointed to the notebook and the drawing-pad on the corner of his writing-table. 'They're here. And the note he wrote –' Tom went to his bathroom, where his dressing-gown hung on a hook. The note was still in the pocket. *I hang myself in effigy* ... Tom handed it to Webster, and went downstairs.

Mme Annette saved boxes, and there was always a variety of sizes. 'What is it for?' she asked, trying to help him.

'This will do very well,' Tom said. The boxes were on top of Mme Annette's clothes cupboard, and Tom pulled one down. It held a few remnants of knitting wool, neatly coiled, which he handed to Mme Annette with a smile. 'Thank you, my treasure.'

Webster was downstairs, talking in English on the telephone. Heloise had perhaps gone up to her room. Tom took the box upstairs and put the little bundle into it, and wadded some newspaper to fill out the box. He got string from his workroom and tied it. It was a shoe box. Tom took the box downstairs.

Webster was still on the telephone.

Tom went to the bar and poured a neat whisky for himself, and decided to wait to see if Webster wanted a Dubonnet.

'... the Buckmaster Gallery people? Can you wait till I'm there?'

Tom changed his mind and went to the kitchen for ice to make Webster's Dubonnet. He got the ice and, seeing Mme Annette, asked her to finish making the drink and not to forget the lemon peel.

Webster was saying, 'I'll ring you again in about an hour, so don't go to lunch ... No, not a word to anyone just now ... I don't know yet.'

Tom felt uneasy. He saw Heloise on the lawn, and went out to speak to her, though he would have preferred to stay in the living-room. 'I think we should offer the Inspector lunch or sandwiches, something like that. All right, darling?'

'You gave him the ashes?'

Tom blinked. 'A small thing. In a box,' he said awkwardly. 'It is wrapped. Don't think about it.' Tom led her by the hand back towards the house. 'It's appropriate that Bernard should give his remains to be thought of as Derwatt.'

Maybe she understood. She understood what had happened, but Tom did not expect her to understand Bernard's adoration of Derwatt. Tom asked Mme Annette if she would make some sandwiches of tinned lobster and things like that. Heloise went to help her, and Tom rejoined the Inspector.

'Just for formality's sake, Mr Ripley, can I have a look at your passport?' Webster asked.

'Certainly.' Tom went upstairs and came down with his passport at once.

Webster had his Dubonnet now. He looked slowly through the passport, seemingly as interested in months-old dates as in the recent ones. 'Austria. Yes. Hm-m.'

Tom recalled, with a sense of safety, that he had not been to London as himself, Tom Ripley, when Derwatt had shown himself for the second time. Tom sat down tiredly on one of the straight chairs. He was supposed to be rather weary and depressed because of the events of yesterday.

'What became of Derwatt's things?'

'Things?'

'His suitcase, for instance.'

Tom said, 'I never knew where he was staying. Neither did Bernard, because I asked him – after we'd – after Derwatt was dead.'

'You think he just abandoned his things in a hotel?'

'No.' Tom shook his head. 'Not Derwatt. Bernard said he thought Derwatt had probably destroyed every trace of himself, left his hotel and – Well, how does one get rid of a suitcase? Drop the contents in various rubbish bins or – maybe drop the whole thing into the river. That's quite easy in Salzburg. Especially if Derwatt had done it the night before, in the dark.'

Webster mused. 'Did it occur to you that Bernard might have

gone back to the place in the woods and thrown himself over the same cliff?'

'Yes,' Tom said, because in some odd way this idea had crossed his mind. 'But I couldn't bring myself to go back there yesterday morning. Maybe I should have. Maybe I should have looked longer in the streets for Bernard. But I felt he was dead – somehow, somewhere, and that I'd never find him.'

'But from what I understand, Bernard Tufts could still be alive.'

'That's perfectly true.'

'Had he enough money?'

'I doubt that. I offered to lend him some – three days ago – but he refused it.'

'What did Derwatt say to you about Murchison's disappearance?'

Tom thought for a moment. 'It depressed him. As to what he said – He said something about the burden of being famous. He disliked being famous. He felt it had caused a man's death – Murchison's.'

'Was Derwatt friendly towards you?'

'Yes. At least, I never noticed any unfriendliness. My talks alone with Derwatt were brief. There were only one or two of them, I think.'

'Did he know about your association with Richard Greenleaf?'

A tremble that Tom hoped was invisible went through his body. Tom shrugged. 'He never mentioned it, if he did.'

'Nor Bernard? He didn't mention it either?'

'No,' Tom said.

'You see, it is odd, you must agree, that three men disappear or die around you – Murchison, Derwatt and Bernard Tufts. So did Richard Greenleaf disappear – his body was never found, I think. And what was his friend's name? Fred? Freddie something?'

'Miles, I think,' Tom said. 'But I can't say Murchison was very near me. I hardly knew Murchison. Or Freddie Miles for that matter.' At least Webster was not yet thinking of the possibility that he had impersonated Derwatt, Tom thought.

Heloise and Mme Annette came in, Mme Annette pushing the cart that held a plate of sandwiches and a wine bottle in an ice bucket.

'Ah, some refreshment!' Tom said. 'I didn't ask if you had a lunch engagement, Inspector, but this little —'

'I have with the Melun police,' Webster said with a quick smile. 'I must ring them shortly. And by the way I'll reimburse you for all these telephone calls.'

Tom waved a hand in protest. 'Thank you, madame,' he said to Mme Annette.

Heloise offered Inspector Webster a plate and napkin, then presented the sandwiches. 'Lobster and crab. The lobsters are these,' she said, indicating.

'How could I resist?' said the Inspector, accepting one of each. But Webster was still on the subject. 'I must alert the Salzburg police — via London because I can't speak German — to look for Bernard Tufts. And perhaps tomorrow we can arrange to meet in Salzburg. Are you free tomorrow, Mr Ripley?'

'Yes — I could be, of course.'

'You've got to lead us to that spot in the woods. We must dig up the — you know. Derwatt was a British subject. Or was he, in fact?' Webster smiled with his mouth full. 'But surely he wouldn't have become a Mexican citizen.'

'That's something I never asked him,' Tom said.

'It will be interesting to find his village in Mexico,' Webster remarked, 'this remote and nameless village. What town is it near, do you know?'

Tom smiled. 'Derwatt never dropped a clue.'

'I wonder if his house will be abandoned — or if he has a caretaker or a lawyer with the authority to wind things up there, once it's known he's dead.' Webster paused.

Tom was silent. Was Webster casting about, hoping for Tom to drop a piece of information? As Derwatt, in London, Tom had told Webster that Derwatt had a Mexican passport and lived under another name.

Webster said. 'Do you suppose Derwatt entered England and travelled about with a false name? A British passport possibly but with a false name?'

Tom replied calmly, 'I always supposed that.'

'So he probably lived in Mexico under a false name also.'

'Probably. I hadn't thought of that.'

'And shipped his canvases from Mexico under the same false name.'

Tom paused, as if he were not very interested. 'The Buckmaster Gallery ought to know.'

Heloise presented the sandwiches again, but the Inspector declined.

'I feel sure they wouldn't tell,' Webster said. 'And maybe they don't even know the name, if Derwatt sent his paintings under the name Derwatt, for instance. But he must have entered England under the false name, because we have no record of his comings and goings. May I ring the Melun police now?'

'But of course,' Tom said. 'Would you like to use my phone upstairs?'

Webster said the downstairs telephone was quite all right. He consulted his notebook, and proceeded to speak with the operator in his adequate French. He asked for the *commissaire*.

Tom poured white wine into the two glasses on the tray. Heloise had her wine.

Webster was asking the Melun *commissaire* if they had any news about Thomas Murchison. Tom gathered not. Webster said that Mrs Murchison was in London at the Connaught Hotel for the next few days, anxious for any information, if the Melun police would pass it on to Webster's office. Webster also inquired about the missing painting 'L'Horloge'. Nothing.

When he had hung up, Tom wanted to ask what was happening in the search for Murchison, but Tom did not want it to appear that he had listened to Webster's words over the phone.

Webster insisted on leaving a fifty-franc note for his telephone calls. No, he thanked Tom, he did not care for another Dubonnet, but he sampled the wine.

Tom could see Webster speculating, as he stood there, as to how much Tom Ripley was concealing, *where* was he guilty, how was he guilty, and where and how did Tom Ripley stand to gain anything? But it was obvious, Tom thought, that no person would have murdered two people – or even three, Murchison, Derwatt and Bernard Tufts to protect the value of the two Derwatt paintings which hung on Tom's walls. And if Webster should go as far as to investigate the Derwatt Art Supply Company, through whose bank Tom received a monthly income, that income was sent without name to a numbered account in Switzerland.

However, there was still Austria tomorrow, and Tom would have to accompany the police.

'Can I ask you to ring for a taxi for me, Mr Ripley? You know the number better than I.'

Tom went to the telephone and rang a Villeperce taxi service. They would arrive at once, they said.

'You'll hear from me later this evening,' Webster said to Tom, 'about Salzburg tomorrow. Is it a difficult place to get to?'

Tom explained the changes of planes at Frankfurt, and said he had been told a bus from Munich to Salzburg, if one landed at Munich, was quicker than waiting at Frankfurt for the plane to Austria. But this would have to be co-ordinated by telephone, once Webster found the time of the plane from London to Munich. He would be travelling with a colleague.

Then Inspector Webster thanked Heloise, and Heloise and Tom accompanied him to the door as the taxi arrived. Webster saw the shoe box on the hall table before Tom could fetch it, and picked it up.

'I have Bernard's note and his two notebooks in my case,' Webster said to Tom.

Tom and Heloise were on their front doorsteps as Webster's taxi drove away, with Webster smiling his rabbit smile through the window. Then they walked back into the house.

A peaceful silence reigned. Not of peace. Tom knew, but at least it was silence. 'This evening – today – can we just do nothing? Watch television tonight?' This afternoon Tom wanted to garden. That always straightened him out.

So he gardened. And in the evening they lay in pyjamas on

Heloise's bed and watched television and sipped tea. The telephone rang just before 10 p.m. and Tom answered it in his room. He had been braced for Webster, and had a pen in hand ready to take down the schedule for tomorrow, but it was Chris Greenleaf in Paris. He had returned from the Rhineland and wondered if he could visit with his friend Gerald?

Tom, when he had finished talking with Chris, came back to Heloise's room and said, 'That was Dickie Greenleaf's cousin Chris. He wants to come to see us Monday and bring his friend Gerald Hayman. I told him yes. I hope it's all right, darling. They'll just stay overnight, probably. It'll be a nice change – a little tourism, nice lunches. Yes? Peaceful.'

'You are back from Salzburg when?'

'Oh, I should be back Sunday. I don't see why that business should take more than one day – tomorrow and part of Sunday. All they want is for me to show them the spot in the woods. And Bernard's hotel.'

'Um-m. Très bien,' Heloise murmured, propped against her pillows. 'They arrive Monday.'

'They'll ring again. I'll make it Monday evening.' Tom got back into bed. Heloise was curious about Chris, Tom knew. Boys like Chris and his friend would amuse her, for a while. Tom was pleased with the arrangement. He stared at the old French film unreeling before them on the television screen. Louis Jouvet, dressed like a Vatican Swiss guard, was threatening someone with a halberd. Tom decided he must be solemn and direct tomorrow in Salzburg. The Austrian police would have a car, of course, and he would lead them directly to the place in the woods, while it was still light, and tomorrow evening directly to Der Blaue Something in the Linzergasse. The dark-haired woman behind the desk would remember Bernard Tufts, and that Tom had once asked for him there. Tom felt secure. As he was beginning to follow the soporific dialogue on the screen, the telephone rang.

'That's no doubt Webster,' Tom said, and got out of bed again.

Tom's hand stopped in the act of reaching for the telephone – only for a second, but in that second he anticipated defeat and seemed to suffer it. Exposure. Shame. Carry it off as before, he thought. The show wasn't over as yet. Courage! He picked up the telephone.